BAD COMPANY

LESTER BLEICH

Luminary
Legends

ISBN 979-8-9906880-2-5 (Hardcover)
ISBN 979-8-9906880-1-8 (Paperback)
ISBN 979-8-9906880-0-1 (e book)

Library of Congress control number 2024909445

Book Cover by Alexander von Ness
Book design by Damonza

1st Edition: 2024
Published by Luminary Legends
Printed in the United States of America

To Elane*

* There is no "i" in Elane, that's what makes her so special

"Man plans and G-d laughs"

Yiddish Proverb

PROLOGUE

JONAH WAS FRANTIC.

Just a few short minutes ago, he was standing on a busy midtown street. Within seconds, he found himself in the back seat of a car that sped off before he could do or say anything.

His pilot and copilot looked like they had just come from a boxing match where they were the featured attraction. The guy driving the car held the wheel with hands that looked like cleavers. He sported a scar that occupied the right side of his face from ear to chin, and his nose looked like it had been used for batting practice but not by the local little league team. His associate occupying the front passenger seat looked like a card-carrying member of the Tattoo of the Month Club. The tiger staring out from the back of his neck looked ready to lunge at the slightest provocation. He did most of his yelling with a pronounced lisp.

Jonah wriggled experimentally, but the rope holding his wrists behind his back held firm, and the tinted windows were sealed shut. There was no point in yelling for help; no one would hear him. He felt like a trapped animal being taken to the slaughterhouse.

The two Harvard grads up front worked their way through busy midtown traffic. The meaty one with the large hands did the driving. The navigator beside him kept yelling, "Fassssster! Fassssster!" They also weren't big on conversation. Jonah tried to get their attention, and the better-looking one in the passenger seat (though not by a lot) waved a gun at him and yelled at the top of his lungs, "Sssshhut up!"

Jonah thought back to all that had occurred over the last few weeks and how much promise his new career once held. His first thought was about Hannah.

Did she make it back to the office, or did they catch up to her too?

This is all my fault; how did it come to this?

1

JONAH MARK WAS a single, 24-year-old business student in gritty 1980s New York City. He had worked in an accounting firm for the last three years while pursuing an MBA at night. Most of his colleagues at Waldman, Fernick, and Madison were typical eighties Yuppies, young urban professionals with expensive tastes and dreams of financial success.

Jonah didn't care about any of that. If he could spend all his time reading spy novels and hanging out with his friends at the mystery clubs, talking about the latest comic books, spy novels, and magic tricks, he would do so in a heartbeat.

Looking at numbers all day was not Jonah's purpose on this earth; he was meant to save the world. However, deep under all the useless stuff that occupied his brain, he knew that his hobbies wouldn't pay the bills, so he found himself doing the same thing everyone his age was doing with their lives: going to work every day.

It had been a very long three years.

For three years, he dragged himself out of bed every morning and took public transportation to wherever he was sent to do an audit. As the junior-most employee, the senior accountants took every opportunity to give Jonah the grunt work.

"Hey, Jonah, run across the street and get us some coffee."

"Hey, Jonah, run off 150 copies of this report."

"Hey, Jonah, you'll have to come in Sunday this week; we're just not done with this audit, and corporate wants us to step it up."

He found himself sneaking a peak at a mystery paperback under his desk whenever he got a chance, daydreaming about a life where his afternoon coffee run turned into a high-speed car chase to escape from trained assassins.

The senior accountant on Jonah's latest audit was a guy named Jay Bradley. Jonah didn't think much of Jay from the get-go; the feeling was mutual. But as usual, Jonah kept his head down, did what he was told, and only fantasized a little about Jay falling through a trapdoor in the floor under his desk into a pit of eels.

One Friday morning, Jay called Jonah over to his desk. He had a smug look on his face.

"Jonah, they want you to see Mr. Waldman at corporate this afternoon at 4:00. You better leave now to catch the subway back to the city."

Jay seemed to be particularly satisfied with delivering the message. Jonah knew exactly what it meant and was sure Jay did, too. It didn't take a rocket scientist to figure out that a junior accountant being called into the corporate office to see the managing partner at 4:00 on a Friday afternoon could only mean one thing.

So, they finally got their wish. As soon as I leave, Jay and his pals will be yukking it up at my expense and taking bets on how many minutes Old Man Waldman will take to swing the ax.

Theodore Waldman was the managing partner at the firm and had been there since its inception. He was about five foot eight, sweaty and bald, and tipped the scales somewhere north of 250 pounds. Clearly, the perks of managing partners included lots of lunches. It was also clear that Waldman did not have a clue who Jonah was when he entered his office. Jonah noticed him glancing at the company roster as he walked in. A couple of managers at the firm had probably selected Jonah for dismissal based on his less-than-stellar employee evaluation reports. Waldman was chosen to be the axman.

The old geezer still takes up oxygen here; he should have retired a decade ago. He took the CPA exam when there were only twelve questions, thought Jonah.

"Come in, Jonah," said Waldman, clearing his throat. "Eh, have a seat."

Jonah came in and sat down, wondering if he should even bother taking off his coat. The sight of Waldman's golf clubs sitting at the other end of the conference room table left no doubt what was on his mind.

"Eh, Jonah, we've decided to make a change. We think your talents are more suited for another company. Here's a severance check. See the secretary on the way out; she has some papers for you to sign."

He grabbed his golf clubs and was out the door before Jonah could utter a word. There was no *good luck; it was nice knowing you.*

Jonah was an afterthought before Waldman even hit the elevator.

To add insult to injury, Jonah saw that the severance check was for two hundred and forty-seven dollars and fifty-three cents. He had no idea how they had come up with that amount; maybe they pulled it out of a hat. Perhaps a big partners' meeting was held to discuss the exact amount of his severance check, but he doubted it. It didn't matter; his career at Waldman, Fernick, and Madison had ended, and unemployment was beckoning.

Jonah lived at home with his parents, David and Esther Mark, both Holocaust Survivors, in a small house in the Flatbush section of Brooklyn. After the war, many Orthodox Jewish families like the Marks' had settled in Flatbush, so nearly all Jonah's friends and neighbors had worn kippas on their heads since childhood and kept the Sabbath.

His parents had a strong work ethic, having immigrated with just the clothes on their backs. As he grew up, many conversations around the dinner table were very similar.

"Jonah, we want you to make something of yourself," his father would say.

"But Dad, shouldn't I enjoy my life?"

"Sure, Jonah; we want you to be happy in whatever you do," his mother would chime in. But first, you have to earn enough money to do it… like your cousin Jacob."

Here we go with cousin Jacob again, Jonah would think to himself.

The Boy Wonder of the family. Would it have killed him to be as laid back as I am and not be the poster boy for success?

"You should watch that show, Thirtysomething, Jonah.

The one about those young couples who enjoy their lives but are ambitious and career-driven? That's what we want you to be one day."

"Ma, that's Hollywood. Nobody lives like that and enjoys it."

In his heart, Jonah would have loved to pursue a career as a police detective or with the FBI, fighting crime and bringing justice to the world, just like in the books and magazines that occupied every spare space in his room. But his parents wanted him to do something "solid," as they put it, to be like his cousin Jacob, the bane of his existence, six years his senior, a CPA and financial advisor who drove a fancy car, owned a lovely house in the suburbs, and lived to torment Jonah by just being who he was.

I think he just lives like that to torture me, Jonah would think to himself whenever his name was brought up.

Would it kill him to maybe crash his fancy car once in a while or make a terrible investment that ruined a few lives, something like that?

With no one to finance his ambitions, Jonah put his dreams aside, at least for the time being, and pursued an accounting degree, hoping there'd be room to solve a crime or two somewhere along the way. He eventually found a job on the ladder's bottom rung at Waldman, Fernick, and Madison.

And now it was over.

❧

For the next few weeks, every morning bright and early, Jonah would run down to the corner, grab the newspaper, and head straight to the employment section, looking at all the help-wanted ads for entry-level finance positions.

I wonder why they call it the employment section, Jonah thought as he sat on the subway to Manhattan one morning. *They should call it the unemployment section. After all, the only people reading this are unemployed.*

He sent his resume everywhere, including for positions that required an MBA, figuring that his half-completed program might at least get him through the door. After a while, he started applying for positions he was not very interested in, hoping to get an interview with someone who would lead to a job *somewhere.* In most cases, he never heard from any of those companies again. The few interviews he could get lasted no more than ten minutes.

He even resorted to visiting office buildings and checking out the lobby directories for finance-related companies. He would make a list of the company names and room numbers. Dressed in a suit with his briefcase in hand, he looked like he worked somewhere in the building. He would then enter the reception area of his target company and try all kinds of strategies to get past the gatekeeper, usually, a receptionist who had seen this game played countless times before. Not only did this method not work, but he also found himself being escorted out of buildings by so-called security officers who were eager to do anything but stand around in a uniform with a tin badge all day doing nothing.

"Why don't you try your cousin Jacob?" his mother remarked one day. "Maybe he knows somebody."

I'd rather sell my body to science, Jonah thought to himself.

"Thanks, Mom; I'll keep that in mind."

The whole extended Mark clan was starting to panic about their wayward son's future. Then, at a family dinner party where the topic of his employment was always fodder for conversation, a family friend suggested a small employment agency.

"A couple of wonderful ladies run the place; they've been in the business for decades," he said.

"Why don't you call them?" said Jonah's mom anxiously.

"I will, Mom."

Jonah had nothing to lose, and it would keep his mother at bay for a few days, so he made the call. An elderly-sounding woman answered, listened to his story, and replied in a husky voice, "Come in, we'll talk."

Success Employment, Inc. was located on the fifth floor of a tiny office building in gritty downtown Manhattan. The street was sprayed with graffiti and garbage, and if you walked down the block too fast, you would probably miss the whole building.

Jonah arrived for his appointment on a Monday morning and was greeted by two women: Millie Cohen and Sally Berkowitz. They could have passed for any woman in his mother's mahjong group. Their voices were loud, and the smell of cigarette smoke permeated the air. The office looked like a train wreck with piles of paper and boxes everywhere; there was barely a place to sit down. He couldn't tell if they had just moved in or were packing to leave. The two women looked him up and down as if setting him up for a date.

"Ya got a resume?" asked Millie, the larger of the two robust women.

Jonah set himself the delicate task of fishing two copies out of his attaché case while he remained standing, as there were no chairs to be found. It was as if Millie was asking for one of the Flying Wallendas to fill out a form as they were doing one of their highwire acts between two buildings. But miraculously, Jonah managed to extricate the resumes without spilling the entire contents of his briefcase on the floor. Just as well, because he had visited the novelty store the night before on his way home from a day of job searching and had the rubber mask lying on the bottom of the case spilled out, it might have caused the interview to end prematurely.

He handed one to each of them. Sally quickly started perusing her copy while at the same time rummaging through a card file with the latest jobs, while Millie, clearly the one in charge, grabbed a bunch of files off a worn-out chair in a lovely duct tape trim and pointed at it. Jonah took this as a cue to sit down for his "talk."

Millie's desk was strewn with paperwork and cigarette butts, one of which was smoldering; she reached for another cigarette as she was reading the resume. The smell of smoke, mixed with the stench of her overpowering perfume, had Jonah almost gasping for air. He was starting to regret the visit.

When have I ever gotten a good idea from a family friend? he wondered. Then, his thoughts were interrupted by Millie's raspy voice.

"Have you ever been on a job interview, young man?"

"Yes, I have," said Jonah indignantly.

Millie noticed his tone.

"Listen, young man, I've been doing this since you were

in diapers. You look like a nice kid, but it's a tough world out there, and you need to know what you're doing; otherwise, they'll chew you up and spit you out… got it?"

Jonah did not respond; he couldn't think of anything to say and wasn't interested in being berated by this woman again. Sally suddenly waved an index card she had pulled from her Rolodex.

"I think he'd be perfect for this job, Millie."

"Lemmee see the card," rasped Millie.

She grabbed it, read, and broke into a big smile that displayed her coffee-stained teeth.

"Nice, Sally!" she said approvingly.

"OK, young man; listen closely. Franklin Heart is the CFO of a company called Tyler Technologies. He is looking for an executive assistant to help manage the company's day-to-day operations. He wants someone with a business degree that he can mold into his assistant. It's not exactly a finance position, although you will help him in that area; it's more like being the assistant to the CFO for whatever he needs to run the company on the finance end. And I think you might fit the bill perfectly."

Jonah was all ears.

"Now, let me tell you about the company. Tyler Technologies is an 80-year-old second-generation company managed by three brothers and a brother-in-law. Are you listening?"

"Of course, I'm listening."

I'm starting to feel like a piece of meat, thought Jonah.

"Just making sure," said Millie.

Jonah was starting to plan an exit strategy. Nothing was

worth the mental gymnastics he was going through to converse with this woman. He was also choking to death and figured he had about three or four minutes of clean air left before his lungs collapsed.

"Now, here's the deal with the company. Their headquarters are on Fifth Avenue, just a few blocks from here. There are about 75 employees in their corporate office, where you would work if you got the job. Are you following me?"

Jonah didn't answer; he just prayed the rest of the information wouldn't be disbursed piecemeal as it had been up to that point.

Mercifully, she continued, but at this point, she began to read from a card with information about the company.

"They manufacture high-tech weapons parts and explosives and depend on government contracts for the bulk of their business. The company has manufacturing plants in Baltimore, Maryland and Philadelphia, Pennsylvania, where they have about 500 employees building parts for high-tech weapons systems used by America and its allies."

Millie looked up from the card.

"You got all of that?"

"Yes, I've got all of that," shot back Jonah.

While this woman was annoying the hell out of him, inside, he could barely contain his excitement.

High-tech weapons parts and explosives, now we're talking! Who knew that accounting could be my pathway to my ultimate dream of saving the world?

Millie gave Jonah another look and decided to move on.

Jonah was starting to feel faint. His oxygen level was teetering between overdose and comatose. Through the fog that now enveloped the room, he couldn't help but wonder: *Why would such a major corporation be doing business with such a small employment agency?*

Millie lowered her voice as if she were about to give Jonah the nuclear codes.

"Now, let me tell you upfront: Franklin Heart is no easy cookie if you know what I mean. He likes things done a certain way. If it's not done the way he wants, he is not very happy. And if he is not very happy, he will let you know. But my instincts tell me he'll like you, and I trust my instincts. You fit the mold that he's looking for… interested?"

Despite the three-ring circus he found himself sitting in the middle of, Jonah had absolutely no prospects on the horizon. Not only did this sound like a great opportunity, but the thought of working for a company involved with national security would be a dream come true.

"Yes," said Jonah, "I am interested."

"Good, now for the hard part," said Millie. "I'm not just sending you in willy-nilly to this interview; if you want the job, you need to learn the interview process taught by the chief trainer at Success Employment, Inc."

"And who is that?" asked Jonah.

"Me."

That figures, Jonah thought.

"If I decide you are ready, you go for the interview. If not, we wish each other a pleasant day and say goodbye. Tomorrow morning, you will show up here at 9:00 promptly, and I will teach you how to interview and, more importantly, how to get the job. And most importantly, I will teach you the magic sentence that will get you any job if you say it right. That is the key, Jonah. You must find the right moment in the interview, and when that moment comes along, you spring the sentence… got it?"

Jonah couldn't wait to get out of there. He'd had dental work that was less stressful than this. Still, the opportunity was the best he had come across since he started looking for employment, and he would seize it. He promised to be there at 9:00 the following day and quickly exited.

Jonah arrived at Success Employment Inc. the next morning at a quarter to nine. It was a beautiful sunny day outside, in stark contrast to the storm raging in his stomach that had kept him up all night. The more he thought about it, the more he realized how great an opportunity this could be and the less sure he was that Sally and Millie were in any way qualified to help him get the job.

Millie got right to work on Jonah when he arrived.

"OK, Jonah," said Millie, "let's see your interviewing style; tell me about yourself."

Jonah proceeded to give her the usual stock answers to the typical questions. What are your strengths? What are your weaknesses? What interests you about Tyler Technologies, etc.? Millie spent all day training Jonah to answer those questions and more.

"We have to drill, drill, drill, over and over again until it comes out natural and not rehearsed," said Millie. "There's nothing worse than a candidate who sounds like he memorized his answers. Once again, let's take it from the top."

"What are your strengths? What are your weaknesses?

What interests you about Tyler Technologies?" Jonah answered each question repeatedly; he felt like a trained seal.

When Millie was satisfied that Jonah was ready, she said. "Be here tomorrow morning at 9:00 in your best suit, and get a haircut on your way home tonight. Sally has set up an interview for you for tomorrow morning at 11:00 sharp with Mr. Heart. Before you go, we will do our final prep, and at that time, I will teach you the most important question. This question will get you the job if asked at the right time and in the right manner. Are you ready, Jonah?"

"Yes," said Jonah. And off he went.

❧

Jonah showed up promptly the following day at 9:00. He could tell the ladies were impressed with how he cleaned up. On his way out of the house that morning, Jonah checked himself in the mirror.

Not bad... not bad at all!

He dressed like a dynamic young executive that any company would love to hire. Millie added the final touches for Jonah's interview. At 10:00, he left the office in plenty of time for his 11:00 appointment on Fifth Avenue. Sporting his new haircut, best suit, and the big smile he was told to flash when greeting anyone at the company, he was on his way. He entered the fancy office building, checked in with the doorman, and took the elevator to the tenth floor.

Tyler Technologies was the only company on the entire floor. He exited the elevator to a gleaming reception area with the company's name emblazoned on the mirrored wall behind the receptionist. Jonah was psyched; *this is it*, he thought to himself. The receptionist asked who he was there to see, and he tested his brand-new smile as he replied.

"I am here to see Mr. Franklin Heart for an 11:00 appointment."

The receptionist smiled back and asked him to take a seat. He caught his reflection in the mirrored wall and was quite impressed with himself.

What are your strengths? What are your weaknesses? What interests you about Tyler Technologies, etc.? I got this, thought Jonah.

After a brief wait, there was a short buzz at the receptionist's desk, and she rose and looked at Jonah.

"Please follow me."

Jonah was led down a large hallway that had offices on either side. The place was buzzing with activity; people were busy working. The *cacophonous* sound of a chorus of typewriters gave the atmosphere its rhythm. But as he passed each office, he felt eyes looking up and checking him out. He wondered if they all knew why he was there. However, it didn't matter; all he cared about were the answers to all the questions Millie had trained him to answer and when to land the big question Millie had taught him to ask at just the right time. The question wasn't a big deal, just an old interview trick, but if that's what the ladies wanted him to ask, and it would land him the job, then that's what he would ask.

He was finally escorted into Franklin Heart's large office. Mr. Heart shook his hand firmly, and Jonah made eye contact just like the ladies taught him. He was a large, well-dressed, and imposing individual; all Jonah could think was that this man was a presence. He exchanged smiles with the receptionist one more time before she left. Jonah noticed the large mahogany desk was empty except for a marble pen holder and a calendar. On the blotter sat a single sheet of paper, Jonah's resume.

"It's nice to meet you, Jonah," said Mr. Heart in an unexpectedly strong German accent. The accent somehow threw him off his game for a moment. As he locked eyes with Mr. Heart, there was a pregnant pause until his brain processed that Mr. Heart had just said, "Nice to meet you," which required a response.

He took a deep breath and calmed himself down, just as Millie taught him if the interview was getting away from him.

"It's my pleasure," said Jonah," making sure Mr. Heart had a good view of his smile.

If Mr. Heart noticed his hesitation, he kept it to himself. He then motioned to Jonah to sit at the other side of his desk. Jonah was a mixture of confidence and nervousness; he felt his knees shake. Mr. Heart had what could be described as a very kind smile, which went a long way toward calming Jonah down. He took a few minutes to explain what the position entailed and what was expected of the person chosen for the job. Jonah sat attentively and listened to every word. He couldn't help but be impressed with how Mr. Heart carried himself; his demeanor was unlike anyone he had ever met. He was kind but confident.

Mr. Heart began the interview process with a series of questions that allowed Jonah to talk about his background, why he was applying to Tyler Technologies, and what he could bring to the job of being his assistant. Jonah was well prepared for these questions and answered them just as Millie taught him. At some point, Jonah started to relax; things seemed to be going well.

It's in the bag, Jonah thought to himself.

This is going so well; I can't believe it.

He was waiting for an opening to spring the question Millie had taught him to ask when Mr. Heart handed it to him on a silver platter.

"Well, young man, you've answered all my questions. Do you have anything you want to ask me?"

This is it. The next words I utter will determine if I get the job at this prestigious high-tech company or if I'll be back pounding the streets in about ten minutes, thought Jonah.

It was a trick question designed to put the interviewer on the spot. It was meant to turn the tables with the only out, for the interviewer to offer the applicant the job.

I've got to get every word out exactly as Millie taught me, Jonah thought. *Here goes nothing…*

Jonah looked Mr. Heart in the eye, making sure to make direct eye contact.

"Mr. Heart, do you believe I possess the qualifications you are looking for to assume this position?"

There it was, right there, hanging out like a big matzoh ball. Mr. Heart stared straight at Jonah without so much as batting an eyelash. Jonah looked right back at Mr. Heart and held his stare for what felt like an hour.

Inside, he felt sick… *did I just ask that? I can imagine Franklin Heart thinking to himself.…*

Did he just ask me that silly question that any experienced interviewer has probably heard countless times?

I can't believe I blew it on the one-yard line, thought Jonah.

Inside, Jonah was a big pile of mush.

Why did I ever listen to that woman? Am I out of my mind? He must think I'm the most pompous idiot who ever sat across his desk. Do you believe I possess the qualifications you are looking for to assume this position? Who am I, Shakespeare? How about, will you let me live, Mr. Heart? Is there a trap door under this chair, Mr. Heart? I'm sorry I wasted your time, Mr. Heart. Can I rephrase the question, Mr...?

And then he heard it; his knees were banging so hard he almost missed it.

"Well, young man, I guess we will find out. Be here Monday morning, 9:00."

Jonah was so frozen in his seat that it took a few beats to realize what he had just heard. He jumped up, grabbed Mr. Heart's hand, and stammered.

"Thank you, Mr. Heart, thank you so much, Mr. Heart, I look forward to working with you, I mean... *for* you."

He thought he spotted a tiny smile cross Mr. Heart's face. He quickly left the office before he might have second thoughts. He practically ran down the hallway, past all the offices into the lobby, passing the startled receptionist, skipping the elevator, and galloping down the steps.

And then it dawned on him, almost like a flashback in a movie. It had registered in his brain, but the adrenaline didn't quite process it... until now. He was so excited racing down the hallway that his eye captured it, but as the adrenaline started to ease, his mind was beginning to process it. The name plaque on one of the office doors... "Hannah Weinberg: Engineer."

Could it be?

2

JONAH STILL LIVED at home with his mother. He couldn't wait to get home and tell her the good news. He knew how much this would mean to her; she would be so proud.

"Ma, I got the job!" Jonah proudly announced as he entered the house that night. "And these are for you."

He handed his mother a bouquet. Her eyes were filled with tears.

"I knew you would be a success one day. Oh, if your father could see you now!"

Jonah was proud of himself. He had given his mother the one thing she craved more than anything else: a modicum of success. If he could give his mother something to be proud of, even for a day, it was well worth it to make her happy, even if he wasn't the ambitious type and had no genuine desire to work in finance. If it were up to him, he would be handing out business cards that read: Jonah Mark: Spy. Reality was just an albatross around his neck.

Someday, he would figure out a way to get back to what he really wanted to do… what was in his heart.

❧

Jonah walked into his new office bright and early on Monday morning. The receptionist seemed to have an extra smile for him as if he had joined the club. He proudly knocked on Mr. Heart's office.

"Come in," said Mr. Heart.

Jonah found Mr. Heart sitting behind his large desk with just a copy of the New York Times spread across.

"Good morning, Jonah. Welcome to Tyler Technologies."

Jonah could not wipe the grin off his face.

"Thank you, Mr. Heart." For added measure, he asked, "How was your weekend?"

Mr. Heart did a double take, and there was a pregnant pause before his response.

"Fine, Jonah… fine."

Jonah thought to himself that he had probably been a bit too familiar, a little too cocky for his first day, and he wished he could have taken that last sentence back. He would dial it back a little, he thought to himself.

"Well, Jonah, it's time for your tour."

Mr. Heart took Jonah to the various offices to introduce his new assistant to everyone. Jonah was anxious to know if the "Hannah Weinberg: Engineer," whose name he briefly saw on one of the office doors as he left his interview, was the same Hannah Weinberg who was studying engineering when they dated. Jonah had not dated anyone seriously since Hannah broke up with him a few years earlier. He just never found anyone that attracted him as much as her. He regretted how things ended between them because they had such a strong connection, but time had passed, and they had both moved on; at least, that's what he thought.

Jonah had no idea where she worked or even lived these days, but seeing her name on that door brought a rush of memory and emotion that he thought he had left behind. The last time he had seen Hannah, there were tears on her face. He had blown it big time with her and wondered what would happen if they did meet again someday.

As Mr. Heart took him around the office, Jonah looked anxiously down every hallway and held his breath as he walked toward each office. Would he see her again? Did she really work here? It was hard to concentrate on anything else.

As Mr. Heart ushered Jonah around the office, he proudly wore his black knitted kipa, also known as a yarmulke, the religious symbol Orthodox Jews wear on their heads as a matter of course. Jonah came from a family that classified themselves as Modern Orthodox, which meant they followed the strict tenets of Orthodox Judaism while integrating with the secular, modern world.

As they walked the office hallways together, Mr. Heart asked Jonah about his background, birthplace, and family. Jonah told him about his family life, leaving out his obsession with spy novels and mystery clubs. Mr. Heart took particular interest in the story of his parents as Holocaust Survivors. Given his German ancestry, Jonah wondered how Mr. Heart would react to these stories. He was struck by the empathy he showed, the questions he asked, and how kindhearted he seemed to be. It was a vibe he picked up as they passed various employees walking past them.

"Hey Joe, how's Sally doing after that knee replacement?" he called out to an older employee as he was about to pass by.

"Doing great, Mr. Heart, thanks for asking."

"Let me know if you need an extra day or two."

"I sure will, Mr. Heart. Thanks so much."

"Hey Frank, how's Jimmy doing in little league?"

"Pitched a no-hitter the other night, Mr. Heart. I think I saw some scouts from the Yankees in the stands checking him out."

They both laughed.

"You tell Jimmy I want to see that arm at the company picnic."

"You can count on it, Mr. Heart, and thanks for that picture of the Babe; he really loved it!"

"You send him my best, Frank."

"Will do, Mr. Heart."

It was the same wherever he went; everybody loved the guy. He seemed to love the employees genuinely, and the feelings were mutual.

He was also struck by how the employees all referred to him as "Mr. Heart," as opposed to his first name like everyone else. He seemed to have earned a different level of respect.

Mr. Heart then headed down a hallway leading to the partner's offices. Jonah noticed the fancier carpeting and paintings on the wall.

The first door they encountered had a plaque that read: "Simeon Tyler: Vice President." Mr. Heart knocked on the door. A man was standing behind a large table in a fancy office. He was short and plain-looking and carried a few extra pounds in his midsection. He was looking at a spreadsheet behind a pair of half-reading glasses. He looked up and saw Mr. Heart and Jonah standing at the threshold. He gave Jonah an extra look.

"Who's this?"

"Simeon, I want to introduce you to my new assistant, Jonah Mark."

Jonah stuck out his hand, but Tyler ignored it.

"I'm swamped, Franklin; can't you see that?"

His terse reply and unfriendliness took Jonah aback.

Mr. Heart chose to ignore it.

"I'm sorry, Simeon; we'll catch you when you're less busy."

"Good idea, and next time, how about knocking?"

He placed his half glasses back on the tip of his nose and continued with his spreadsheet.

What a jerk, thought Jonah to himself.

As they exited his office, Jonah noticed that Mr. Heart seemed to take it in stride, as if nothing new. Jonah did not know what to say, so he decided to say nothing. They passed a few more employees in the hallway and exchanged pleasantries. Mr. Heart introduced Jonah to all of them, and they each wished him luck in his new position.

Mr. Heart then steered them to another partner's door. The plaque read: "Joel Tyler: Chief Executive Officer."

I guess this is the Big Honcho, Jonah thought to himself.

The man sitting behind his large desk looked tanned and fit. His feet were propped up with the morning's Wall Street Journal in his well-manicured hands. Jonah spotted what looked like a protein shake on his desk. Mr. Heart knocked on the door.

"Come in," he said as he looked up from his paper.

"Good morning, Joel. I want to introduce you to my new assistant, Jonah Mark."

Jonah stuck out his hand and received a rather cold stare followed by a limp handshake.

"So, this is what all the excitement is about."

Mr. Heart did not respond.

Joel's eyes were trained on Mr. Heart when he said it. It was as if Jonah wasn't even there.

"OK, so I met him. Will there be anything else? As you can see, I'm busy here."

"No problem, Joel, we'll catch you another time."

Talk about a welcome wagon! Jonah thought to himself.

Mr. Heart started to walk out of the office. Jonah felt awkward; he glanced back at Joel Tyler one more time. He had returned to his newspaper as if nothing happened. Jonah couldn't help but look back at him. Joel looked out from behind his paper, and they made eye contact for about two seconds. It felt like an hour for Jonah. It was a deadly stare, one that Jonah would not forget soon. He quickly looked away and continued to follow Mr. Heart.

They passed a few more employees who shared pleasantries with Mr. Heart. They enthusiastically shook Jonah's hand as they were introduced. The next partner's office had the name: "David Tyler: Vice President" on the door plaque.

He was pecking away at a keyboard as they knocked on his door. He looked thin in build with slumping shoulders. When Mr. Heart said "Good morning," he was so soft-spoken that you could barely hear his response.

"David, I'd like to introduce you to my assistant, Jonah Mark."

David's handshake was so light and cold that it was as if Jonah had shaken the hand of a ghost. He seemed to lack the confidence of the other partners Jonah had met.

"I'm in the middle of something here, so you'll have to excuse me."

There was no "nice to meet you, Jonah," but none of the other partners he had met had uttered those words.

"I'll leave you to your work, David," said Mr. Heart.

"OK then," said David softly as they left the office.

Seems like unfriendliness runs in the family, thought Jonah.

From the company roster, Jonah knew that there were four partners. He had already met Joel, Simeon, and David Tyler. The name that matched the plaque on the door at the end of the hall read: "Irving Carter: Vice President."

He must be the brother-in-law, Jonah thought to himself.

They heard the man shouting on the phone as they approached the door.

"You tell that sonofabitch that if I don't have that contract signed by tomorrow, he can kiss this deal goodbye!"

The entire conversation, including his slamming of the phone receiver, could be heard down the hall. The employees who sat at their desks right outside his office didn't seem all that stunned; it was as if they had seen this movie a thousand times. They all just went about their businesses.

Mr. Heart looked like he was about to pivot away when he heard Carter's voice.

"What do *you* want?"

The body language was unmistakable. It was clear to Jonah

he didn't like Mr. Heart; he could practically see the venom spew from his mouth. But while Mr. Heart was determined to act professionally, this guy clearly had no intention of doing so.

Jonah noticed some papers on his desk that he suddenly seemed to want to hide. He quickly gathered them together and shoved them into a desk drawer. He then took out a key and locked it. Jonah's Spidey Sense was alerted immediately. It was an expression from the Spiderman series, one of the many comic books he read, where he would sense danger before it occurred, and Jonah was always on alert.

Loudmouth has something to hide, thought Jonah to himself.

Mr. Heart ignored the side show and forged ahead as if this was their regular course of business.

"Irv, I wanted to come by and introduce you to my new assistant, Jonah Mark."

Jonah didn't get the chance to reach out his hand.

"Are you kiddin me, Franklin? I'm up to my ass in morons that don't know which end is up, and you're bothering me with this?"

Before they could say another word, he picked up his phone.

"Evelyn, get me a cup of coffee, and how about making sure it's hot this time."

He slammed down the phone.

"I swear, I don't know what that woman does all day, but she can't make a hot cup of coffee, that's for damned sure!"

He looked at both of them. Jonah felt the man's eyes pierce his skull, but Mr. Heart looked cool as a cucumber.

"Are we done here, or was there something else?"

"I think we're done," said Mr. Heart.

As they turned to walk away, he yelled out to Jonah.

"Hey!"

Jonah turned around.

"What was your name again?"

"Jonah Mark."

Jonah noticed the smirk on the man's face.

"If you can make a hot cup of coffee, you might just have a career here… and how about shutting the door on your way out."

Jonah was a little flustered, but he wasn't about to get into it with this lunatic, at least not on his first day. But he had a feeling that opportunity would present itself at some point. He quietly closed the door and continued to walk down the hall with Mr. Heart. Once again, Mr. Heart said nothing, but the look on his face was a different story. While he may have been embarrassed in front of his new employee by all the partners they had met, it seemed to Jonah that Mr. Heart had chosen this exercise to let him formulate his own opinions. And Jonah's mind was working overtime.

Jonah would have to process everything he had witnessed at a later time. Right now, however, his mind was preoccupied by one thing. He kept looking up and down the hallway for a possible glimpse of Hannah. They were heading toward the area where Jonah had seen Hannah's name on that door when he ran out of the office after his interview. Every female employee they passed got an extra glance from him. The thought that her appearance may have changed after all this time had crossed his mind. However, there were certain traits about Hannah that he knew would never change. The single freckle at the end of her nose, the elegant curve of her neck, the way she reacted when she was surprised; she would quickly cover her mouth with her hand to suppress a laugh or a scream. That was the Hannah he remembered, and as they walked down the hallway, a plaque on a door came into view. He had seen it before: "Hannah Weinberg: Engineer."

Jonah's heart was banging as they reached the door.

3

HANNAH WAS OUT the day Jonah was hired and knew nothing about it. She was reaching for a stack of files on an upper shelf when Mr. Heart knocked on her door. Jonah's suspicions were confirmed when Mr. Heart opened the door.

It's Hannah, as pretty as the day we broke up, thought Jonah.

Even as her back was turned, Jonah knew it was her by the elegant curve of her neck. She was startled by the knock, and the sight of Jonah standing next to Mr. Heart sent the stack of files scattering all over the floor. Jonah found Hannah's shocked reaction humorous but suppressed a smile as Hannah looked utterly flustered. The first thing she did was quickly cover her mouth with her hand; it was Hannah, no doubt. The freckle was still prominently displayed at the end of her nose. Mr. Heart smiled at her reaction.

Jonah and Hannah exchanged pleasantries as if they had never met before. They both knew to act professionally, and they did. Hannah craned her neck as Jonah and Mr. Heart left the room to get one more look. She thought about their past relationship. She really liked Jonah and regretted how things ended.

As they left her office, they each thought back to the night they met.

◈

Hannah Weinberg was two years younger than Jonah. She lived with her parents in the small town of Trumbull, Connecticut, where she attended a local Jewish day school as a child. Her father was an insurance salesman, and her mother stayed home and cared for Hannah and her two younger brothers. They were a Modern Orthodox Jewish family in a town of primarily gentiles. Her parents kept an observant lifestyle, following all the kosher dietary laws and attending synagogue on the Sabbath.

Hannah was always very bright and did well in school. As she grew older, her excellent grades allowed her to pursue a degree in technological engineering at Columbia University in New York City. She rented an apartment in Queens with a friend from high school and would take the subway every morning to class. Her parents were always concerned that she was too busy with her studies to pursue a serious relationship. Whenever she came home to her parents to visit, they would ask her how her dating life was.

"Meet anyone new this week, Hannah?" her mother would ask within minutes of walking in.

"It's been pretty busy, mom," Hannah would reply. "I've got a lot of reports to finish, so I don't have much time for a social life these days."

Her mother would practically sing the following line.

"Someone out there is missing out on a very special girl."

Hannah would usually steer the conversation elsewhere and get past the awkward moment. One weekend, her roommate was invited to a Jewish singles mixer on a Saturday night in Manhattan, and she asked Hannah if she would like to join her. Hannah decided to go so that she could tell her parents that she went.

Jonah and his best friend, Josh Silberstein, used to love going to singles events and meeting girls, so when Josh saw the event advertised in their synagogue newsletter, he told Jonah about it.

"Hey Jonah, check this out," said Josh, hanging around Jonah's room one night just shooting the breeze.

"What is it?"

"It's an ad for a singles event; take a look."

He took a quick look.

"Nah, I don't think so."

"Why not?"

"Not for me."

"Not for you?" said Josh.

"Nope!"

"How come?"

"I don't like the vibe."

"What vibe?"

"Well, you see here where it says where it's taking place?"

Josh looked at the ad again.

"It says it's taking place at the Biltmore Lounge on 60th Street; what's wrong with that?"

"I have no luck with girls anywhere north of 57th Street."

"Are you nuts, Jonah?"

"I'm telling you, whenever I go to a singles event north of 57th Street, I strike out with the ladies. Remember that mixer we went to last year at that coffee house on 59th?"

"Yeah?"

"I used my best lines, guaranteed to attract any woman, and I was driving women away from me in droves."

"And you think it's because of the address."

"What else can it be?"

"Jonah, did you ever think it might be your approach?"

"My approach? What's wrong with my approach?"

"How about… everything!"

"I'm speechless. You can blow me over like a feather."

"The truth shall set you free, buddy. Did you ever try to just walk up to a woman and say hello instead of those lame pickup lines of yours?"

"Why would I do that? And what lame pickup lines?"

"What lame pickup lines? Are you kidding me? How about when you told that girl at the synagogue social last month that you were a Nuclear Proctologist?"

"What's wrong with that?"

"You told another girl at Mark's birthday party last June that you invented scissors; who comes up with stuff like that!?"

"I don't see why I can't impress a girl with my background."

"Why can't you just be yourself?"

"Be myself? I'm not sure I understand what you're driving at?"

"Look, Jonah, we're not twelve years old anymore, and I know you're into all your mystery clubs and all that magic mumbo jumbo you spend your time with…."

"I'm wounded!"

"Nevertheless, try to act normal for once and see how that works for you. Why not let them see the real Jonah Mark? They may just like what they see."

"Hmmm, be myself, a novel thought. I'll never pull it off; it's much too complicated."

"I'm making two reservations; you'll join me at the mixer north of 57th Street. You will *not* be a nuclear proctologist or a NASA Supersonic Jet Test Pilot like you told those girls we met last week at the science fair, and for heaven's sake, you did *not* invent scissors!"

"Well, that's where you're wrong, buddy. I once cut a piece of paper with two knives going in opposite directions…."

"No scissors!"

"OK… OK, no scissors."

✍

The singles event took place in a crowded room with lots of music and lots of singles. At some point, as they had done so often, Josh and Jonah decided to split up and mingle with other friends. The night was boring for both of them until Jonah spotted Hannah from across the room; she was a vision. He had never seen someone so beautiful.

This is why I am here tonight, thought Jonah to himself.

He was trying to figure out how to meet her when he noticed her heading to the refreshments table. That was his cue. He made a beeline to the table just as she was reaching for a soda cup.

"Can I help you with that?" said Jonah as he reached for a cup and handed it to her.

"Thank you," said Hannah with as pretty a smile as Jonah had ever seen.

"You know that's very dangerous," said Jonah.

"What's dangerous?"

"The way you reached for that cup."

"What do you mean?"

"Well, if you don't reach for that cup at just the right angle… well, you don't want to know."

Hannah looked up to see a nice-looking young man with a bright smile. *Not bad,* thought Hannah. *Maybe it was worth coming after all.* She was intrigued, so she decided to play along, as he was clearly making things up on the fly.

"Well, I do want to know because it sounds *very dangerous.*"

"It is… it most certainly is… very… very dangerous."

"And how would you know that?" asked Hannah.

"I'm sorry. I should have introduced myself, but given the circumstances, I had to act first."

Hannah had a dubious look on her face, but she went along.

"Of course… and you are?"

"Jonah Mark, NC."

"NC?"

"…eh… Noted Cupologist."

"A Cupologist! I don't think I've ever met a Cupologist before."

"Well, we usually work undercover… and your name?"

"Hannah Weinberg, regular person. And what might that danger be?"

"What danger is that?"

"That I reached for the cup at a dangerous angle."

"Right… well, you can damage your flaganoid if you reach for a cup at that angle."

"Really, my flaganoid! I never knew that. I guess I'm lucky to have run into you."

"Oh, without a doubt. And I'm so glad to have run into you… eh… to save your life."

"You've got some line there. Do you use that on all the girls you meet?"

"Only the pretty ones. By the way, I notice you have something there on the tip of your nose."

"And what might *that* be?"

"Well, I should tell you I am also a Certified Freckologist."

"A Freckologist… really!"

"And what do you see, Mr. Freckologist?"

"I see a very cute freckle perched right there at the end of your nose."

"And what would you suggest I do about it, Mr. Freckologist?"

"You can call me Mr. Freckles for short."

"OK, I'll bite; what would you suggest… Mr. Freckles?"

"If it were me, and I looked like you, I'd leave it right there; it's definitely too cute to do any procedure."

"Did you make all of that up?"

"Oh no, *I am a noted Cupologist*; I dabble in freckles on the side."

"You dabble in freckles on the side; how interesting. Is it *Doctor* Mark?"

"My friends call me Jonah. As do my family and everyone else I know. I do my best work undercover."

"I bet you do."

They both laughed; there was an instant attraction between them. As they spent the next couple of hours talking, they discovered that they both came from similar backgrounds and knew many of the same people, so it was a natural fit for them. Jonah thought she was beautiful, and Hannah also thought he was attractive. The conversation flowed easily, and the night went by quickly. Their friends noticed.

"Nice looking girl," said Josh at the end of the night. Are you going to pursue this?"

Jonah flashed Hannah's phone number on a napkin he withdrew from his pocket. He asked her out the next week, and they dated steadily for about a year and a half. They spent a lot of time with each other and spoke on the phone on nights when they were apart. Hannah took Jonah to her favorite museums while Jonah took Hannah to his favorite bookstores, which featured readings from well-known mystery writers. Jonah wasn't big on museums, something Hannah noticed, and Hannah found the readings to be boring.

But they loved each other's company. Jonah could stare at Hannah's smile all day long, and Hannah found Jonah to be very entertaining, but getting used to his corny jokes might take some time. On Hannah's birthday, he surprised her with a beautiful locket. Jonah engraved it with the words: "To my favorite future engineer from your favorite Cupologist." Hannah loved it. They introduced each other to their best friends and enjoyed movies and pizza together. Hannah often wondered what it would be like to be married to Jonah. There would be many laughs, but would that be enough for her?

⤙

The story of Mr. Heart's introduction of Jonah to Hannah got around the office very quickly. While no one knew of their past, it made for excellent office gossip. Everyone in the company knew that Hannah was a young and pretty religious girl, so there was always gossip about a match for Hannah. Hannah ignored it, as she had been through this before, every time a young Jewish man entered the office.

The previous week, Jane from data entry was waiting in line to make copies when Hannah walked by.

"Hey Hannah, how's it going?"

Hannah was so used to this routine that her antennas immediately went up.

"Fine, Jane; how are you?"

"Great, Hannah. Did you see the cute guy who dropped in to see Simeon for a lunch meeting yesterday? I spotted him from down the hall."

I need to get through this, thought Hannah.

"No, I missed it; I was in my office… working."

Jane lowered her voice.

"Well, the guy was adorable… lemee tell you. And he had one of those yamaha's on his head, you know like the Jewish guys wear."

"I think you mean a yarmulke."

"Yeah, that's it! And I bet he had a bar mitzvah too!"

Hannah held her tongue and hoped to find a way to extricate herself from this conversation smoothly and quickly.

"And I think they ordered bagels and lox and everything."

"Really!"

"Yeah, I passed his office to do a little reconnaissance for you. I may have heard him humming Hava Nagila when he walked out, but I could be wrong."

"That's really nice of you to check this guy out for me, Jane, but I usually like to…."

"And did this guy have a head of hair! He looked like that Alex Keaton on Family Ties. You know, he's got some mop on his head… a little too conservative for my taste… I don't think he's Jewish, but ya never know."

"Uh, thanks, Jane. I appreciate you looking out for me. I just remembered; I forgot something in my office."

"Always happy to help, Hannah; you just let me know."

Hannah had trouble concentrating at work ever since Mr. Heart dropped into her office with Jonah. In her mind, that chapter of her life was over. Now, here he was again, and those feelings she had worked so hard to suppress after their breakup were also back.

And it was such an awful breakup.

After many months of spending so much time together, it became clear that they had hit a bump in the road. As Hannah continued her educational career, it was becoming difficult for her to carve out time for Jonah. They were on different career tracks, and her busy schedule left less and less time to spend with him. She had tests to study for and research papers to do. She could not give up that precious time to hang out with him and talk about his mystery books or the latest movies, like ET, that she had not found the time to see.

What finally ended it for Hannah was that she had become increasingly uncomfortable with Jonah's lack of seriousness about his life. He seemed stuck in a world of spy novels, comic books, and mystery clubs; it was as if he hadn't found the right balance in his life.

Does he know where the line is between mystery and reality? thought Hannah to herself one day as they were walking through the park. All he could talk about was the movie Return of the Jedi and how he couldn't wait for her to see it.

It bothered her that he didn't have the ambition she possessed for the future. He didn't seem interested in his job and wasn't career-minded enough for her. His interests and her interests were very different. Hannah often voiced her concerns to Jonah, but he didn't take them seriously. Instead, he seemed to take her concerns for granted, like how he ran his own life. She wished there was a way to get Jonah to focus more on the essential things. But Jonah was oblivious to those concerns.

Hannah thought back to Jonah's birthday. She had taken him to one of his favorite restaurants, Kosher Delight. Although Hannah wasn't into fried chicken, she knew how much Jonah loved chicken wings. She was happy there was a salad on the menu and went with that. Hannah handed him an envelope from her pocketbook as Jonah was busy munching on his wings and fries.

"What is it?" asked Jonah.

"Two tickets to the Met."

"Just what I always wanted; I love the Mets. Where are

the seats located, behind home plate or along one of the baselines?"

"No, Jonah, not the Mets, the Met."

"I don't get it; we're seeing one Met? You know *it is a team sport*, Hannah; they don't play one at a time."

"It's the Metropolitan Museum of Art, Jonah, one of the largest museums in the world.

"Well, I think it's pretty sneaky of them to steal the name of a revered sports team in this city. Couldn't you have gotten tickets to the Mets?"

"You'll love it, Jonah; we're going to see an exhibition of European paintings by the Masters."

"When is it?"

"Tomorrow night."

"Can't go."

"Why not?"

"We're getting together at the mystery club. They're doing an exhibition on lock picking by the Masters."

His humor wasn't hitting the mark with Hannah, at least not that night.

"Jonah, these tickets weren't easy to get."

"Then maybe you should have checked with me first."

Hannah stood up to leave.

"I was just kidding, Hannah."

"Does that mean you'll come?"

"How about we duck into this Met place for like twenty minutes; we check out these masters you're talking about, and then we hop the train to Flushing, where we can see the real Mets playing the Dodgers."

Hannah was out the door.

He called Hannah later that night to apologize and agreed to join her at the Met the following night. Still, as they walked through the exposition, it was clear that he was going through the motions. After about an hour of witnessing his total disinterest, Hannah waived the white flag.

"Jonah, you're not interested in any of this, are you?"

"That depends."

"On what?"

"If you'll get angry at me again if I tell you the truth."

Hannah felt exasperated.

"Jonah, this isn't working."

"I agree. We can still catch the train and make it to the third inning."

"I meant us, Jonah… or maybe just me. This isn't working for me. All you care about are magic tricks, mystery books, and a whole lot of things that make me feel like I'm going out with a guy from high school."

"Hannah, don't say that; I love you."

"Maybe that's just not enough for me anymore, Jonah?"

"I'm sorry, Hannah; I really am. Give me a chance to do better."

They walked and talked for the next two hours. Jonah promised to ease up on his hobbies and to be more attentive to her interests. The following week, he surprised her with tickets to the opera and sat through the whole evening with a big smile.

And then came the final straw for Hannah.

Things had gotten better between them until Hannah met a well-known college professor at a school function one night. He was nearing retirement and had recently started mentoring business students, helping them figure out a career path. He did it all for free on his own time. Hannah was impressed that someone would be willing to help others this way, and she told Jonah all about it the next day as they were taking a lunchtime walk.

"He's a busy guy, Jonah, but I think I could schmooze my way in and get you an appointment. What do you say?"

Jonah was noticeably less enthusiastic about it than Hannah, but the anxious look on her face seemed to convince him.

"Sure, I'll see him."

Hannah was so excited that she searched the entire building for the professor the next day at lunch. She spotted him just as he stepped out for a bite and broke into a dead run to catch him before he stepped into the restaurant he was standing in front of.

"Professor Mendelson," she called out, reaching him entirely out of breath.

"Are you OK, young lady?"

"It's Hannah Weinberg; we spoke the other day."

"Sure, sure, Hannah, how are you?"

"I'm fine, Professor; I hope I'm not interrupting you."

"Well, I was about to step inside for a bite, but it can wait another minute. What's on your mind; you seem very anxious?"

"Do you remember telling me how you mentor young business students?"

"Sure."

"I was wondering if you could help my boyfriend. His name is Jonah Mark, and he is an aspiring business student who can use some good advice on a career path."

"I'd be happy to, Hannah. Here's my card; have him call my secretary tomorrow, she has my calendar. She's only there until 1:00, so make sure he calls in the morning. I'm going away next week, and when I return, we will start the new semester, so I will have to fit him in in the next two days. After that, I won't be mentoring for another six months. Just tell him to mention your name, I'll leave word, and she'll set something up."

"Thank you so much, Professor; this really means a lot to me."

"Not at all."

He walked into the restaurant as Hannah wished him a nice lunch.

Jonah and Hannah got together that night, and she couldn't get the words out fast enough.

"Professor Mendelson is willing to meet with you; isn't that great?"

"Professor who?"

"Professor Mendelson, the professor I told you about who mentors students on the side."

"Eh… of course, how could I forget? That's great!"

His response sounded a little forced to Hannah, but she ignored it and handed him the business card.

"OK, call his secretary at this number tomorrow morning and mention my name; she'll know what it's about. She's only there until 1:00, so make sure you call in the morning. Remember, tomorrow is the last day to get an appointment before he leaves and starts a new semester. He'll slip you in before he leaves."

"Got it."

"Jonah, this is serious stuff. I need to know we are on the same page regarding furthering our careers."

"I'm right there with you," said Jonah.

"Make sure you call tomorrow."

"Will do."

"OK, I've got to get home to study," said Hannah. They exchanged a quick "good night," and she was off.

&

Hannah was so lost in thinking about her breakup with Jonah that she accidentally knocked into Becky, who was carrying a box of letters to the mail room.

"Are you OK, Hannah?"

Hannah had suddenly come back to reality.

"Eh… sorry Becky… I had something on my mind."

"No problem, Hannah. But next time, I'll have to issue you a ticket."

"Uh… sure, Becky; next time."

Becky walked away, confused.

That's it. I have to get him out of my mind.

Hannah headed to her office. She would have to finish her daydream later.

&

About three months after Tyler Tech hired Jonah, he found out about a position that was about to become available in their accounting department. They were looking for a young accounting grad that they could train who would grow with the company. His best friend Josh Silberstein had graduated with an accounting degree from Columbia University in

New York City. He was working in a small firm and looking for a new opportunity. Jonah thought he would be perfect for the job. Josh and Jonah attended yeshiva, an Orthodox Jewish day school, together as kids and became great friends; they were inseparable in their youth. They attended the same yeshiva, the same high school, and the same college together. They spent most of their free time together when they were young. They both loved the Mets, who played their home games at nearby Shea Stadium in Queens, and used to attend games whenever their parents would let them.

As it turned out, they lived just one block from each other, so they always hung out together. They hadn't spent as much time together in the last couple of years as they were busy trying to get their careers going. Still, they kept in touch and would share a pizza occasionally. At one of those get-togethers, Jonah told Josh about the position. He was excited about the opportunity to work for such a well-known firm in the same office as Jonah.

"Wow, that's great, Jonah; I'd love to work with you. It would be like old times!" said Josh.

"One more thing," said Jonah, "Hannah works here too."

"You're kidding me!" said Josh. "Hannah Weinberg works there too?"

"Yes," said Jonah. "It's been a little awkward."

"I can imagine. How are you handling it?"

"To tell you the truth, I'm unsure how to handle it. I've tried to keep a low profile. The other day, we were both in the elevator heading to lunch. There were other employees on the elevator, too, and I felt them staring at me.

"They were probably looking for some gossip, Jonah;

that's what employees do. And everyone loves an office romance."

"I guess so, but I wasn't about to sweep her off her feet in an elevator filled with employees."

"So, what did you do?"

"Nothing, I just stared at the floor numbers."

"You'll have to teach me that move, Jonah. What did she do?"

"She stared at the floor numbers."

"Why didn't you say something?"

"Well, like I told you, other people were on the elevator, and I couldn't think of anything to say. I was so flustered I had to stop myself from announcing the floor numbers. I even toyed with mentioning how quickly the elevator was traveling."

"Riveting."

"The other people on the elevator would have probably thrown me out."

"I would have. Do you still like her?"

"*Yes, I still like her, Josh; we're talking about Hannah.* I never stopped liking and thinking about her, but if you remember, she dumped me. So, I'm not sure what to do."

He thought back to the breakup....

❧

Things had not been going well between them; Hannah had told him she wasn't happy that he didn't take things seriously. Their relationship had been hanging by a thread, and he had been doing everything he could to improve things. He had even surprised her with tickets to the opera the week before.

Then, Hannah ran into this professor who helped aspiring business students with their careers. Hannah managed to convince the man to meet with him. All Jonah had to do was call his secretary the following day and set up the appointment. She would only be there until 1:00. The professor was going away the following week, so this was the only chance to see him until the following semester. Jonah promised to make the call.

The phone rang on his night table at 7:00 AM. He felt around for the phone and knocked over a cup of water.

"Hello?"

"Hey buddy, it's Josh."

Jonah was all groggy; he hadn't gotten a good night's sleep.

"Josh, what time is it?"

"It's baseball time!"

"It's what time?"

"I got these great box seats at Shea Stadium for today's game. A friend of mine had to cancel. The guy's got an impacted molar that's killing him, so he's going to see the dentist, and we're going to the ball game. Talk about luck!"

"That sounds great, Josh, but there's something I gotta do for Hannah… actually, it's for me. Anyway, I've got to call a number to make this appointment."

"What appointment?"

"I'll explain later."

"The game is at 1:00. I want to get there for batting practice and shag some foul balls before the stands get filled up. The gates open at noon, and we will be the first ones on line."

"Yeah, that means we need to leave here by eleven to beat the traffic. I'll make the call before I leave."

"Sounds like a plan, buddy; I'll pick you up at 11:00; make sure you're ready. We're going to the Mets!"

Jonah figured he had time to catch a few more winks, so he set his alarm for 10:00. That would give him enough time to get dressed and make the call before Jonah honked his horn outside.

Jonah awoke to the sound of a horn outside his window. He looked at his alarm clock; it was 11:15. He jumped out of bed.

My alarm didn't go off!

Jonah heard Josh yelling outside his window as he frantically tried to get dressed.

He looked out the window as he was hopping around in one shoe.

"Hey buddy, where are you?" yelled Josh from outside.

"My alarm clock didn't go off!"

"Well, that sucks, we're gonna miss batting practice."

"OK, give me five minutes to hit the bathroom and another five for everything else."

"Everything else? What else is there?"

Jonah ignored him and headed for the bathroom, where he did his morning routine in record time. Before he ran out of the house, he looked around the room quickly. Something bothered him, but he couldn't figure out what it was.

Am I forgetting something?

There was no time to figure it out; he would deal with it when it came to him. He ran down the stairs and saw his mother at the kitchen table.

"It looks like you slept late, Jonah, but don't worry, I've got some hot pancakes on the stove."

The pancakes smelled great, but he'd have to grab something at the game.

"Sorry, Mom, I'm really late. Can we save them for tomorrow?"

Before she could reply, he grabbed a few pancakes off the plate; they were a little hot to handle. He gave his mom a peck on the cheek and ran out the door.

He handed Josh a hot pancake as he entered the car.

"Ouch, what are these?"

"They're called pancakes, Josh; maybe you've heard of them."

"You had time to eat?"

"Just drive Josh, I'll explain later."

The game was great, although they didn't catch any foul balls because they missed most of batting practice. The Mets were winning, and they were having a great time. It was about the fifth inning when Jonah suddenly bolted out of his seat with a look of terror on his face.

"What's wrong, buddy? You look like you've seen a ghost."

"The call… I forgot to make the call!"

"What call?"

"I was supposed to call that professor's secretary for Hannah… actually for me."

"Forget it, you'll call tomorrow."

"No, no, no, you don't get it; this meant a lot to Hannah; she will be livid. I was supposed to call this woman by 1:00, and it's 2:30. Maybe I can still reach her from the phone booth."

Jonah started rifling through his pocket for the business card and realized he left it on his dresser at home. His mother would be at her mahjong game by now, so there was no sense calling her for the number; he was too late to call anyway.

"My goose is cooked," said Jonah.

"Come on, it can't be that bad."

"It can't be worse. She went through all this trouble to get this professor to do her a favor, actually to do *me* a favor, and she went over the instructions with me like I was operating on half a brain."

"Well, she got that right. Maybe you should have done it while dining on pancakes while I was waiting for you."

"I wasn't dining on… forget it. You don't understand, Josh; how will I explain that I couldn't do it because I was late to the ballgame and forgot to make the call?"

"At least enjoy the rest of the game, Jonah; we'll come up with a plan on the way home."

"I'm not interested in the game anymore, Josh. Things are already rocky with Hannah; she thinks I'm not taking my career seriously, and this will not help. I already got her pissed with me when I didn't want to go to the Met."

"You just went to the Mets."

"Not the Mets, the Met."

Jonah, there is more than one Met; they don't play the game one guy at a time, you know."

"Forget it, Josh, just forget it. The bottom line is that she thinks I'm not serious enough about my life."

"*Well, she got that right,*" Josh mumbled under his breath.

Jonah shot him a look.

"What's that supposed to mean?"

"Face it, Jonah, you don't have the intellectual curiosity Hannah seeks."

"And who are you, Sigmund Freud?"

"I know things."

"You know things?"

"Yes, Jonah, I have a gift."

"Really? Let me hear this one."

"On a superficial level, to the eye of the simple beholder, you are perfect for each other. You tell a joke, she laughs; you tell her another joke, and she laughs again. But to a trained appraiser of the human spirit like yours truly, this relationship can only go so far. When it comes to the serious stuff, on an intellectual level, you just don't fill her needs."

"I see, professor; please continue."

"Well, she doesn't strike me as the comic book, slash mystery club slash spy novel kind of girl."

"And you know this from your years of experience as an observer of the human condition."

"I know this from my years of experience as your friend who happens to have this gift."

"Well then, I would think your love life must be going swimmingly for a man with such gifts."

"Well, I wouldn't say swimmingly."

"That women can't wait to go out with you and drink from your fountain of knowledge."

"Well, I didn't say anything about knowledge."

"That your calendar is filled with dates from the intellectual types you speak of. After all, who wouldn't want to go out with someone blessed with such a gift!"

"Well… maybe a gift was a little strong."

"Earth to Josh, reality just arrived."

Josh sat back in his seat and said nothing.

"Look, Josh, I'm in a mess here; I think I blew my last chance with Hannah."

Jonah moped in his seat for another half hour before Josh decided to put him out of his misery and take him home. He pulled up in front of Jonah's place.

"Cheer up, buddy, it'll all work out."

Jonah didn't respond; he just headed upstairs to his room. His mom hadn't come home from mahjong yet. When he walked into his room, the first thing he saw was the business card sitting on his dresser. It was like rubbing salt into his wound.

What am I going to do?

He sat on his bed all afternoon trying to come up with something to tell Hannah when they met at the deli for dinner that night. He decided that Hannah would see through any story he came up with. So, he decided to go with the truth and hope for the best.

Jonah pulled up in front of Hannah's apartment in Queens at 6:30 and honked the horn. Hannah came running out about a minute later with a big smile on her face. Jonah had come around to her side of the car and held the door open for her. As he got back in the car, he could see the excitement on Hannah's face. He was doomed, and he knew it.

"Well," said Hannah, "what happened? Did you get the appointment; was she waiting for your call?"

This had disaster written all over it; he would have rather had to eat a plate of poison.

"Hannah, I'm really sorry I didn't make the call."

Hannah looked stunned. The smile on her face had disappeared.

"You didn't make the call? Why not?"

"I guess I can tell you how my alarm didn't go off; I was late for the ball game with Josh and left the card at home. But the truth is I screwed up, Hannah. I never made the call."

Hannah looked the most upset he had ever seen her.

"Are you telling me that after all I went through to get you this appointment after I went over exactly what you needed to do so that this man, who owes you nothing, can do me, actually *you,* a favor to help you further your career, you just blew that off?"

"Well…."

"And what am I supposed to tell him that my boyfriend, who has absolutely no ambition for the future, who thinks life is all about comic books, mystery clubs, and going to baseball games, forgot to make a simple call to make an appointment for someone to help him set his head straight?"

"Hannah, I'm really sorry; I really meant to make the call, it's just that …"

"Forget it, Jonah; this was a mistake."

"You mean the appointment?"

"No, Jonah, I mean everything."

Hannah reached for the handle on the door.

"Hannah, you can't be serious!"

"No, Jonah. It's you who can't be serious. I can't see spending the rest of my life with someone so shallow."

"Just because I missed making a call?"

"It's more than that, Jonah. It's the Met; it's all the time you spend on superficial things. It's your total lack of intellectual curiosity."

Thought Jonah: *Josh finally got something right, and this is what it turns out to be.*

"I'm sorry, Jonah. I thought we had something special, but I guess I was wrong."

"I'm sorry Hannah… I can change."

"That's the problem, Jonah; I don't think you can."

Jonah was speechless; he could not come up with anything to say. There were no clever lines to use; it was over, he knew it, and it was all his fault. Tears were rolling down Hannah's cheeks as she exited the car.

Jonah tried calling her at various times of the day over the next week, but she ignored his calls and never picked up the phone. It was over, dead and buried.

Jonah resolved to make something of himself going forward. There would no longer be time for his mystery clubs and comic books; he would spend his time reading textbooks instead, and although Hannah would probably never know it, shortly before joining Tyler Technologies, he not only finished his MBA at night but graduated summa cum laude with a 4.0-grade point average. Although his love for comic books, mystery clubs, and spy novels would forever be inside him, he would try as hard as he could to suppress those thoughts and feelings and strive to be a Yuppie like everyone else his age… as much as it killed him.

Josh could see Jonah was lost in thought about his breakup with Hannah and apparently still upset about it. He tried to get his attention.

"Jonah, she dumped you a while ago; maybe her feelings have changed. Back then, you were drifting along with no future. She hated that and that you spent all your free time with those comic books and mystery clubs."

"Yeah, well, I was so upset with the breakup, I dumped all those books and stopped going to those mystery clubs too. But the truth is that it's still a part of me, Josh; it's still who I am."

"What's the deal with that Jonah?"

"With what?"

"Those mystery clubs you always used to talk about; what did you guys do there?"

"It was pretty much like a book club; only we talked about mystery books."

"So, name me one of them."

"Huh?"

"Give me the name of one of your mystery clubs; I wanna hear a name."

"You're pulling my chain, Josh; you don't care about a name."

"So, you spent all those hours talking about mystery books, and you can't name a single club."

"Yes, I can."

"No, you can't."

"It's not happening, Josh; I'm not getting sucked into another one of your crazy, yes, I can, no, you can't, verbal gymnastics."

"Because you can't."

"Yes... I... can... now leave it alone, you pain in the neck...."

Jonah realized that he had been shouting and felt silly about it.

"OK, Josh, I'll give you a name under one condition."

"What's that?"

"You leave it alone. Not a sentence… not a word… not a syllable… nothing… nada… zero; you got it?"

Jonah noticed he was shouting again and shot Josh the death stare.

"OK, what is it?" said Josh.

"Are we in agreement?"

"We are in agreement."

Jonah looked Josh in the eyes as he said the name, using his hands for dramatic effect.

"The Plot Thickens!"

Josh was quiet for a few seconds as he contemplated the name.

"That's actually pretty good."

Jonah felt relief and pride at the same time.

"Now, are we all done with that?"

Josh was looking humbled.

"I suppose so."

"Good. Now, where were we?"

"You know what, Jonah?"

"What?"

I'm impressed; you really *have* changed. I'm proud of the new you, buddy. Now, you've got an MBA with honors, and this great job at a great company. Maybe if Hannah met the new you, she might be interested in getting back together?"

"I don't know, Josh; we pass each other in the hallway occasionally and do the awkward smile thing, but I don't know what's going on in her head."

"Well, you might think about having a conversation

with her one day and gauge her interest. No sense in tortur-
ing yourself; if she's not interested, at least you'll know where
you stand and be able to move on."

"You're probably right, Josh; I just have to find the right
time and place. Meanwhile, let's get you this position. And
by the way, what was wrong with the *old* me?"

"How much time do you have?"

"I take offense to that."

"Offense noted."

Jonah knew that Personnel was about to advertise the position he wanted Josh to get; having him around would be
great. So, he dropped Josh's resume on the desk of the HR
department head the following day and told him that the
resume somehow got routed to him instead of HR. Jonah
didn't want anyone to think that if Josh got the job, it was
because he was friends with Jonah, so he asked Jonah to keep
their past relationship private. Josh got called into the office
two days later for an interview. He was the only candidate
at that point, and if he fit the bill, he would save the HR
department a lot of time, effort, and money. He was hired
the following week.

Jonah was thrilled to have his best friend working with
him at Tyler Tech. And the thought of possibly rekindling
his relationship with Hannah put some extra pep in his step.

Everything is falling into place; I couldn't be happier,
thought Jonah.

The next day, Jonah had just returned from grabbing some takeout lunch when he felt a pair of eyes focusing on him. It was the same pair of eyes he had thought he had noticed from the other end of the office the day before but had written off as his own paranoia. But this time was different. This time, he was sure he was being watched by the same person who made no attempt to look away when Jonah looked back at him. It was an uncomfortable three seconds.

What the hell? thought Jonah.

That's the Director of Corporate Security, Ryan Schapp; why is he looking at me that way?

He hurried into his office and tossed his lunch on his desk. He felt a cold sweat on the back of his neck. Jonah's Spidey Sense had never left him, even though he had stopped reading his spy books.

There's something strange about that guy, and one way or another, I'm going to find out what it is.

4

IT DIDN'T TAKE long for Jonah to get used to the office dynamics; the partners' disdain for Mr. Heart and Smokey was easy to see. He saw Mr. Heart eating lunch in his office every day with Smokey, and from where his office was situated, he could hear more than he probably should have. They would sit and shoot the breeze and lament how things used to be and how the children were ruining the company that Noah Tyler had created.

"Noah would have turned over in his grave if he had known how they were running the company," he once heard Mr. Heart say to Smokey.

"It's not like the old days, Franklin, that's for sure," said Smokey. He was the only person in the company besides the partners who called Mr. Heart by his first name.

Jonah could see they were both bitter about what the children had done to their father's legacy in a few short years. He could also see the partners' body language when dealing with Smokey. They clearly didn't like him. Jonah imagined that to them, he was just another Franklin Heart to deal with, someone looking over their shoulders. And Jonah witnessed little things the partners did to make him uncomfortable. He remembered seeing Mr. Heart and Smokey heading for their usual Tuesday lunch one day when he heard Joel Tyler call out to Smokey.

"Hey Smokey, I need you to review this file for me; it's on that shipment to France next week."

Smokey stole a glance at Mr. Heart.

"Can it wait until after lunch? I was just going out."

"I really need it now, Smoke, sorry."

He glanced at Mr. Heart, who clearly looked irritated.

"You better go without me, Franklin. I gotta do this thing."

As he headed toward Joel to get the file, he looked past Smokey at Mr. Heart with a little smirk.

Jonah remembered another time when Mr. Heart could not get into his office one morning. Jonah tried to help him get the door open. After a half hour of struggling, Irv came strolling down the hallway. Jonah could see the delight on his face when he passed them, struggling with the door. He made a show of turning around with an expression of remembering something.

"Oh, Franklin, I forgot to tell you; we had to change the locks on the office doors last night. The security people recommended we change them after that theft from petty cash last month."

"They could have given me a new key before I left last night."

"I suppose they could have; I guess they forgot."

He smiled at both of them as he continued down the

hallway to his office when he suddenly heard a voice from behind that startled Irv and Mr. Heart.

"You know, it wouldn't kill you to show Mr. Heart some respect."

"Jonah!" said Mr. Heart, who was clearly taken aback by his comment.

Irv turned around and confronted Jonah.

"What did you say, young man?"

Jonah had seen enough disrespect shown to Mr. Heart and decided to throw caution to the wind.

"I said it would be nice to show Mr. Heart some respect; is that too much to ask?"

Irv looked directly at Mr. Heart.

"I suggest you teach your little sidekick here to mind his manners."

He turned around and headed down the hallway.

"My office, now!" said Mr. Heart. Jonah never saw him look this angry.

He closed the door behind them as they entered Mr. Heart's office. Jonah realized he had made a mistake and started to apologize.

"I'm sorry, Mr. Heart, but Mr. Carter was …"

Mr. Heart cut him off in mid-sentence.

"You will never do anything like that again; do you understand me?"

"Yes, sir."

"Now, leave my office."

Jonah was upset with himself for his indiscretion and tried again to apologize.

"I'm sorry, Mr. Heart; I should have thought before I spoke."

"Close the door behind you, Jonah; that will be all."

Jonah left the office and quietly closed the door.

As he started to walk away, he heard a voice a few feet behind him.

"You better watch your place if you know what's good for you."

Jonah spun around and found himself face to face with Irv; his face was as red as an apple.

Jonah had caused enough trouble for himself with his one outburst; he had no fight left in him for more. He just turned away, headed to his office, and didn't look back. His heart was racing.

What have I done? Jonah thought. *With one sentence, I screwed myself with Mr. Heart and Irv, and for what?*

He thought back to something Josh had told him the night before when they had gone out for pizza.

❧

Josh worked in the accounting department, which gave him a perspective on the company that Jonah did not have. As Josh chomped down on his first slice, he looked up at Jonah, who seemed engrossed in watching him eat. Josh looked a little self-conscious and decided to broach something that had been on his mind lately.

"I've been meaning to tell you this, Jonah."

"What's that?"

"I'm not sure, but there's something screwy happening in my neck of the woods."

"What do you mean?"

"From what I can see, the Tylers seem to watch every

penny lately. It wasn't that way when I started. I don't have all the facts because I don't get to see all the books, but it's pretty obvious, even from my limited perspective, that something has changed."

"That's strange," said Jonah. "From what I can see from my end, the elaborate vacations and expenditures by the partners haven't changed at all. They each take two or three vacations to far away and exotic locales yearly. They rarely can be found in the office after 5:00. They order big lunches daily. You once told me that the expense reports they file show that they charge them to the company as office expenses."

"That's true, not to mention their fancy cars that are written off as business expenses because they see clients from time to time. And I know that each of their offices is furnished with the finest leather upholstery and upscale furniture, all charged to the company. The company is like a piggybank to them."

"They are living the life, Josh, that's for sure. We working stiffs should be so lucky. So that's why what you're telling me about their watching every penny seems so out of place. It does seem strange. I think we need to get a closer look at those files?"

That got Josh's attention.

"What do you mean? We need to get a closer look at those files; this isn't one of your spy novels, Jonah; this is real life. I just told you that because I found it interesting; the rest is above my pay grade and yours. Let's not stick our noses where they don't belong."

But Jonah's mind was elsewhere.

"Right, Josh, sure thing."

"I know that look, Jonah; I shouldn't have said anything."

"Relax, Josh, I'm just exercising my mind, that's all."

"Yeah, well, it sure can use it."

Jonah was lost in thought when the waitress came around.

"Will that be all, boys?"

"I'll have another round," said Josh.

"Another round of what?" said Jonah.

"Another round of pizza."

"You mean, two more slices?"

Josh was starting to feel embarrassed in front of the waitress.

"Yeah; what's wrong with two more slices?"

"Humans don't eat four slices, Josh," said Jonah. "We save some for the rest of the species."

"Well, this one does."

The waitress hid a smile, wrote down the order on her pad, and turned to Jonah.

"Will there be anything else for you?"

"I'm good, thank you."

As the waitress walked away, Josh looked at Jonah.

"You know, you didn't have to embarrass me that way."

"You're right, Josh; I'm sorry."

"All is forgiven, and I've got my eyes on that piece of cheesecake on the counter for dessert."

"You know, you're hopeless, Josh."

"A man's gotta eat, Jonah. Hey, have you caught Raiders of the Lost Ark yet? Everyone says it's the thrill of a lifetime. Maybe we can catch it Saturday night after Shabbat ends."

"Yeah, maybe Josh."

But Jonah's mind was miles away; he was just wired differently. The spy novels and mystery clubs had found a permanent home in his brain even if they no longer existed in real life.

He knew that whatever Josh was privy to, Mr. Heart was undoubtedly aware of, and more than likely, so was Smokey, who Mr. Heart confided in. He imagined how Mr. Heart and Smokey felt seeing decades of work and pride by Noah Tyler going up in smoke while they kept spending on the company's dime. Jonah felt for them and was determined to do something about it.

I'll get to the bottom of this one way or another.

Jonah figured that Irv probably shared their little confrontation with the other partners. The disdain on their faces as they passed him in the hallway over the next few days confirmed it. He was determined to keep his nose clean and watch his back around them. But, at the same time, his Spidey Sense was vying for his attention again, and Jonah had to feed the beast.

There's more than meets the eye at Tyler Tech, and Jonah Mark will figure it out one way or another!

Jonah noticed two new people visiting the partners every few days. They were a couple of large Mediterranean-looking guys, the type you don't mess around with. He had never seen them before, yet they acted like they owned the place. There was something about them that he didn't like, and he knew that they were a concern to Mr. Heart as well because he saw the look on his face one day when their laughter could be heard all the way down the hall to his office.

I wonder who these guys are and what they're up to, thought Jonah.

Jonah always knew when Mr. Heart was upset about something, his face would tense up, almost as if he were trying to calm his nerves. One day, as Jonah walked down the hall, he noticed the two new guys enter Joel Tyler's office along with the other partners. As he passed by, Jonah couldn't help but turn back around and look. He was pretty sure he heard the names Marco and Carlos being addressed by the others. They were in deep discussion and did not notice him at first. One of the strangers had his feet up on the other side of Joel Tyler's desk, almost as if he was a Tyler Tech partner.

Jonah's Spidey Sense was calling again; he just had to get a peek at what was going on in that office. So, without thinking of the implications, he simply dropped the pile of papers he was holding right in front of their door. As he reached down to retrieve them, he looked into the open door and found the partners and their two new friends had stopped talking and were staring at him. He awkwardly tried to look away, but not before they locked eyes with him.

"Did you lose something, Jonah?"

It was the unmistakable voice of Irv.

"Uh, no, I just dropped these papers and ..."

Before he could finish his sentence, the door slammed in his face. Jonah panicked, and he hurried into his office. But he could not undo what just happened. He felt a chill run through him.

Those two new guys looked pretty menacing, thought Jonah. But he did not know who they were and what they were up to. He debated in his mind about telling Mr. Heart, but what would he say?

Mr. Heart, I saw these two new guys with the partners, and I think they're up to no good. I don't think so, thought Jonah. *I don't have proof of anything going on. Besides, I'm already in enough hot water with him with my Irv outburst the other day; I'll keep this to myself for a while and see if it leads to anything.*

Jonah felt a certain loyalty to Mr. Heart, and although he was his assistant, in this case, he felt more like his protector.

Tyler Tech's Security Director was Ryan Schapp. He was an ex–New York City police officer hoping to be promoted to detective but kept getting passed over year after year. He was not cut out to be a police officer in the first place, and his superiors at the police department knew that. It was just a matter of time before another bad review would end his police career in its infancy. His home life wasn't the greatest. He lived with his wife, Sue, in a small apartment on the lower east side of Manhattan; they had no kids, and the financial pressures strained their marriage. He was always looking for an easy way to make money. He would buy lottery tickets, play the horses, and bet on the New York Knicks.

Ryan came home one night looking dejected. Although they didn't have the best marriage, Sue felt sorry for him. He didn't seem to have much luck in whatever he tried.

"Hi Ryan, you look a little beaten up."

"It's been a rough day, Sue."

"Wanna talk about it?"

Ryan looked up at Sue. It had been a rough day because

he had bet big on a horse that a friend told him was a sure thing; it wasn't.

Why do I do these things? thought Ryan to himself. *It's really not fair to her.*

"Sue, I'm just gonna grab some leftovers and a beer if that's OK."

"Suit yourself; I'll be in the bedroom."

As Sue walked away, Ryan felt a lump of guilt in his throat. It could have been so different. They were childhood sweethearts, and when they got married, life was full of promise. Sue worked as a physical therapist, and Ryan worked as a police officer. Things looked so promising at the beginning. But Sue had problems conceiving, and their hope of having kids was not in the cards. Ryan had his own demons that he could not conquer. His love of sports led him to gambling. He wasn't very good at it, but he couldn't stop looking for that big score that would change their lives. The bills started piling up, and Sue figured out what was going on one day when she found a pile of betting slips on the floor next to his dresser. They had apparently fallen out of Ryan's pocket, and he hadn't noticed. Sue confronted him when he got home from work that night.

"What are these?" Sue asked when he walked in the door.

Ryan was startled to see what Sue was holding.

"Oh, a friend told me about a horse running at Belmont that was supposed to be a sure thing. So, I thought I'd surprise you with a nice dinner for your birthday."

"Ryan, these slips are for different races on different dates running over a few weeks; what's going on; are you gambling? Is that why we seem to be short of money every month?"

"I'm not gambling, Sue; I can stop anytime I want."

"I want you to stop now, Ryan."

"OK, Sue, I will."

"Gambling is an addiction, Ryan, and I don't want you doing it."

Ryan knew she was right, and he realized he probably had a problem he wasn't admitting to himself. He didn't tell Sue he was up to his ears in gambling debts to some very unsavory characters. He hoped to pay them off and be rid of them, but that's not how it worked out.

"You're right, Sue; I promise to stop."

"I mean it, Ryan; I want things to be like before we married."

Sue burst into tears and ran into the bedroom; she had made her point. Ryan wished things could go back to when they married, too. He decided that once he could come up with a way to pay those guys back, he would never gamble again.

Easier said than done, thought Ryan to himself.

Irv called Ryan into his office the next day. He did not know why he was being called into a partner's office, which made him very nervous. The thought of being called in to be fired had crossed his mind. As he knocked on Irv's office door, all he could think about were his gambling debts and all the people he owed money. Unemployment was not an option.

"Close the door, Ryan," said Irv, "and take a seat."

"Yes, Mr. Carter."

Ryan sat at the other side of Irv's large desk. He felt a

small bead of sweat as it made itself down the side of his face. He quickly brushed it off with his sleeve.

"Ryan, do you know anything about internal security?" said Irv.

Ryan had to think fast. *Internal security could mean almost anything*, thought Ryan. But he knew he had to remain calm because he had no idea where this was going. *Had they caught him doing something he shouldn't have been doing?*

"Eh, yes sir, Mr. Carter," said Ryan.

"Good, we've been looking for someone to keep an eye on things for the partners here at Tyler, someone we can trust to look over our shoulders if you know what I mean. You can call it our own internal affairs position; interested?"

"Wait… whaa?"

Interested? thought Ryan. *Here, I thought I was about to be fired, and instead, I was being offered a promotion; how about that?*

"Yes sir, of course!" said Ryan. "Anything for the company."

"Good Ryan… very good indeed."

Although Irv did not tell Ryan anything about why he was being given this assignment, he said he wanted him to keep an extra eye on Mr. Heart and his new assistant, Jonah Mark, and Smokey. He told Ryan he wanted to know anything that seemed unusual.

"You see any of them stick their nose where it doesn't belong, you report it to me. I want all the details, understood?"

"Yes sir, Mr. Carter," said Ryan.

"You do a good job with this; a nice bonus is in the offing."

That's all Ryan had to hear. Maybe this was the way he

would pay off his gambling debts once and for all. He had no idea what those three did to tick off the partners, and Ryan couldn't care less.

If that's what he wants, thought Ryan, *that's what he gets.* He was going to keep his eyes glued to them.

Ryan Schapp, Director of Internal Affairs; it has a nice ring to it… yes indeed!

Tyler Technologies was heavily involved in the future of defense: military space technology. US armed forces increasingly relied on satellite technology for surveillance, weather tracking, communication, and navigation. The Air Force regularly launched GPS and missile-defense tracking satellites. The protection of all these assets in orbit from countries that may try to blind them, particularly at a time of war, was something that Tyler's research and development team had been working on for many years.

One day, Jonah arrived a few minutes late for work, out of breath and dripping wet, as he slid into the elevator right before the door closed. The two women sharing the elevator shot him a glare and edged out of the danger zone where he might get them damp. He recognized them as Belinda and Phyllis from M&A and shot them a sheepish smile of apology. Still, they quickly went back to ignoring him, heads bent together deep in conversation.

"I heard," said Belinda quietly, "isn't it exciting? And they're announcing promotions at the meeting at 3:00."

"Promotions?" asked Jonah, surprised.

"You didn't hear it from me," said Belinda, sliding out as soon as the doors dinged open.

All morning, Jonah walked past similar, half-whispered conversations that seemed to be cut short as soon as he tried to ask for more details. Finally, Josh knocked on his door.

"Hey, did you hear the news?"

"You mean, what everyone in the office is whispering about except me?"

"That would probably be it."

"No, Josh, I haven't."

"Boy, for a guy I thought was clued in about everything around here, you don't have a clue, do you?"

Jonah was starting to get annoyed.

"No, Josh; what's the big news?"

"What's it worth to you?"

"Your life."

"You know you've lost your sense of humor, right?"

"Hanging around you can do that; now, what's the big news?"

Josh ignored Jonah's remark.

"The company has announced the launch of a new division: Tyler Space Technology."

"That *is* big news. Now, that wasn't so hard; was it Josh?"

"It wasn't much fun either."

"You've outlived your usefulness, Josh; you can go now."

"Sourpuss."

"I'm wounded."

The news was indeed big, and Jonah wondered what all the ramifications would be. He remembered the ladies in the elevator earlier talking about promotions. He began to wonder who would be transferred to the new division.

⊷

Later that day, while Jonah was in Mr. Heart's office going over some paperwork, he remarked to Mr. Heart about how the news about the new division was all the employees were talking about.

"I guess you must be excited, Mr. Heart," said Jonah.

But the look on Mr. Heart's face spoke differently.

"Jonah, I am not involved in the new division… and so aren't you."

"But… I don't understand, Mr. Heart, I…."

Mr. Heart's silence was deafening. *How could the CFO of Tyler Technologies be left out of something this important?* thought Jonah.

"Eh, sorry, Mr. Heart, I just thought …"

"I'm going to need that paperwork before you leave tonight."

"Sure thing," said Jonah.

As Jonah left his office, Mr. Heart recalled the day he discovered he was left out of the new department. He had stormed into Joel Tyler's office.

⊷

"Joel, as CFO of Tyler Technologies and the person who suggested this idea in the first place, I expect to be in charge of the new division."

"What can I tell you, Franklin? We're stuck living up to the letter of the agreement we signed with our father, but we have no obligation to do anything more. We had a partner's meeting and took a vote. Guess what? We're in and you're out!"

Mr. Heart knew exactly what agreement Joel was talking about. As his last act before transferring the company to his children, Noah Tyler drafted legal papers defining how the company would be run after he retired or passed away. As part of that agreement, and as his own insurance policy to ensure the company was run the way he built it, he ensured that Mr. Heart would have a lifetime contract that his children could not break. The children didn't like that clause in the agreement, but they didn't have much choice if they wanted to be partners one day, so they reluctantly signed on the bottom line. It also stipulated that if Mr. Heart needed to hire an assistant to help him, that person would only answer to him.

Mr. Heart was more than frustrated by being left out of the new division, but there was little he could do. As he quietly left Joel's office, Joel called out to him.

"Hey, Franklin. Do you mind closing the door?"

Jonah left Mr. Heart's office wholly bewildered.

What exactly is going on around here? Mr. Heart is the CFO of Tyler Tech; why would they leave him out of such a significant development?

He had no time to think about it; he had to take care of the paperwork Mr. Heart had asked him to work on. So, he grabbed it off his desk and headed to the main copy machine in the middle of the office. He punched in his employee number, put the first 150 sheets into the feeder, and pressed start. After about a minute of waiting, Irv showed up behind him. He looked like he was in a rush, but Jonah could do nothing to make the machine go faster. He could feel the annoyance on Irv's face behind him without turning around. He seemed to make a show out of grunting.

"How long is it going to be?"

Jonah heard Irv's voice from behind and turned around. He was determined not to get into another confrontation with him.

"I'm sorry, Mr. Carter, I need to get this done for Mr. Heart."

Suddenly, the machine started making noises that he had never heard before. It was as if it had swallowed a mouse. There was grinding and churning and a piercing sound that was as annoying as it was loud. It abruptly stopped copying, and a red light started flashing, the dreaded paper jam. The timing could not be worse. Jonah opened the top of the machine and started trying to fish out the jammed paper, but he was only making things worse.

"Are you kidding me?" said Irv. The drama was now the focus of everyone in that part of the office.

"It's a paper jam; you're not having a baby there, Jonah."

Jonah gave Irv an annoyed look, but Irv's look was worse.

"Let's go," yelled Simeon to Irv from down the hall. "The meeting's starting."

"Yeah, well, I'm dealing with Heart's assistant here, who is having trouble extricating a piece of paper from the copy machine."

That got everyone's attention, including Smokey, who

had looked up from what he was doing when he heard Irv's voice harassing Jonah. He walked out of his office and straight to the copier. Jonah stepped aside as Smokey quickly dislodged the culprit from the machine, closed it, and hit a few buttons; it continued making copies.

"Thank you, Smokey," said Jonah.

"All you have to do is ask; there's no need to make a federal case out of a jammed copier; it happens every day."

Irv looked annoyed with the two of them and embarrassed in front of all the employees watching.

Jonah grabbed his copies from the machine and stepped around an irritated Irv without saying a word.

"Smokey, do you have a minute for me?" asked Jonah.

"Sure thing, kid; come to my office."

They both walked into Smokey's office and closed the door behind them.

"A couple of real smartasses," muttered Irv for all to hear.

He turned around and spotted Smokey and Jonah busy in conversation.

❧

Jonah had formed a good relationship with Smokey since he joined the firm. He appreciated Smokey's honesty. He was a clone of Mr. Heart in some ways, and he treated him like a son. He was like a big teddy bear. Occasionally, Jonah would drop into Smokey's office to chew the fat a little. It was a way for Jonah to get a lay of the land, and he genuinely loved talking to the guy.

As Traffic Manager, Smokey had a unique vantage point of seeing what was happening in the office from a global perspective. So many things passed his desk. That and his relationship with Mr. Heart made him Jonah's go-to person to get info from if he was willing to share it. Their increasingly close relationship certainly helped. Smokey liked Jonah, and Mr. Heart must have said good things about him.

He remembered a story Mr. Heart told him about when a young employee working under Smokey in the traffic department had made an error that sent a shipment meant for a port in the United States to a European port. It was not a small error, and very costly to the company. Irv got wind of it, and all hell broke loose. Everyone in the office could hear him ranting and raving to the other partners; he wanted the young lady immediately fired. Smokey had been on vacation that week and didn't know what had occurred while he was gone. The morning Smokey returned and heard what had happened, he went straight into Joel's office. He told him he had made a terrible mistake the afternoon he left and gave the young lady the wrong instructions. It was all his fault. As CEO, Joel could have fired Smokey for such a major error that would have cost the company a tremendous amount of money. However, losing an experienced traffic manager differed greatly from losing a young employee. Things eventually blew over, but Irv had another thing to add to his list of reasons to hate Smokey.

Jonah also loved to talk to Smokey because he had a very interesting way of speaking.

"What's up, kid?"

That's how Smokey addressed Jonah, and Jonah enjoyed the nickname.

"Mind if I run something past you?" said Jonah.

"I'm all ears, kid; lay it on me?"

"If I'm out of line, just tell me, OK?"

"What's on your mind, Jonah? You look a little troubled."

"Well, I heard about the new division, and when I mentioned it to Mr. Heart, he told me he had nothing to do with it and seemed pretty upset. I just don't get it, Smokey; why would they leave Mr. Heart, the CFO of Tyler Technologies, out of the biggest thing around here since sliced bread?"

Smokey had a resigned look on his face as if it was a fact that could not be changed. Jonah could tell that Smokey was being careful with his reaction. Jonah knew there was a bond between Smokey and Mr. Heart, so there probably was little he could say. What he could surmise, based on Smokey's relationship with Mr. Heart and what he was able to overhear from Smokey's conversations with him, was that they both were bothered by what was going on in the office. He had overheard them talk about the partner's exorbitant corporate expenses. Based on Mr. Heart's look when he broached the subject of the new division, he could imagine that they were both unhappy that Mr. Heart had been left out of the loop.

"You know what kid?"

"What?" said Jonah.

"I think you're pretty smart and perceptive, which will serve you well as long as you work here. So let me give you some advice. Sometimes, it's good to watch and observe Jonah. Not everything is always spelled out. But things can make themselves clear if you step back and let them. I think you'll get my drift soon enough."

And with that, Smokey grabbed his coat and pipe, walked out of his office, and made his way down the hall, leaving Jonah to figure out what he meant by that.

Jonah thought to himself about how *Smokey-like* that answer was.

I'm not just going to let this go. I think Smokey was trying to tell me something. So, I will watch and observe, just like he said, and act when the right time comes.

His Spidey Sense had come alive again.

⁓

As Smokey left Jonah at his office door, he noticed Irv had been staring at him the whole time. The annoyance from earlier at the copy machine was still clearly with him. As he watched Smokey walk out of his office and down the hall, Jonah also spotted Irv glaring at him.

He could hear Irv say to Simeon, who had just entered his office:

"I don't like that little kid. I told you what he said to me outside Heart's office the other day."

"You're making a big deal out of nothing, Irv; he's just a kid."

"Yeah, well, I don't trust him, and you know what I'm thinking?"

"What?"

"I'm thinking that little weasel is probably passing info to Smokey, who's probably passing it on to Heart; he's always hanging around Smokey's office. Remember how he strategically dropped those papers outside our office when Marco and Carlos were here the other day?"

"Yes, I remember Irv; I was right there. But wouldn't it be easier to tell Mr. Heart what's on his mind instead of through Smokey?"

"Well, maybe Heart doesn't talk shop with the kid, so the nosy little bastard uses Smokey as his carrier pigeon."

"Irv, he just joined the firm a few months ago; just because he tried to listen in to a partner's meeting doesn't mean he's clued into what's happening here. Maybe he was just curious; you know how employees are. I think you're starting to get a little paranoid."

"Maybe so, but like Reagan says about the Soviets, trust but verify. We're stuck with Heart and his little carrier pigeon; we can't get rid of either of them. But why must we put up with Heart's miserable sidekick, Smokey? You know they're always talking about us behind our backs; I don't like it. It's like they're plotting against us. I swear, if I had a two-by-four, I'd smack that smokin' bastard clear across the office!"

The words sent a chill down Jonah's spine.

"OK, calm down, Irv; no one's smacking anyone."

"Yeah, well, I don't trust the old bastard; maybe it's time our friends come up with an exit strategy to clear the air of any smoke around here. You get my drift?"

Jonah could see how red Irv's face had gotten, and he couldn't miss the veins bulging from his neck. He clearly possessed an explosive temper, and his hatred for Mr. Heart and Smokey was palpable.

Jonah's Spidey Senses were in overdrive. Questions were rapidly coming to mind, like who were the "friends" Irv referred to, and why did they say they couldn't get rid of him or Mr. Heart? The talk of coming up with an exit strategy for Smokey scared the hell out of him. He hoped his little drop-in to Smokey's office wouldn't cause him any trouble.

That's it, thought Jonah. This wasn't another spy book; this was the real thing.

I need to get some intelligence on these guys. The vibe around this office is giving me the creeps. I need to know what's going on, and then I need to fix it!

The announcements about promotions were made, and Jonah learned that Hannah had been transferred to the new division to work under Irv because of her strong technological engineering background. Jonah hated that idea, not only because of what he had witnessed outside Smokey's office but because he knew that Irv had an overbearing personality and would probably take advantage of Hannah being a young female, and Jonah still worried about her. But he figured that Hannah didn't have much choice; he was her boss, and that was that. But he decided to keep an extra eye on Irv from then on.

The newly promoted employees were moved into a brand-new area outfitted with the latest high-tech computers. Jonah could see the new department whenever he walked down the hall. He could also see that Hannah's desk was right outside Irv's office.

That lecherous bastard better keep some distance from Hannah if he knows what's good for him.

∾

One day, as Jonah was walking down the hall facing the new division, he noticed Irv leaning over Hannah's desk and pointing at something on a piece of paper Hannah held. He could see how close they were and how uncomfortable Hannah looked, and Jonah didn't like it.

Yeah, well, that doesn't work for me, buddy.

Without thinking, he walked straight down the hall toward Hannah's desk in a department where he didn't belong. Adrenaline had taken over as he headed full force toward Hannah's desk. Both Hannah and Irv looked up in time to see Jonah crash into Irv, knocking him to the ground with his papers scattered all over the place. Hannah looked shocked to see Jonah, and Irv was enraged.

"What the hell was that about?" demanded Irv as he tried to get back on his feet.

Jonah had to think fast, as his mind had just caught up with reality.

"Eh, I'm sorry, Mr. Carter, I didn't see you."

"Didn't see me; are you blind? And what the hell are you doing in this department anyway? Did you lose your way to the Men's Room?"

Jonah was still desperately trying to think on his feet when he heard Simeon calling Irv from the door.

"Irv, I've got Jack on the phone; he needs those figures for the staff meeting. And what are you doing there on the floor?"

Irv looked back at Jonah with disgust; the familiar red face and neck bulge he was starting to get accustomed to displayed prominently.

"You might want to grab a map of the office and study it, you moron. I'm not through with you!"

As he stormed off while straightening out his jacket and tie, Hannah tried to suppress the grin on her face with her hand.

"What was that all about?" she asked.

Jonah stood there awkwardly; words weren't coming fast enough.

Come on, think of something… anything… anything???

"Eh… I better go."

He quickly brushed off his jacket and high-tailed it out of the department. His mind was racing a thousand miles an hour; he was starting to think he might have overreacted. But it was now clear to him that his feelings for Hannah were still very strong.

Nice going, he thought to himself. *She either thinks I'm some kind of lunatic or that this is my way of trying to rekindle our relationship. If I were her, my bet would be on lunatic, but I wonder what she really thinks.*

Sitting in his office a short time later, Jonah found himself lost in thought. He remembered Josh's advice about having an honest conversation with Hannah to gauge her interest in him. The idea of asking her about her feelings like a normal person did not appeal to him. He had convinced himself that it would make for an awkward work environment for both of them if she rejected him, given all the busy bodies in the office.

I am going to do this my way.

Borrowing an idea from one of his spy novels, he decided to follow her on her way to work, on her way out to lunch, and on her way home after work until the opportunity presented itself to *run into her accidentally*; the perfect plan!

Although *accidentally* running into Irv, which he just did, didn't work out too well the last time he tried it, he felt that his improvisational skills needed a slight improvement and would make the necessary adjustments.

In his mind, that was not wired like everyone else's; his plan was genius.

I'll just be calm and quiet and let my skills do the talking. Calm and quiet… like a cat in the night.

Jonah's first attempt at *accidentally* running into Hannah on her way out to lunch the next day was less than encouraging. As soon as Hannah passed his office door on her way out, Jonah grabbed his coat and counted to ten. As he began to ease out of his office quietly, he tripped over the wastebasket next to his desk, sending it crashing against the wall, eliciting a large bang that could be heard outside his office by anyone within shouting distance.

Now he had everyone's attention; heads started to glance in his direction. As he was extricating himself from the wastebasket, he managed to kick his chair, sending it spinning out into the hallway and slamming into the copy machine. Hannah may have heard it all, but she kept walking and exited the office.

"Eh… sorry… I just got a little tangled up here," he announced to those who did not bother to hide their faces and just smiled at him. The jig was up; this was anything but cool and quiet. It seemed everyone noticed the entire scenario, from when Hannah had passed his office to his clumsy attempt to follow her.

"Masterful," called out one of them.

"Great technique," yelled another, "I should take notes."

He heard a few claps, then a few more. Pretty soon, it seemed the whole office had joined in.

"Yes… well… thank you," he stammered.

He awkwardly pointed to the front door leading out to the elevators.

"I'm… going to… go now."

"Go get her, Jonah," yelled Jack from the mailroom.

Jonah was embarrassed; this was not how it went in the spy books.

"Let's just keep this between us, everybody."

"Sure thing," yelled Hal from HR.

"It's exactly how Harrison Ford would have done it," yelled someone he didn't even recognize from the back of the office.

Jonah threw caution to the wind and dashed for the exit amid much good-natured laughter. He was well-liked around the office because he was Mr. Heart's assistant. And everyone enjoyed a good love story.

Jonah's plan to ease down the hall had become more of a trot, quickly becoming a sprint. He entered the lobby just as the elevator door was closing, with Hannah facing him. Their eyes met briefly. Jonah couldn't tell if Hannah noticed him trying to catch the elevator, but by the time he got down to the street, Hannah was gone.

Nice going, Jonah, he thought to himself; *well done!*

He did remember how much Hannah loved pizza, so he decided to take a chance and head to the only kosher pizza shop in the area.

If, at first, you don't succeed… thought Jonah.

❧

Hannah had indeed caught the look on Jonah's face as he raced to the elevator. She also saw him grab his coat as she passed his office and heard things crashing behind her, but she was determined not to turn around. She also noticed the smiles on some faces and filled in the blanks for herself. Coupled with what happened the day before when he smashed into Irv while he was leaning over her, things were starting to clarify themselves. The new Jonah still had some of the old Jonah inside. But one thing was beginning to make itself clear; besides being a klutz, he obviously still had feelings for her.

Yep, he's following me, thought Hannah. *I saw him watching me from across the street as I entered the building this morning. He needs to brush up on his spying skills; he's either stopped reading those spy books, which would be great, or he needs to start reading up on how to attract women before he kills himself.*

Hannah had thought of Jonah since Mr. Heart brought him into her office. She was completely shocked and flustered when she looked up and saw him standing there. So many conflicting feelings raced into her mind at that very instant. She had thought a lot about him since they broke up. The breakup was terrible, and she regretted some of what she had said to him. She knew how much she had hurt him then, but Jonah did not know how much it had hurt her to end the relationship. His lack of seriousness about his future and all the time he wasted with his spy novels, comic books, and mystery clubs were hard to ignore. She wanted a serious relationship with Jonah, but not *that* Jonah. She agonized over her decision for days after, but she had decided she had done the right thing, to lead with her head instead of her heart, but her heart was still calling.

The version of Jonah she had been witnessing over the last few months since he joined Tyler Tech was the one she had been hoping for back then. She had a friend who took the same MBA course as Jonah did, and remembering that Hannah once went out with him, she told her when he got his MBA and that he had graduated summa cum laude. She could not believe it; this was not the Jonah who couldn't even make an appointment to see someone who could help him with his future.

He must have really buckled down after we broke up, thought Hannah. *Maybe he's not practicing his spying skills after all; perhaps he is just a klutz. I can work with that!*

He now had a serious job with significant responsibilities, and she had taken notice. She would have loved to give it another try; she did not know how Jonah felt until now, and she didn't want to hurt him again or get hurt herself. Hearing him clumsily chase after her put a smile on her face. And she could not forget how he had knocked Irv off his feet when standing over her.

Poor guy, maybe I'll let him catch up with me and see what develops, thought Hannah as she headed toward the pizza shop.

❧

As Jonah quickly made his way down Fifth Avenue, he suddenly felt he was being watched. He couldn't put his finger on it, but his instincts were usually pretty good. So, he used one of the tricks he learned from his spy books. He stood in front of a shoe store window as if he were looking at the display and quickly checked out the reflection behind him in the afternoon sun. No doubt about it, there he was, across the street, standing behind a streetlamp, wearing a pair of sunglasses, looking right at his back.

Was it Marco or Carlos? He wasn't sure, and it didn't matter. *Why would one of those guys be following me?*

5

JONAH WAS SPOOKED. He completely abandoned catching up with Hannah; he was in danger.

Why the hell are these people following me? thought Jonah.

He glanced behind him, and when he was sure he wasn't being followed, he ducked into the lobby of another office building. He ran over to an unused payphone and quickly called Josh, who answered on the first ring.

"What's up, buddy?"

"Josh, can you meet me after work at our usual spot?"

"Is everything OK, Jonah, you sound spooked?"

"That's because *I am spooked, Josh*; can you meet me at 6:00?"

"You got it, buddy; see you then."

"And Josh… make sure you aren't being followed."

"Being followed? Why would I be followed? Who would want to follow me? For what reason would anyone want to…"

Jonah had already hung up. He looked up and down the block from the lobby window. When the coast was clear, he slipped out of the building and headed back to the office. His nerves were shot. He took the elevator back up to the tenth floor. He slipped back into his office, making sure to avoid being noticed by his busybody employees/cheering section. When he took his coat off, he saw his shirt was sweaty. He had completely forgotten about Hannah and hoped she didn't notice he was following her. All he could think of were those two menacing guys and how one of them had followed him down Fifth Avenue at lunch. The same two guys that had been hanging with the Tylers recently. The same two guys that Mr. Heart was concerned about.

What was it that Smokey said? Sometimes, it's good to just watch and observe. Maybe he's been reading the same spy books as me.

From that moment, Jonah decided to do just that: watch and observe.

Hannah had sat in the pizza shop longer than she needed to for a quick bite. She was sure Jonah would be coming through the door at any moment. But as the time ticked by, she wondered if she had misread Jonah's actions. Maybe all of this was just a series of coincidences. She felt a somewhat surprising sense of regret creeping into her thoughts.

Am I misreading this, or do I miss him more than I'm willing to admit to myself?

There was a kosher deli five blocks from the office on a small side street. Josh and Jonah had shared many sandwiches there, but corned beef and pastrami were not what concerned Jonah at that point. Jonah sat at a table in the back and nervously waited for Josh to arrive.

Josh got there about ten minutes late and casually strolled over to Jonah's table in typical Josh fashion, as he had all the time in the world. He was wearing a hoodie and sunglasses.

"What the hell are you wearing?" asked Jonah.

"What do you mean, these are clothes?"

"Yes, I know what clothes are; I wear them myself."

"So?"

"You're wearing sunglasses and a hoodie."

"Again, so?"

"So, it's cloudy outside; it's 6:00 in the evening, and I asked you to make sure no one was following you, not to dress like the Unabomber."

Josh ignored the comment; he thought he looked pretty cool.

What's going on, Jonah, is everything OK?"

"No, Josh, everything is not OK."

"What's up buddy; you look a little green around the edges?"

"Listen, Josh, some strange things are happening in the office, and I'm unsure what to make of them."

"What strange things?" said Josh, feeling a little nervous. "What are you talking about?"

Jonah filled Josh in on everything that had been happening in the office recently, the vibes between the partners and Mr. Heart, Smokey, and himself. He told Josh what he overheard from Mr. Heart and Smokey about how the partners were ruining the company, the fact that Mr. Heart was left out of the new division, and Mr. Heart and Smokey's reaction when he broached the subject. He also told him about his verbal confrontations with Irv and his threat to smack Smokey on the head with a two-by-four, which caused Josh to cover his mouth. He also told him about the two tough guys hanging around with the partners lately, the menacing look he got from the men in the office when he stared too long at them, and finally, how one of them had followed him at lunchbreak earlier that day.

"Wow, that's a lot of stuff, Jonah, especially that last part about being followed, although you had me at the two-by-four story."

"It's more than *stuff*, Jonah; the place gives me the creeps. And I'm not happy that Hannah is now working in the new division with Irv breathing down her neck."

"Well, did you speak to Hannah about how you feel about her like I told you to?" asked Josh.

"I think I jumped the gun on that."

"What do you mean?"

Jonah told him about what he did to Irv the day before at Hannah's desk in the new department.

"Nice going, Jonah; very smooth. That guy is a psycho from what I can tell; the whole office hears him yelling like a banshee on the phone."

"Yeah, well, it was a miracle I didn't get myself killed."

"Did Hannah realize what you were doing?"

"I have no idea; she actually asked me about it."

"And what did you tell her?"

"I wish I knew; the whole thing was a blur. I just knew I needed to get out of there fast."

"So, what did you do?"

"I got out of there… fast."

"So, you never spoke to Hannah about how you feel about her."

"I was too busy running into garbage cans and chairs and then being followed in the street by one of those menacing-looking guys who doesn't look like he's much into small talk."

"You ran into what and what?"

"It figures out of all the harrowing things I just told you about, you zero in on me tripping over a few things in the office."

"Actually, I heard about it from Karen in Accounting; everyone is talking about it. They can't wait until you try something else. There's actual wagering going on about when you'll try something else. I took the under on forty-eight hours max."

"Thanks, Josh; I guess I'm a celebrity now."

"Ya think? You're bigger than Dynasty; everyone is waiting for the next episode."

"OK, Josh, I want you to concentrate. I don't care about any of that stuff as compared to everything in my dialogue that preceded it… comprende?"

"Sounds like a mess, Jonah; what are you gonna do?"

"That's kind of why I called you; I'm not sure *what* to do."

"You see, that's where you lost me, 'cause I haven't got a clue. Are you sure this isn't all that spy stuff running through your head again? For all you know, that guy you say followed you could have been shopping for shoes."

"From across the street?"

"It's possible."

"Right, the guy is looking at a shoe store window from across the street; it makes perfect sense to me."

"Have you ever heard of long-distance running? Well, this is long-distance shopping."

"I don't know why I bother."

"It's because deep down you love me, Jonah."

Jonah gave Josh a look, but he did his best to ignore it.

"And what's the deal with how you pursue Hannah? Does that make any sense at all?"

"What do you mean?"

"What do I mean, Jonah? Normal people don't do these things."

"I was going to try and accidentally run into her at the pizza shop when I noticed one of those two goons following me."

"What's with all this *accidently running into her* stuff? Did you ever consider the novel idea of meeting her for lunch and telling her how you feel? Do you want her to think you're still the same old Jonah doing his spy thing or that you've finally grown up and put all that stuff behind you?"

Jonah stopped to think for a moment.

"You're right, Josh; I guess that does make sense."

"And by the way, just for the record, I wasn't trying to look like the Unabomber, whoever that is."

"Forget it," said Jonah.

"I was going for the Muhammad Ali look after a big fight."

"Well, you certainly nailed it," said Jonah sarcastically.

Josh was feeling his mojo coming back when Jonah interrupted his thoughts.

"Let me ask you a question, Champ."

"What's that?

"Big celebrity fighter; how come nobody in this restaurant came rushing over for your autograph?"

Josh pondered Jonah's point for a moment and decided the better part of valor would be to retreat.

"What did you say the names of those two thugs were?" said Josh, quickly changing the subject.

"Marco and Carlos, or something like that. That's what it sounded like from outside Joel Tyler's office. And by the way, I saw what you did there."

Josh ignored the last comment.

"Jonah, what you're telling me sounds like a lot of random stuff, but nothing you can really put your finger on. The two-by-four thing sounds a little scary, but maybe Irv was just letting off some steam; it's not like anyone in the office hasn't heard it before. I get the same vibe about the partners; they don't seem like the Heart and Smokey type, but I'm not sure that's a crime. And maybe that guy following you on the street was just a coincidence, too, although I still like my shopping for shoes from across the street theory. I don't know, Jonah; I hope this isn't one of your spy fantasies; you told me you left that stuff behind."

Jonah looked dejected.

"I don't know what to think anymore, Josh."

Josh thought about how they were such close friends that they could practically read each other's thoughts. It had been that way since they were kids....

∾

"…Hey Joshie," said an excited nine-year-old Jonah; look at that!"

"At what?" asked Jonah.

They had been playing stoopball in front of Mrs. Lichtenstein's house, down the block from where Josh lived. They used to walk home from school together and loved using Mrs. Lichtenstein's stoopball steps because they were so big. The idea of the game was for one of them to throw the ball against the edge of one of the steps, "the stoop," while the other would have to catch it. Mrs. Lichtenstein loved all the kids on the block, so she let them play on her steps, but as time went by, she would always remind them that their mothers were waiting at home for them with supper, and they still needed to do their homework.

"What are you looking at?" said Josh.

"Right there, under the car, it's all crumpled up, but it looks like a dollar!"

Josh looked as amazed as Jonah.

"Hey Jonah, would you look at that, a real dollar!"

Jonah picked it up and flattened it out against Mrs. Lichtenstein's stoop. There he was, George Washington, staring right back at them.

"Worth a slice and a soda, that's for sure," said Jonah. "Race you to the pizza shop."

They ran down the block straight into Berger's Kosher Pizza Shop. Old man Berger stood behind the counter in his big white apron as the kids ran in.

"Hey boys, where's the fire?" said Mr. Berger.

They showed Mr. Berger the treasure they had found.

"Wow, that's some haul!" said Mr. Berger.

He loved the two boys and would often banter with them when their parents brought them in for a treat.

"How about a slice and a Coke?" said Jonah. Looking over at Josh, he said, "Make that two half slices and two half cups of Coke," said Jonah, who felt like a millionaire.

"You're a genius, Jonah," said Josh.

"We're having a special today, boys," said Mr. Berger; "two for the price of one."

Jonah did a quick calculation in his mind.

"That means we can each have a whole slice and a whole cup of Coke!"

"Double genius!" said Josh.

They sat on their stools at the counter for the next half hour and felt like a million bucks.

"Ya know Jonah, you're a great friend. Let's make a pact: best friends forever!"

"You got it… Josh…"

⟊

"… Josh… earth to Josh!"

Jonah was trying to get Josh's attention; his mind was clearly elsewhere. The spell was finally broken.

"Listen, Josh, this is really important," said Jonah.

Josh looked at Jonah and realized he had been daydreaming. He put on a serious face to try to hide it.

"Like I said, Jonah, I'm not sure any of this stuff is connected."

Jonah thought of what Smokey had told him.

Sometimes, it's good to watch and observe. Not everything is always spelled out. But things can make themselves clear if you step back and let them.

"You're right, Josh. How about we keep our eyes open and see what develops."

Mr. Heart had a doctor's appointment the next day; his office door was closed but never locked during the day. While away from the office, Jonah noticed Simeon and Joel Tyler hanging around Mr. Heart's office when most of the company was out to lunch. They didn't realize Jonah saw their reflection off a glass window outside his office. One of them was clearly keeping watch while the other was inside. Mr. Heart was always meticulous in keeping his drawers and cabinets locked, and his desk was always empty of paperwork. This disturbed Jonah. He wondered what they might have been looking for or what they were up to. He debated whether to tell Mr. Heart when he returned but kept it to himself.

Just another strange occurrence to add to my list, thought Jonah.

The next day, there was a safety seminar that everyone in the office was required to attend once a year. Someone from the fire department would go over the procedures to evacuate the building quickly and safely in case of fire or another emergency. It was held in the main conference room around a large oval table. It was held in shifts so everyone could comfortably fit around the table. Ryan saw it as an opportunity to get close to Jonah and maybe glean some information for Irv.

So, he grabbed a seat next to him. Jonah noticed as they were all being seated and found himself very uncomfortable, but it was too late to change his seat. Throughout the thirty-minute presentation, Jonah could feel Ryan stealing glances at him.

What's with this guy? thought Jonah. *Why is he always staring at me? And now he's practically sitting in my lap.*

And then an idea that was straight out of one of the many spy novels he read crept into his head.

Jonah couldn't wait to get out of there. The seminar mercifully came to an end. When Jonah got home that night, his mother greeted him at the door.

"Are you OK, dear? You look a little green around the edges."

"Have you been speaking to Josh?"

"No, why?"

"Never mind; I'm fine, Mom, just a little tired."

"Well, supper will be ready in about a half hour."

"There was a meeting in the office today, and they served sandwiches, so I'm not really hungry tonight, Mom; is that OK?"

"I guess so, dear, but I'll leave some leftovers in the fridge if you change your mind."

"Thanks, Mom."

Jonah's mother worried a lot, and he understood why.

∾

David and Esther Mark saw life as no one should see it. Born in Budapest, Hungary, they enjoyed a quiet life before World War Two. The Holocaust in Hungary was the final act of mass murder of a Jewish community by Nazi Germany during the 1939 - 1945 genocide of European Jewry. New restrictions against Jews were imposed soon after Germany occupied Hungary in March of 1944. The invading troops were led by SS officer Adolf Eichmann, who arrived in Budapest to supervise the deportation of the country's Jews to the Auschwitz concentration camp in occupied Poland. Between May 15th and July 9th, 1944, over 434,000 Jews were deported on 147 trains, most of them to Auschwitz, where about 80 percent were gassed on arrival.

David Mark's family and Esther Weiss' family met the same fate. They were herded into suffocating cattle cars with no food or water and little room to breathe. Many died on their way to the notorious concentration camp. When the suffocating doors were finally opened, they found themselves forcibly separated. Those who could work to one side, those who were too young or old or not physically able, were ripped from their families as they screamed and cried and were sent to the other side.

David Mark never saw his parents or six-year-old sister again. Esther Weiss saw her parents and three younger siblings, aged five to ten, beaten and dragged away, a scene she would never forget. At the height of the Nazi concentration and extermination camp's operations, an average of 6,000 Jews were gassed and cremated each day. After the war, many Survivors ended up in displaced persons (DP) camps set up in Western Europe under Allied military occupation at the sites of former concentration camps.

David Mark and Esther Weiss met at a DP camp in Germany in 1946. Neither of them had any family left. It was a difficult and tedious process, but eventually, they were able to make their way to the United States. A few years later, they were married in a religious ceremony before a Rabbi in a small synagogue in Brooklyn, New York, where many other Survivors had settled. They both worked for meager wages in a garment factory in downtown Brooklyn. They would come home every night after a hard day at the sweltering factory to their tiny basement apartment in the Borough Park section of Brooklyn.

Jonah was born in 1961; he was the light of their lives. They always believed that one day, they would make a better life for themselves. They did, after toiling in the factory for many years. Esther always loved clothing and design; she dreamed of opening a little dress shop in Borough Park. A store was going out of business on a busy street on the main thoroughfare. Esther had her eyes on that store; she would pass it every day when she got off the bus to walk the last few blocks home.

One day, she saw a going out of business sale sign on the window and decided to go in and speak to the owner. That night, when her husband David came home from the factory, she was waiting for him at the door.

"We must take a chance, David, and this might be it. The owner is willing to sell us the store and take payments over time. He would train me to run it for an extra six months. You told me your cousin Golda is looking for work; maybe she can come and help me as a saleslady. You always told me she had a great way with people; maybe we could make it work."

David mulled it over for a few minutes; he turned to Esther and said:

"Esther, you were always good at everything you put your mind to. If you're willing to take a chance, then so am I."

The store became successful, and after a year, David left his job at the factory to join his wife. The store became a fixture on the main street in Borough Park for over twenty-five years. It put Jonah through college and taught him the value of hard work and never giving up on your dreams. His parents were a real rags-to-riches story; from the depths of the Holocaust, they made a life for themselves. Jonah was always so proud of them.

Jonah's father, David, passed away five years earlier from a heart attack he suffered when he was in the store one day. Esther retired and closed the store a year later. Jonah lived with just his mother and always cared for anything she needed. She was slow on her feet, but her mind was still sharp as ever.

Jonah was exhausted from all the pressure he was under at work. Having Ryan sitting right next to him at the seminar that day and staring at every move he made didn't help. But his Spidey Sense had kicked in just as the seminar ended, and now he was sitting in his room staring at something on his desk.

Each employee had been issued an attaché case with the Tyler Tech logo engraved on the front when hired, with their name etched next to one of the buckles. It was another extravagance the partners wasted money on that annoyed Mr. Heart. Jonah always made sure to keep his locked. The last thing he needed was to lose any paperwork Mr. Heart had given him. At the end of each day, he would lock the case and spin the two little dials next to the buckles each with three little zeros to remind him it was locked.

He looked again at the name etched into the corner next to the right buckle. The name Jonah Mark was nowhere to be found. Instead, the name engraved on the briefcase he was staring at sent both a thrill and a chill down his spine. "Property of: Ryan Schapp."

He had fed the beast.

6

JONAH SAT AND stared at the briefcase for what felt like an hour; he was afraid to do anything with it, at least not yet.

He decided to call Josh at home.

"Josh, I need you to drop everything and come over here ASAP."

"What's wrong, Jonah?"

"I can't talk about it on the phone. Can you come? It's really important."

"Sure, buddy; I'm on my way."

It felt like an hour, but it only took a few minutes; Jonah heard Josh downstairs.

"Hi, Mrs. Mark."

"Hello, Josh. It's so nice to see you."

"So nice to see you too, Mrs. Mark. I'm just here to help Jonah with a work assignment."

"Well, he's upstairs in his room. If you boys are hungry, there's plenty of leftovers in the refrigerator."

Josh loved Mrs. Mark's cooking and would have gladly sat down to a plate of her leftovers, but Jonah was waiting upstairs.

Mental note to self: make sure to attack the leftovers on my way out of the house.

"Thanks, Mrs. Mark," said Josh, "maybe later."

Josh continued to hurry up the stairs; this sounded important.

"What's the emergency?" said Josh as he entered Jonah's room.

"You're looking at it," said Jonah as he pointed to the briefcase sitting on the table.

"That looks like your company-issued briefcase."

"Nice, Sherlock; I'm sure glad I called you. Looks can be deceiving, Josh; look at the engraving next to the right buckle."

Josh glanced at the engraving and almost jumped out of his shoes.

"What are you doing with Ryan Schapp's briefcase? More importantly, Jonah…"

Josh looked him squarely in the eye.

"What are you *planning* to do with Ryan Schapp's briefcase?"

"I guess you know how I think, Josh."

"That's because your brain is still wired for spying. I take it you switched briefcases with, of all people, Ryan Schapp, the Director of Security, at the seminar. And now you are contemplating opening said case, which, as you know, is illegal in all fifty states, including the District of Columbia."

"Yeah, well, the guy was practically sitting in my lap; it serves him right. Besides, maybe what's inside this briefcase can explain why this guy has been staring at me lately, and maybe …"

"…The thought of spending the next twenty years in jail hasn't occurred to you yet, Jonah."

"I'm willing to take the chance. What's in this briefcase may explain many things that have been happening in the office lately. Aren't you in the least bit curious?"

"Not *that* curious."

"Well, I'm different than you are."

"You don't say!"

"Besides, I didn't exactly plan it in advance; the briefcases look exactly the same, and I just seized the moment."

"No, you seized the briefcase."

"It's all I could think about the whole seminar; I'm gonna find out what I need to find out and teach him a lesson at the same time."

"Is that what they teach you in spy school?"

"Well, not exactly; I never saw this scenario in any of my spy books. This kind of just happened."

"It just happened."

"Right."

"No, Jonah, just happened is like being hit by a car when you cross the street. What you did was like running out into traffic."

Josh looked at Jonah with a look of resignation.

"You're going to do this, Jonah, no matter what I say, right?"

"Right, said Jonah; it's how I roll."

"Jonah, have you ever been to prison?"

"No."

"Have you ever seen one on TV?"

"Yes, Josh, I've seen one on TV?"

"Would you say the prisoners look happy when you see them on TV?"

"No, Josh, they don't look particularly happy."

"Why do you think they don't look happy, Jonah? Do you think it's the food, the lack of freedom, the décor, or maybe being beaten up by a 300-pound gorilla every night just for the hell of it? Am I getting through to you yet?"

"What's your point, Josh, that I'm going to wind up like some prisoner that gets beaten up for the hell of it?"

"You catch on fast."

"I'll take my chances, so either help me or leave me to do this myself; what's it gonna be?"

"It's your party," said Josh, "just don't say I didn't warn you. And I just want to say that if you do wind up in prison, I won't be visiting!"

"Is that a promise?"

"You can take it to the bank."

"The best news I've heard all day. As soon as I finish this, I'll be crossing you off my prison visitors list."

"OK, Jonah, for the sake of our friendship, I'll pretend I didn't hear that. What do you want from me?"

"Right now, moral support. And I can use an idea for what to tell Ryan when I return this to him tomorrow."

"You do realize that he probably has *your* briefcase," said Josh.

"The thought has crossed my mind."

"Did you try to open it?"

"Not yet," said Jonah.

"Why not?"

"I'm not sure."

"Do you even know if it's locked?"

"Nope, but I'm guessing it's not if he had it with him the rest of the day and planned on going straight home with it."

"I bet you're having second thoughts, cold feet, doin' the Hesitation Waltz. I bet my words to you about going to prison are starting to worm their way through that little spy brain of yours, contemplating prison for the next ..."

"Bang... zoom!" said Jonah, as he popped open the two buckles, with a look of satisfaction written across his face.

The case was open, and there it sat on the table right in front of them. Neither of them moved; it was as if they were staring at the latest Michael Jackson video.

"You didn't just do that?" said Josh.

"I sure did," said Jonah. "And I was right about him not locking it."

"You know, Jonah, we can still stop. Just close the brief-case, and you can return it tomorrow; he'll never know you opened it."

"I'm a sucker for a good mystery; what can I say."

"And the stuff I told you earlier about going to prison, has any of that entered your mind yet?"

"Prison, shmison; let's check this baby out."

Jonah could feel the adrenaline pulsating through his body; he loved a good mystery.

"Prison... shmison?" said Josh. "Well, that changes every-thing now that you put it that way. Why didn't you just say that in the first place? Future... shmootcher. Life... shmife. Maybe while you're busy committing a federal offense, I can sit here and rhyme away what the rest of my life will look like if we get caught and they arrest me for being an accomplice. Let's see…. Feds… shmeds…."

"I get the point, Josh, but *we* need to know what's in the case."

"*We* need to know what's in the case? *I* don't. I'm the kind of guy that likes to let sleeping dogs lie. I don't have to know what's buried under every tree. I don't remember signing up for the same fantasy life you've got going on up there in your curious little spy brain. How about we close the briefcase, get it back to the guy that owns it, and call it a day?"

Jonah had already started rifling through the papers; it all looked like gibberish to him.

"This looks like serious stuff," said Jonah.

"How do you know?" said Josh.

"Because I don't understand any of it."

"Let's check out the little compartment in the cover behind that big snap," said Josh.

"I thought you wanted to let sleeping dogs lie?"

"And I thought you weren't listening to me?"

"I can do two things at once, and besides, I kinda enjoyed your little speech."

"I'm sure glad I can provide you with some entertainment," said Josh.

Jonah popped open the snap and out poured a bunch of floppy disks. They both stared at the disks; things had suddenly gotten serious. The floppy disks added a whole new dimension to what was in the briefcase. It was like anyone could write things on paper, but grownups used floppy disks.

"Well," said Josh, "I guess that's that."

That's what?"

"Jonah, once we place those disks into your Mac, we're dealing with a whole new level of crime."

"Says who?"

"Says who? Says US Penal Code number 6656960 eh… dash 47"

"You just made that up, Josh."

Josh looked frustrated.

"I knew I shouldn't have added the 47."

Jonah rolled his eyes.

"Yeah, that's what convinced me you were making all that up, the 47."

"Well, I still think looking at computer disks that don't belong to you is more serious than looking at papers."

"Why?"

"I… don't… know."

"Gotta admit; you make a strong argument, Josh. Now, let's check out these little plastic babies."

Jonah loaded his startup disk, and his brand-new Macintosh 128K, which he had blown practically all his bar mitzvah gifts on, came to life. Next, he loaded the application disk for his word processor program. It was now time to see what Ryan had in his briefcase.

"OK, Josh, hand me one of those disks."

"You realize that by handing you one of these disks, I am now an accomplice to whatever crimes you will be charged with if you are caught."

"We won't get caught, Josh. Hand me a disk, please."

"You think we'll be in adjoining cells?"

"With any luck, we'll be in different prisons; the disk, please."

Josh handed him the first disk, and Jonah loaded it into the computer. There were a series of humming noises and some technical mumbo jumbo in small letters. Finally, his screen came to life.

The first page read:

"Ryan, these are the files we discussed earlier that contain the various shipments we will be making in the next 60 days to the port in Izmir, Turkey. Please make sure you forward them to the right parties as we discussed."

There followed a list of shipments with dates and other technical information about what was being shipped.

"Any clue what we are looking at?" asked Josh.

"No idea."

"So, what do we do?"

"Hand me a blank disk from on top of the dresser behind you."

"What are you doing?"

"I'm going to make a copy of everything on this disk and print it out later. I bet those other disks have more of the same stuff on them."

Jonah was like a runaway train; there was no sense stopping him from doing whatever he planned. So, Josh just handed Jonah the disks.

For the next half hour, Jonah carefully copied all the information on each of the disks in Ryan's briefcase.

"All done," Jonah finally announced.

"What are you going to do with those disks you just made?" said Josh.

"I'm going to show them to someone who can understand them."

"And who might that be?" said Josh.

"The one person we know that works in the new division and understands all the technical jargon these files contain."

"And, once again, Jonah, who might that be?" said Josh.

"Hannah Weinberg," said Jonah, with a crooked smile.

"I knew you'd say that," said Josh.

"I'm also thinking that I might want to get a look inside Irv's office," said Jonah.

Josh did a double-take.

"Come again?"

"I said, I'm also thinking …"

"I heard what you said; I'm right here."

"Then why am I repeating it to you, Josh?"

"Because I want to make sure my brain correctly processed the words that just came out of your mouth."

"Yeah, that's what I said, Josh."

"Are you crazy? Are you out of your mind? You want to get a look into Irv's office?"

"That's right."

"And how do you propose to do that?"

"Tonight, I'm going to sneak into Irv's office and have myself a little look-see."

"A little look what?"

"A look-see; it's an expression I just picked up; it's really cool. You can use it in all kinds of sentences …"

"What the hell is wrong with you?"

"Whaddya mean, Josh?"

"What do I mean? You tell me you plan on waltzing into Irv's office in the middle of the night and having a look-see, and you're wondering why I think you've lost your mind?"

"Look, Josh, I don't know what's on those disks, nor do I know why he's sharing them with the Security Director, and Hannah may or may not be able to figure it out. But I still have the keys to the office from when Mr. Heart had me close it up when he left early the other night; he told me to hang on to them for future use. The partners are long gone after five, so I'm going to look around Irv's office and see what I can find."

"Listen, Jonah, what we are doing now is called real life. In real life, people don't put their lives in danger when they look-see anything, not if they want to live to tell about it. Unfortunately, that brain of yours is built differently than that of most mortal men. You're still lost in your world of spy novels and mysteries; in that world, people go have *look-sees*, not here on earth with us regular humanoids."

"Well, Josh, the way I see it, there are the humanoids, like yourself, that choose to have the world come at them and then react. And then there are those like yours truly who have that extra gene that mere mortals like you have not been blessed with. Men like us choose to climb the highest mountain, reach for the brightest star, and go where few men choose to go. I choose to grab the bull by the horns… come what may."

"I can't believe I'm hearing this."

"Believe it, Josh. Tonight, I am going on a mission. Now, what do I do about getting this briefcase back to Ryan without him being suspicious that I looked through it?" said Jonah.

Josh was exasperated; there was no point in arguing any further. Like Jonah said, he was wired differently, and when he got his mind on something, there was no point in trying to dissuade him.

"That will require some thinking time; I suggest we have a serious talk."

"With whom?" said Jonah.

"With your mom, about those leftovers, I'm hungry," said Josh.

"You haven't changed a bit."

"The first rule of business," said Josh. "Never pass up a meal."

✧

Earlier that afternoon, as everyone was leaving for the day, Hannah took a quick trip to the Ladies' Room near her desk in the new division. Most of her coworkers had either left or were on their way out. As she was washing up, she heard the distinct voices of Irv and Simeon talking right outside the bathroom door. It was clear to her that they must have thought everyone in the division had left for the day. At first, everything seemed normal, but that changed quickly.

"The next shipment is early next month," said Irv.

"Are our people in Izmir ready?" said Simeon.

"They better be, and if someone opens up their big Turkish mouth, I'll personally fly down there and deposit a bullet in their head."

Uh… oh!

That last comment sent chills up Hannah's spine and sent her scurrying quietly into one of the stalls.

What the hell was that? thought Hannah.

"Relax," said Simeon, "we have everything under control."

"And if Heart or Smokey stick their necks where they don't belong, they'll each get one too."

"OK, Irv, you made your point," said Simeon, who sounded noticeably annoyed.

"We are talking about high-tech weaponry, not pea shooters, Simeon. This is technology the Soviets don't have. Heart doesn't trust us and looks more suspicious of us every day, and the same goes for his sidekick, Smokey, that nosy bastard! If they find out where these shipments are really headed, not only can we forget about another big payoff like the ones we've been getting, but we'll be pushing up daisies faster than we can say, Marco or Carlos. And those two guys are not ones to be messed with," said Irv.

Hannah had heard Irv being nasty before, but this was downright chilling. And the thought that these people were selling America's sophisticated technology to the Soviets was beyond belief. She wished she had left earlier, but unfortunately, it was too late. She quietly recited a silent prayer that they didn't suspect someone hiding in the bathroom. As she lifted her feet above the toilet seat, her elbow hit the toilet paper roller ever so slightly. But in the quiet of the office, she could not tell if the noise had been loud enough to be heard outside the ladies' room.

"Did you just hear something?" said Irv.

"Yeah, that was your mind playing tricks on you; you're just being nervous," said Simeon.

"Well, that happens when you're selling out your country for cash. I'm just going to have a look around. And if I catch someone that doesn't belong here, that will be just too bad for them."

Hannah felt beads of sweat pouring from her forehead; she was in tears. She heard one of them start walking around the office.

"Let's get out of here before your paranoia takes over," said Simeon. "Everyone knows how much fun that can be."

Irv kept walking around the office, looking under desks and behind doors. He spotted the closed ladies' room door. Hannah heard footsteps as he came closer to the door. She put her hands over her mouth to suppress the sound of her breathing. There she was, perched on top of the toilet seat, praying for her life. Irv swung the door open and gave a quick look under the stalls. He was about to walk in when Simeon called from outside.

"That's it, Irv; I'm leaving. Do you want this report, or should I shred it?"

"Shred it," said Irv as he let the door swing shut. "I've got a copy on my computer, and I gave some floppies to Ryan."

"What's the deal with Ryan; do you think you can trust him?" said Simeon.

"He's the perfect patsy to take the fall for what we're doing if we ever get caught. I promised him a nice raise to keep his eyes open for snitches and believe me, this guy needs the cash."

"So, he has no idea what we are really doing."

"All he has is a list of shipments to Izmir. The real dirt is on the floppies I keep in my briefcase; I don't even trust the computers here. I take them with me wherever I go. They have all the contacts and strategically missing info the Feds would need to assemble the plot. Ryan is going to be our insurance policy. Wait till he finds out what he's really going to be doing for us."

"You've got a devious mind, Irv; now, let's get out of here," said Simeon.

Hannah breathed a sigh of relief as the voices started getting lower. She didn't move a muscle until she heard the door close down the hall. She had just spent the longest ten minutes of her life in that bathroom.

I've got to get out of here!

Hannah snuck down the hallway as quietly as possible; she had her shoes in her hand. All the lights in the office were still on because the maintenance crew would come in a few minutes. She stepped out into the vestibule and headed down the stairwell and out of the building, constantly looking over her shoulder to ensure the coast was clear. She quickly made her way home. The phone rang as soon as she walked in the door; it was Jonah. Before she could say anything, he said:

"Hannah, it's me, Jonah."

He sounded very serious.

Why is he calling me? thought Hannah.

She tried to sound relaxed.

"Hi Jonah, what's up?"

"Hannah, I need to talk to you about something in person; can you meet me at our old place tomorrow night after work, say six?"

"Um, I guess so. What's this about Jonah?"

"I'll see you then."

And with that, the line went dead. Given the mixed signals she had gotten the day before, Hannah was confused about Jonah. Her mind was also preoccupied with the ordeal she had just gone through. She needed to speak to someone she could trust.

Maybe Jonah is the right person, thought Hannah. *At least I know I can trust him. I wonder what's on his mind.*

She couldn't wait until tomorrow night.

Hank was the nighttime security guard at the building for the last twenty-seven years. He had missed only two nights at his front desk in all that time. One was for his daughter's wedding over ten years ago, and the other for a kidney stone about five years ago. He knew everyone in the building, and everyone knew him. He was parked at the front door as always when Jonah arrived; it was just after 9:00 at night, and he knew the office would be empty. Jonah had psyched himself up for his mission to have a "look-see" around Irv's office, but he was still nervous. He greeted Hank and told him he had forgotten something upstairs earlier. Hank knew him, so he didn't ask too many questions.

"Still gotta sign in, ya know," said Hank, handing Jonah a pen. Jonah quickly signed the log and took the elevator to the 10th floor.

Being the only company on the floor, Jonah expected it to be completely dark as he had left it hours earlier, so he was surprised to see lights on as the elevator door opened. He could also see lights on in Joel Tyler's office; that's where the partners' meetings were usually held, and it was close to the front of the office. The partners, as usual, had left by 4:00 in the afternoon that day, so he was puzzled by what he saw.

Why would they return after everyone had left for the day?

He suddenly heard the distinct voices of the partners as

someone opened Joel Tyler's office door. Not knowing what to do, he hid himself behind a large plant. He couldn't hear much, but he heard someone step out of Joel's office to make himself a cup of coffee. He distinctly heard one of them saying, "…the next shipments to our friends behind the curtain better be on time; they're paying us a lot of money for this."

It was a strange expression, one that Jonah had never heard before.

Our friends behind the curtain: what are these guys up to? Jonah thought.

He also heard Irv complaining about Mr. Heart always sticking his nose where it didn't belong and how he "hopes Smokey dies of cancer really soon."

Those words sent chills up Jonah's spine.

I've gotta get out of here fast, Jonah thought to himself. *Mission aborted.*

He needed to make his escape before they noticed his presence. He decided to skip the elevator this time and snuck down the stairs. He quietly slipped out through a back door without Hank noticing.

But the words he heard chilled him to the bone.

The next shipments to our friends behind the curtain; what did that mean? And the rest of it about Mr. Heart always sticking his nose where it didn't belong and how he hopes Smokey dies of cancer really soon. I hope Hannah can make heads or tails about those disks cause these guys sound like they're playing for keeps.

He called Josh as soon as he got home. Josh was waiting for the call.

"How did it go?" asked Josh.

Jonah told him everything that happened; Josh could not believe it.

"It's a good thing you got yourself out of there before anyone noticed."

"You're not kidding; these guys scare the hell out of me."

"You and me both; how did you get out of the building?"

"I ran down the stairs and slipped out the back door so no one would see me."

"What about the register?"

"The register?"

"Yes, Jonah, you signed the register on your way in but not on your way out. If any of those guys noticed your name while signing themselves out and the fact that you made a one-way trip during the meeting, don't you think that would raise some suspicions?"

Jonah suddenly froze.

"The register!"

7

RYAN SCHAPP SAT at his kitchen table at home that night with a perplexed look. He had waited for his wife Sue to fall asleep before sneaking out of the bedroom so she wouldn't ask any questions. She was a heavy sleeper, so he figured she wouldn't wake up with the noise of him sneaking out.

He had brought home his briefcase to work on the files Irv had given him without anyone looking over his shoulder. As per Irv's instructions, tomorrow morning, he was to fax the files they discussed earlier that contained the various shipments that would be made in the next sixty days to their contacts in Izmir. He was then to follow up with them by phone.

I can't seem to be able to get into my briefcase, thought Ryan. *That's strange; why is my briefcase locked?*

Ryan examined the briefcase closely. It looked the same as everyone else's in the company, except that he noticed that the numbers next to each buckle were set at three zeroes, something he did not do.

And then it occurred to him: *Is this my briefcase?*

He looked closely next to the right buckle for his name. He could not believe what he was staring at. "Property of: Jonah Mark."

What the hell am I doing with this guy's briefcase? Ryan was having cold sweats. *And more importantly, where is mine?*

Ryan went over the day in his mind. He thought of the various instances when he may have run into Ryan.

Of course! The seminar. I sat right next to him, practically breathing down his neck. We must have grabbed each other's briefcases on our way out. I wonder if he even knows I have his. But it's not his briefcase I'm worried about. Irv entrusted me with some vital information; if that information gets out, it's not just Irv's neck on the line....

Ryan flashed back to a meeting in Irv's office a week before. He could not shake it from his mind. It was all he could think about for days.

"Ryan, you're doing a good job keeping your eyes open for me," said Irv. "Your reports on the comings and goings of the three people I asked you to keep an eye on have been detailed and thorough."

Ryan was more than thrilled to hear those words. He was particularly delighted with the extra bonuses he had received in his paycheck that helped keep him ahead of his gambling debts. Marco and Carlos had been breathing down his neck. They did not like waiting for their money.

"Just doing my job, Mr. Carter."

Anything for those bonuses, thought Ryan.

As far as I am concerned, I'm Irv's new ventriloquist dummy, with his hand stuck firmly up my back. Any secrets he tells me are in the vault. I'm not going to mess with the golden goose.

Ryan knew that Irv knew what a financial mess his life was and how important his new assignment was to him. The last person Irv needed to worry about was him.

"Ryan, I am going to tell you something that I need you to keep in the strictest confidence."

"Of course, Mr. Carter."

"If any of this gets out, I will hold you fully responsible; do you understand me?"

"Yes, of course, Mr. Carter; you have nothing to worry about."

Just keep those checks coming, and I don't care what secrets you have; they are safe with me, thought Ryan.

Irv could practically read his mind.

"Ryan, we have been making shipments of high-tech weapons parts and explosives to countries in the Soviet Union; do you understand the implications of what I am saying?"

Ryan was stunned.

Do I understand the implications of what he is saying? I may be naive when it comes to certain things, but I'm not a moron. The partners are doing some nasty stuff, and now he's buying my loyalty with a gun to my head.

"Eh, yes, sir, Mr. Carter."

Now that he told me what he just told me, I just became a party to it, and if I don't report it, I'm in it up to my neck should things go south. Great way to buy my loyalty, Irv, thought Ryan; *nicely done.*

"Ryan, I want you to listen carefully. Tyler Tech has been

shipping these high-tech weapons to some satellite countries in the Soviet Union through their port in Ukraine. Because there are no direct shipments from the US to Odesa, the main seaport in Ukraine, the cargo must first be shipped to Izmir, Turkey, which is on the Aegean Sea, where it is discharged and transloaded onto other ships bound for Odesa. Got me so far, Ryan?"

"Yes, sir," said Ryan.

"Good," said Irv, as if he were talking to a complete idiot.

"I've got a crew of Turkish dock workers that are being paid handsomely to transfer the cargo that is marked for Turkey and place it on ships bound for Odessa."

Ryan couldn't believe what he was hearing. *This guy is essentially telling me that the Tylers are committing treason for money; why is he telling me this?"*

"Ryan, I think you have what it takes to be more heavily involved with this endeavor. I want you to act as our point man for this crucial operation."

I guess what it takes is to have the word "shmuck" written across my forehead, thought Ryan.

"Ryan, I am going to give you some floppies with lists of shipments that we will be making in the next sixty days that are officially bound for the port of Izmir. I want you to coordinate with our friends in Turkey and make sure those shipments are taken off the cargo ships and transferred to the ships that we designate. Here is a list of our contacts in Turkey. Make sure to keep them in a safe place. Can you handle the job, Ryan?"

Ryan's mind was flying a hundred miles an hour. *I am essentially being told to handle the dirty part of the operation, to coordinate with the crew in Turkey to transfer some of our country's high-tech weapons parts and explosives to our enemies. If I don't, I will be held responsible by Irv and whichever other partners are in on this scheme, not to mention that I can wind up in the slammer for who knows how many years. I'm not sure I'm ready to be the point man, i.e., the sacrificial lamb here, no matter how much I owe in gambling debts. I've got to get away from this guy and think. For now, I'm just going to play it cool with this maniac until I can make my exit.*

"Yes, sir, Mr. Carter, you can count on me."

"I knew I could, Ryan; that will be all."

Ryan could feel Irv staring at him as he left his office. What Irv could not see was the revolution taking place in his stomach.

As Ryan sat and stared at Jonah's briefcase, he knew he was in big trouble. There were floppies in his own briefcase that Irv had sent him, which contained lists of illegal shipments to US adversaries to which Ryan was now a party. He assumed Jonah probably figured out they had switched briefcases just as Ryan did. The question was, did he open it?

Relax, thought Ryan. *There is no reason he would want to open my briefcase. Jonah will probably just bring it back in the morning, no harm, no foul.*

Jonah decided he would have to come up with a story if anyone asked him about his visit to the office last night; right now, he had more pressing things to deal with. He ensured he had copied all the floppies for his meeting with Hannah the next night. He decided that in the morning, he would go with the most plausible explanation to Ryan for what he was doing with his briefcase, one that Ryan probably already expected. He would arrive at the office early and get rid of the briefcase and the Ryan issue ASAP.

There was a knock on Ryan's door at about a quarter to nine the following day.

"Come in," said Ryan.

Ryan knew whom to expect, and Jonah walked in. Ryan decided to be abrupt with him so they wouldn't get into any small talk, which he very much wanted to avoid.

"Good morning, Ryan."

"You've got my briefcase."

"How'd you guess?" said Jonah, hoping for a smile. He didn't get one.

"Next time there's a seminar, how about you give me some space," said Ryan.

"Give *you* some space! You were practically sitting in my lap, Ryan."

"Look, just gimmee the briefcase, and I'll give you yours, and we'll call it a day," said Ryan.

"Fine," said Jonah.

They exchanged briefcases, and as Jonah turned to leave, he turned back around to Ryan and said:

"Hey Ryan, what's the deal; did I ever do something to you that I'm not aware of? What's with all the hostility, bro?"

"Just get out of my office... bro!"

They glared at each other, and Jonah made his exit.

What a jerk! he thought to himself.

Ryan felt bad about being such a jerk to Jonah; he had nothing against him personally, but his relationship with Jonah was not at the top of his mind at that moment. He quickly went through his briefcase; it looked the same as the day before. He breathed a sigh of relief and promptly pulled out the sheet of paper with the contacts in Izmir that Irv had given him to check on the shipments.

Once I do this, I'm in bed with these people, thought Ryan. *I've got no choice; my next payment to Marco and Carlos is due next week.*

Ryan perused the sheet of paper. There were about a dozen Turkish-sounding names on the list. On top of the list was the guy he needed to call, the Port Director's assistant. Ryan had no idea if everyone on the dock was part of the conspiracy or just the people on the list. He dreaded making the call but had to do what he was told. He dialed the number at the top of the list.

Ahmet Bayar picked up the phone after two rings.

"Ahmet, eh, this is Ryan Schapp at Tyler Technologies in New …"

"What you want?"

His response was direct and to the point.

"I'm sorry to bother you, Mr. Ahmet. I'm just calling to make sure everything is all set for the next shipment."

"You crazy? Why you people call me every week about same damned shipment, you think I'm stupid, eh?"

"Uh, no sir, Mr. Ahmet…."

"My name is Ahmet Bayar, you idyot, not Mr. Ahmet, you understand?"

"Uh, yes sir… Mr… uh… Mr. Bayar, I …"

"You no call me again, or I throw your damned shipment into the sea, you understand?"

"Uh, yes sir Mr… uh… Bayar …"

The line went dead. Ryan sat there in a ball of sweat; he was never so scared in his life.

What am I going to do?

Hannah left the office a little late and headed to what Jonah referred to as "our old place" for their 6:00 rendezvous. Twenty-four hours before, she could only think about her relationship with Jonah and whether she had gotten mixed signals while heading to lunch. She felt a spark for Jonah; that was obvious, but she was the one who had ended it because the previous version of Jonah was not what she was looking for. Since Jonah joined the firm as an assistant to Mr. Heart, she had been impressed with how he had handled himself. He seemed so much different than he was when they dated. She found herself stealing glances at him whenever she could, but she had no idea what, if anything, Jonah was feeling.

She wondered why Jonah asked her to meet him.

Was it to explain his actions the previous day at lunch? Was it to try and rekindle their relationship? Or was it the opposite? thought Hannah. *Maybe he just wants to clarify to me not to get my hopes up because he's moved on. Perhaps he's seeing someone else? Hannah thought that would be pretty devastating.*

Unfortunately, whatever it was about would have to wait. Her close encounter with Irv and Simeon the previous night had really rocked her world. She needed someone to confide in, someone she could trust to tell what happened.

I need to get this off my chest and figure out what to do, thought Hannah. *No matter how Jonah feels about me romantically.*

Our old place was Bernie's on Essex Street on the Lower East Side. It was their favorite place to steal away whenever the opportunity arose. They loved to sample the incredible array of delicacies from deli to Chinese food; they had it all. It had been their go-to spot whenever they were hungry. Hannah grabbed the subway for the short trip downtown.

Too bad this isn't a date, thought Hannah.

Jonah called Josh earlier in the day.

"Listen, Josh, I called Hannah to meet me tonight at Bernie's at 6:00 so we can go over what we have."

"Does she know why?"

"Why, what?"

"Why you are meeting."

"No, I kept it brief."

"How brief?" asked Josh.

"Very brief… cryptically brief."

"Why'd you do that?" asked Josh.

"Because I didn't want to get into it on the phone; I figured it's safer that way."

"Jonah, did it ever occur to you that Hannah may think this is about something else?"

"What do you mean?"

"What do I mean, knucklehead? She has no clue what you want to talk to her about, and you asked her to meet you at your favorite dating place; what do you think she might be thinking?"

Jonah realized that Josh had a point.

"I didn't think about that," said Jonah.

"Really, Einstein! Are you ready to spill your guts about how you feel about her?"

"I was hoping to feel her out first at the pizza shop yesterday; I don't want to make a fool of myself."

Did she ask you what the meeting was about?" said Josh.

"She did."

"And what did you say?"

"Nothing; I hung up on her."

"You really have this relationship thing nailed down, Jonah. I must say, I'm super impressed!"

"I guess I'm out of practice. Besides, I have a secret weapon that will surely kill the mood."

"What's that?" said Josh.

"You!"

"Me?"

"Yes, you, Josh. She'll know it's not about our relationship when she sees you. Besides, I need all the help I can get to figure this out. See you at Bernie's at six."

"Wait a minute…"

It was too late; Jonah had hung up the phone.

I'm getting pretty adept at that, thought Jonah.

Josh arrived first. Bernie's smelled like… Bernie's. From the salami hanging on the wall behind the deli counter to the huge hot dogs and knockwursts sizzling on the grill to the smell of corned beef, pastrami, and other deli favorites, to the aroma of Chinese food emanating from the rear of the store.

The place was packed with wall-to-wall patrons eating their Chinese and deli favorites. It was a strange combination, but it worked. Josh waited in line to be seated. After about fifteen minutes, he was ushered to a table in the back that was set for three, as he requested. The smell of the place was driving Josh crazy.

Jonah and Hannah better come soon, thought Josh, *or I'm ordering.*

Jonah arrived a few minutes later and was ushered to the table.

"I'm not sure this was such a great idea," said Josh. "Besides, the smell of this place, which can be pretty distracting, brings back lots of memories. I'm surprised Hannah agreed to meet you here."

"She didn't have a choice, Josh, remember; I hung up the phone on her."

"Yes, you did do that, and may I once make note of how impressed I am with your relationship skills. Now, I say we order."

"We wait," said Jonah in a firm tone.

"Listen, Jonah, I'm all for waiting, but this is Bernie's, for heaven's sake!"

"We wait."

"Maybe just an eggroll."

"No," said Jonah.

"One little eggroll; who's it gonna hurt?"

"We wait, Josh!"

"Fine," said Josh … "since you're paying."

"Who said anything about paying?" said Jonah.

Before they could argue any further, Hannah walked

in, looking frazzled but *as beautiful as ever,* thought Jonah. Hannah spotted Jonah in the back. She said something to the Maître D', who hustled her to the table. She looked over at Josh with a puzzled look and then at Jonah.

"I didn't expect *you* here, Josh."

Josh felt embarrassed as if he were intruding on a date. Hannah looked flustered and didn't know what to make of the scene. It was up to Jonah to speak first since this was his rodeo.

"Hannah, why don't you have a seat? I'll explain everything."

Hannah, still looking confused, took a seat opposite Jonah and Josh. Jonah thought to himself, *she looks like she's feeling ambushed; I better say something.*

Before he could say anything, the waiter arrived wearing one of Bernie's famous trademark oversized yarmulkes with a Chinese tassel hanging from the side. He looked to be in his early seventies and apparently recognized Jonah and Hannah, who used to be regulars. As soon as Jonah spotted the waiter, he knew he was in trouble, but it was too late. Jacob was off to the races.

"Jonah… Hannah, welcome back; it's so nice to see you again!" said Jacob, soon to be their formerly favorite waiter. "You know, I was wondering if I'd ever see you two again, such a perfect couple. Just the other day, I asked Bernie what happened to Jonah and Hannah. They were such a perfect couple; how long has it been?"

Jonah, looking for a hole under the table to climb into, had to come up with something. He glanced over to Hannah, who looked totally bewildered. Josh had a grin on his face from ear to ear; he was starting to enjoy this. Jonah gave him his killer look, and the grin magically disappeared.

"Uh… Jacob, it's been a little while. We're kind of in a rush. Can we just order?"

Jacob looked confused but forged ahead; it was like trying to stop a freight train.

"I get it, a little bump in the road to happiness; I see it all the time. Don't worry. Things always work themselves out. You know what they say: love conquers all!"

Great, I've been coming here for years; suddenly, my waiter turns into Cupid, thought Jonah.

"What'll it be?" he said in his trademark hoarse voice. "Wait, don't tell me; let me see if I remember. For you young man, it's pastrami on rye with mustard, some kishke on the side, and an order of cole slaw with a Doctor Brown cherry soda. I got that right, didn't I? Jacob never forgets. Remember the time you both walked in from a big storm? Hannah, you were wearing Jonah's jacket and-"

"Uh… Jacob… the time?" Jonah pointed to his watch.

"I guess we could do memory lane next time; such a cute couple!"

Jonah was looking for a sharp object… any sharp object.

Jacob winked at Hannah with a big smile as if he was there to save the day.

"And for you, young lady, sliced turkey breast on club with Russian dressing, some well-done fries, steamed vegetables, and a diet Coke."

Jonah and Hannah shook their heads in agreement, careful not to say a word that might prolong the ordeal. What Jacob lacked in couth, he made up in memory.

He looked over at Josh.

"And what'll it be for you, young man?"

They all looked at Josh as if they had noticed him for the first time. Looking at the three faces suddenly turned in his direction, all he could think of was what form of retribution he would inflict on Jonah when the evening was over.

"Uh… I'll have the Sino Steak, with fried rice, a roast beef egg roll, and a celery soda."

"Excellent, sir," Jacob quipped. And for good measure, he added, as he looked at Jonah and Hannah, "I'll leave you two lovebirds alone."

"There goes his tip," said Jonah as Jacob mercifully left their table. But no one was laughing.

Hannah looked like she was in shock; no words were coming from her mouth. Jonah needed to say something. He couldn't ignore the last five minutes as if they never happened.

"Hannah, I apologize for making you feel uncomfortable; I never expected that to happen."

Hannah put her hand in front of her mouth as she tried to suppress a grin fighting to make it to her face. She was starting to enjoy Jonah's pain.

"It's OK, Jonah, life happens."

"Also, the food here is terrific," said Josh, hoping for a laugh, but his attempt at humor landed with a thud.

Jonah shot him another look before clearing his throat.

"Hannah, I chose this place because it's sufficiently noisy, and what Josh and I have to say needs to be kept between us."

"What is it, Jonah?" said Hannah. Her look became serious; she had enough of the formalities.

"OK, here goes," said Jonah.

He then proceeded to tell Hannah everything that had been going on in the office over the last few weeks; he didn't leave anything out. He caught a break when another waiter helping with the busy crowd brought them their orders.

Hannah listened intently, only stopping to take a bite or two of her turkey sandwich. Josh did most of the eating, as he already knew what Jonah had to say, and he had built up a rather large appetite that he was in the midst of satisfying.

As Hannah listened to Jonah's story, she wondered if Jonah had indeed changed, given his recklessness in taking on Irv, stealing Ryan's briefcase, and sneaking into the office late at night. She thought his running into Irv next to her desk and knocking over some garbage cans was just him being a klutz; now, she wasn't so sure.

Is this the spy novel Jonah I thought I left behind, or is this the new Jonah I have been admiring that still has not entirely left his fantasy world behind?

As she listened to Jonah's narrative, she couldn't help but think of what she had gone through the previous night herself, and their stories seemed to fit together. She wondered whether what was in Ryan's briefcase might clarify things for her.

Hannah had not spoken as she listened to Jonah's detailed story. When he was done, he asked Hannah to examine the files on the floppies he had placed in a large envelope on the table. Hannah let them sit there, at least for the time being.

"As long as we have stories to tell, I have one of my own," said Hannah.

Both Jonah and Josh looked puzzled. She had not yet

commented on the story Jonah had just related. She then told them everything that occurred the previous night in the office. Hannah became emotional as she related the story for the first time; it sounded like she had gone through quite an ordeal. The guys listened intently, hanging on to every word. When she got to the part about where the Tylers were sending the shipments listed on those floppies, they looked stunned.

"Hannah, are you telling us that the Tyler partners are using the company Noah Tyler created to send our greatest technological secrets to the Soviets?" asked Jonah.

"I'm afraid so."

"This is worse than anything we could have anticipated."

As she finished the story of her ordeal, Jonah fished a tissue out of his pocket and handed it to Hannah. It was a nice gesture that Hannah appreciated. She dabbed at her eyes.

"That was quite a story," said Jonah. "I am so sorry about what you went through, and what these people are doing is downright treasonous."

"I was going to call you before I got your call," she sobbed. "But when you called me, I figured we would meet anyway, and you hung up so quickly."

Josh glanced at Jonah but said nothing. Jonah felt the glance and chose to ignore it; his eyes were lost on Hannah. He was surprised by his own emotions, which he seemed to have momentarily lost control of. He looked at Hannah while trying to hide a tear with a quick swipe of the back of his hand.

"Don't worry, Hannah, we'll figure this out."

There was a connection there that neither of them had felt in a long time. Hannah somehow felt better after telling her story to Jonah. They each realized how much they missed each other, but the relationship talk would have to wait another day; this was serious business.

"I'm going to take these floppies home tonight and see what I can glean from them. I'll contact you after I've gone through everything," said Hannah, "then we can meet again."

Josh felt a little out of place, so he just stayed quiet. Hannah looked at him and said, "Thank you, Josh, for being here and lending your support."

"Sure, Hannah; whatever you need. I'm so sorry you went through what you did."

"Thank you," said Hannah. Standing up to leave, she looked at both of them.

"And let's make the next meeting at Starbucks."

There was no argument from either of them.

"Let me walk you to the subway," said Jonah.

Josh gave Jonah a quick smile, which he chose to ignore.

"That sounds like a good idea," said Hannah.

They both said goodnight to Josh and walked out the front door. It was only four blocks to the subway. They both felt a little awkward and didn't say much.

Jonah thought of different things to say, but he could not come up with anything that would not sound like he was taking advantage of her vulnerable state; this wasn't the right time to bring up their relationship; it would have to wait another day.

"Are you sure you'll be safe down there? I can call you a cab?"

"I always take the subways, Jonah; a little graffiti never killed anyone."

Hannah sensed Jonah's predicament, unsure where they were in their personal lives. There was an awkward silence as they reached the train station stairway. They each said goodnight, and Hannah was gone.

There was one more unpleasant chore Ryan felt he had to do before it came back to bite him on the nose. He had gotten in early the following day after a sleepless night of worrying. He had gone over the proposed dialogue in his head repeatedly. He doubted Jonah had accessed his briefcase and found the floppies. Still, with the minute chance he might have, he was hoping to get out in front of the problem, a proactive way of handling it, which might impress Irv. He would soon find out whether that was a good idea or not.

He finally got the courage together and knocked on Irv's door. He was sitting at his desk going over some paperwork.

"Mr. Carter, do you have a minute?" said Ryan.

Irv looked up from what he was doing.

"What's up, Ryan?" said Irv.

"I'm not sure, Mr. Carter, but there is a tiny possibility that we may have had a security breach."

Irv looked up from his desk with a look of concern; *not a promising start*, Ryan thought.

"What kind of security breach?" said Irv, as Ryan suddenly had his full attention.

"Someone may have gotten into my briefcase and accessed the floppies you sent me."

The look on Irv's face had changed from extreme concern to alarm to panic in seconds. The more Ryan spoke, the worse it was getting. Although the entire plot was not revealed on the disks he gave Ryan, any loose evidence could prove dangerous.

"Explain," said Irv, "and I want *all the details.*"

Ryan was starting to doubt his *getting out in front strategy*; so far, it was not yielding any dividends, but it was too late to make any adjustments; as the old saying goes, in for a dime, in for a dollar.

"Well, Mr. Carter, there was an apparent mix-up of briefcases yesterday between Jonah Mark and me."

"Details, Ryan, I asked for details."

"Sure, Mr. Carter; Jonah and I sat right next to each other at the safety seminar yesterday; it was my way of staying close to Jonah, just like you had asked."

Irv didn't seem as impressed as he had thought he would be when he had practiced this dialogue in his office earlier.

"Don't tell me," said a visibly angry Irv; "he took home your briefcase, didn't he, Ryan?"

"And I took home his, Mr. Carter."

Somehow, that part didn't seem to appease him.

"But he brought it back first thing in the morning, and it looks perfectly intact."

"I see," said Irv, who was looking remarkably like a volcano about to erupt.

"And you would know if anyone accessed the briefcase's contents because…?"

"Well, Mr. Carter… it didn't appear to have been accessed… because…."

There was no because, because there was no way to know. Irv knew that, and it was beginning to dawn on Ryan.

Ryan had a unique vantage point from where he stood; he could see each vein bulging from Irv's neck; his face was red as an apple. No, it turned out his strategy of getting out in front of the problem put him right in the line of fire.

"You imbecile!" shouted Irv. "Do you know how important those floppies are?"

"Actually... I do sir... but ..."

"How can you be my Director of Security if you can't even secure your own briefcase!?"

"Well, sir... I... guess that's a fair point... but-"

"Get out!" shouted Irv at the top of his lungs as he sprang out of his desk like a pellet out of a slingshot. Irv didn't have to ask twice; Ryan was already out at the word "how."

It was clear to him that the *get-out-in-front strategy* was definitely *not* the way to go.

Two offices away sat Jonah, who heard the whole thing.

So, there is a connection between the partners and those floppy disks. This confirms Hannah's story. I need to get to the bottom of this.

Three offices away sat Smokey, who heard everything as well. He watched Ryan run past him to his office like he was shot out of a cannon.

As Irv sat at his desk trying to catch his breath, he couldn't help but notice as Smokey got up from his desk and headed straight for Mr. Heart's office, closing the door behind him.

From Ryan's vantage point, he could see that Irv witnessed the same thing. He could also see the look on Irv's face as Smokey disappeared into Mr. Heart's office.

If looks could kill, thought Ryan.

∽

The next day, Jonah got to his office at precisely 9:00. Everything about the office these days gave him chills. As he was sitting at his desk, he heard a muffled argument coming from behind Mr. Heart's closed office door, which was usually kept open. Suddenly, the door opened, and he heard the words, "This is your last warning Franklin; you better wise up and mind your own damned business, and the same goes for that smokin' friend of yours," as he witnessed Irv storming out and walking down the hall to his office, which was across from Jonah's. He glanced across at Jonah with a menacing look and slammed the door.

Jonah sat frozen at his desk; he did not know what to do. It was apparent to him that Mr. Heart and Smokey had irritated Irv somehow. He was sure it had something to do with Smokey's visit to Mr. Heart's office the day before. It had been clear to Jonah that the partners didn't like Mr. Heart and Smokey very much, but the level of animosity was even more than he thought.

What the hell was that? thought Jonah.

Irv was a hothead; having an office close to Jonah's, he was always carrying on about something or other, but most of the yelling was done behind closed doors, so he didn't hear much from where he sat. One thing he was sure of was that there was much going on beneath the surface at Tyler Technologies, and he didn't plan on waiting to find out.

He remembered the expression he had heard while hiding in the office the other night.

Our friends behind the curtain….

It was time to do some espionage of his own, and his first stop was Smokey's office. He was hoping to get some clues from him. He noticed Irv staring coldly at him as he knocked on Smokey's door. Jonah was in spy mode; he looked straight back at Irv.

It's a free country, buddy. I can visit whomever I want, he thought to himself.

"Come in, kid," said Smokey. "What's on your mind?"

"Hi, Smoke. I hate to bother you, but I'm a little concerned by what I've witnessed from my office the last few days. I was hoping you could clue me in."

"Close the door and have a seat."

Jonah stared straight at Irv as he closed the door and sat down.

"I was wondering when you'd show up, kid."

Jonah loved it when Smokey asked him to sit down; it usually meant he would get the inside scoop on something interesting.

"Listen, kid, whatever I tell you is just between us, OK?"

"Sure thing, Smokey."

"There's a lot of stuff beneath the surface that I'm not prepared to get into right now because it's all speculation. Maybe some nerves are frayed, and guys like Irv lash out when they feel the heat. I don't have to tell you he has a temper, so I would stay as far away from him as possible."

"I got the vibe, but he's always glaring at me; I can't figure out why."

"Alright, kid, I will tell you something that may make you feel better."

"What's that?"

"They can't fire you."

Jonah was startled.

"Why not?"

"The same reason they can't get rid of Mr. Heart. It was in the contract the partners signed with Noah Tyler when he handed off the company. Mr. Heart stays no matter what, and his assistant can only be fired by him."

"Why'd he do that?"

"I guess he knew their capabilities."

"No wonder Irv's always glaring at Mr. Heart and me, but what about you?"

"I guess you can say I'm twisting in the wind, kid, flying without a parachute."

"Doesn't that make you nervous? I mean, everyone knows you and Mr. Heart are best buds."

"I've had a long career, Jonah; if they give me the pink slip, I'll be fine."

"I get the feeling there's more that you're not telling me, Smokey."

"There is, Jonah, but that's all I can discuss now. Remember what I told you."

"I know... not everything is always spelled out. But things have a way of making themselves clear if you just step back and let them."

"Exactly. Now, if you don't mind, I've got an appointment I need to get to."

He grabbed his coat and hat and shoved his pipe in his mouth.

"You take care of yourself, kid."

"You too, Smokey; you too."

As Jonah left Smokey's office, he saw Irv glaring at him.

"Lose something?" yelled Jonah, who suddenly didn't feel so scared of him.

Maybe I shouldn't have said that. The guy can't fire me, but I guess there's nothing in their contract that says that he can't kill me.

Irv looked even angrier if that was possible.

The hairs on the back of Jonah's neck began to rise as he hurried back to his office.

Ryan sat in his office shaking like a leaf. He did not sleep at all the previous night. Not only did he fear for his job after being thrown out of Irv's office the day before, he was now part of a treasonous conspiracy, which scared the hell out of him.

And for what? thought Ryan. *He'll probably fire me anyway for exchanging my briefcase with Jonah. And if he hears from Bayar in Turkey about how well our phone call went yesterday… I don't even want to think about it.*

He had also heard the commotion from outside Mr. Heart's office earlier. He remembered how Smokey visited Mr. Heart yesterday immediately after he was thrown out of Irv's office. And now he could distinctly hear Irv threatening Mr. Heart and Smokey as he stormed away. *That guy has some temper,* thought Ryan.

He heard Irv tell Mr. Heart to mind his own damned business, and he mentioned Smokey too.

Ryan thought to himself, *Was he referring to the same*

treasonous business Irv was involved in? Were Mr. Heart and Smokey on to what Irv and the partners were doing in Turkey?

Like everyone else in the company, Ryan respected Mr. Heart, even though Irv had told him to keep an eye on him. Smokey seemed like just a friendly old guy that everyone liked.

I never had an issue with either one of them, thought Ryan. *I don't even have it in for Jonah; I'm just following orders. What have I gotten myself into?*

Jonah noticed an envelope sticking out from under his desk blotter as he walked into his office. As he slowly pulled it out, he saw his name written on it in Hannah's unmistakable handwriting. *She must have gotten in extra early this morning in order not to be seen leaving the envelope,* he thought. He opened it up. Inside, there was a small sheet of paper that read simply:

"Starbucks on 57th at 6:00 tonight; bring J."

8

JONAH DROPPED A note on Josh's desk during lunch break about the meeting at Starbucks that night. They left the office separately at about 5:30 and took separate routes in case someone was watching them. They saw Hannah leave at 5:00 and didn't acknowledge each other. All three kept looking over their shoulders as they walked the street. Jonah wore a baseball cap, and Josh wore sunglasses. Hannah threw on a hoodie and arrived first. The place was busy as the rush hour crowd grabbed their final caffeine jolt of the day.

Jonah arrived next. He scanned the crowd for a minute before noticing a scared young woman sitting at a table in the back corner of the coffee shop. He recognized her fear before recognizing her face. *She looks worried,* thought Jonah. Hannah looked up from her cup of coffee and noticed Jonah right away. *He's still as handsome as ever, even with the baseball cap,* thought Hannah. She had asked Jonah to bring Josh, not only because he was part of this, but as a buffer so that Jonah would not feel uncomfortable being alone with her.

There was no way to think clearly about their relationship with everything happening.

Jonah approached the table and sat down.

"Did you make sure you weren't followed?" said Hannah.

"No sweat," said Jonah.

Just then, they noticed Josh entering the coffee shop in his sunglasses and heading to their table.

"Here comes Ray Charles," said Jonah.

Hannah suppressed a smile with a hand to her mouth.

"What's wrong now?" asked Josh indignantly.

"Did you bring your sunblock; it's six o'clock in the evening. Do you even understand the concept of sunglasses?"

"I was thinking of going with one of those plastic glasses with the big nose and fake mustache attached; would that have suited you better, Mr. Disguise Expert?"

Hannah cleared her throat loudly to get the guy's attention.

Men are like children, thought Hannah.

"OK, let's get into this," said Hannah.

Josh shot Jonah a wounded look.

"I looked at the disks you gave me; those files were scary as hell," said Hannah. That got the guys' attention.

"So, first things first. What is in these shipments has enough firepower to blow a whole city off the map," said Hannah.

The guys sat stoically, listening to Hannah's presentation.

"My biggest concern is those shipments cannot fall into the wrong hands. I know we are working on technology the Soviets don't have."

"That sounds pretty scary, Hannah," said Josh.

"If you ask me, this has already gone too far," said Hannah. We need to call the authorities."

"I agree," said Josh.

"I don't," said Jonah. They both looked at Jonah at the same time.

"Why not?" said Josh.

"Because neither of you have seen Marco or Carlos up front. If they find out that we told on them, they could exact revenge against us, not to mention Mr. Heart or Smokey or any of our families. Hannah, you told us about your encounter with Irv and Simeon in the office the other night. Did Irv sound like someone to be messed with? I heard him threaten Mr. Heart and Smokey with my own ears, and I have been the recipient of some of the worst glares I have ever seen; believe me, this guy is scary."

"But we have proof of the shipments on these disks," said Hannah.

"We have proof of shipments of parts and explosives we sell going to countries approved by the US; there is nothing on those disks that speak about removing those parts in Turkey and shipping them elsewhere. We have nothing," said Jonah.

"He's right," said Josh to Hannah.

Hannah thought about what Jonah had said.

He has a pretty valid argument. If the police came snooping around the office, it could scare Irv enough to run to Marco and Carlos, and all their lives would be in danger.

"What do you propose?" said Hannah.

"If we want to go to the authorities," said Jonah, "we need proof."

"Proof of what?" said Josh.

"We need to prove that there is a conspiracy to ship illegal weaponry and explosives to the Soviets. And we need to connect the Tylers and Irv to the conspiracy."

"How are we going to get that proof?" said Hannah.

"I suggest we take a little time and think about it," said Jonah.

"We don't have much time; that first shipment is scheduled for early next month," said Hannah.

"I know," said Jonah. "Look, we all have different jobs in different parts of the company. I say we keep our eyes and ears open and see if we can come up with an idea. Let's meet here again when we have some solid info to work with. But time is of the essence."

"I don't know, Jonah, this sounds a little like one of your spy novels," said Josh. I bet you'll try and come up with some crazy stunt you read in one of those books."

"You can stand to read some yourself, Josh; maybe you'll learn something."

That got Hannah's attention.

I thought he was done with the spy books; does he think this is some kind of game? What am I dealing with here?

"And what about that crazy stunt you tried in the office late last night?" said Josh.

Jonah gave Josh the death stare, but it was too late; he felt Hannah looking at him. He turned to face her.

"It was nothing, Hannah."

But Josh wasn't done.

"Nothing? Do you call sneaking into the office in the middle of the night nothing?"

Hannah did a double take and looked squarely at Jonah.

"Jonah, what did you do?" said Hannah.

Before he could clean it up, it all poured out of Josh's mouth. Jonah thought about leaping across the table and strangling Josh but did not think it would be a good look for Hannah.

"Jonah, you didn't!"

"I did what I felt had to be done, Hannah. Besides, I got out in time; no harm, no foul."

"What about the register?" said Josh.

"What register?" said Hannah.

Jonah looked directly at Josh.

"You're on borrowed time, buddy."

Hannah looked at Josh.

"Josh, you'll fill me in later; we've got enough to deal with right now."

She then looked at Jonah.

"Alright, Jonah, we'll try your way, but remember that time is not on our side."

"OK, said Jonah; let's keep all our senses open."

"What does that mean?" said Josh.

"It means start wracking our brains for anything we can come up with that we may have missed, and if we can, snoop around a little in our departments."

"Why do you keep dragging me into these life-threatening situations?" said Josh.

"Because there's a little spy in all of us, Josh."

That got Both Hannah's and Josh's attention. They both looked at each other sharply but said nothing.

They each left the coffee shop separately.

I didn't offer to walk Hannah to the subway, thought Jonah. *I don't want to endanger any of us if someone is watching; I hope she didn't read anything into it.*

Hannah did wonder about that, but she was too nervous about what they were now dealing with to dwell on it, and she was starting to have doubts about where Jonah's head was. The thought of Jonah sneaking into the office in the middle of the night scared the daylights out of her, but for now, she had to keep her head in the game.

The next morning, Josh and Hannah nervously sat at their desks, trying to figure things out. They knew they did not have much time. They were worried about being caught doing anything out of the ordinary that would attract the attention of the partners, Ryan, or anyone else involved in the conspiracy. They also worried about what Jonah was up to.

Jonah sat at his desk, deep in thought. There was something the Tylers did that never made much sense to him that came to mind. There was probably a reasonable explanation, but suddenly everything was suspect. The partners used an outside accounting firm named Bartowski and Company to prepare their financial reports. This never made sense to Jonah; a big company like Tyler Tech should not need the services of an outside accounting firm to prepare their reports.

Max Bartowski, the CPA and owner of the company, would take the raw data the accounting department put together and prepare the needed reports. He was a big, sweaty type of guy with a combover, not the kind Mr. Heart cared for. Jonah watched Bartowski dropping in on Mr. Heart every Wednesday like clockwork for so-called courtesy visits after first meeting with the partners to discuss the company's financials. They were both about the same age.

This guy's not interested in chewing the fat with Mr. Heart, he would think to himself. *The partners probably told him to drop in and say hello to Mr. Heart every week to make him feel like he's part of the loop. He's not fooling Mr. Heart one bit, and he's not fooling me either.*

Jonah often heard them from his office when he paid his weekly visit. Bartowski would knock on Mr. Heart's door and walk in.

"Hello, Franklin."

"Hello, Max."

"How are the grandkids?"

"Oh, the usual Max, you know how kids are."

"Yup, got a couple of 'em myself, you know."

Jonah could tell from Mr. Heart's body language after these drop-ins that he probably didn't like Bartowski and had no use for him. But for appearance's sake, he would "shoot the breeze," as Bartowski would put it. At some point, Bartowski, who was prone to sweat like a geyser, would excuse himself and go to the Men's Room to freshen up while Mr. Heart would cool his heels, waiting for the ordeal to end. A few minutes later, he would return to Mr. Heart's office, say his goodbyes, and be on his way.

Jonah sat at his desk and thought about the entire scenario. The whole idea of using this outside company bothered him in the first place, plus he hated watching Mr. Heart go through this ridiculous charade every week.

There's something about this that just doesn't feel right.

He decided to drop in on Smokey and try to get his take on the whole thing. He knocked on Smokey's door; he was fiddling with his pipe.

"Hey, Smokey," asked Jonah.

"What's up, kid?"

"Can I ask you something?"

"Sure thing, kid, what's on your mind?"

Jonah stepped into Smokey's office and watched as Smokey banged his pipe against the inside of his trash can to remove the old tobacco. He noticed Jonah watching his ritual and placed the pipe in his ashtray. He then looked at Jonah.

"What's up, kid."

Jonah realized he now had Smokey's complete attention.

"I was just wondering: why does Tyler Tech use an outside accounting firm to prepare its financial reports when we are a large company perfectly capable of doing the work ourselves? Isn't that a big waste of money?"

Smokey looked impressed.

"Good question, kid; it shows you're using your head, and not just for a hat rack, as my late wife Becky used to say."

He seemed to look over his shoulder before he spoke and lowered his voice. Jonah knew something big was coming.

"Let me put it to you this way, Jonah. If you ran a company and did not trust your CFO but were bound by an agreement that kept you married to each other, what would you do to keep that CFO from looking over your shoulder?"

"Hire someone whose shoulder he couldn't look over?"

"Bingo, I told you you're a smart kid. This guy Bartowski

was hired by the Tyler partners two years ago after Noah Tyler passed away."

"Pretty sneaky, don't you think?" said Jonah.

"Jonah, there's much beneath the surface at Tyler Technologies. Now, do me a favor and let you and me keep this little conversation under our proverbial hats, OK?"

"Sure thing, Smokey; my lips are sealed."

As Jonah left the office, he thought to himself.

Smokey knows that certain things around here don't sit well with me. Maybe he wants me to get the lay of the land. I'm not sure why; perhaps he's looking to protect me. But protect me from what?

✑

Jonah walked down the hall and knocked on Josh's office door; he was sitting at his desk, deep in thought.

"What's up Jonah? Are you looking for some gunpowder to blow up the office 'cause I'm fresh out?"

"Huh?"

Jonah looked confused.

"Never mind; what's up, buddy?"

"Josh, I just had a conversation with Smokey that blew my mind. I was thinking that maybe it might help us somehow."

Jonah closed the door behind him. He looked at Josh like his head was about to explode.

"Lay it on me, buddy."

He then filled Josh in on everything Smokey said. Josh listened to what Jonah had to say as if someone had hit him with a bowling ball.

"You know what, Jonah?"

"What?"

"The next time you invite me to join a company you're working at, you might want to fill me in on all the little skeletons in the closet."

"And ruin all this fun we're having?" said Jonah. "Not a chance!"

But Josh was no longer listening; he seemed miles away. He remembered something that happened the other day in the accounting department where he worked that didn't sit well with him at the time. Thinking back to it now after listening to Jonah's story, it suddenly stood out.

"Listen, Jonah, I just remembered something; I gotta go."

"Gotta go? Where to?"

"I just remembered something I forgot to do."

"I do that all the time, Josh, but I don't let that ruin a perfectly fine argument."

"If anyone asks, tell them I think I lost my wallet downstairs, and I went looking for it."

"Is that the best you could come up with?"

But Josh left Jonah sitting in his office as he ran out. He hit the elevator and was out of the building in five minutes. As he ran down the street, it all came back to him, and things were suddenly making sense. He thought back to all the events of that day.

Joel Tyler would visit the accounting department regularly to oversee the raw data collected so Bartowski could prepare his monthly reports. It always struck Josh as strange how they would both step to the other end of the department to talk whenever Bartowski visited. The other employees in the department would notice but didn't seem to care.

What's the big secret? Josh would think to himself. *It's just an accounting department; we aren't splitting the atom here.*

Nevertheless, it was always the same scenario. Bartowski would show up, Joel would enter the department, and within a few minutes, Joel would say: "Max, let's discuss this privately." They would then move to a private office at the other end of the department.

Fred Watkins was a staff accountant in the department; he sat one desk over from Josh. He was a great worker, and from what Josh could tell, he was highly regarded at the company. Fred's job was to review the raw data Bartowski used to prepare his reports. A few days earlier, Joel walked into the department, and Fred called him over to ask a question about the numbers he was working on. Suddenly, Joel grabbed the papers out of his hand and said:

"Where did you get this?"

"From you, Mr. Tyler."

"That's impossible!" said Joel as he stormed out of the office with the papers.

Josh had witnessed what happened and the bizarre reaction. He turned to Watkins.

"Is everything OK, Fred?"

Fred looked shaken.

"I'm not sure, Josh, but something strange is happening here?"

"What do you mean?"

"Joel gave me this set of numbers to review and look for errors."

"What's wrong with that?"

"Well, it's something I've been noticing lately, but I figured I just didn't have the full picture, so I kept quiet about it. I took a course in financial fraud when I worked at the Department of Justice before taking this job. So, by force of habit, I look at things from a different angle sometimes."

"And?" said Josh, curious to hear what Fred had to say.

"Well, one of the things we were taught to look for when examining books and records was a sudden growth in revenues unsupported by additional business. For example, lately, there are tens of thousands of dollars every month that are classified as various types of revenue appearing in these accounts. Still, there's no business or cash flow increase to support it. It's like money has suddenly started flying into these accounts for no discernable reason."

"That *is* strange, Fred. But if they were doing something wrong, why would the Tyler's want to let anyone see that data?"

"Good question, Josh; I've been trying to wrap my head around that lately."

"And?"

"There can be only one reason why anyone would do that, I can figure. And Joel's reaction makes it all the more likely."

"What's that?"

"Well, you saw the reaction when I pointed out the issue to Joel. He grabbed the papers from my hand and asked who gave it to me as if I was not supposed to see it. I think no one was supposed to see those papers, Josh. We've all seen the reports Bartowski generates for the firm; they are public knowledge. The revenues on the public reports are not the same as the reports I've been looking at for Joel Tyler."

"What are you saying, Fred? Give it to me in plain English?"

"Josh, I think there are two sets of books: one that Bartowski prepares for the public and one the Tylers keep privately. I think Joel has been giving me the wrong set of numbers lately by accident. He must have realized it when I asked him about the revenues not being supported, and you saw his reaction; it was pretty clear and over the top."

The next morning, Josh arrived and saw that Fred was gone and his desk had been cleaned out. The story that was fed to the employees in the department was that Fred had left the company for a greater opportunity elsewhere, but Josh didn't buy it. Fred would have told him he was leaving, as they had become pretty good friends. It also happened the morning after the incident with Joel, and that was just too convenient.

As he ran through the streets, Josh thought about all the secret meetings between Bartowski and Joel at the private office in his department and what Jonah just told him about his meeting with Smokey. Smokey told Jonah that the Tylers were using Bartowski as a layer to hide the books from Mr. Heart, who was the company's CFO and was entitled to see them. Now, it was all starting to make sense. They were hiding the revenues they were making selling illegal high-tech weapons and explosives to the Soviets and using a second set of books to hide them from Mr. Heart, Smokey, and the public. Fred Watkins had gotten too close, and it cost him his job.

Josh glanced around to ensure he wasn't being followed; Jonah had completely creeped him out. He ducked into a busy office building lobby and looked for a phone. He had Fred Watkins' number in the little pocket phone book he carried because they had spoken a few weeks back after office hours when Fred had to leave early for a funeral.

He remembered the call just after 5:00. He saved Fred's number in case the same thing ever happened to him. Fred dialed straight through to Josh's extension, knowing the receptionist would be gone after 5:00.

"Hi Josh, I'm so glad I caught you before you left."

"Still here, Fred, what's up?"

"Josh, I need you to do me a big favor. I left a report on my desk when I had to rush out early this afternoon; do you see it?"

Josh looked over at Fred's desk; the report was sitting there.

"I see it, Fred; what do you want me to do with it?"

"Josh, do me a favor and lock it up with your papers; I'll get it from you in the morning. If Joel or Max find it on my desk, they'll kill me."

"No sweat, Fred; consider it done."

"Thanks, Josh, I owe you one."

"No biggie, Fred, forget it ever happened."

Fred sat at his desk the next morning, looking very

nervous as Josh entered the department. He went straight to his desk drawer, unlocked it, and handed the report to Fred.

"You're a lifesaver, Josh," said Fred. "I owe you big time."

"Forget it, Fred; it never happened."

❧

It was time to call in the favor.

Josh looked around the lobby to ensure he wasn't being followed. He spotted two payphones on the wall next to each other with a small wooden privacy divider between them. One had an "out of order" sign pasted on the front, and the other was being used by a large individual engaged in an animated conversation with what sounded like his wife.

"Sweetheart, you know I love you; please give me one more chance."

Josh looked around the lobby; there were no other phones. He debated whether to try another office building but decided it would be faster to wait the guy out than to hunt for another phone. The guy on the phone seemed to be pleading for his life.

"Honey, I was out with the boys and lost track of time."

Josh was quickly losing patience; he had to get back to the office before anyone noticed. The excuse he told Jonah to use if anyone was looking for him was not great, but this was very important. So, he subtly made the guy aware he was waiting. He began to clear his throat a few times, so the guy knew there was someone behind him waiting for the phone. The man heard him and turned around; he looked much larger and more intimidating from the front than from the back, but Josh was in a rush, so he tapped his wristwatch.

The guy looked at him and then turned around to continue his conversation.

"Baby, I don't hate your mother; we just don't see eye to eye on everything. I love your mother."

Josh cleared his throat again, this time a little louder. The guy turned around again with a look that said Josh might be living on borrowed time.

"Hey, what's your problem, buddy?"

His breath practically knocked Josh over. He was beginning to think that starting an argument with a guy twice his size who had clearly been drinking and was in the middle of a fight with his wife was probably not a great idea. Still, he needed the phone desperately, so he had no choice but to tempt fate.

"Uh, sorry, sir, I was just …"

"Who are *you,* buddy, the pay phone police?"

"No, I just really need to use the phone."

"Well then, I suggest you use one squirt."

He then turned back around and continued arguing with his wife. Josh had no choice and tapped the man on the shoulder. This time, the guy turned around with a look that scared the hell out of him.

"Listen, buddy; I don't know what your problem is, but I'm thinking of wrapping this phone cord around your neck. Whattaya think of that?"

"Ten bucks."

"What?"

"I'll give you ten dollars if you hang up the phone right now."

He turned back to the phone and said, "Listen,

sweetheart, I've got some moron here that's looking to get his head realigned …"

"Twenty."

The guy turned back to Josh.

"I'll give you twenty dollars if you hang up the phone right now."

"Fifty."

"Are you kidding me? Fifty dollars to use a phone?"

"Going once."

"I'm not paying you fifty dollars to use that phone."

"Going twice."

"Okay… okay… I'll give you thirty."

"Forty bucks, and you've got five seconds before I continue the longest phone call you've ever heard, buddy. And believe me, I've got lots of quarters."

He lifted his sweater and revealed a quarter dispenser attached to his belt, filled with hundreds of coins. Josh looked at the dispenser and then back to the guy who was suddenly sporting a devious smile.

"I work at the laundromat… what are the odds, huh?"

"OK, forty," said a defeated Josh.

Eight million people in the City of New York, and I run into Norm from Cheers, who works at the laundromat.

"This'll take a second, buddy."

The guy turned back to the phone.

"Gotta go honey; regards to your mama."

Josh searched through his wallet; he had forty-three dollars in it. He handed the guy two twenties.

"Nice knowin' ya, bud; a pleasure doin' business. Maybe we can do this again sometime."

The guy ran off as if he had just won the lottery.

I feel like a real shmuck!

Josh had to compose himself before dialing the phone; he was worked up about what had just happened, but this was too important. He needed to exorcise the last ten minutes from his mind. Fred answered on the first ring.

"Fred, it's Josh."

Fred sounded happy to hear his voice.

"Josh, it's so great to hear from you; I never got a chance to say goodbye."

"I know Fred. I was shocked to see you were gone; what the hell happened?"

"Those bastards fired me. Imagine, I gave them six years of hard work, nothing but glowing personnel reviews, and the first mistake I make, I'm history."

After what Fred told him previously about what happened that day, Josh wasn't surprised.

"That really sucks, Fred," said Josh.

"And they didn't even have the decency to can me in person. I got home from work, and the phone rang before I could even get my coat off; it was Joel Tyler. He tells me they decided to make some personnel changes due to budget cuts, and my services were no longer needed. He said they would mail me a severance check. He hung up the phone before I could even respond; I couldn't believe it."

"That's crazy, Fred; do you think it had anything to do with what happened with Joel?"

"You bet I do, Josh; it was the same night. I know you don't work on the Bartowski reports; that was my own bad luck. But as I told you, I've been suspicious of those jackasses for months. All those private meetings between Joel and Max, ensuring we didn't hear anything, never sat well with me. But as I told you in the office, I started noticing strange deposits with nothing to back them up. It's not the first time they accidentally gave me the wrong paperwork. My mistake was allowing my suspicions to get the better of me and asking Joel about it. I didn't expect him to fly into a rage and fire me, but you live and learn."

"You sure do; I'm really sorry that happened. Listen, Fred, do you have time to meet me tomorrow at lunch or after work? I want to talk to you about something, not on the phone."

Josh could hear a few beats of silence before Fred finally responded.

"My calendar has suddenly become very empty, Josh."

Josh felt a little embarrassed.

"Yeah, sorry about that, Fred; a little slip of the tongue."

"It's OK, Josh; you can help me brush up on my gallows humor," said Fred sarcastically.

"How about tomorrow night at six at the little kosher deli on 53rd and 5th?"

"Kosher, huh?"

"You'll learn how the other half lives… or at least the other one percent."

"Sounds like a plan, Josh; see you then."

As he hung up the phone, Josh thought to himself.

That second set of books, along with the information from Fred Watkins, could be critical evidence to prove that the Tylers are receiving illegal money from outside sources. And that could be who's paying for what they're doing overseas.

It was a start, Josh thought to himself. They would still need to find the trail of where that money was coming from, which could be locked up somewhere in the department's filing cabinets, on someone's computer, or someplace else. And even if they did find that trail, without proof of a crime being committed to connect to those funds, they probably still didn't have a case. And without an airtight case, they could not go to the authorities and take the chance of them asking a lot of questions, or the partners putting one and one together and figuring out where the feds were getting their information from, which could put their lives in danger.

Fred Watkins could go a long way in helping to connect those dots. If Hannah and Jonah can come up with proof that the Tylers are selling illegal high-tech weapons and explosives to the Soviets, this evidence of being paid for it could seal the deal.

Josh now had something concrete to bring to their next meeting.

9

JONAH PASSED JOSH'S office the next morning.

"What happened to you, Josh?"

"When?"

"When? What do you mean when? Yesterday, you practically ran out of the office."

"I did?"

"Are you nuts? You ran out of here like a bat out of hell?"

"Are you sure that was me?"

"Let me think… are you out of your mind?"

"OK, Jonah, I thought I lost my wallet on the street, so I went down to look for it. Funny thing, it was in my back pocket the whole time."

"Josh, you're feeding me the same alibi you asked me to use if anyone was looking for you."

"I am?"

"Josh, I'm starting to worry about you; get some help."

"If I told you I spent forty dollars to make a phone call yesterday, would that help?"

"If you were calling Mars, I suppose; what are you talking about?"

"I'll explain later; can I borrow some money from you to get home?"

"Didn't you tell me you would buy subway tokens on your way home tonight?"

"I did?"

"What is this, the Twilight Zone?"

"Forget about that; I thought of something that might help us big time."

"What is it?"

"It's kinda long and involved; let's save it for the meeting."

Jonah had an exasperated look on his face. He needed to deal with Josh in smaller doses.

"Fine, Josh, whatever; here's some cash. I gotta go."

He grabbed some bills out of his wallet and handed them to Josh.

"Thanks; are you *sure* that was me yesterday?"

Jonah thought of arguing but decided to just head to his office.

Jonah had not spoken to Mr. Heart about everything that had been going on in the office. It was one thing to bounce his thoughts off Smokey; it was another to go to his boss, even if he respected him. He was sure Smokey must have kept Mr. Heart in the loop about his feelings, even if he didn't repeat their conversations word for word. With all that had been going on recently, things had escalated to the point that he felt it would be best to bring Mr. Heart into the loop, at least to a certain extent.

He knocked on Mr. Heart's open door.

"Come in, Jonah."

Mr. Heart, as usual, sat at an empty desk with a single sheet of paper. No doubt the sheet of paper was the item he was working on.

Everything else must be locked away, thought Jonah. *I've never seen anyone work like that.*

"Jonah, how can I help you?"

Jonah wasn't sure how to start. *I should have had a plan drawn up about how to do this,* thought Jonah.

Jonah began to stammer.

"Mr. Heart… I… well…"

"You want to talk about what's been happening in the office."

Jonah breathed a sigh of relief. It was so much easier when Mr. Heart took the lead.

"Yes, Mr. Heart, I do."

"Jonah, please close the door behind you and have a seat."

Mr. Heart picked up his phone and said something Jonah could not hear. Then he hung up. He then turned to Jonah.

Jonah could suddenly feel his heart beating hard inside his chest; he had no idea how this would go. But at this point, there was no turning back. Before he could say anything further, there was a light knock on the door, and Smokey slipped in. He glanced at Mr. Heart. Jonah suddenly felt uneasy. It felt like an ambush, even if he was the one who initiated it.

"Hey, kid," said Smokey in his usual manner of speaking.

He had taken a seat in the chair beside him. There was something about Smokey that always made Jonah feel at ease, but not this time.

"Jonah," said Mr. Heart. "I asked Smokey to join us because I know you have voiced concerns to him. He did not divulge the nature of your conversations; he just said that you were under some stress working here, and I can understand why. I want you to know that I appreciate how difficult it must be for you to be thrown into this situation without warning. I probably shouldn't have hired an assistant at this time."

Jonah was struck by that statement but stayed silent.

"You have by now figured out the family dynamics, and although they have existed for the last two years since Noah's passing, the boys, as I refer to them, seem to have recently been playing at the deep end of the pool."

I don't know how much he knows, and he doesn't know how much I know, thought Jonah. He decided to sit tight and see where this led.

"Jonah, as I said, I think it is unfair to you to have been put in this position, so I would like to make you an offer. I would like to allow you to resign from your position, or I can terminate you to allow you to collect unemployment, and I would offer you a nice severance check. This way, you can free yourself of any pressure you may feel under. And I truly apologize for putting you in this situation."

Jonah sat stone-faced; he felt like he was underwater and could not get any words out of his mouth. Mr. Heart was giving him a get-out-of-jail-free card. He could walk away from all of this and be safe. But would it be fair to Mr. Heart and Smokey? And what about Josh, his best friend? As for Hannah, there was no way he was leaving her alone with Irv.

He knew too much at this point, and he was in a position to help Mr. Heart and Smokey restore the legacy Noah Tyler had left, and he was determined to see it through. The one lesson he learned from Mr. Heart and Smokey was the lesson of loyalty.

It was time for Jonah to speak, and he chose his words carefully.

"Mr. Heart, I appreciate your generous offer, I really do. There is much that I have learned in the last few weeks that points to some reckless actions by the partners of this firm. This is no longer just about how they treat certain people, out-of-control spending, or how the partners run the business. If that were the case, and I simply felt uncomfortable working for these people, I would accept your generous offer and get on with my life. Unfortunately, it is no longer that simple."

Mr. Heart and Smokey glanced at each other, but he could not read their body language.

"I have learned about things that neither of you may be aware of that the partners are involved in. They include issues of national security, fraud, and deception involving outsiders as well. I and others in this company now find ourselves in similar circumstances. With the information we have learned so far, we may be able to stop some very dangerous people from using this company to do some very bad things. I wish we could simply tell the authorities and walk away. But we are still gathering evidence, leaving us no choice but to pursue this further for our own protection. Without that evidence, if they were to find out that we were somehow involved in stopping them, our lives would be in danger."

"Respectfully, while your offer is tempting, I believe by leaving now, I would not be doing right by this company, the others I have mentioned, and either of you. I need to see this through."

Both Mr. Heart and Smokey said nothing; it was as if the air had been sucked out of the room. It seemed to Jonah that all Mr. Heart and Smokey knew was that the partners were squandering the company's assets. The words "national security" and "very dangerous people using this company to do some very bad things" seemed to get their attention.

"Would you care to share what you have discovered with us so far?" said Mr. Heart.

Jonah thought for a minute; he was not yet ready to do that.

"Respectfully, not yet," said Jonah. "And it's not because I don't trust you; I trust you both implicitly. I just don't want to put you in any danger. The less you know at this point, the better. Please take what I said about outsiders being involved seriously. They may also have at least one person in the company watching out for them besides the partners."

Jonah stood up and said: "Thank you again, Mr. Heart, for your generous offer."

Jonah looked back at Smokey as he began to leave, and their eyes met. Little did he know that that was the last time he would see him.

⁓

As Jonah left Mr. Heart's office and closed the door behind him, he noticed Irv sitting in his office with the two guys he had come to know as Marco and Carlos facing him from the other side of his desk. His Spidey Senses were tingling again.

If I could just hear what those people are talking about… I've got an idea.

Jonah made a quick right turn instead of taking a left to his office. He headed past Irv's office and stopped at the office right behind Irv's, which he knew was unoccupied and used to store extra furniture. He ensured no one noticed and quickly entered and closed the door behind him. There was no time to lose. He put his ear against a wall not quite behind Irv's desk because he would have had to move some furniture to get closer and was afraid he might be heard. The sounds coming from Irv's office were muffled, but he did hear them talking about shipments that were about to be sent out. He also heard Smokey's name mentioned a few times but couldn't make out what they were saying.

He decided the only way to hear exactly what they were saying was to get his ear pressed against the wall directly behind Irv. The only way to do that would be to climb on a desk and lean over to the wall. As he approached the desk, he accidentally knocked over a chair he had not noticed earlier. Before he could do anything, the chair banged against the wall behind Irv.

Jonah knew they all must have heard it; this was not good. The loud bang coming from an unoccupied office would raise Irv's suspicions, given how paranoid he was. He scrambled for the door, hoping to escape quickly, but it was too late. As he opened it, Irv and the other two men stood there.

"Lose something?" said Irv, with a smirk. He had him dead to rights.

Jonah could feel the hairs on his neck standing at attention; he needed to come up with something quickly. How would he explain what he was doing in an unoccupied office right behind Irv's? He decided to go full spy mode. If caught, act cool and admit nothing.

"No sir, I did not lose anything," he said as casually as he could.

Irv wasn't buying whatever he was selling and ignored his response.

"I'll ask you again: what are you doing here, Jonah?"

There was no time to think; whatever came to mind came to mind. He was working without a script.

"Uh… I needed a step stool and remembered seeing one in this office."

A step stool? Really? That's what I came up with, thought Jonah. *Is that what James Bond would have said?*

"A stepstool," said Irv, repeating Jonah's response with an incredulous look. "You came all the way down to this end of the office to borrow a stepstool."

Yeah, I know how lame that sounds, thought Jonah to himself. *There are like twenty stepstools between my office and here, and this is what I came up with… nice… really nice!*

It was obvious what he had been up to, and Irv had caught him in the act. His mind raced a thousand miles an hour as he anticipated his next move. He couldn't remember this exact scenario in any of his spy books, so he had to improvise.

Irv looked Jonah straight in the eye with the scariest look he had ever seen.

"You know, young man, I don't like you. I didn't like your smart-ass comments to me the other day, your sneaking around the office in the middle of the night, your hanging around in Smokey's office while glancing over your shoulder at me, your secret meetings in Mr. Heart's office with Smokey, and your privileged character status around here. And when I don't like something, Jonah, I eliminate it; get my drift?"

Yup, I got that drift; nooo doubt about it—angry, deranged person staring me in the face. Neck red, veins bulging… no mystery here.

The other two men looked at him hard but said nothing; it was Irv's party. Jonah was having trouble standing up straight because his knees were shaking so much, but he was determined not to show any fear to this maniac. He was numb with anxiety but was determined not to show it.

OK, here goes nothing …

Jonah looked Irv straight in the eye with the most fearless look he could muster.

"You know what?"

"What?" said Irv.

"You don't scare me. And if I make you nervous, get a dog!"

Jonah quickly spun around and headed down the hallway; he could feel six eyes follow him all the way back to his office. He quickly closed his door and threw himself onto his chair. Sweat was cascading from every pore on his face. He was breathing hard and shaking like a leaf.

This is not good, not good at all. This guy is talking about eliminating people. And the other two scared the hell out of me just as much, and they didn't even say anything. Maybe I should just take Mr. Heart's offer and get the hell out of this looney bin.

But I can't; I'm in too deep. He also just confirmed that he knew I was in the office the other night. He must have been saving that for a special occasion. Now, Marco and Carlos have a firsthand look at what Irv must have told them about me, and they don't seem like the type to let me ride off into the sunset with my severance check. Plus, I've got this guy Ryan watching every move I make, probably for the partners.

His thoughts turned to Hannah.

I can't bear the thought of her working for this guy. I need to protect her, thought Jonah.

If that lunatic ever lays a hand on her…!

Hannah sat at her desk and pondered her situation. She had overheard the general plot that was discussed between Irv and Simeon. She had seen the files that showed the dangerous cargo to be shipped by Tyler Technologies to a Soviet Union satellite. There was no way those shipments could get into the wrong hands. The information they had so far was uncorroborated and useless without proof of a connection between the partners and foreign bad actors on the one hand and criminals that the partners were dealing with on the other. As Jonah had pointed out, they needed proof of those connections if they were to be taken seriously. And they would need protection if they found the evidence and shared it with the authorities. She needed to gather as much information as possible to help them find those connections. She was also worried because Jonah was being watched, and she feared for his life.

I don't know what I'd do if anything happened to Jonah, thought Hannah.

∾

Smokey had been a widower for the last five years since his wife, Becky, passed away from cancer. They had one son who lived alone in Phoenix, Arizona, and would visit them occasionally. Smokey and Becky led a nice but quiet life in a small apartment in Flushing Queens. When Becky died, the doctors had told him that it was most likely from secondhand smoke. Becky didn't smoke, but Smokey certainly did, a bitter irony he would have to live with for the rest of his life.

Smokey took the subway to and from work every day. His joy in life was to sit home with the newspaper every night and look after his dog, Gabe. Gabe was a large Doberman mix with black and brown spots. He was a very loving dog. He was probably too big for the apartment, but Smokey adored him, and Gabe returned the favor every day.

Smokey was a creature of habit; he had the same daily routine. He left the office at 5:00, bought a copy of the New York Post at the corner newsstand, and grabbed the F train to Flushing. He would stop at the deli on the way home, exchange pleasantries with Paul, the store owner, pick up two packs of Marlborough's, a deli sandwich, some chips, and a beer, and head to his apartment building, where he took the elevator to the fourth floor. He looked forward to opening the door and being greeted by Gabe, who would practically knock him over as he jumped on him and licked him all over his face. It was a nice routine for an older bachelor living a simple life. Unfortunately, it was an all too predictable routine for anyone watching him.

Ryan sat at his desk with a sick feeling in his stomach, and it was not from anything he ate. He had reported on the same goings-on at Mr. Heart's office that Irv had witnessed. Irv's reaction was one that he had seen all too often; it was anger. And when Irv was angry, most people headed to the exits. This was not a man to be messed with. What particularly bothered him were the words he spoke with such fury just before he was dismissed from Irv's office.

"Maybe a warning isn't good enough," said Irv ominously. "Maybe it's time we really got their attention."

Ryan didn't like the sound of that, not one bit. He had nothing against the three people he was ordered to follow; it was just a job.

Irv is crazy enough to do anything, and I may be responsible for whatever happens, thought Ryan. As he left the office that evening, he had an uneasy feeling that weighed heavily on his mind.

Jonah arrived at Starbucks first; he took the same table at the back and waited. Josh was the next to arrive. Instead of sunglasses, he wore a hoodie. He sat down next to Jonah and waited for him to speak first.

"Not a word about your wallet… got it?"

Josh glared back at him, but he got the message.

They looked up just as Hannah had entered the coffee

shop and headed to their table. All three of them had serious looks on their faces. Each of them had much on their minds.

At the same time, a fire escape window was quietly being opened from outside a fourth-floor apartment in Flushing, Queens. The smell of cigarette smoke was unmistakable as it permeated the air.

10

RYAN GOT HOME to his apartment at 6:30 that night; his wife Sue was watching TV in the den.

"Ryan," she called out, "is that you?"

"It's me," said Ryan.

The sound of his voice was softer than usual. He entered the den, threw his coat on the couch, and headed straight for the Lazy Boy. He reclined it like a dental patient waiting for a filling.

"What's up, Ryan?" said Sue. "You look like something the dog dragged in."

"Just a rough day, Sue, that's all."

"Seems like that every night lately."

"You can say that again; anything for dinner?"

"There's some leftover casserole on the table."

Ryan dragged himself off the recliner and headed to the kitchen. He threw the casserole into the microwave, grabbed a beer from the fridge, and sat at the kitchen table. Sue sat down across from him.

"Look, Sue, whatever it is, how about we wait for the weekend?"

"Ryan, I was feelin' a little sorry for you, seein' how you looked when you came home. I just thought you might wanna talk about it."

The last thing I want to do is rehash my day, thought Ryan.

"Listen, Ryan, I'm not looking to complain, but it's the same thing every night. You come home and drag yourself into the house like you just done ten rounds in a prize fight. The bills are pilin' up, and we still live in this miserable apartment with no prospect of things gettin' any better. Why can't you let me help you?"

She's right, thought Ryan. *I've got bill collectors up my ass and all the crap going on at work; maybe talking things out with Sue might not be a bad idea.*

He thought back to when he met Sue in college. They were so much in love; all they could think about was getting married, having lots of kids, the picket fence, and all that went with it. It all changed with the gambling. They used to fight all the time. Ryan knew that he had dealt Sue a lousy hand, but the more he tried to escape it, the deeper he fell.

"Sue, it's been a rough day, and I have a lot on my mind. How about we retreat to our neutral corners, and we can have ourselves a real barn burner this weekend," said Ryan sarcastically.

"Come on, Ryan; I don't want to fight. I just wanna talk, that's all."

Ryan felt bad about his response; he knew she didn't deserve it.

"I'm sorry, Sue; maybe we can talk sometime over the

weekend. I want things to be the way they used to be… before all the nonsense."

Sue got the message; she got up and left Ryan in the kitchen with his beer, leftover casserole, and thoughts.

As Sue left the room, Ryan wasn't sure who to feel worse for, himself or her.

He pondered his thoughts. His mind went back to everything that had been happening lately in the office; he was scared. He felt like he'd been sucked into a vortex that he could not find a way to escape. He was now fully aware of what the partners were involved in, which put him in a difficult position. Like it or not, he now knew the plot, which, from what he could tell, was treason against the United States. He remembered when he worked for the police department, where detectives worked on a case with some international implications. He was pretty sure that one of them had said that it was the duty of every American citizen to report knowledge of suspected treason to the authorities, and if a person did not, they could be brought up on charges or even thrown in jail.

What am I going to do? thought Ryan. *On the one hand, I now know something that I have a duty to report, or I can wind up in prison, and on the other hand, betraying Irv can get me killed by whoever the partners are working with. Great choice, Ryan, great choice indeed!*

"OK, where do we start?" said Jonah. "Has anyone learned anything new?"

Hannah looked visibly uncomfortable; this is not why she went to engineering school.

"Well," said Hannah, "just as Irv said, the floppies contain lists of shipments to Izmir but nothing about them being rerouted elsewhere, no information about contacts or anything else that would be incriminating. I remember him saying that the real dirt was on the floppies he keeps in his briefcase that he carries with him wherever he goes; they've purposely ensured that nothing in the office links anyone to those shipments. We need to focus on Irv's floppies; that's where the proof we are looking for resides."

"That's actually pretty good thinking, Hannah," said Jonah, with a little more excitement than he meant to convey. Hannah blushed; she had not heard Jonah speak to her in such a positive way in a while. And even though this was so important, her heart skipped a beat. Jonah's eyes rested on Hannah a drop longer than he had intended. He quickly looked away and tried to ignore his feelings.

Josh noticed the look on both their faces; he cleared his throat. They both glanced at Josh and realized their eyes had probably lingered on each other for too long.

"Well, I think I've got something significant," said Josh, trying to ignore the moment that had just passed.

"What is it?" said Jonah and Hannah simultaneously. They both realized their excitement didn't match the moment and felt slightly embarrassed. Josh then told Jonah and Hannah everything that had occurred in the accounting department recently. They listened intently as Josh described the actions of Joel Tyler and Max Bartowski. They paid particular attention to the story of Fred Watkins.

"That's great that you're meeting him tomorrow night," said Jonah.

"If we can somehow get our hands on proof of the partners being paid by outside sources and connect that to proof of shipping illegal cargo to the Soviets, I think that would complete the circle," said Hannah.

"This is great, Josh," said Jonah. "It also confirms something Smokey had told me a while back."

He then told them about Smokey's comment about the partners keeping information about the new company away from Mr. Heart, and a separate set of books would make sense if they were going to do that.

"I have something to share with you guys as well; it has to do with Mr. Heart and Smokey," said Jonah.

He then told them about his meeting in Mr. Heart's office and Mr. Heart's offer to him to resign. They both looked stunned.

"That's quite a story," said Josh. "How did you respond?"

"I was taken by surprise, so I kind of played it cool. I told Mr. Heart I was putting myself and some others, whose names I did not divulge, in serious jeopardy by leaving now. I told him there were things that neither of them may be aware of that the partners are involved in and that they have to do with issues of national security, fraud, and deception involving outsiders. I also told him this is not just about me; others in the company are in similar circumstances. I thought it was important that they understood that things were worse than they might have thought. I felt like they needed to know how dangerous things were."

"Wow, Jonah, you must have scared the hell out of them," said Josh.

"The looks on their faces said it all," said Jonah. "Smokey and I exchanged looks as I left the office. I don't know how to explain it. It was almost as if he was proud of me or something. Neither of them said anything after that; I don't know what they are thinking."

"That's some story," said Hannah.

"There's actually some more."

"More?" said Josh.

Jonah knew what he was about to say would not sit well with either of them, but he needed to unburden himself to someone, and they were all in this together.

"When I left the meeting in Mr. Heart's office, I noticed Irv in his office meeting with Marco and Carlos, the two guys that have been hanging around with the partners lately."

"What did you do?" asked Josh. He looked like he didn't want to hear the answer.

"Well, I couldn't let the opportunity go by, not with all that's happening."

"You didn't!" said Josh.

"I did; it's just how I roll, Josh. I need to feed the beast."

Josh and Hannah sat there with their mouths open. The expression left them speechless.

Feed the beast?

Jonah then told them how he had snuck into the empty office behind Irv's and what happened when he tried to listen in on his meeting with Marco and Carlos.

"Are you out of your mind?" said Josh. "You're lucky you didn't get yourself killed."

"Yes, the thought crossed my mind as Irv was listing all the things he didn't like about me. And let me tell you something: we will never be best buds."

"Really!" said Josh. And what did you do after that? I assume you walked away and didn't do anything about it?"

"I answered him in kind."

"You did what?" said Josh and Hannah simultaneously.

"I told him if I make him nervous, he should get a dog?"

Josh looked like he had been run over by a truck.

"Are you trying to get yourself killed, Jonah? Because this is how you would do it, you know?"

"Look, Josh, we need answers and don't have much time, so sometimes we need to step out of our comfort zone."

"It's that crazy spy gene you've got that's wrapped around your brain."

"Maybe it is, Josh. At least now he knows that I will not be pushed around."

"Do you hear yourself, Jonah? This guy is *crazy* and liable to do much worse than push you around."

"Well, I guess I'll just have to be a little more careful next time."

"Next time? Do you plan on trying something like that again?"

"It's a day-to-day thing, Josh. The beast needs to be fed."

Hannah had sat quietly, listening to the two guys arguing. She was too stunned by Jonah's words and actions to speak. It was apparent to her that he was still working under the notion that life was a big spy novel. While he may have changed in many ways for the better, some things were still part of his being, so if she wanted Jonah in her life, she would have to accept that. She couldn't ignore the chemistry between them that had become obvious during their meeting; what to do about the spy side of him was a question she would have to address. For now, she tried to steer the ship back on course.

"Listen, guys; can we just stick to what's happening in the office for now and address these other issues later? What is our plan going forward?"

They both looked at Hannah as if they had just noticed she was there.

Josh looked like he had run out of gas and was ready to move on. Jonah felt like he had probably just blown his relationship with Hannah, and maybe he should not have had this argument in front of her, but he didn't plan it. It just happened. Maybe, somehow, it was for the best.

Jonah cleared his throat.

"Yes, so… I'd like to hear about what happens in your meeting with Fred Watkins tomorrow night, Josh."

"Yeah, I've been thinking about that. I think he feels like he got a bum rap, so that may work in our favor. I think he's a straight shooter, and he was willing to share his theory of the Tyler's having two sets of books. I hope that means we've developed a rapport because the next thing I'm going to ask him is to help us find the proof we need to nail these guys on the revenue side."

"OK, guys, let's do this," said Jonah. "Josh, you meet with Watkins tomorrow night and gauge how helpful he may be. Meanwhile, I need to start figuring out a plan to get those floppies out of Irv's hands for enough time to get them copied without his knowledge."

Josh and Hannah shot him another look; it was becoming a habit.

"Wait, you want to do what with what?" said Josh.

"Let's face it unless we get a copy of that info, this book will not have a happy ending."

Josh and Hannah gave each other another look; *did Josh understand this was real life, or did he think he was acting out another one of his books?*

Neither was in the mood for another argument, so they kept quiet.

"Josh, when you're done with your meeting, let us know, and we'll get together again to hopefully put together a plan," said Jonah.

They decided to leave separately, and Josh got up to go first.

As he passed Jonah out of Hannah's earshot, he said.

"Nice going, buddy. And that relationship thing; I think you nailed it."

Jonah looked at Josh with a puzzled look as he left the restaurant.

As Hannah got up from the table, Jonah felt he had to say something.

"Hannah, wait a minute." Hannah slowly turned around.

"I… I'm not sure what I want to say, Hannah, but I think it's obvious something is going on between us."

"I'm a little confused myself, Jonah; I didn't expect this; I thought we were over."

"So, what do we do now?" asked Jonah. "I think just ignoring our feelings puts a lot of pressure on ourselves, and we've got a lot going on."

"With all that's going on, I haven't had much time to process my thoughts," said Hannah. "And now there are other things I need to consider after all I just heard."

Jonah was afraid of that.

"I understand," said Jonah. Maybe we can grab some coffee somewhere in the next couple of days and have a heart-to-heart. One way or another, I think we'll both feel better."

"I think that's probably a good idea," said Hannah.

"I'll call you soon," said Jonah.

They said their goodbyes and each left the table separately. They both headed home with much to think about.

Jonah entered his office the following day and threw his coat on the rack. It had been a long night with little sleep, and he was hoping for a quiet and uneventful day so he could think things out. There was so much going on. Whatever was going to happen with Hannah, the thought of spending time with her had a calming effect.

As he was about to sit behind his desk, Mr. Heart's voice came over his intercom, asking to see him. As he exited his office, he noticed Mr. Heart's door was closed. He knocked lightly and walked in; Mr. Heart looked white as a ghost. He told Jonah to close the door behind him and sit down. With trembling hands, he reached into his lower desk drawer and took out a bottle of scotch and a glass. Jonah had never seen him do that before. After gulping down some scotch, he turned to Jonah and said,

"Smokey is dead!"

Jonah was stunned. He could not get any words out

of his mouth. The best he could offer was a soft murmur. "Whaat?"

"They found him in his apartment late last night. The neighbors called the police because his dog, Gabe, wouldn't stop barking the whole night, which was unusual for him, and Smokey wasn't answering the door. When the super let them in, they found Smokey lying on the kitchen floor in a pool of blood; a bloody knife lay next to him."

Jonah did not know what to say; he just sat there with his mouth open.

Mr. Heart continued.

"They noticed the fire escape window was open, and it appeared as if he put up a struggle. They think there must have been more than one assailant, and Smokey was in no shape to fight back. The police don't think it was a robbery; it did not appear as if anything was missing from the apartment, and they found his wallet and cash still sitting on the table next to the door. The prints on the knife had been wiped clean."

Mr. Heart had a faraway look in his watery eyes, the tears of someone who had lost an irreplaceable friend. Jonah could not find words to console him. He knew how close the two of them were and how much pain he was in. They had gone through so much together. And now he was alone.

Mr. Heart looked off in the distance and talked about the decades Smokey had given to the company, how, with Noah Tyler, they had worked so well together to build a great company, and what a special person he was. He said Tyler Tech was family to him, even if he wasn't enamored with all the family members. Mr. Heart said Smokey was his confidant, the person he could talk to about anything.

Someone killed Smokey! Jonah thought to himself.

He thought back to Irv's chilling words the night he hid in the office about hoping Smokey died from cancer and his warning to Mr. Heart from outside his office the other day that included a threat to "that smokin' friend of yours." He also remembered Irv's threat to smack Smokey on the head with a two-by-four.

Did it have anything to do with my confrontation with Irv when he told me about my hanging around in Smokey's office while glancing over my shoulder at him or what he referred to as my secret meetings in Mr. Heart's office with Smokey?

Jonah remembered how his eyes met Irv's as he left Mr. Heart's office the night before.

Did I get Smokey killed?

He quickly shook off the thought.

Get it together, he told himself.

"Mr. Heart… I… don't know what to say," said Jonah.

Jonah could feel Mr. Heart's pain as they looked at each other with watery eyes.

"Jonah, this thing you spoke to us about yesterday, do you think it cost Smokey his life? There was no reason to kill Smokey; was it a warning to me?"

Jonah did not know what to say. He did not want to lay such terrible guilt on a man that did not deserve it. At the same time, Mr. Heart would see right through him if he lied. So, he answered him with the only truth he knew.

"Mr. Heart, I have no idea who did this, but one thing I

do know. There will be a time when whoever did this terrible thing will be discovered and punished; I am sure of that."

"You know Jonah, you seem much older and wiser than the young man I hired a few months ago."

Jonah was finding it hard to keep it together. He looked at Mr. Heart as his voice choked. He could barely get the words out. It was almost a whisper.

"Mr. Heart, I am so sorry for the loss of your dear friend."

Mr. Heart looked at Jonah as if he were taking his measure.

"Thank you, Jonah; that means a lot."

Jonah walked out of Mr. Heart's office and slowly closed his door. He couldn't help but notice the reaction from employees just arriving for work. They were huddled together in front of a table with a flower arrangement and a framed picture of Smokey, along with an announcement the partners had posted on the office bulletin board with the sad news of Smokey's passing. Some were sobbing together while others stood off in the distance, dealing with the news in their own way.

There was nothing about how Smokey met his demise, but word had gotten out. The office would be closed the following day as a Day of Reflection. Anyone who needed to take an additional day off was welcome to do so, and grief counselors would be available all week for those who needed one. The partners donated ten thousand dollars to the American Cancer Society in Smokey's memory. There would be a memorial for Smokey at a time to be determined.

How ironic! thought Jonah. *They know he was murdered, but you'd think he died of cancer; these guys are really slick. As for the Day of Reflection, it sounds more like a day for the part-ners to get their act together. They're not fooling me!*

Jonah noticed the partners huddled together in Joel's office as he returned to his office. No doubt they were busy talking strategy for looking sufficiently mournful. The idea that they could sit there without a care in the world made Jonah's blood boil. Without thinking, he headed toward Joel's office and stood outside the door. His next words were loud enough for those in his office and all the other employees milling around.

"A good man who cared about this company lost his life last night; why did that happen?"

He could hear the partners stirring in Joel's office, and the employees in the area stopped what they were doing.

"People don't get murdered by accident!"

Mr. Heart came out of his office.

"Jonah, this is not the place!"

Jonah looked around at the startled faces of the employees and, from the corner of his eye, caught Joel Tyler at his office door. He called out to Mr. Heart.

"Franklin, I think you need to teach your assistant some manners; if he's got something to say, there are proper channels to do so."

Mr. Heart glared back at Joel as Irv suddenly appeared beside him; you could hear a pin drop.

"Alright, everyone, back to work," yelled Irv.

Employees started slowly moving away, but they kept their eyes and ears open.

Jonah realized he had acted impulsively, which didn't

help Mr. Heart, and may have put a target on his own back if he didn't already have one.

"My office," said Mr. Heart to Jonah.

Jonah walked past Mr. Heart into his office while he continued to stare at the two partners.

He stood frozen in fear as Mr. Heart finally closed his office door. The look of sadness on Mr. Heart's face was now replaced with anger.

"What was that Jonah?"

Jonah's lips were frozen; he could not get a word out.

"That's not how we handle things here."

"I… I'm sorry, Mr. Heart… I truly am."

"Look, Jonah, I will overlook what just happened out there and attribute it to grief. But I will not tolerate anything like that again. Do you understand me?"

"Yes, sir."

He had never seen Mr. Heart this angry. He pointed to the door, and Jonah slowly made his exit. He could feel the eyes of the employees on him. He noticed Josh and Hannah off in the distance, looking very concerned. Joel's door was now closed; he could only imagine what they were discussing. He practically accused them of murder in front of the whole office.

Yep, Jonah Mark, you screwed up big time, thought Jonah to himself. *Nice going!*

He sat at his desk with his head buried in his hands. The intercom on his phone buzzed; it was Josh.

"Hey buddy, are you OK?"

"What do you think, Josh?"

"I think you need to get some fresh air, Jonah."

"Thanks, Josh; I'll be OK. I've got a nice cup of poison hemlock here that I am about to drink; make sure I get a proper burial."

And with that, Jonah hung up the phone. He could not undo what he just did any more than he could unring a bell. He may have punched his ticket with the partners and scared Mr. Heart even more than yesterday. But he needed to keep his head in the game. What just happened happened. He still needed to put an end to what was going on at Tyler Tech and find out who killed Smokey.

Mr. Heart was right, thought Jonah. *There was no reason to kill Smokey, as much as Irv may have hated him, but there was every reason to make it clear to Mr. Heart to stay out of the way.*

Smokey was just the Traffic Manager, but Mr. Heart was the company's CFO; he knew as much about the company as the partners did. Indeed, he was there even before they arrived. He was in a position to cause trouble for the partners. They would only need a second set of books to hide it from Mr. Heart. Smokey would have nothing to do with the company's records. They knew Smokey was his closest friend, so they threatened Mr. Heart about him.

But why? What was it about Mr. Heart that scared the partners so much?

A thought occurred to Jonah.

Does Mr. Heart know more than he is letting on? After all, he has been here a long time, and if something sinister was going on, he was in a position to know and do something about it. The partners had to know that. Maybe they thought he was getting too close and threatening him was not deterring him anymore.

Perhaps they decided that this one extreme act would finally get their message across. Or maybe someone else was involved who was sending this message.

Jonah sat and thought to himself.

What does Mr. Heart know?

11

THE REST OF the day dragged on for Josh, anticipating his meeting with Fred Watkins after work. He chose the small kosher deli on 53rd and 5th because if the wrong person spotted him with Fred, an employee who had just been fired, they could suspect something was up. There was little chance any of the partners would be found there. He scheduled the meeting for 6:00; the partners would be long gone by then. Josh figured he'd leave the office at 5:30 and head straight for the deli, lost in the rush hour crowd.

At about 5:15, as he was getting ready to leave, he was startled to see Irv passing the accounting department as he made his way down the hall. Josh quickly hid himself behind one of the filing cabinets. Irv didn't seem to notice Josh's presence. He quietly watched Irv enter Joel's office. He could hear the voices of other partners as the door closed.

An after-hours meeting of the partners is unusual enough, thought Josh; *the same day Jonah called them out in front of the office and on the night after Smokey's murder. Oh, to be a fly on the wall!*

As he was about to leave the office, Josh noticed two men who fit the loose description that Jonah gave him of Marco and Carlos slip into the meeting.

I guess the gang's all here, thought Josh. From the corner of his eye, he saw Mr. Heart standing at his office door, watching the same scene. He then stepped back into his office and closed the door.

It seems everyone is up late tonight, thought Josh. It was time to make his exit. He quickly snuck down the hallway without making any noise and slipped out of the office as quietly as a mouse.

He was running late due to the last-minute appearance of Irv, so he sprinted through the streets and arrived at the deli just in time. Josh waited a few seconds to catch his breath before he stepped in so he didn't look too anxious. He spotted Fred sitting at a table in the back as soon as he walked in. The deli was not that big. But what it lacked in size, it made up in noise, with people talking loudly and plates clanging as tables were being bussed off. It had a very homey atmosphere, and the smell of the place was intoxicating. It was like this is where salami, corned beef, and pastrami went to heaven.

Fred waived Josh over as soon as he stepped in; he headed straight to Fred's table.

"Great to see you, Fred." Josh leaned over to shake his hand.

"Same here, Josh, although I wish it were under better circumstances."

"Why don't we order something, Fred? It's on me."

"Thanks, Josh, that sounds like a good idea."

They both checked out the menu, although Josh could cite it by heart. It was a kosher deli; it didn't require a brain surgeon to figure out what to order, at least not for Josh. Fred perused the menu like a tourist in a foreign land. He did not understand the food or the culture. Josh noticed.

"Have you ever had kosher deli?" asked Josh.

"No," said Fred, "but this place smells incredible."

"If you're OK with it, why don't I order for both of us? I won't steer you wrong," said Josh.

Fred looked relieved as Josh waived over a waiter wearing a clean white apron and sporting a pad of order slips and a pencil behind the ear, the tools of the trade.

"We'll take two corned beef and pastrami sandwich combos on rye with mustard and Russian dressing, two orders of extra crispy fries, two orders of kishke with gravy on the side, and a couple of black cherry sodas," said Josh.

Fred was impressed. The waiter slid away, and before either could say the next word, someone dropped off two plates of cole slaw and an assortment of sour and half-sour pickles.

Fred looked puzzled.

"This isn't health food, ya know, Fred."

"I'll survive," said Fred as he dug into the cole slaw. The sauce was soon dripping down the sides of his mouth, but he hardly noticed.

"Why don't we start while we're waiting?" said Josh.

"Sure thing, Josh; what do they call this stuff?"

"Cole slaw."

"Damn, that's good."

Josh tried to get him to focus, but it was apparent that it would be an uphill battle.

"You told me about your theory about the two sets of books on the phone."

Fred wiped his mouth, and words finally started to form.

"Yeah, I'm pretty sure about that, Josh. I'm unsure what they are into, but the revenues are unsupported."

The waiter came by with their orders as Josh was about to speak. Fred looked stunned by the size of his sandwich and seemed to be mulling a strategy to get his mouth around it. He took one big bite and looked at Josh with a smile.

"Are you kidding me?" said Fred. "From now on, you order!"

There was a little more banter about the food before Josh got back into it.

"Fred, there is something screwy going around at the company; I'm sure you heard about Smokey."

"Yeah, that's awful. I ran into Mary from bookkeeping in the coffee shop this morning; she told me about it. She said everyone at the company was sick over it. Why would anyone kill Smokey?"

"I wish I knew," said Josh. He was being careful about what he was willing to talk about. At the same time, he would need a reason to ask Josh these questions.

"Fred, the unsupported revenues and the second set of books, and now the murder of Smokey, tell me that there's something not right at Tyler."

"And the way Joel blew up at me doesn't sit well either," said Fred. "I agree, but what can we do about it? Call the authorities?"

"We probably should do that at some point, Fred, but unless we have proof, the feds will probably just throw out the case. The partners will probably figure out pretty quickly who told on them; it's not that big of a department. You just got fired, and they know we're good friends. And now, with the murder of Smokey, who knows what these people could be into."

"What are you suggesting, Josh?"

"I'm not sure yet, Fred."

Josh did not let on that others were working with him so as not to scare him off.

I've gotta tread lightly here, thought Josh.

"Fred, if we could figure out where that money was coming from, the unsupported revenues, I mean, maybe that might help us figure this thing out." Josh was careful to use the word "we" a lot to make Fred feel like it was just the two of them working on the problem.

"How could we do that?" asked Fred.

"I was thinking maybe if we can get a look at that other set of books, with your knowledge of their financial operations, that would be a great start."

"Josh, you're talking about doing something illegal; do you realize that?" said Fred.

"I suppose it is," said Josh. "Maybe you're right; we should just forget about it. I'm sorry I wasted your time, Fred."

"And let those jackasses who fired me for no reason get away with this… no way!"

It was the kind of reaction Josh had hoped for, but he still had to take it slow.

"Are you sure, Fred? I mean, this could land us in some pretty hot water."

"Well then, I guess they shouldn't have fired me in the first place, should they!"

Josh could see how angry Fred was, and the idea of revenge clearly had some appeal.

I was hoping to convince him, but he doesn't seem to need much convincing, thought Josh.

"OK, Josh, I'm in; what do you have in mind?" said Fred, who was conquering the last of his sandwich with a new-found vigor.

"Fred, if we can figure out where that second set of books is, or at least get a look at some of that paperwork, it will tell us all we need to know about who's pumping cash into their accounts."

Fred sat there thinking, the only sound coming from the crunch of a sour pickle he was finishing. Josh watched him as he sat in deep thought. Suddenly, he looked up with a look in his eyes and a smile that looked so sinister it almost scared Josh.

"What?" said Josh, looking sideways at Fred; he did not know what to expect.

Fred's face had turned red as an apple, but the crazy smile remained. Josh had never seen such a look on his face. Fred's voice had changed completely as he uttered the next words. He looked Josh straight in the eye.

"You find that paperwork, and with everything I know, they'll wish they never hired me, let alone fired me."

Josh did a double-take at the expression on Fred's face. Undoubtedly, when the time came, he could count on Fred. He then grabbed Josh by the arm....

❧

Ryan headed home after another long day at the office. He wasn't looking forward to being confronted by Sue again, but it was home base, and he needed a place to think. He was about two blocks from the office and headed toward the subway when he heard a voice from behind. The words were clearly directed at him.

"Don't turn around."

The voice hit Ryan like a clap of thunder in the night, so suddenly, he felt a jolt through his body. *Who the hell is that?* thought Ryan. Suddenly, a car pulled to the curb, and the back door swung open.

"Get in," someone with a gun in his hand barked from the back seat. Ryan had little choice, so he eased into the back seat slowly. He quickly looked back to see who had called from behind him on the street, but whoever it was was gone. He found himself sitting next to an imposing figure who didn't appear as if he was much for conversation, so he just sat there quietly as the car lurched forward.

For Ryan, it could be any number of people who would take him off the streets. He owed money everywhere due to his obsessive gambling; it could have something to do with what was going on in the office, or worse, it could be none of the above. Ryan felt the beads of sweat making their way down the sides of his face and the back of his neck. Sitting to his left, his host was silent, leading him to believe he was just an underling doing an assignment. *Bring me Ryan Schapp,* thought Ryan.

He began to think about his life and what a mess he had made of it.

When he married Sue, they were really in love; *whatever happened to that?* he thought. He had big plans when he graduated from the police academy. He hoped to pass the sergeant exam one day and buy a home in the suburbs where he would enjoy a nice life with Sue. Instead, he got caught up in gambling. It was a vice he never should have picked up, but the lure of easy money was his downfall. Before he knew it, he was in over his head. Not only did he lose at horses and gambling on sports, but he lost big, and he found himself borrowing money from the worst kinds of people. He could barely make the interest payments he had to come up with every week, let alone pay down the principal. The people he borrowed from had no interest in his excuses. He found himself being beaten constantly. They were always careful not to leave marks so he could return to work the next day and not attract the attention of his superiors at the police department.

Nobody suspected what was going on, but the worries on his mind, along with the physical pain he was hiding, were starting to wear on him. At home, he was different to Sue as well. There was constant arguing.

"Why don't we have enough money to pay our bills, Ryan?" Sue would nag.

"I don't know, Sue; I'm doing my best."

"Well, maybe your best isn't good enough, Ryan. How are we ever going to get ahead?"

It's the question Ryan kept asking himself. His superiors had long since written him off as sergeant material. He knew it was a matter of time before he lost his job. That's why the Tyler opportunity couldn't have come at a better time; it was a chance for a fresh start. Marco and Carlos would still come around every week for their weekly vig, as they called it. Ryan was making a little more money with his new salary and could make his minimum payments. He had promised himself never to gamble another dime and stuck to it. When he got the job at Tyler, he ran home to tell Sue.

"Things will be different from now on, babe, I promise."

Sue gave him the old *I'll believe it when I see it,* look. But things did get better for a while. He was making his interest payments and slowly whittling down at the principal. Sue was happy with the new Ryan; he even bought her flowers for her birthday.

But old habits die hard, and a friend had an extra ticket to a Knicks game one night. He was feeling so good about himself that he decided one harmless little bet for old times' sake would allow him to prove to himself that he was in complete control of his vices. Unfortunately, the worst thing that could happen happened; he won a few hundred dollars. He decided the new Ryan indeed had the magic touch. So, he started betting more and more. Before too long, he found himself in basements being kicked around like a football all over again.

He came home one night to find Sue standing in the kitchen with a suitcase.

"Babe, what are you doing?"

"What I should have done long ago: I'm going to stay with my mother."

"Sweetheart, just give me another chance: I can make things right."

"When that day comes, we can talk about it. Right now, I need some safety and security. Speaking of security, for both our sakes, don't tell anyone where I've gone so they can't use me to get to you."

She still loves me, thought Ryan.

"Babe, don't leave me this way… please!"

But Sue headed out the door; she had reached her breaking point. Ryan knew she had made up her mind, and he would not talk her out of it, not tonight, anyway.

And now he found himself involved in a treasonous criminal conspiracy that could cost him his freedom and who knew what else. As the car raced through the streets of Manhattan, all he could think of was what a mess he had made of his life. The fear that accompanied him as he spent his life looking over his shoulder and the pain he endured through all those beatings were nothing compared to the one thought he had in the back of his mind as the car rapidly made its way to wherever it was headed. It was a feeling he could not escape.

Is this where it all ends?

12

"OK, LISTEN TO me, Josh."

Josh was all ears. This lowkey, dependable guy sitting across him at the deli table who had been sharing the same area of the accounting department with him since he joined the firm, who would punch in at 9:00 and head home at 5:00 every day, was clearly furious at the Tyler company. And that anger was fueling a boatload of motivation. There was nothing Josh needed to do to convince Fred to help him.

This guy is all in, thought Josh.

"I'm listening, Fred."

"You know how Bartowski comes to the department every Wednesday, and he and Joel head to the other side of the department to talk?"

"Sure, it happens every week like clockwork; it's like Bartowski is carrying the winning Lotto numbers in his briefcase."

"Close enough," said Fred. "Only his briefcase is probably empty when he comes in."

"What do you mean?"

"One day, a few weeks ago, curiosity got the better of me. I casually snuck around the filing cabinets for a peak about two minutes after they took off for the other end of the department."

"That was a pretty dangerous move, Fred."

"I know, Josh, but as I told you, my previous job was working for the justice department on criminal fraud cases, and I just knew those unexplained revenue items that were in the raw data we generated were evidence of something that was not on the up and up; I could just smell it."

"OK, Fred, what happened when you snuck over to the other side of the department?"

"I nudged myself between two filing cabinets. The two of them sat at a table, and Joel Tyler was loading Bartowski's briefcase with papers. They were the same papers I had just given Joel Tyler because they were still in his hands. Josh, those papers were among the most suspicious papers I had worked on."

"So, what happened next?"

"I watched the two of them in deep discussion, and then Bartowski closed his briefcase and started to grab his coat. That's when I scurried back to my desk. Bartowski passed my desk a minute later on his way to Mr. Heart's office for his usual courtesy visit before he left the office."

"So, what are you thinking, Fred?"

"I'm thinking the Tylers are not putting anything that has to do with those unexplained revenues on any computer or filing cabinet at Tyler Tech, so there will be no evidence to be found at the Tyler company. That's why Joel got so upset when he saw me with that paperwork the other day."

Josh thought for a moment.

"So Bartowski is acting like a carrier pigeon. He takes the raw data, puts it in his briefcase, and works on the reports at Bartowski and Company. There is no second set of books to be found, at least not at Tyler Tech."

"That's correct, Josh."

"So, to get hold of that incriminating evidence, we have to infiltrate Bartowski's company; fat chance of that happening," said Josh.

"Or," said Fred, with that menacing look again, "intercept it from the big fat carrier pigeon."

"Fred, that's an interesting take; I hadn't thought about that possibility, but it would make sense. No one will likely check the accountant's office unless there's a good reason. All eyes would be on Tyler Tech. But it's just a theory. Let me kick it around a little bit."

As they both got up to leave, Fred said:

"One more thing, Josh."

"What's that, Fred?"

"Can you get me the recipe for that kishke with gravy? I never tasted anything like it; I think I might convert."

"Easy, buddy," said Josh, with a concerned look. "Let's not do anything hasty."

As they left the deli, Josh and Fred agreed they would keep in touch, and they each went their separate ways.

On his way home, Josh called Jonah and filled him in on his meeting with Fred. Jonah expected that the Tylers were doing something underhanded to fund their scheme. They had already discussed the unusual circumstances that led to the firing of Fred Watkins and were hoping they could get some solid information from Josh's meeting with him.

"OK, Josh, this is good information; I'll keep Hannah posted."

They both were quiet for a beat too long; the mention of Hannah's name felt awkward at that moment and seemed to throw them both off.

"What's the next step?" asked Josh.

"Wait… what are we talking about?" asked Jonah, sounding slightly flustered.

"What are *you* talking about?" asked Josh.

Jonah wasn't even sure himself. The unsettled Hannah relationship situation was messing with his mind, and Josh sounded confused.

"Josh, we need to figure out what to do next with the information we have so far. *And that's all I want to deal with at this moment.*"

Josh picked up the annoyance in Jonah's tone as if Jonah's complicated relationship with Hannah was somehow *his* fault.

"Hey buddy, it's not my fault your brain and heart are not in sync; don't blame the innocent here. Do you think it's easy sitting through a meeting with the two of you? *That's actually pretty good thinking, Hannah! Great choice of food, Hannah!* And the looks the two of you were giving each other across the table; I thought I would lose my dinner right there."

"Yeah, well, there was no chance of that."

"Not at those prices," Josh sounded too much like he was enjoying himself, and Jonah noticed.

"You think this is funny, Josh?"

"Actually, Jonah, watching you handle women can be quite entertaining, so I plead the fifth."

"Yeah, well, not from this end."

"I suppose not," said Josh. "All the more reason to get your relationship in gear."

Suddenly, there was quiet coming from Jonah's end.

"Jonah, are you still there?"

"I've got an idea," said Jonah; "I need to make some calls."

"Wait!" said Josh… "about what?"

But Jonah had already hung up.

Here we go again, thought Josh. *Are we talking office crisis or relationship crisis? I can't take much more of this.*

It felt strange to Jonah that while they were dealing with some very high-stakes life-and-death drama, the mere mention of Hannah's name seemed to throw their conversation off. But he had been toying with an idea and decided it was time to implement it.

The car carrying Ryan sped through the streets; he had no idea where he was going. Oddly enough, he felt a sense of calm. Whatever was going to happen to him was inevitable, he thought to himself. He faced trouble every which way he turned. It was as if he was mired in quicksand. There was trouble at work and trouble at home. He had no money and was quickly losing his self-respect. Multiple people would be happy to end it all for him. This was not life; it was barely existence.

I might as well get this over with, thought Ryan.

As the car began to speed up, Ryan noticed that the

streets were less busy with commuters. As he looked further through the front window, it was clear that he was headed to the docks.

Where are these people taking me? thought Ryan. The thought of being dumped in the river sent a chill up his spine. Ryan decided to play it cool; showing fear was not a good idea. The car finally pulled up to a quiet area near the docks.

"Get out," barked the man sitting to his left. The sound of his voice had jolted Ryan; these were the first words he had heard in about a half hour, and they were spewed at him with such venom that he could only imagine what was waiting for him.

Before he could reach for the handle, the door swung open, and a large man in a black leather jacket lifted him off the car seat and out into what was now the cold night air. He first noticed the deep scar on the man's pockmarked face. He simply nodded to a black Chevy Tahoe with its windows blackened, the kind he had seen before ferrying celebrities and politicians to famous places. He was not a celebrity or a politician. He was someone who had gotten in well over his head. The only good thing he could think of was that whoever was in charge wouldn't need a big car to dump him into the sea. There had to be more to this, as he would soon find out.

After telling his mother he had grabbed a late lunch at work and wasn't hungry for supper, Jonah headed upstairs to his room. It was time to act on the idea he had been kicking around in his head the last few days. He took a list from his desk drawer, although he knew all their names and numbers by heart. There was Mack Leibowitz, AKA Mack the Knife, Peter Rosenberg, also known as Sneaky Pete, and Marvin Goldberg, who liked to call himself Marvelous Marv. All of them were old friends and card-carrying members of one of the mystery clubs he loved so much in high school and college.

They called themselves the Motley Crew, for lack of a better name. Every weekend, they would sit around and talk about the latest spy novels, computer hacks, magic tricks, and anything else they thought was cool. Their days of getting together were behind them; they were all into more serious endeavors, like jobs and family. But they still kept up with each other. It was a time in their lives that they all looked back at fondly.

What Jonah needed was a lot more serious than the stuff they were into back then, but it required the type of expertise these guys possessed, and he needed help from people he trusted. With those criteria, who would be better to bounce things off than them? Jonah wanted to get them all in a room and let their creative juices flow. It had been a while, so he decided to entice them with a reunion. There'd be lots of hot dogs, wings, and beer, the three irresistibles for any grown male. He grabbed the phone and started making calls. All the calls went pretty much the same way.

"We're getting the gang together at my house tomorrow night at 8:00."

"What for?"

"A reunion."

"A reunion for what?"

"A reunion to celebrate."

"To celebrate what?"

"Dogs, wings, and beer."

"I'll be there; don't let them start without me!"

"Done!"

Jonah had another call to make, one that he had put off for too long. He dialed Hannah's number; her voice sounded a bit apprehensive.

"Hi, Jonah; how are you?"

"As well as can be expected, Hannah, given all that's been happening."

"I know, Jonah, there's so much going on; are you sure this is a good time for us to deal with our personal issues?"

"I think we've put this off long enough, Hannah. I am starting to learn that life doesn't happen one thing at a time; my priorities are not what they should be."

Maybe he has changed, thought Hannah.

Would you like to grab a cup of coffee at lunch tomorrow?"

"I'd like that," said Hannah.

"How about the Starbucks on 33rd and Fifth at 1:00? Does that work for you?"

"Sure."

"I'll see you then."

As she hung up the phone, Hannah couldn't help but think about how much Jonah had changed since they went out. He seemed so much more confident, so much more of what she wanted in him back then. He clearly hadn't dropped the spy stuff from his repertoire, and it was troubling to her, but maybe now she had more to work with. As she went to bed that night, she passed the mirror and couldn't help but notice a slight smile on her face.

It was the same one Jonah had after he hung up the phone.

✍

Ryan approached the Tahoe with trembling hands and started to reach for the door handle. Another hand twice the size of his own beat him to it and swung the door open.

"Have a seat, Ryan," said the well-dressed man, who was already seated on the opposite side. Ryan slowly took a seat, and the door closed behind him. The man beside him waved his hand, and the two men sitting in the front seat exited the vehicle. He was not very well built, but he had a look on his face that was so intense that Ryan felt his dark eyes looking right through him.

"My name is Angelo."

"Uh… well, I guess you know; my name is Ryan."

"Yes, I do," said Angelo. "I know a lot about you."

"Why am I here?"

"I will ask the questions, Ryan."

This man with the dark eyes looked a lot scarier than anyone he had ever seen before. Ryan's knees buckled at the sound of his voice; he would not be talking out of turn again.

"Ryan, you present a dilemma for me."

Ryan felt like saying, How so? But he decided the best way to live through whatever this was was to stay silent and let the man talk.

"I can probably dispose of you as I did with Mr. Smokey, or I can let you live. Which option would you prefer?"

Ryan sat dumbfounded. The fact that this man just took credit for Smokey's murder, as if it was nothing more than an errand he needed to take care of, scared the hell out of him. But right now, he was being asked if he chose life over death, and for Ryan, that was of immediate concern.

"I… I want to live… of course."

"Good, Ryan… very good."

He reached for a leather box from the seat pocket before him. He opened it, took out a cigar, and clipped off one end with a device Ryan had never seen before. He then fished a gold lighter from his pocket with the letter "A" engraved on it and lit the cigar. He turned on a small exhaust fan in the ceiling above them. It was almost as if he didn't notice Ryan as he went through this routine. He then looked at him.

"So, you want to live, Ryan."

"Yes, sir."

"Ryan, I'll be very straight with you," he said as he took another puff of his sweet-smelling cigar.

"I look at people as assets or liabilities. Mr. Smokey was a liability; do you understand what I am saying, Ryan?"

"Yes, sir."

There was silence in the car as Angelo smoked his cigar while Ryan trembled in his seat, too scared to move a muscle. Finally, he looked straight at Ryan with those piercing dark eyes.

"I want you to do something for me, Ryan."

"Yes, sir."

"I don't trust the Tyler's, and I don't trust Irving Carter either; do you understand me?"

"Yes, sir." It was all Ryan could say.

"I have a big investment in that company you work at."

"Yes, sir."

"And what does one do to protect their investment, Ryan?"

"Insurance?"

It just popped out of his mouth.

"Now you're catching on, Ryan. You get yourself an insurance policy; very good."

Ryan sat frozen in his seat; not a syllable would be uttered by him going forward unless asked.

"Guess what?" said Angelo. "You are my insurance policy."

Ryan just sat there dumbfounded; he did not know what to say.

"Here's the deal, Ryan. I want you to be my eyes and ears at Tyler Technologies. Specifically, you will keep your eyes and ears trained on Irving Carter. I believe he is affectionately known as Irv at the company, but I don't tend to be very affectionate."

Ryan said nothing; he just sat there thinking about how Irv had asked him to spy on others, and now he was being asked to spy on him, a double agent of sorts.

"One more thing," said Angelo. "You will place this listening device in Carter's office."

He showed Ryan a small disk the size of a nickel.

"How do I do that?"

"Observe, Ryan. You just pull off this adhesive backing and place it under the surface of Carter's desk; it's that simple."

"I meant, how do I do that without getting caught?"

"Oh, you'll find a way, Ryan; I know you will. Just do it as if your life depended on it. Do I make myself clear?"

Yes, sir," said Ryan.

"Good. You know Ryan, that's what it is about insurance policies; some pay off, and some get canceled."

Ryan swallowed hard.

"And Ryan, your wife Sue seems like such a nice young lady; I'd hate to see anything happen to her if you made the unfortunate decision of going to the authorities."

Ryan froze in his seat; he wasn't even sure if he was breathing.

"Assets and liabilities, Ryan."

Angelo reached past Ryan and knocked on the window. The man with the large hands opened the door and lifted Ryan out of his seat before he could say anything. He was then deposited into the back seat of the car that had brought him there. He looked back at the Tahoe just before being thrown into the car.

New York plates, 565-LOAN. I guess he's proud of being a loan shark, thought Ryan. He also memorized the plates on the car that brought him there and into which he was unceremoniously deposited.

It was second nature to him. When he was a kid, his dad would take him and his brother on long car trips while his mom was in the hospital getting treatment for her terminal illness. It was a way to give his mother some rest and keep the kids from watching her fade away. She died when Ryan was in the seventh grade. They would memorize the license plates on cars that would pass them on the road to pass the time. When they stopped for a soda, his dad would test them on what they remembered, and Ryan discovered he had a pretty good memory. Old habits die hard, and for some reason, he continued to memorize license plates even as an adult. He would try to figure out what it meant if it were some sort of word combination.

◈

The same friendly guy sat next to him for his return trip. They sped through the streets for another ten minutes until the car abruptly stopped at a set of stairs that led down to the subways.

"Get out," said the man sitting to his left.

As soon as Ryan's feet hit the sidewalk, the car took off with a screech.

Ryan Schapp, Double Agent, Ryan thought to himself. *Just great!*

He quickly ran to the phone at the corner and called his wife Sue, who had been staying at her mother's house.

"You need to get out of there, Babe," he said as soon as she answered the phone.

"Why, Ryan?"

"I've got some guys after me, and I don't want them to use you as a bargaining chip or harm you in any way."

"No, Ryan, how could you do this to me; where will I go?"

"You have that uncle in Virginia; there's no way they'll figure it out. Just go."

"That's great, Ryan; I must live like a fugitive."

"Listen to me, Sue. Go out the back door and cut through some yards until you get a few blocks down; there's a phone booth on the corner of Elm and Maple; call for a taxi. And don't tell your mom where you're going."

"Nice job, Ryan."

"I'm so sorry, Babe."

The phone line had gone dead.

⁂

Per the partner's notice, the office was closed the following day to reflect on Smokey's passing. The following morning, as Jonah walked into the office, he noticed two men in suits; they looked like police. He asked around and found out that they were detectives asking questions about Smokey's murder. They spent a lot of time in separate meetings with Mr. Heart and the partners.

I'd love to know what questions they are asking, thought Jonah. It made sense that they would go to Smokey's place of employment and speak to the people in charge.

Is this a routine visit, or are there any leads they are checking out?

Jonah did not have time to contemplate it further; he had many other things on his mind, such as his lunchtime meeting with Hannah and meeting with the Motley Crew that night. The closer it got to lunchtime, the more nervous he grew.

I will tell her how I feel, no pretenses or games, thought Jonah. *I need to get this off my chest and work it out one way or the other. I really have feelings for Hannah; I felt a connection at our meeting, but if I got it wrong, I might as well know it now.*

⁂

Hannah sat at her desk, nervously shifting papers around. It was hard to work. She had no idea where Jonah's head was, although she thought she noticed some interest the other night at her meeting with the guys. At the same time, his reckless actions recently regarding Irv were concerning and would have to be part of the discussion. The fact that he suggested they meet to talk about their relationship gave her some relief. She hoped that things could be worked out between them, but even if they decided otherwise, she could at least move on with her life one way or another, although she hoped to make it work. She looked at the clock on her office wall; it was only 10:45. She looked at her watch to make sure: 10:46. She would use the watch going forward.

Ryan sat in his office, dazed and confused. He had tossed and turned all night, trying to figure out how to get the little disk he was fingering in his right hand stuck beneath the surface of Irv's desk.

What am I supposed to do? thought Ryan to himself. He thought of all the possibilities and came up with three options… really two. Option 1A would be to knock on Irv's door with some benign question and try to shimmy up to his desk, remove the backing from the disk, and somehow reach under his desktop and do the deed. Option 1B was the same plan, except he would wait to be called in by Irv the next time he needed him. It would be the preferred option because it would be less suspicious but would take longer to get done because he had no idea when Irv might ask him to come to his office.

Option 2 was to sneak into Irv's office during lunch and do the deed. That was the most dangerous option because anyone in the office, including Irv or the partners, might see him if they returned early or didn't go out for lunch. And he would have no excuse for being there. So, he decided that Option 2 was off the table. It would be 1A or 1B. He started thinking about changing the name of the options in his mind to Option 1 or 2 since the original Option 2 no longer existed. Or he could change the name of the options to just A or B. That's when he realized he was starting to lose it.

Damn, I'm really freaked out. Who cares about the option numbers, he thought to himself, *just get it done!*

He was feeling sick just thinking about it. The life of a double agent was not for him, but he had to do something quickly. The thought of having to meet the guy with the dark eyes again did not appeal to him. So, he decided to test out the feasibility of the former option 1A, which was now option 1, which he had decided would be called option A from now on, and find some pretext for knocking on Irv's door.

I'm starting to lose it!

Ryan placed the little disk between his thumb and fore-finger and headed down the hall. He hoped his sweaty fingers would not do anything to reduce the adhesive. The thought of trying to do this with scotch tape did not appeal to him.

As he made his way down the hallway, he was trying to come up with a reason to knock on his door when Irv made it easy for him. He was sitting at his desk as he yelled out.

"Ryan, come in here a minute."

Well, I guess it's Option 2, the former Option 1B, now option B, thought Ryan.

Damn, I'm a wreck!

"Yes, Mr. Carter," said Ryan as he entered Irv's office.

As he glanced down at his desk, he immediately realized that neither option 1, 2, 1A, 1B, A, B, or any other option could ever work. Irv's desk was only open from the side he was sitting on; there was no way to reach under and place the disk unless he got behind the desk where Irv was sitting. Even Houdini couldn't do that.

"Is something wrong, Ryan?"

Ryan realized that Irv noticed him staring at his desk.

"Eh… no, Mr. Carter. I was… eh… thinking about something… not important, sir."

Irv ignored whatever Ryan was babbling about; he seemed to have other things on his mind.

"Ryan, there were some detectives here this morning asking about Smokey's murder; did they talk to you?"

"No sir, Mr. Carter."

"Well, they were asking many questions as if someone here had anything to do with it. I think they were just sniffing around. Anyway, if they should question you, I want to know about it. Do you understand?"

"Of course, Mr. Carter."

"The last thing we need are cops or the feds sniffing around here."

"Yes, sir, Mr. Carter."

"OK, that's all; I've got to get to a lunch appointment."

And with that, he grabbed his coat off the rack, passed by Ryan, and headed down the hallway and out the door.

I can't believe this, thought Ryan; *he left me alone in his office!*

He quickly fished the disk out of his pocket and was about to peel off the backing when he was startled to hear his name."

"Ryan, what are *you* doing here?"

He looked up and saw Simeon Tyler standing in the doorway, looking at him. He quickly slipped the disk in his pocket.

"I… uh, was just talking to Mr. Carter when he realized he was late to a lunch meeting and had to run out; I was just leaving."

Ryan awkwardly slipped past Simeon and quickly left Irv's office. As he walked down the hallway, he could feel Simeon's eyes still on him.

If he asks Irv, my story will check out, thought Ryan. *But how am I going to get that disk under Irv's desk?*

Angelo's words rang in his ear; "assets and liabilities." He was not going to wind up a liability like Smokey. Getting caught in Irv's office by one of the partners would be bad, and he would have to explain his way out of it. But it would not be as bad as getting murdered. The saying "dead men tell no tales" suddenly came to mind.

It was lunchtime at Tyler Tech and time for Ryan Schapp to make his move.

13

Hannah looked at her watch; it was finally time to leave for lunch. She had decided to leave extra early so there would be no office gossip if someone spotted her heading to lunch with Jonah. She was tired of everyone in the office keeping track of her relationships, so the less they saw her with Jonah, the better. Jonah noticed Hannah as she passed his office; they did not acknowledge each other. Jonah thought to himself, *I'll give it another ten minutes and then make my exit.*

Hannah got to Starbucks quickly, looking over her shoulder to ensure no one in the office saw her. This Starbucks was not the closest one, so the chances of anyone in the office having lunch there were more remote. She ordered a latte and took a table at the back with her seat facing the front windows.

⁊

For Jonah, the sight of Hannah passing his office triggered memories of the night they first met at the singles event.

He remembered how pretty she was that night; that hadn't changed. He thought about how much had changed in his own life and how the fact that he was so uninvested in his future back then had probably cost him the relationship. Although he had made changes to his life, he still wasn't sold on finance as his profession. His heart still required intrigue; he could no longer ignore it. It was a part of him that would probably never change. Hannah was surely aware of that, having witnessed his argument with Josh the other day. Yet she still agreed to meet, maybe a hopeful sign. But he still expected her to bring it up. The real question was how she felt about it. He had missed Hannah since they broke up, but he didn't realize how much he had missed her until Mr. Heart brought him into her office on his first day on the job.

And now he wanted her back.

Hannah sat nervously at her table at Starbucks and thought about Jonah. She remembered how difficult it was to break up with him, even though she was so upset with his unseriousness about his future. She also could not forget how hurt he looked when she ended things. But *that* Jonah was not *this* Jonah; something had changed. The Jonah that came to work at Tyler Tech was a much more confident Jonah, the Jonah she hoped he would become back then but never did.

She had spent much time in the office over the last few months thinking about him; she did not expect him to come back into her life. Walking past him in the hallway all these months was awkward; she had not sorted out her feelings and felt like the ball was in his court if he wanted to try again. She was still old-fashioned that way.

With all that had happened lately, she got to see him more closely, and her heart and mind were more in sync this time. Yes, he still seemed to have that spy novel side of him and almost seemed reckless with some of his actions. She would surely bring that up when they met. Maybe she could try and balance that out somehow. She realized that she would have to take the complete Jonah if she was interested in him; he would not be available a la carte.

Jonah looked at his watch; it was time to leave. He stood up from his desk and grabbed his coat. His phone buzzed as he was about to step out into the hallway. It was Mr. Heart.

"Jonah, can you step into my office for a minute?"

Jonah had no option, even if Hannah was waiting for him. Hopefully, this was just a momentary thing, and he'd just be slightly late to meet Hannah.

It wasn't, and he would not be.

Jonah tossed his coat back on the rack. He knew that making Mr. Heart wait was never a good idea. He went to Mr. Heart's office and knocked on his open door. Mr. Heart was sitting at his empty desk.

"Come in, Jonah, and close the door behind you."

As Jonah stepped into Mr. Heart's office and closed the door, Ryan, who had been monitoring the hallway until the coast was clear, realized that this would be his best chance of hiding the disk in Irv's office. The partners all seemed to have left for lunch. Mr. Heart and Jonah were behind closed doors, and the rest of the office staff were either out for lunch or busy at their desks at far-off ends of the office.

This is my chance, thought Ryan. *It's now or never.*

He slowly and quietly headed to Irv's office door, disk in hand. He was sweating profusely and trying to keep the tiny disk dry as he balanced it between his right thumb and index finger. He quickly approached Irv's desk and slowly pulled the chair out from behind it. Suddenly, he heard voices from the hallway outside Irv's office. They were the voices of Simeon and Joel Tyler returning from lunch.

"Where is that report, Joel?"

"I think Irv has it," but I thought I saw him leave for lunch a little while ago."

"Well, I need it, and I'm not waiting for him to return; let me check his office."

Holy crap, what do I do? thought Ryan, who was now totally drenched in sweat.

With no time to spare, he quickly ducked under the desk, and as he did, the little disk slipped unnoticeably from his fingers. It was now sitting on the carpet right in the middle of the office.

Ryan could see Simeon's feet as he entered the office. He walked straight up to the desk and started to rifle through Irv's desktop. He continued to sweat beneath Irv's desk, not moving a muscle as tears of fear streamed down his face.

That's it, I'm toast, " thought Ryan as he trembled beneath Irv's desk. There would be no way to explain to Simeon why he was back in Irv's office alone a second time in a half hour and what he was doing under Irv's desk. He heard Simeon murmuring to himself, "Nothing here; let me check his drawers."

As Simeon's feet moved toward him, Ryan decided there was no point in hiding; he would let fate do its thing. He was about to step out from under the desk when he heard Joel's voice from down the hall.

"I've got it, Simeon; he must have left it here in my office."

Ryan froze as he saw Simeon's feet turn in the opposite direction and head out of the office. He was numb with fear but had to make his move; it was now or never. He would place the disk under Irv's desk and slip out of the office as quickly as possible. And that's when he saw it… sitting on the carpet in the middle of the office just a few feet away; with all that was happening, he did not realize he had dropped the disk.

Ryan thought to himself, *I'll have to break for it, grab it off the floor, scoot back behind the desk, stick it beneath the surface, and get the hell out of here.*

He could not believe his predicament, but he had to do what he had to do.

I lost the disk in Mr. Carter's office, will not be an acceptable excuse for Angelo.

Soaked from sweat and paralyzed with fear, Ryan scooted out from beneath the desk and headed straight for the disk. As he reached down to retrieve it, he heard the unmistakable sound of Irv's voice from down the hall; he was headed back to his office.

I can't believe this is happening, thought Ryan. There

would be no time to install the disk and no time even to pick it up. All he could hope for was enough time to escape Irv's office before he was spotted. With no options, he left the disk where it was and broke into a dead run, making a sharp left as he exited Irv's office so that no one in the hallway would see him.

He made it…

…and now he was officially toast.

"Jonah, please have a seat," said Mr. Heart.

Jonah sat opposite Mr. Heart with his empty desk between them. All he could feel was empathy toward him for the loss of his very best friend. Had it not been for Smokey, he probably would have left the company years ago. The two of them most likely felt that their presence was the only way to keep the partners in check and Noah Tyler's legacy intact. And now, here was Mr. Heart alone, probably a lonely place to be.

He seemed to have put Jonah's behavior outside Joel's office earlier behind him. It felt to Jonah as if Mr. Heart had to admonish him for what he had done, but that he understood where it came from.

"Jonah, a detective came to see me this morning; he asked if I knew anything to help them solve Smokey's murder. I didn't have much to tell them."

Jonah knew about the two men in suits who had interviewed Mr. Heart and the partners, so this was not news to him. He wasn't sure what Mr. Heart was getting at, but he was waiting for a response from Jonah.

"You can only answer what you know," said Jonah.

Jonah, Josh, and Hannah had decided early on that it was likely that if the feds suspected the partners of any crime, they would most likely suspect Mr. Heart would have had something to do with it. So, they decided to protect him by giving him plausible deniability, another way of saying that you don't know what you don't know.

Mr. Heart was pretty sharp, and he wasn't buying it.

"Jonah, I don't need protection. Whoever killed Smokey was probably connected to the outsiders you referred to and what you termed a threat to national security, using fraud and deception."

Wow, he remembered every word, thought Jonah. His collar started to feel a little sticky, and he began to fidget in his chair. Mr. Heart's eyes bore right into him. He wasn't sure what to do.

Suddenly, Mr. Heart's phone buzzed.

Saved by the bell? prayed Jonah.

"Mr. Heart, I have Jim Thompson on the phone for you, returning your call from earlier; should I put him through?" said the receptionist.

Mr. Heart glanced at Jonah. This was clearly an important call he had to take. He looked Jonah squarely in the eye and then at the door.

"To be continued," said Mr. Heart.

Jonah quickly stood up; he felt like he had been facing the electric chair and had just received an eleventh-hour reprieve from the governor. He walked out of the office briskly as Mr. Heart lifted the receiver.

Jonah glanced at his watch; he could still make it to

Starbucks, but his shortened meeting with Mr. Heart had completely thrown him for a loop. His relationship with Hannah meant a lot to him; he wanted to be in the best frame of mind when he met her. He decided he would just have to explain things to Hannah when she returned. He hoped she would understand.

Hannah had sat at her table at Starbucks, nursing her coffee for the last half hour. She was perplexed. *Was I wrong about Jonah after all?* she thought to herself. *Maybe this was the old Jonah, the same one I broke up with.*

She left Starbucks and headed back to the office.

Jonah sat at his desk and kept looking into the hallway, anticipating Hannah's return; he would explain his no-show to her when she passed his office. Finally, the lobby door opened, and Hannah walked in; the look on her face said it all. Jonah knew he was in deep trouble.

"Hannah!" he yelled as he ran into the hallway to cut her off and explain his actions. Unfortunately, he ran straight into Andrea, a middle-aged woman from personnel, who was carrying a large pile of papers.

She yelled, "Watch out!" But it was too late, as he barreled into her, and they both hit the floor hard; the papers were strewn everywhere.

Not only did Hannah notice, but so did most of the office. He had now cemented his reputation as a total klutz. He could see some people covering their mouths to keep from laughing. Hannah stepped around the two of them and kept on walking, which was not a good sign for Jonah.

"Ya gotta teach me that technique, 'cause I haven't seen that in any dating handbook I've ever read."

It was Hal from HR again.

Smartass! thought Jonah.

He finished helping Andrea collect her papers and gave her an embarrassed apology. All eyes were still on him.

"That's OK, dear; you seem to have enough to deal with right now," she patted him on the shoulder and walked off.

"Maybe you should think about pursuing someone else before you kill somebody," yelled Hal.

Jonah had had enough.

"Sorry, buddy; you're not my type!"

That elicited a sympathetic cheer from the rest of the employees who were still watching and sent an embarrassed Hal retreating to his office. The show was over, and the rest of the employees went back to work.

Jonah felt a sense of deep regret. He had blown it with Hannah again. It seemed like they just weren't destined to be together; the fairy tale he had concocted in his mind was turning into a nightmare. He wished he could drop everything, run into Hannah's arms, and tell her how he felt about her as unambiguously as possible. Unfortunately, he kept messing things up. He promised himself that when things got back to normal in the office, he would prove to Hannah that his love for her was real.

But he had little time to waste; he was supposed to host his friends from the Motley Crew at his place that night. He had to put off dealing with Hannah for at least another day. While the Crew would be munching on hot dogs, wings, and beer, he had his own fish to fry. It was time to devise a plan for what to do next, and these guys were his secret weapon. He left the office at precisely 5:00 and headed straight to the supermarket to get all the fixings. His mother was visiting her cousin in Connecticut for a few days, so the house was his. He would get the supplies, head home, and start cooking. On his way out the door, he tried Hannah again on her desk phone. He hoped she would listen to his explanation of what happened, but the call went unanswered. Hannah saw Jonah's name on the intercom, but she felt so conflicted that she decided not to pick it up, rather than having to come up with something on the fly.

Jonah seemed pretty upset; maybe he had a good reason for standing me up, thought Hannah.

She needed to think things through.

Irv fingered the little silver piece of electronics in his hand. It had what appeared to be an adhesive backing on one end and some tiny electronic circuitry on the other. He spotted it lying on the carpet in his office as he returned from lunch. It was shiny and easy to notice, so he knew it was not there when he left for lunch. It appeared to be a listening device or "bug," as they were known for short. The question was, what was it doing in his office? Obviously, someone dropped it, but who? A professional would not have been that careless. He was pondering two overriding questions at that moment. Who would want to be eavesdropping on him, and who lost the bug?

He thought back to the last person in his office before lunch. It was Ryan, and he remembered him acting a little strangely.

"Did you lose something, Ryan?"

"Eh… no, Mr. Carter. I was… eh… thinking about something…not important, sir."

Irv remembered leaving Ryan alone in his office as he left for lunch. Now, he was back from lunch and found a tiny listening device lying on the carpet. Ryan was suspect number one. But who would he be placing the listening device for, and who *loses* a listening device and leaves it right where it can be easily spotted?

Someone very nervous who's in a rush thought Irv; there really is no other suspect. Suddenly, Irv was very nervous, too.

Someone doesn't trust me and must have forced Ryan to place the bug; no other explanation makes sense.

Was it Mr. Heart? Not his style, thought Irv. *And I doubt he trusts Ryan very much, either.*

What about the other partners? They were all on the same page, which didn't make much sense either.

All roads pointed to Marco, Carlos, or the big boss that he had never met but knew so much about. He was afraid to even think about him.

Angelo Papatonis: International arms dealer.

The thought of his name sent shivers up Irv's spine. According to Marco and Carlos, he was itching to kill someone just to get everyone's attention at Tyler Tech. It was just a matter of time. When Irv heard about the brutal murder of Smokey, he knew it had to be Angelo. As much as Irv hated Smokey and ranted about him, he never would have gone that far.

And now he has his sights on me, but why?

There was only one way to find out. He reached for his phone and pressed the intercom button to Ryan's office.

"Ryan… in my office… now!"

14

RYAN SAT AT his desk, frozen by Irv's demand that he come to his office immediately. He was trembling with fear because he knew that Irv must have found the bug and surmised that he had dropped it. He was the last person Irv saw in his office before he left for lunch, and it was an awkward scene to begin with. It must have been clear to Irv that he was hiding something.

What should I do?

The best idea he could come up with was to stonewall, making it seem like he had no clue what Irv was talking about. He would probably continue to suspect him, but he had no other option. He would lie as if his life depended on it because, in many ways, it did.

As Ryan entered Irv's office, he spotted him fingering the little disk in his hands; it was now clear that Irv was about to grill him about it.

"Have a seat, Ryan."

"Yes, Mr. Carter."

"Do you recognize what I am holding in my hand?"

"No sir," said Ryan.

"I will ask you again, Ryan; do you recognize what I am holding in my hand?"

"No sir, Mr. Carter; should I?"

"Is that the way you want to play this, Ryan?"

"Play what, sir?"

Ryan had no choice; he would lie through his teeth and hope for the best. His stomach made him feel like he was on the Coney Island roller coaster.

"Ryan, I will ask you again for the final time: do you recognize what I am holding in my hand?"

"No sir," said Ryan. "It looks like some sort of disk to me. I'm sorry, Mr. Carter, is this some kind of test? Am I supposed to know?"

"Ryan, do you value your employment here at Tyler Technologies?"

"Very much, Mr. Carter."

Irv was looking more frustrated by the minute, and Ryan was bracing for the explosion that would inevitably come. But while he needed his job, he valued his life much more. There was no way he would cross Angelo, so he had no choice but to lie, and he was starting to feel like he was gaining a little traction. Although the circumstantial evidence pointed to him, there was no smoking gun. All he could hope for was a tiny seed of doubt to plant itself in Irv's mind.

Irv looked Ryan squarely in the eyes.

"Ryan, if I find out you lied to me, you will not only lose your job but there will be serious consequences; do you understand me?"

"Yes, sir, but I'm not sure what you are talking about. I have never seen-"

"Get out!" shouted Irv as he suddenly leaped from his desk and pointed to the door. A second invitation would not be needed.

Ryan had just crossed the door threshold when he turned back to Irv to say something. It was a good thing he had cleared it because the slam was loud and strong. Ryan literally ran to his office and quickly closed the door behind him. He was sweating profusely and was having a hard time catching his breath. This was by far the craziest thing he had ever done, and while he knew this wasn't the end, he was still standing, a small victory of sorts.

The doorbell rang. Mack Leibowitz arrived first. Tall and lean, the name "Mack the Knife" fit him well because he was sharp as a knife; nothing got past him.

"Hey Jonah, long time no see," said Mack as he walked past Jonah holding the door.

"It's been a while," said Jonah; what have you been up to, Mack?"

"You know," said Mack. "A little of this, a little of that."

"That line is getting a little tired."

"Hey, Jonah, it's who I am and what I do. Now, tell me the real reason you invited us for this little shindig."

"In due time, Mack, in due time. Why don't you grab some grub while we wait for the other guys?"

"Don't mind if I do. Wait just a second and let my nose be my guide."

He made a show of breathing in the air.

"Yep, I can smell some hot wings due north. I suppose the executive dining room is straight ahead; am I correct?"

Jonah chuckled—*same old Mack.*

As Mack made his way to the kitchen, the doorbell rang again. Jonah headed to the door.

Peter Rosenberg was known to the guys as "Sneaky Pete" because he was slightly built. He could steal the watch off your wrist, your lunch out of your briefcase, and a dollar out of your wallet and be gone before you noticed.

"Hey compadre," said Pete. "Aren't ya gonna let me in?" he said with a smile as he walked past Jonah, holding the door.

"Now, where are those wings you were talkin' about?"

He spotted Mack standing at the kitchen door with a wing in his hand.

"You lettin' *anyone* in these days, Jonah?"

Before Jonah could answer, Pete headed to the kitchen; he gave Mack a big bear hug.

"Que pasa, big guy; you saved some for me?"

"I've got a nice plate of bones waiting for you, little guy," said Mack.

They both attacked the spread on the table.

Before Jonah could close the door, "Marvelous Marv" Goldberg walked right past him and headed for the kitchen.

"Hey, are you guys starting without me again? Why am I always the last to arrive?"

Marvin Goldberg called himself "Marvelous Marv" because of his marvelous ability to crack open a safe or pick any lock. He also loved junk food and had the belly to prove it.

Jonah joined the three of them in the kitchen and

watched his three old friends attack the food with abandon. There was lots of talk of old times and stories they remembered from a time in their lives they all missed. They were like a group of veterans that had gotten together to tell war stories. Whether it was the latest computer game, bank heist, or mystery novel, they loved getting together and discussing it all. Over time, they had moved on but kept in touch. Through the years, when one of them was in a jam, they would contact each other and try to help. They were more than just friends; they had a bond they were convinced others would not understand. Finally, the last wings were devoured, and the rest of the food was attacked and conquered. For Jonah, it was time to get down to why they were there.

"Hey guys, the war stories were great, and I can do this all night, but as much as I love spending all this time with you…"

"I knew there was a catch!" said Pete. "The food was too good."

"Well," said Jonah, "There *is* something I wanted to talk to you guys about.."

"I knew it too," said Mack; "there's gotta be a payoff here somewhere."

"OK, guys, you got me; I do need your help with something."

"Like old times," said Marv, "OK, Jonah, let's have it."

Jonah's face betrayed that what he was about to tell them was more than fun and games, so they all stopped talking and gave him their attention.

"What's up Jonah?" said Pete; "this sounds a little serious."

"It is, guys; it really is."

And with that, Jonah launched into a narrative that took about twenty minutes to relate. He covered everything going on at Tyler Tech from the day he arrived. The guys all listened intently as he told them about the company's history and his relationship with Mr. Heart. He told them about the partners, the office dynamics, and even what was happening with Hannah. They all knew about her but thought she was out of the picture as far as Jonah was concerned. When he got to the part about what had been happening in the office lately, including his meeting with Watkins and the murder of Smokey, their ears all perked up.

"Good thing I had my last wing," said Pete; "I would have choked on it."

"Holy crap!" said Marv, "you weren't kidding. This is serious."

"Listen, fellas, I called you guys together tonight because you're my most trusted friends."

"What about Josh and Hannah?" said Mack.

"Well, them too," said Jonah.

"So, what do you need from us?" said Marv. "You know we'd do anything for you."

"I know you guys have always been there for me, and I appreciate that. But I am looking for some out-of-the-box thinking, and you guys have always fit that bill," said Jonah.

"We're talking some international conspiracy here," said Pete. "This is serious stuff with people getting killed. Jonah, are you sure you aren't in over your head?"

"I'm sure I am, Pete, but while I might have been able to bail earlier, I don't think I have much choice anymore.

I promise you guys, I will not put any of you in danger; I would never do that," said Jonah. "That's for Josh, Hannah, and me 'cause we're all stuck in it. And maybe Watkins, who's looking for revenge. What I'm looking for is a plan, that's all."

"Well, we'll talk about the danger part later, Jonah," said Pete. "It seems you've got two separate problems here. You've got this Bartowski guy, who's got the proof of where the money is coming from to fund this international scheme, sittin' in his briefcase while he carrier-pigeons it back and forth to the Tyler place on at least a weekly basis. And then you've got this Carter guy, running point with the Tyler Partners and his contacts overseas, and he's got the keys to the kingdom in his briefcase; do I have that right?" said Mack.

"That's about it," said Jonah.

The three guys huddled in a corner and began to whisper and murmur. They glanced over at Jonah a few times as he intently watched them. Finally, after about ten minutes, they broke up their little meeting.

"Jonah, we've got some ideas to hash out," said Mack. "But we need you to do something."

"What's that?" asked Jonah.

"When's your mom coming back?"

"Thursday."

"Good," said Mack. "You need to fill this house with dogs, wings, beer, and all the other accouterments needed for a serious meeting; we'll be back tomorrow night, same time. And make sure Josh, Hannah, and Watkins join you."

The boys left Jonah standing in his kitchen as they exited the apartment. The dining room looked like the Romans had been there. It made sense that they should all be there the next night, but getting Hannah there would be awkward; he wondered if she would even show.

❧

Jonah got to the office early the next morning and called Josh from his desk phone.

"Josh, it's Jonah."

"Hey, buddy, what's up?"

"I spoke to my guys from the Crew and filled them in on all the shenanigans going on in the office. They want to help us with a plan. We're meeting at my place tonight at eight for another round of dogs, wings, and beer."

"You mean there was a first round? *I love dogs, wings, and beer?*"

He really sounded wounded.

"Forget about the food, Josh, and start thinking about the mess we are in. I need you to call Watkins and Hannah and make sure they come too."

Jonah tried to slip it in, but Josh wasn't buying it.

"Wait a second, I saw what you did there."

"What do you mean?"

"I mean, how you slipped in Hannah; how come you're not calling her?"

"I'm not getting into it now, Josh; just call her."

There was an extra beat of quiet on the line.

"Trouble in paradise?"

"I said leave it, Josh; make sure you're all there at 8:00."

"I'm not in the habit of coming late when there's food around, Jonah; I think you know that."

244

Jonah had already hung up the phone. Josh was struck by how stressed out Jonah sounded. With everything happening in the office and his struggles with Hannah, his fuse seemed much shorter these days.

Josh called Watkins; he picked up after the first ring.

"Hi Fred, it's Josh."

"Hey Josh, great to hear from you."

"How's the job market?" asked Josh, who suddenly realized how bad that sounded.

"I'm talking to you on the phone, Josh, during working hours, and I answered on the first ring."

"Uh… yeah, sorry about that." He swallowed hard.

Josh decided that small talk was probably not the best approach and delved into why he called.

"Listen, Fred. Jonah, Hannah, and I are getting together tonight at 8:00 at Jonah's place, along with a couple of guys, to discuss what the two of us discussed at the deli the other night."

"What, guys?"

"Some good friends I would trust with my life that can help us with what we discussed. Are you still interested in getting involved in this?"

"I sure as hell am; what's the address?"

"320 Wilson Street, apartment 3K."

"I'll be there," said Fred.

Fred couldn't help but think of the food he ate with Josh at the deli the last time they met.

"Hey Josh… any food?"

"Hot dogs, wings, and beer."

"Man, you really know how to throw a party!"

"See you at 8:00."

"You can count on it."

Jonah found it hard to work; so much was on his mind. He kept his head low whenever a partner passed his office. He was also hiding from Mr. Heart to the extent that he could to avoid conversation. He had not yet seen Hannah and figured she had come in earlier than him.

He stared at the clock all morning long. He planned on taking a walk when lunch hour hit to clear his mind. When the time finally came, he grabbed his coat, squeezed into the busy elevator, and spilled into the street with the lunchtime crowd.

It was a crisp fall day, and he figured the fresh air would benefit him. It was useless; it wasn't like he had an on/off switch. After walking about four blocks from the office, he had the uneasy feeling that he was being followed. It wasn't for any specific reason. It was his Spidey Sense calling again. As he walked along the crowded sidewalk, he suddenly stopped short in the middle of the block and did a complete 180.

And there he was.

15

THERE WAS NO place for him to hide; Jonah was staring face-to-face with either Marco or Carlos. He didn't know who was who, and it didn't matter. He was trailing about a half block behind him with a crowded lunchtime crowd between them. As Jonah stared directly at him, he looked like he got caught with his hand in the cookie jar. The only question for Jonah was which one of them should run.

Jonah didn't wait; he spun back around and broke into a dead run, shoving people out of his way as he ran as fast as his feet could take him. He noticed the traffic light at the corner was about to turn red; this was his chance. As he ducked so the man couldn't see him, he darted across the street just as cars started moving. Horns were honking, but he knew he could make it across, while his pursuer would have no chance and would have to wait until the light changed. Jonah ran back toward the office while glancing across the street simultaneously. He did not see the man again, but that was of little comfort. He kept his eyes on the traffic lights for his chance to do the same trick again. He looked both ways and ran across the street again. Horns honked, and tires squealed as he headed back into his office building.

He was drenched in sweat and completely winded as he entered the lobby. Not wanting to attract anyone's attention, he made sure the man was gone, ran into the men's room, and ducked into one of the stalls to give himself a chance to catch his breath. After a few minutes, he peeked into the hallway to ensure the man wasn't there. He then washed himself off at the sink and slipped back out. As he exited the elevator on the 10th floor, his heart was beating, and his legs were shaking. He headed straight to his office and closed the door.

So much for the relaxing lunch.

The afternoon was as long as the morning. Jonah planned to leave the office at 5:00 on the button, head over to the supermarket, get the food, and head back home as quickly as possible. It would be a long night. He had no idea what he would say to Hannah, but that wasn't his biggest problem. At the moment, a guy on the street was taking precedence over everything. Mercifully, Mr. Heart did not call him into his office, and nothing major happened for the rest of the day.

At exactly 5:00, he grabbed his coat and made his way out of the office. He would have to keep his eyes open to avoid a repeat performance of his lunchtime activities. He grabbed the subway home and spent his time looking over his shoulder.

So far, so good, he thought as he left the subway station near his home and entered the supermarket. He grabbed a wagon and filled it with everything he needed, constantly looking east to west and north to south. At a couple of points, he suddenly left his filled shopping cart on its own and hid in a corner to watch for any unusual activity, an old trick he had read about in one of his spy novels. As far as he could tell, he was on his own. He was sweating and would need a shower before he started cooking. He certainly did not want Hannah to see him like this.e H

❧

"Hannah, it's Josh."

"Hi Josh, what's up?" said Hannah as she answered her office phone after several rings.

"Jonah has gotten his old friends from the Crew together. He filled them in on everything happening, and they want to help."

"That's fine, Josh; what does that have to do with me?"

Josh noticed an edge to her voice; it was not the usual Hannah. He decided to ignore it and move on.

"Well, we are meeting at Jonah's house tonight at 8:00 to work out a plan. Fred Watkins, the guy fired from my department for apparently getting too close, will be there too. Can you make it?"

"Who's doing the inviting?"

Josh knew he was treading in dangerous territory.

"Well… Jonah is… I guess."

"Well, then, why are you the one who's doing the calling, Josh?"

Yikes!

Josh cursed Jonah under his breath for putting him through this; he had no choice but to forge ahead.

"He asked me to make the calls."

"So, you've been calling all his friends from the Motley Crew to come tonight?"

Josh felt like he was sitting on the witness stand at a murder trial, and he didn't like it.

"Well, actually, Jonah already invited them."

"I see," said Hannah, "*Jonah* invited them."

"Um… yes."

"So, who else did Jonah ask you to call?"

"Well, there's Fred Watkins."

"Fred and who else, Josh?"

"Uh, just Fred and you."

"I see; Jonah invited the guys from the Crew and then asked *you* to invite *me* to *his* house. Do I have that right?"

Josh swallowed hard.

I love him, but I'm going to kill him!

"Um… well… I guess, in a manner of speaking, but..-"

"I've got other plans tonight, Josh; thanks for calling."

As Hannah hung up, Josh started to look for sharp objects.

Hannah thought things were getting better between herself and Jonah, but after having stood her up at Starbucks, asking Josh to invite *her* to *his* house struck her as something the old Jonah would do. Maybe she was being a little harsh on Jonah, not to mention Josh, but a lady was entitled to play a little hard to get.

Jonah got home, tossed the beers in the fridge and the wings and hot dogs in the oven, and was about to hit the shower when his phone rang. Wrapped in a towel, he grabbed the phone.

"Hey Jonah, it's Josh."

"Hi Josh, what's up?"

"Watkins will be there."

"That's great, Josh. We really need him. What about Hannah?"

"What *about* Hannah?" said Josh.

"She's not coming, Josh, is she?"

"No, she's not."

"Did she say why?"

"Did she have to?"

"I guess not."

"You guessed right."

"I'll see you later, said Jonah; I've got a lot to do before the meeting."

"I bet you do."

Jonah could hear how upset Josh was.

"Hey, I'm sorry, buddy; I shouldn't have put you in that position. I owe you one."

"I'll add it to your tab."

Jonah hung up the phone and headed to the shower. He was upset with himself for stupidly asking someone else to invite Hannah instead of picking up the phone to do it himself and for putting his best friend, Josh, in the middle of it. He grabbed a quick shower and then checked on things in the oven. It was hard to concentrate on anything with the situation with Hannah hanging over him.

How could I be so stupid?

There was too much to do and no time to dwell on it further; he had to keep his eye on the ball.

I'll have to fix things later somehow.

At ten to eight, Josh rang the bell; he was the first to arrive. He seemed to have quickly gotten over their earlier conversation with one sniff of the food.

"Smells great in here, Jonah. Did you really have another one of these meetings last night with all that food and didn't invite me?"

"I'm sure you'll make up for it tonight. Josh. And I'm sorry I put you in the middle of my issues with Hannah."

"Jonah Mark, you truly have changed."

"Unfortunately, *you* haven't."

"There was no call for that, Jonah."

Before he could answer, the doorbell rang again: Fred Watkins. Jonah had seen him in the office but had never had any contact with him, given that they worked in different departments. He knew his story as Josh had related it to him.

"Jonah, I'd like you to meet Fred Watkins. Fred used to work in the accounting department at Tyler Tech," said Josh.

"Good to meet you, Fred," said Jonah as they shook hands.

"Likewise," said Fred. "I understand we've got a nice spread here tonight." His eyes were pointed at the dining room, where all the smells came from.

Jonah and Josh looked at each other.

"Sure," said Jonah. "Help yourself; it's all in the dining room."

"Don't mind if I do," said Fred. And off he went.

"That boy must have some appetite," said Jonah.

"You wouldn't believe it if I told you."

"Did you tell him why we're here tonight?" asked Jonah when Fred was out of earshot.

"All I had to do was mention the food. What can I say? The man has an appetite."

The bell rang again; it was Mack, Pete, and Marv.

"Smells like the right place," said Pete as they walked past Jonah and Josh.

"Does anyone care why we are here tonight?" asked Jonah.

"The way to a man's heart," said Josh.

"I know all this food will clog their arteries; I just hope it doesn't clog their brains," said Jonah.

But they were already busy in the dining room. The guys stuffed themselves on the food for the next half hour and washed it down with the beer. Josh and Fred enjoyed listening to all the stories the Motley Crew guys were telling about all the cool things they were involved with in the past. Jonah had heard it all before, and with everyone having such a good time, he wasn't sure how to break things up, but it was time to get down to business.

"Alright, everybody, let's simmer down," Jonah called out a few times until he finally got everyone's attention.

Just as things got quiet, there was another knock at the door. Josh looked at Jonah.

"Did you invite anyone else?"

"No Josh, just Fred and Hann…."

He dropped what was in his hands, lunged at the door, and swung it open. There stood Hannah; Jonah was speechless.

"Hannah, you came!"

The room suddenly became hushed; Hannah looked Jonah in the eye.

"From the smell of the food, I guess you weren't expecting me."

"Actually… I was hoping you would come. So, just in case, I kept your favorite warming up in the oven."

"You didn't!"

"I did… fried Oreos!"

"You remembered!"

"How could I forget?"

Everyone in the room did a double take. Hannah felt their eyes on her.

"And who are all these fine-looking gentlemen?" asked Hannah as she entered the dining room; Jonah was almost too stunned to talk.

"Well, you already know Josh, and this is Fred Watkins from accounting."

Fred discreetly dropped the half-eaten hot dog he was holding onto his plate.

"Nice to meet you, Fred; I've heard much about you. Thank you for helping us out."

"To tell you the truth, it's been a culinary delight," said Fred. "But I have other reasons to be here besides the food… of course."

"So, I've heard. I hope you get the satisfaction you are looking for."

Hannah walked past Fred.

"Are you going to introduce me to the rest of your guests?" said Hannah to Jonah.

The guys were drenched in oil from the chicken wings and were quickly trying to clean themselves up. Jonah made his way into the room, still shaken by Hannah's appearance.

"Hannah, I think you remember me mentioning the Motley Crew before."

"Indeed I have, but I never had the pleasure of meeting them in person."

"Well, I'd like you to meet, from left to right, holding the chicken bone, Mack Leibowitz, who also goes by the moniker Mack the Knife."

"Mr. Knife."

Mack quickly wiped the side of his mouth with a napkin.

"Eh, you can call me Mack."

"Sure, Mack; it's a pleasure to meet you."

"The pleasure is mine, believe me."

"And who, may I ask, is this handsome fellow?" asked Hannah, who was staring at Pete.

Pete looked a little self-conscious and straightened the collar of his shirt.

"Peter Rosenberg, but my friends call me Sneaky Pete."

"I can't wait to find out why," said Hannah.

Pete, for the first time in a long time, did not have a comeback.

"And finally, you are?"

"Marvin Goldberg."

"Just Marvin Goldberg?"

"Well, Marvelous Marv," he answered sheepishly.

"Well, it's a pleasure to meet all of you, said Hannah. Don't let me interrupt the party."

"Uh… guys, I'm just gonna take a few minutes with Hannah in the kitchen," said Jonah. "Why don't you all just eat some more."

The noise started again as Jonah escorted Hannah to the kitchen.

"You came, Hannah; why?"

Hannah looked Jonah in the eye.

"Jonah, I'd like to believe that what I've seen in you ever since you came to Tyler Tech is real, that you are a better version of yourself, someone I am starting to have feelings for. I don't know what happened the other day when you didn't show up at lunch, but I'd like to give you the benefit of the doubt."

There were tears in Jonah's eyes, which also brought a tear to Hannah's.

"Hannah, I don't deserve you," said Jonah.

"Maybe we deserve each other," said Hannah with a smile.

They suddenly noticed that the apartment had gotten quiet again, and all eyes were on them. They both felt a little awkward.

"Let me get you those Oreos before they burn," said Jonah as he grabbed an oven mitt. He carefully placed the food on a plate and handed it to Hannah.

"Well done, just the way I like it," she said with a smile.

"I guess my timing hasn't improved."

"We can work on that," said Hannah.

Jonah felt a little embarrassed with everyone watching them.

"OK, everybody," said Jonah. "Let's get started."

Ryan sat at his desk, frozen in fear; his encounter with Irv shook him to the core. He thought to himself, *I'm screwed at every turn. Not only did I not place the bug as Angelo instructed me to, but I actually managed to lose it. And the guy whose office I was supposed to bug now has possession of it. I couldn't make this stuff up. And on top of all that, I obviously lied to Irv's face, and he knows it.*

Think! said Ryan to himself. *How do I get out of this mess? After a day or two, Angelo and his pals will realize something's not right when they aren't getting any signal from that bug. Then they'll come looking for me.*

Ryan considered his options. Confessing to Irv was not a great idea; his temper was utterly unpredictable, and there was no telling what he might do. Telling Angelo that he lost the bug after they inevitably pulled him off the streets and hauled him back to the limo was another non-starter. Angelo didn't strike him as a man who allowed for mistakes. He also remembered how close the limo was to the river. The thought of running away and disappearing crossed his mind, but he figured Angelo's men were keeping their eyes on him and would track down Sue. As he quietly left the office, he knew he needed a plan, and he needed it quickly.

Mack was the first to speak.

"Jonah, as you indicated, this is a two-part problem, so the guys and I have been trying to come up with two separate solutions; let's focus on part one first."

Everyone in the room was quiet and listening intently to what Mack had to say.

"Part one concerns this Bartowski guy, the carrier pigeon, as you referred to him. He visits the office at least once weekly on Wednesdays and meets with Joel Tyler in the accounting department. Joel supplies him with the raw data collected from the previous week regarding the revenues they are making selling illegal high-tech weapons and explosives to the Soviets. Bartowski then puts it all in his briefcase, drops in on Mr. Heart for a courtesy visit, and presumably brings the paperwork back to his accounting firm, where he keeps the second set of books. As far as we know, there are no copies of this data kept at the Tyler office, so what he is carrying in his briefcase are the crown jewels, so to speak. Do I have it right, Jonah?"

"I would defer to Fred, who has firsthand knowledge from his vantage point in the accounting department," said Jonah.

Fred was busy working on a wing when he noticed all eyes were on him. He slowly lowered the wing onto a plate and wiped his mouth with a napkin.

"Eh… yes, that's all correct," said Fred. "As I told Jonah when we met the other day, I have watched this routine repeat every week for months. I am as sure as I can be that Joel gives him all the data we run. That's why he got so upset and fired me when he realized his error in giving me the wrong data to review."

"OK," said Pete. "So, the plan the three of us have been discussing is a work in progress, and your knowledge of what goes on in the office is where we need your help. This will be a three-step process. Step one: We need to get Bartowski's data while he is occupied. Step two, we need enough time to copy everything in his briefcase and step three, we need to return it all to his briefcase without his knowledge."

"And how are we going to accomplish that?" asked Josh.

"Relax," said Pete. "We have a plan. We just have to separate him from his briefcase long enough to copy everything inside it and return it all before he notices," said Mack.

"Oh, is that all? I thought we might have to do something complicated," said Josh.

Mack ignored Josh and continued.

"The way we see it, the only window we have from the time he loads his briefcase in the accounting department with the data until he leaves the office is when he visits with Mr. Heart."

"Jonah, have you ever dropped in on Mr. Heart while Bartowski made one of his visits?"

"About two or three times," said Jonah. "Usually, when Bartowski hits the Men's Room. Mr. Heart, who considers the whole ordeal a big waste of time, has called me in to discuss something I've been working on or something he needs; I can see the annoyance on his face."

"Yes, you did mention that he hits the Men's Room."

"Whenever Bartowski visits Mr. Heart, at some point, he excuses himself to freshen up in the Men's Room while Mr. Heart has to sit there cooling his heels."

"OK, Jonah, I want to clarify what you told me earlier because this is very important. Does he take the briefcase with him to the Men's Room, or does he leave it in Mr. Heart's office?"

"Well, every time I've been called in while Bartowski was out freshening up, his briefcase was sitting on one of the two chairs in front of Mr. Heart's desk with his jacket folded over it. He knows Mr. Heart is honest and has no reason to suspect what's in his briefcase, so he must let his guard down."

"And there you have it, guys," said Mack. "The optimum moment when we have the opportunity to copy the contents of his briefcase."

"Easier said than done," said Josh.

"Your skepticism is noted," said Mack to Josh.

Josh looked a little uncomfortable.

"We are going to need Mr. Heart's help," said Mack. "Jonah, you need to tell Mr. Heart everything you have discovered about what the Tylers are into. From what you have told us about how he feels about what the partners have done to Noah Tyler's company and what happened to his best friend Smokey, I think there's enough motivation for him to help."

"How do we know we have enough time to remove the contents of his briefcase, copy it, and return it without him coming back too early?" said Hannah.

Everyone turned to look at Hannah; it was the first time she had spoken, confirming that she was all in.

"Great question," said Mack. "We have come up with a little diversion to stall him until the task has been completed."

"Wait a second," said Fred. "Aren't you forgetting something?"

"What's that?" said Jonah.

"He may trust Mr. Heart not to go through his briefcase, but don't you think he would keep it locked until he returned to his office just the same?"

"You're right, I forgot about that," said Jonah. "We need

to be able to get into that briefcase before we can think of making copies."

"We've got that covered, too," said Pete.

"And how, may I ask, do you have that covered?" asked Josh, quickly turning into the designated skeptic.

"Marvelous Marv here, can pick a safe lock in minutes; do you think an attaché case with two spinning combination locks will be a challenge?"

"Guys, I told you, I won't let any of you risk going to prison to help us," said Jonah. "Besides, how are you going to bring a guy who doesn't work at Tyler Technologies into Mr. Heart's office at the precise moment he is needed to pick the lock?"

"One step ahead of you, buddy," said Marv. "At about the time Mr. Heart usually gets his Wednesday visit, at the signal, his old friend Mr. Perkins will enter the vestibule for an unscheduled visit with Mr. Heart. The receptionist will call Mr. Heart over the intercom, announcing that Perkins is there to see him. As soon as Bartowski heads to the Men's Room, Heart tells the receptionist to let him in."

"As for any of us taking a risk, Jonah. You've been there for all of us in the past; we're just returning the favor," said Pete.

Jonah was speechless.

"Guys, I don't know what to say."

"OK," said Watkins, "what about this diversion you were talking about to give Marv a chance to pick the lock plus get everything copied and returned to Bartowski's briefcase?"

Mack turned to Jonah.

"Jonah, do you remember how they stole the manuscript

from Sir Michael Tucker in the Great London Opera House Caper?"

Jonah was quiet for a few seconds when suddenly a smile began to form on his face.

"You're kidding me, right?" said Jonah.

"I kid you not," said Marv. "It's a little messy, but this Bartowski guy seems like the perfect clam for this."

"Brilliant!" said Jonah. "Josh, I'll need your help on this one, and we'll need a few props."

Hannah, Fred, and Josh looked puzzled.

"I'll need all of your help in setting this up."

"What kind of help?" asked Josh.

"I'll explain later," said Jonah. "Right now, I've got to figure out what to say to Mr. Heart tomorrow morning. We've got a lot of prep work to do. Today is Monday; that gives us two days to rock and roll."

"We still have to work on part two, you know, getting the info we need out of Irv's briefcase; that won't be a cake-walk either," said Josh, who was starting to feel more and more self-conscious about his skepticism.

"One thing at a time," said Pete, who gave Josh an annoyed look.

"I had a feeling you'd say that."

Jonah looked at Josh and Hannah.

"I'll fill you guys in on what we need."

Jonah turned to his old friends.

"You guys, I can't thank you enough."

"No thanks necessary," said Pete. "What are friends for?"

Hannah was impressed by their friendship and loyalty to each other. As Jonah stared straight at Hannah, he said to

Watkins and the Crew, "Guys, let yourselves out when you're done with the food; I'll be in touch."

Jonah then turned to Hannah.

"No way I'm doing this without you, come on."

"No way I'd let you," said Hannah.

With a smile from ear to ear, Hannah grabbed her coat and joined Jonah as they were about to run out of the apartment.

Josh was just standing there, not sure what to do.

Jonah turned to him and said:

"What are you waiting for, Josh?"

"Well… I… wasn't…sure…."

"Let's go, buddy," said Jonah.

Jonah was back in his element; this is what he loved to do. They both looked at him and remembered what he had told them when contemplating doing something dangerous.

There's a little spy in all of us.

16

"HANNAH, CAN YOU pick up a few things from the market?" said Jonah as they hit the street.

Hannah could see how excited Jonah looked. It was clear that there was a part of him that would never change, and if this was what it would take to make him happy, maybe a little intrigue was just what the doctor ordered for their relationship.

"Sure, what do you need?"

"Got a pen?"

"Right here."

"OK, I need two boxes of crackers, some ready-made oatmeal, a large jar of apple sauce, three cans of vegetable soup, a quart of milk, two cans of cat food, and three jars of baby food; make it baby carrots, peas, and yogurt."

"Sounds like some meal!" said Hannah.

"I'll explain later."

"Josh, I need you to go to the hardware store and get five feet of clear tubing, about a half-inch diameter. I also need a rubber bladder about twenty-four inches on each side."

"What in the world do you need all this stuff for, Jonah?"

"Like I said, I'll explain it all later; do you still have that fake wig and mustache you used at that singles party we attended last year?"

Josh looked a little embarrassed in front of Hannah; she tried to cover up a grin with her hand.

"Must you remind me, Jonah? That silly singles event where I made a fool of myself because you told me it would be a masquerade party, and all the guys were doubled over in laughter when I showed up trying to impress the ladies by trying to look like a suave, sophisticated man about town. Would that be the one?"

"Yeah, that's it," said Jonah, ignoring Josh, reliving his embarrassment.

"I think so."

"Bring it."

"What for?" said Josh. "I know… later."

"You've got it, buddy. Right now, I've got a meeting with Mr. Heart to plan for. We meet again at my place tomorrow night after work for a run-through. It's good that my mom decided to stay with her cousin in Connecticut for another two weeks. I'm going to ask the other guys to join us again."

"More dogs, wings, and beer?"

"If that's what motivates everyone, and I'll get some Oreos for you, Hannah."

"I'll fry them this time, if you don't mind, Jonah," said Hannah.

"We'll have to go over that recipe again."

Before they could say anything further, Jonah was half-way down the block.

"I guess some things never change," said Hannah to Josh.

"He's a good man, Hannah; maybe a little unconventional, but you'll never be bored with him."

"Thanks, Josh… thanks a lot!"

They said their goodbyes and headed in different directions to complete their assignments.

Josh and Hannah spent the rest of the night picking up the items Jonah requested from the stores that were still open. The rest would be picked up the following morning and during lunch.

Jonah returned to the supermarket the next day after work, buying more hot dogs, chicken wings, beer, and some Oreos for Hannah. He was so excited that Hannah was back and couldn't stop thinking of her gesture the day before. He found himself at the same checkout for the third day in a row and started feeling a little self-conscious, as the college kid that rang him up for the third time with the same items had a funny look on his face.

"Throw a lot of parties, do you?"

"How about you concentrate on hitting the right buttons on the register instead of playing detective, Sherlock!"

"Wow, man, someone didn't have his Wheaties this morning."

Jonah felt bad about unloading on a kid just trying to make conversation. His nerves were on edge, and there was no reason to take it out on someone else.

"Hey, kid, sorry about that. My nephews are over for a few days, and this is pretty much their diet."

"Sure, man, whatever; just doing my job, dude. This is not what I plan on doing for the rest of my life, you know."

"I'm sure it isn't," said Jonah, who was starting to feel like a heel. He spotted an elderly woman on line behind him who had obviously heard the conversation; she was glaring at him with a dour expression. He reached into his pocket and pulled out five dollars.

"Here, kid, for your education fund."

"Thanks, man, that was very generous of you."

"Forget it."

As Jonah grabbed his bags, he noticed the woman behind him with a slight smile on her face. Their eyes met, but no words were exchanged as Jonah left the store.

Hannah had one more store to visit to complete her strange shopping list. She couldn't get Jonah out of her mind. She was so glad she decided to join him and the guys the night before. She had a warm feeling whenever she thought of him, especially after last night. This was the version of Jonah she always wished for, someone responsible with a take-charge attitude. As for the spy stuff… it was a package deal.

Who knows where this could lead? she thought to herself.

She was hopeful that whatever this plan was, it would put the Tylers where they belonged, behind bars in a prison cell for many years. What they had done to Noah Tyler's legacy was despicable in her mind. Knowing the illegal activities they were involved in just for the sake of money made her feel sick.

She couldn't stop thinking of Smokey. She considered him and Mr. Heart to be mentors to her in the company. Whenever she had something she needed to discuss, they

were always there for her. The thought of Smokey being murdered was more than upsetting; it was like losing a friend
in the worst possible way. Whatever the plan the guys had
cooked up, she would be with them all the way.

Josh had picked up the items Jonah had asked him to get.
As he left the hardware store and walked down Lexington
Avenue, his mind flashed back to his days at his Yeshiva ele-
mentary school.…

Josh and Jonah sat in the back of the class next to each
other in sixth grade. There was a big history exam one day
that Josh hadn't studied enough for, and he was nervous that
he wouldn't do well. He met Jonah in front of school that
morning after his mom had dropped him off.

"Hey Joshie, ready for the test today?"

"I don't know, Jonah; Mrs. Klein said it would cover five
chapters; I'm really nervous."

"Come on, Joshie, you always do well in history."

Before they could finish talking, the school bell rang, and
they ran into the building with all the other kids. Mrs. Klein
was waiting for them in front of the classroom.

"Good morning, boys; I hope you all studied last night."

"Good morning, Mrs. Klein," they all recited together.

"Now I want you all to put away your books and anything else on your desk. All you should have on your desk is
a number two pencil, a sharpener, and an eraser."

The boys dutifully complied as Mrs. Klein walked down
each aisle of the classroom, handing out the test papers neatly
stapled in the upper left corner and placed face down on

each desk. She carried them like they were the secret recipe for Coca-Cola.

"OK, boys, you have forty-five minutes; you may turn over your papers. Good luck."

Jonah had studied hard, as did most of the other kids, and quickly completed the twenty-five multiple-choice questions. Over at Josh's desk, things weren't going so well. The look on his face matched the color of the walls in the classroom; he was white as a ghost.

I'm gonna fail; what do I do? thought Josh.

As the kids who had finished their test early had placed their pencils back in their cases, Josh just sat there with an empty page in front of him. He couldn't bear the thought of failing history. He couldn't help but notice the boy sitting to his right, filling in his answers as if he were in some race to the finish line; he was already somewhere on page two.

In a panic, Josh did something he had never done before. He started copying the other boy's answers. *9:B, 10:A, 11:C,* etcetera. He looked at the boy on his left, still working through the first page. *1:B, 2:C, 3:A.*

And then he heard it.

"Josh Silverstein, what do you think you are doing?"

Uh, oh. Busted! Think fast.

"Uh… nothing, Mrs. Klein," said Josh in a panic. He could feel the beads of sweat cascading down his cheeks like the water slide at Coney Island.

"Were you looking at that boy's paper?" said Mrs. Klein as she headed toward Josh's desk in a huff.

He could feel the eyes of everyone in the class as they watched the drama taking place. Before he could speak,

Mrs. Klein grabbed Josh's test and returned to her desk in front of the room. He saw everyone staring at him, including Jonah, who looked stunned at this turn of events. Josh's face felt like he had just exited a sauna.

"What am I to do with you?" said Mrs. Klein to Josh. "Looking at someone's answers while taking a test is no better than stealing someone's answers; how could you?"

"I... I..."

Josh could feel his lips moving, but no sound came out. He was in deep trouble. He had no choice but to add another major transgression to his newfound life of crime, and he knew he had to do it well.

"I was not looking at anyone's test paper, Mrs. Klein... I would never do such a thing!"

"But I saw you, Josh."

"I was trying to think of an answer and happened to look in the wrong direction; I would never cheat on a test."

And then, in the thralls of panic, he added this unnecessary but most unfortunate sentence.

"I know the material very well; I do not need to cheat."

There, I said it. If I survive this... I'll get the Nobel Prize for lying.

Josh had done a more effective job than he realized, as Mrs. Klein looked like she was starting to doubt herself. There was only one thing she could do to solve this dilemma.

"OK, Josh, since you know the material so well, I will give you another chance to take the test."

Josh couldn't believe he had gotten away with what he had said. How he would come up with the correct answers this time was another story.

"…at this desk in front of the class. Let's see how well you do this time."

She pointed to an unused desk in the front corner of the room. There would be no one's shoulder to look over; he would be facing the front and left walls of the classroom. And since he foolishly went for overkill by announcing to Mrs. Klein and the rest of the class that he knew the material very well, anything less than an excellent grade and the jig was up.

Josh slowly sat down at the desk Mrs. Klein pointed to as she dropped a fresh test on his desk.

What am I going to do now? Not only will I fail the test because I don't know the material, but I will also prove to Mrs. Klein that I had not only cheated but lied to her in front of the class. How many years do you get for larceny, dishonesty, and, most of all, stupidity? he thought to himself.

As Josh sat staring at the blank pages in front of him, others brought their completed tests to the front of the class to hand to Mrs. Klein. The answers weren't flying into Josh's head as he had hoped. Unless he was the world's greatest guesser, he was looking at a grade somewhere between zero and ten if he was lucky.

After ten minutes of sitting there not knowing what to do, more and more kids were approaching Mrs. Klein's desk with their completed exams, including someone who positioned himself perfectly with his back facing Josh while blocking the view of Mrs. Klein, as he flipped a small piece of paper, it was actually a bubble gum wrapper, between Josh's legs. Josh could not see where it came from, and it took him a few seconds to realize what had just happened. He slowly and carefully opened the tiny piece of paper. "1:C, 2B, 3:A..." Twenty-five tiny little answers. Josh was in shock, and there was no time to figure out who his guardian angel was. He quickly copied the answers and shoved the tiny bubble gum wrapper into his mouth under his tongue. There would be no evidence, and he would swallow it if he had to.

He waited a few more minutes for dramatic effect, stood up, and proudly handed Mrs. Klein his test. She looked surprised by how quickly he had completed the exam, but he decided the better part of valor would be not to say anything stupid this time; the results would speak for themselves. When the bell rang, Josh and Jonah ran out of the classroom with the rest of the kids. Josh would wait until they got behind the school to tell Jonah what had happened. Jonah said nothing at first but then looked at Josh.

"My hand hurts," said Jonah.

"From what?"

"You try writing fifty tiny answers in the back of a bubble gum wrapper; it's not as easy as it looks."

Josh looked at Jonah, who suddenly had a big smirk on his face.

"It was you!"

"You think I would let Mrs. Klein get the better of you? Although, if it were me, I wouldn't have declared myself such a genius."

Josh grabbed Jonah and gave him the biggest bear hug he had ever given him.

"Jonah, you're the best friend a guy could ever have."

"You can say that again; you owe me big time!"

They laughed all the way home. Josh knew what he did

was wrong, and it was not like him to do something dishonest. But things just snowballed after he glanced at the other boy's test. He promised himself he would never do anything like that again.

"Jonah, you took a big chance for me; I'll never forget it."

"Hey, forget about it, Joshie, you're my best friend."

"You can say that again," said Josh.

…Josh's thoughts were interrupted by a car horn blasting as he crossed Lexington Avenue.

"Hey… earth to daydreamer, watch where you're goin'. You're gonna get yourself killed!"

Josh practically jumped out of his shoes as he quickly crossed the street.

I better get this stuff over to Jonah.

Ryan had spent a sleepless night reviewing all the options and considering all the alternatives; there was nothing else he could do. It was time to grab the bull by the horns and finally take control of his life. Whatever the repercussions, he could look at himself in the mirror and know that he did the right thing. He got to the office about a half hour before the regular employees would start to filter in. He knew who else liked to get in early to the office. Before taking his next action, he grabbed a legal pad and began to write. When he was done, he tore the page out, neatly folded it, and put it in his pocket.

He walked down the hall, looked both ways to ensure he wasn't seen, and knocked on the open door.

Mr. Heart looked up from what he was working on. It

looked to Ryan as if he was not very surprised at his appearance at his office door.

"Come in, Ryan; how can I help you?"

Ryan stood still momentarily; Mr. Heart could see how nervous and flustered he looked.

"Why don't you close the door behind you, Ryan, and have a seat."

Ryan sat across from Mr. Heart and tapped his feet nervously.

"Mr. Heart, I'm not sure where to start. I know we don't have much to do with each other here at Tyler Tech, and there is no reason for you to help me. But everyone here, including myself, respects you as a straight shooter, and I have no one else to turn to, no one I can trust. And right now, I am desperately in need of some help."

"What's this all about, Ryan?"

"Mr. Heart, I'm scared… I screwed up."

"Ok, Ryan, why don't you start from the beginning."

And that's what Ryan did. He told Mr. Heart everything. He felt some relief unburdening himself as he told him about his past history, his problems with gambling, what Irv had asked him to do, what the Tylers were involved with overseas, about his meeting with the man named Angelo in the limo, and his disastrous attempt to place the bug he was told to place in Irv's office. He spoke for ten minutes, trying not to leave out any details.

Throughout Ryan's monologue, Mr. Heart listened without comment. He asked Ryan a few questions along the way to clarify things. Still, it seemed to Ryan that he wasn't asking the kinds of questions someone who was hearing about something for the first time would ask.

When he was done speaking, Mr. Heart looked directly at Ryan. Whatever Mr. Heart may have already known was hidden behind his poker face.

"That's quite a story, Ryan; I'd like to think about this a little. I want you to return to your office and lie low for a while. Try to stay away from Irv as much as possible. I will get back to you as soon as I can."

Ryan stood up and faced Mr. Heart.

"Thank you for listening to my story, Mr. Heart. I know I'm no Boy Scout, and I've made many poor choices in my life. But what the Tyler's are into… well… that's just not right."

"Understood, Ryan; I'll be in touch."

Ryan quietly left Mr. Heart's office, looking both ways before stepping into the hallway to ensure no one saw him leave.

About an hour later, Jonah knocked on Mr. Heart's open door.

"Yes, Jonah."

"Mr. Heart, I was wondering if you might have a few minutes to talk about what we discussed the last time we met together with Smokey."

"Come in, Jonah, and close the door behind you."

Jonah entered Mr. Heart's office. He pointed at the seat in front of his desk for Jonah to sit down.

"Mr. Heart, I promised to finish our conversation once I met with the other employees I am working with to get our ducks in a row. I was hoping to meet with both you and

Smokey. Unfortunately, I believe he became a victim of the people behind all that has happened at Tyler Tech."

Mr. Heart looked directly at Jonah.

"Jonah, you alluded to crimes involving national security, fraud, and deception emanating from this company and involving outsiders."

"Yes, sir."

"I think it's time we stop playing cat and mouse. If you came in here seeking my help somehow, you will have to be completely transparent. Otherwise, we are wasting each other's time."

"Fair enough, Mr. Heart."

Jonah took a deep breath.

"Mr. Heart, I have reason to believe that the partners at Tyler Technologies are selling illegal high-tech weapons and explosives to the Soviet Union."

Mr. Heart held his poker face.

"These are serious claims, Jonah; do you have proof to back them up?"

"That's the whole point, Mr. Heart; we know it is happening, we know how it is being done, and we know how we can get the proof, but we don't have it yet."

"Why not just share this information with the FBI?"

"Because unless we have definitive proof, they will be treated as unproven allegations, which will set off an investigation, and we'll be sitting ducks if the FBI starts snooping around and asking many questions. It won't be hard for the Tyler partners to figure out where the information came from, and that will endanger all our lives."

"What have you got so far that makes you believe this has been taking place?"

Jonah then spoke for the next ten minutes about what he, Josh, Hannah, and Fred Watkins had observed over the last few weeks. He told him about his exchange of brief-cases with Ryan that confirmed the plot, leaving out the fact that he had exchanged them on purpose, what Hannah had overheard Irv and Simeon from the Ladies Room speaking about, and the firing of Fred Watkins for accidentally reading the wrong financials that proved there was a source of funds from outside parties that was being funneled into the Tyler accounts to fund the plot. Mr. Heart was impressed with what Jonah and his friends had been able to come up with. It all jived with what Ryan had told him earlier.

Jonah shared his theory of there being two sets of books, which made the idea of Bartowski collecting the weekly numbers directly and being used as a carrier pigeon sound like a brilliant way of hiding a second set of books that did not exist anywhere in the office. It also made sense to Mr. Heart that Irv was driving the bus for the entire scheme. It took someone with absolutely no scruples to do something this corrupt and this treasonous to his own country.

He found it more difficult to believe the Tylers would follow such a scheme. Using the company as their piggy bank was one thing; using it for treason against their country to gain a profit was quite another. But he knew that money corrupts, and he also knew where that money was coming from, based on his own information that Ryan had just verified to him earlier.

"That's pretty impressive work, Jonah; what you have

told me confirms many of my suspicions and what I found out from Ryan Schapp about an hour ago."

"Ryan Schapp?"

Jonah looked at Mr. Heart dubiously.

"I know, it surprised me too, but he is in enough trouble to keep him honest, and he seems to have changed somehow."

"Mr. Heart, I get the feeling you, and I am guessing Smokey as well, have known more than you have been letting on. I think, respectfully, that it is time for you to share that information."

"OK, Jonah, you have kept your end of the bargain, so here is what I know."

Mr. Heart then launched into his own ten-minute dissertation while Jonah sat and listened with rapt attention. He was fascinated with what Mr. Heart had to say. It was clear to Jonah that Mr. Heart knew much of what had been happening in the company lately, just as Jonah did. His information, along with Ryan's, had filled in many blanks. As Jonah would soon learn, Mr. Heart's information came from a different source. He had a trusted friend on the inside of what the partners were involved with, one they would never have guessed.

Mr. Heart told Jonah that the information he and his friends had come up with at Tyler Tech and that he had just received from Ryan that morning confirmed what he and Smokey had gotten from his inside source. Jonah was surprised to hear about Ryan's visit and was suspicious about anything he said. However, once he heard about the hot water Ryan had gotten himself into, his remorse was more believable.

Maybe I misjudged Ryan all this time. Perhaps he treated me the way he did because Irv didn't leave him much choice, thought Jonah.

"Jonah, together with Smokey, we were beginning to close in on the information we needed to bring to the FBI about what the Tylers are involved with, but we too did not feel like we had enough meat on the bones to bring to the authorities just yet. Then you visited my office and told Smokey and me that you and others in the company were working on your investigation regarding crimes that you said involved issues of national security, fraud, and deception. We realized you must have stumbled on the same thing we were working on; that certainly complicated things. We didn't think we could talk you out of continuing your investigation, so we decided to let you continue; maybe you might come up with some vital evidence."

As Mr. Heart related, Smokey's unfortunate demise was devastating and threw him off his game. Still, it gave him a renewed determination to get to the bottom of what he knew were illegal and treasonous activities by the Tyler partners. When they first discovered it, Mr. Heart and Smokey could not believe it was true. They never cared much for the Tyler children or Irv. But what they were involved in was beyond the pale.

"Mr. Heart, please tell me about this inside source."

"Jonah, Marco Moretti is a retired undercover cop who had worked security for me at the pharmaceutical company I ran before joining Tyler Technologies. He was smooth as silk and could ingratiate himself with anyone. I had used him for countless jobs in the past when I needed to check out an employee that I felt was involved in stealing highly sought-after pharmaceutical products for sale on the lucrative black market dealing with drugs. I did a lot of favors for him and paid him well for the jobs he did for me."

"Well, the name Marco certainly rings a bell," said Jonah.

Mr. Heart continued.

"Carlos Martinez is a strongman who works for Angelo Papatonis. Papatonis is a ruthless international arms dealer who will stop at nothing to get what he wants."

"An international arms dealer," repeated Jonah. "How coincidental!"

Mr. Heart continued his story.

"Carlos also dealt in illegal drugs on the black market when I ran the pharmaceutical company; it was a name I heard from Marco many times. When I told Marco that we thought the Tylers might be involved with selling illegal arms and explosives, he did some sniffing around for me, and guess whose name came up?"

"Carlos Martinez."

"That's right, Jonah. Marco had befriended Carlos when he worked undercover for the police. He knew that he hung out at a bar he frequented through previous police surveillance on an unrelated case before his retirement. They became good friends. Carlos thought Marco was an ex-con like himself and never knew he was an undercover cop. Marco spent weeks at the same bar, and at times, he knew Martinez hung out there. He made sure to let Carlos know that he was an unemployed construction worker who needed a job. He kept asking Carlos if he knew of any openings where he worked."

Jonah was taking it all in; he could not believe what he heard.

"All that work finally paid off one day when Carlos told Marco he was working on a job for someone and needed a partner, but Marco would have to meet his boss first. As it turned out, his boss was Tony Romano, an underling of Angelo Papatonis. Tony had been looking for someone to work with Carlos on the Tyler job, and Carlos vouched for Marco as a great guy he knew and trusted. After a brief meeting, Tony hired Marco to pair up with Carlos. It had taken months, but I now had an inside man to keep track of the Tyler partners. Carlos's job was simple: do what he was told and keep an eye on the Tylers."

"And that is why I kept seeing those two guys together hanging out with the Tylers, including the night I hid out in the office and could have gotten myself killed," said Jonah.

"You did what and could have what?"

Uh… oh!

"Uh… that's a story for later."

Mr. Heart shot Jonah a look and then continued his story.

"Jonah, to keep you safe, I had Marco keep an eye on you, Josh, and Hannah as well, even on the streets."

"I guess that explains why he followed me the two times I saw him, but why did he chase after me?"

"Marco told me about that. I had him follow you to keep an eye on you once you told Smokey and me that you were doing your own investigation."

"That still doesn't explain why he chased me through the streets."

"He didn't; you suddenly turned around, stared him in the face, and took off. If you turned around once you started running, you would have noticed that he wasn't chasing you. That was your own paranoia."

Jonah felt a little embarrassed. He realized that if someone was really tailing him, the last place he should be running was straight back to the office.

"One question," said Jonah.

"Marco and Carlos? Romano and Papatonis? These aren't Russian-sounding names."

"Good point, Jonah. And until today, I did not know who they were selling the weapons to, just that they were not friends of this country. Both you and Ryan filled in that blank. But we do know that the mob will deal with anyone if it means making a lot of money, so this is no surprise. The question is, where do we go from here?" said Mr. Heart.

"That is actually what I am here to talk to you about."

"I don't understand, Jonah."

"Mr. Heart, have I ever told you about my friends from the Motley Crew?"

"The Motley who?"

"I think I need to tell you a little bit more about my background."

Mr. Heart had a puzzled look on his face.

"I'm all ears."

✍

Ryan was restless; he had spilled his guts to Mr. Heart earlier in the morning but had not heard from him since. He felt completely exposed. Whether it was Irv or Angelo, he didn't feel safe sitting and waiting for the other shoe to drop. He felt like a sitting duck. He decided to get some air with an early lunch.

He grabbed his jacket and headed down the elevator and out of the building. Stopping by the food cart outside, he grabbed a hot dog and a can of soda and headed aimlessly down the street. It took about five minutes for him to notice the same car that had grabbed him off the street the other day. He remembered the license plate. The same two guys were sitting in front as he passed by the car. They were clearly not expecting him. He tried not to make eye contact but was not successful. Two doors opened simultaneously as he got about half a block from the car, and the two men appeared.

No way these guys are taking me off the street again, thought Ryan.

He dumped his food in a trash can and quickened his pace, but the men were gaining on him. There was nothing else to do.

It was time for Ryan to run.

<h1 style="text-align:center">17</h1>

MR. HEART LISTENED TO Jonah talk about his childhood and the types of friends he hung out with. He found some of it humorous but wondered if he would have hired him had he known where his head was. He described the members of his group and the talents they possessed.

"This is all very nice, Jonah, but what does it have to do with the situation we are faced with now?"

"Mr. Heart, as we have both said, we need evidence to present to the FBI to be taken seriously."

"That's true."

"My friends and I, along with Josh, Hannah, and Fred Watkins, have met a few times to discuss how to handle this situation. We believe the authorities will want evidence of two separate parts to this scheme."

"Go on," said Mr. Heart, listening intently.

"Part one is proving where the funds are coming from to pay for these serious operations overseas to transport the illegal parts and explosives. Based on what you have ascertained, we know Angelo Papatonis, the international arms dealer, is involved. And we probably have enough informa-tion from Marco and Ryan to at least give the Feds a reason to investigate."

"True."

"But we don't have proof of those funds going into the Tyler accounts on any computer, disk, or shred of paper in this office. So, right now, there is no connection. We already know from Fred Watkins that Max Bartowski is working on a second set of books off-premises. We know he takes the reports and places them in his briefcase every Wednesday after he meets with Joel Tyler and brings them back to his office."

"Interesting, so what is your plan?"

"I'm just getting to that. We also know that he pays a courtesy visit to you, Mr. Heart, just before he leaves with the goods; this is the only place he stops before leaving."

"Don't remind me."

"Our plan for part one is to remove the paperwork from his briefcase while he is here visiting you and copy it all before returning it to his briefcase before he leaves."

"And I suppose he will just sit here cooling his heels while you copy the contents of his briefcase and return it to him."

"I don't think so."

Mr. Heart looked intrigued but skeptical.

"I take it your *Crew* has a plan."

"We do."

"And what might that be?"

"It's a little messy."

"Messy?"

"A little bit."

Jonah spent the next few minutes detailing the plan to Mr. Heart and what they needed him to do. He listened intently, if not incredulously.

"You're kidding me, right?" said Mr. Heart.

"I kid you not," said Jonah.

Mr. Heart stared at Jonah with an intense look, one that Jonah had not seen before. Jonah started to get nervous and found himself holding his breath. He needed Mr. Heart's help to make the plan work. If not, they were all out of luck.

Maybe this wasn't such a great idea after all, he thought.

Suddenly, a small smile appeared on Mr. Heart's face.

"I think I'd pay to see it."

Jonah exhaled.

"Are you in?"

Mr. Heart looked at Jonah and waited a few beats.

"I'm in," said Mr. Heart. "You will fill me in on the timing and details when you're ready to go."

Jonah jumped out of his seat and hugged Mr. Heart. It was a spontaneous move that he regretted as soon as he did it. Mr. Heart looked uncomfortably startled.

"Uh… sorry. I got a little carried away. I'm going to leave the office now… I have the meeting with the guys tonight at my place and…."

Jonah walked out of Mr. Heart's office and slowly closed his door. There would be no graceful exit.

Mr. Heart stood there shaking his head. It was evident to him that the Angelo Ryan had referred to was Angelo Papatonis. He buzzed Ryan in his office; there was no answer.

He must be out to lunch, thought Mr. Heart. *I've got to give him hope and calm him down before he makes a mistake.*

❧

Ten stories below and six blocks away, Ryan was running for his life. He knew the terrain well, having worked in Midtown Manhattan office buildings for the better part of his adult life. He knew which buildings he could run through that had exits on the next block on the other side and which department stores had the best hiding places. He could only hope that the guys chasing him were from out of town.

Mr. Heart tried Ryan's intercom an hour later, but still no response. He was getting concerned; Ryan had been gone for two hours. He saw Irv walk into Ryan's office, looking for him. His paranoia was well-placed.

He panicked and took off. This will not end well, thought Mr. Heart.

Ryan had been running out of one building and into another for a long time. He was far away from the office. He had looked over his shoulder dozens of times and felt sure no one was watching him.

These guys must have called Angelo by now, and he probably will have people heading to my apartment to find Sue to use her for bait, he thought to himself. *Her mother's place would be next; hopefully, she got out of there like I told her to. Thankfully, my own mother is on vacation in Europe.*

What am I going to do? he thought to himself. *I have no place to go.*

As he was hiding in an office building, checking outside the window every couple of minutes, shivering from fear, he began to take stock of himself. What had he done with his life, and what had he done to Sue? He was running like a scared rat through the streets of New York in fear for his life. What made it worse was that his wife was forced to hide in fear as well.

As he cowered in that office building lobby, Ryan suddenly found something inside himself that he did not know he had. He knew he had made a lot of mistakes in his life and hurt a lot of people. Talking to Mr. Heart today made him realize what a decent person he was and what a scumbag Irv Carter was.

He was tired of being taken advantage of and tired of running. It was time for him to stand up for himself and hopefully be a better husband to Sue if he ever got the chance again. He told himself that life would change from then on, but first, he had to escape this mess. It was time to stop running; it was time to start fighting back.

It's just you and me, Angelo, mano a mano.

He headed straight to a pay phone in the lobby he was hiding in and made two calls. He also stopped off at a post office he spotted earlier to take care of an important errand.

This may not end well for me, but I will ensure it ends badly for them.

Everyone made it back to Jonah's apartment that evening for the run-through. They were filling themselves with junk food, except for Hannah, who was enjoying her fried Oreos. Jonah filled them in on his meeting with Mr. Heart earlier in the day. They were all very interested in hearing his reaction to the plan and were pleasantly surprised by it.

"That's great," said Josh.

"It's great if we follow through," said Jonah. "Let's review the plan again so everybody knows what to do."

They spent the next hour reviewing the exact details of where everyone who was part of the plan needed to be and when. Josh had his disguise and the other supplies he needed. Hannah's job was to keep watch and signal to Pete when to enter the vestibule and ask to see Mr. Heart. Jonah would enter Mr. Heart's office as soon as Pete passed his door. Once Pete got past the locks on the briefcase, Jonah would grab the paperwork and head over to the high-speed copier in the main office area. Hannah would make sure to be using the copier so that she could step aside and allow Jonah immediate access as soon as he arrived without anyone else taking up any of their valuable time.

"OK, everybody," said Jonah. "I think we have our plan for part one together. We will execute it tomorrow. We need to get this exactly right. Any mistakes… well, there can't be any; let's put it that way."

"By the way, Jonah," said Josh. "Having me leave out that milk in my apartment is really stinking up the joint."

"Then I guess you're glad tomorrow is Wednesday."

"Very funny."

"What about the second part of our plan, tying the Tyler partners to the plot itself?" said Watkins.

"If we do this right," said Jonah, Bartowski will never know the information is missing, which will give us some time to prepare for part two."

Looking at the Crew guys, he said, "I know you guys have been working on a plan for part two."

"We sure have," said Mack.

"Let's just get part one out of the way," said Jonah.

Jonah looked at everyone.

"Any more questions?"

There was silence in the room. All that could be heard was the sound of Fred Watkins munching on some chips. They all looked over at him. He stopped eating and closed the bag.

"Eh… I'm good."

"Great, guys; we meet here again tomorrow night to assess how it went and start working on part two," said Jonah.

"Any food?" asked Watkins. They all looked over at him again.

"Right… never mind. No reason to be thinking of food at a time like this."

❧

The call was picked up on the first ring.

"Sue, it's me… don't hang up."

"Ryan, I didn't recognize this number."

"I'm calling from a pay phone; I can't talk long."

"Where are you, Ryan? I'm so scared."

"I can't say. I am so sorry I put you through this baby."

"Ryan, what do I do?"

Ryan could hear Sue sobbing; it broke his heart.

"There is no reason to worry, sweetheart. I just wanted to make sure you're alright. I promise you, Sue, things will be different if I get out of this. I will never gamble again. We can start all over; maybe even have a kid of our own."

Sue was crying over the phone; words were not coming from her mouth. Ryan realized that the mention of having a baby may have been too much for her. They talked about it often when they were a young married couple with such promise. Deep down, he knew she still loved him.

"Listen, sweetheart," said Ryan. "I will try to call you again when it's safe. Don't contact your mother; they'll be monitoring her calls and be able to trace them to you. Do you understand, baby?"

"Yes," she said as she continued to sob. "When will I see you?"

"As soon as I can, sweetheart, I promise. And these guys that are after me will never be in a position to hurt us again."

"Please be careful."

"I will baby… I love you."

Ryan was about to hang up the phone.

"Ryan, I love you too."

He had a lump in his throat as he hung up the phone. He had not heard those words in a long time.

I will never make Sue cry again.

It was Wednesday morning at Tyler Tech, and it was time to put the plan in motion. Josh sat at his desk nervously. His disguise was in his backpack with the rest of the stuff he needed. He had practiced at home for half the night using water in place of the ingredients he now had with him. It was all a matter of choreography, he told himself. He looked at the clock on the wall of the accounting department. It was ten o'clock. Bartowski would be there in about an hour. It was almost crunch time.

Hannah sat at her desk. In about an hour and a half,

Bartowski would pass her office. She knew what she had to do.

Mr. Heart sat at his desk. His job was to follow Jonah's timeline. Nothing would make him happier than to know that this might be Bartowski's last courtesy visit to his office.

❧

Angelo Papatonis was livid.

"How did you two morons let Schapp get away from you?"

"Sorry, boss, we weren't expecting him."

"Oh, you weren't expecting him, I see. You were doing *surveillance,* you knuckleheads! Were you expecting him to knock on your window and tell you he was there so you could follow him?"

The two looked at each other, but no words came out of their mouths. The temperature in the room had gotten noticeably hotter.

"What about the mother's house?"

"We sent somebody over there, boss. She said she hadn't seen her in two weeks; they don't speak much."

"So, what you are telling me is that what I have got here is a dead end? The bug isn't transmitting, and our link to keep an eye on the Tylers is gone with the wind because you two idiots couldn't follow some simple instructions. Is that what you are telling me?"

"We're really sorry, boss."

"You don't know how sorry the two of you are about to become."

"Vinnie! Joe!"

A couple of heavyset muscular guys weighing about 600 pounds between them walked over.

"Yes, boss?" said one of them.

"I think these guys have earned the no-expense tour of the East River."

Before they could say another word, they were lifted off their feet and were starting to be escorted out when Angelo called out.

"Vinnie!"

Vinnie turned to Angelo. He looked enraged; his face was red, and his neck veins were bulging.

"Before you get rid of those two bozos, I want you to find out exactly where they lost sight of the guy they were supposed to keep an eye on and make sure you get his complete description. Then I want you to take Joey, Whitey, and Sal and start searching for that piece of crap in every rathole he could possibly be hiding in. That means checking every store, talking to every cabbie in the area, and checking every motel or rooming house in a five-mile radius. The next words I hear outta your mouth better be, *we got him*. And when you do, you send him where those other two halfwits are goin'; got my drift?"

There was no need for Angelo to wait for an answer. His face was red, and sweat was pouring from his forehead.

Ryan Schapp, you piece of crap… where are you?

⁓

The clock struck eleven, and Max Bartowski strolled into the accounting department on time as always. Joel Tyler was there to greet him, like every other Wednesday.

"Good morning, Max. How was the traffic?"

"The usual cross-town mess; my driver tried to avoid it, but you know the city, Joel."

"Sure do," said Joel. "Let's get started."

"Bartowski, briefcase in hand, headed over to the office at the other end of the department. The clock was now ticking. In about twenty minutes, they would walk back in Josh's direction and bid each other a good day. Bartowski's briefcase would be filled with the reports that Joel would have filled it with. He would then head to Mr. Heart's office.

And who says accounting is a boring profession? thought Josh.

As soon as Bartowski left the department, Josh reached under his desk, grabbed the equipment and ingredients Jonah told him to bring, and headed to a small bathroom on the other side of the accounting department that was rarely used. When he got inside and opened the bag, he was almost knocked over by the smell. His memories of the previous night turning the ingredients into liquid using his blender came rushing back. Once he assembled everything, he brought a small can of room deodorizer that he would use to hide the smell as best he could. He then returned to his desk.

I could knock Sugar Ray Leonard out with this stuff!

The meeting with Joel and Bartowski was over. They bid each other a good day, and Bartowski headed to Mr. Heart's office. As he walked past Hannah's office, she had visual confirmation that he was headed to Mr. Heart's office. She picked up the phone and buzzed Josh's desk. "Start phase one," she said and hung up.

Josh headed slowly down the hallway toward the Men's

Room in the main office area. He had to move gingerly because of the extra weight strapped to his body under his shirt. The wig and mustache were stuffed into his pockets. As soon as he entered the empty Men's Room, he headed into the last stall at the far end. He then started completing the assembly that he had begun earlier.

Mr. Heart had been sitting nervously at his desk waiting for the knock; it was right on time.

"Come in," said Mr. Heart as he rose from his desk for his ritual greeting of Bartowski.

"Good morning, Franklin. How are you?"

He thrust out his oversized and sweaty hand that Mr. Heart was once again forced to shake.

"Fine, Max. How is the family?"

"Oh, the usual; how about yours, Franklin?"

"The kids are busy with work, and the grandkids are all busy with school."

"Busy lives, Franklin, busy lives. I'd love to take a vacation sometime, but I'm just too piled down with work these days."

⁓

As the ritual continued in Heart's office, Josh was frantically getting his disguise on and running the clear tubing from the rubber bladder containing the most disgusting foul-smelling ingredients he had ever encountered that was strapped under his shirt through his right arm and up to his hand. He prayed that no one else would need the Men's Room, but his prayer wasn't answered.

Suddenly, a heavyset man strode in, heading to the stall

right next to him. After a few coughs, it was clear that it was Irv Carter for whom nature was calling. Josh sat perfectly still, hoping the foul odor would not attract Irv's attention. The one thing he had going for him was that this would be the right place for it to originate from.

There were three words on Josh's mind as he turned to the wall between his stall and the next one that held Irv, and they worked in different combinations.

Get out... now! Now... get out! Now... now... now! Out... out... out!

After a few more minutes of small talk, during which Mr. Heart kept stealing glances at the clock on the wall, Bartowski finally uttered the magic words.

"Franklin, I'm going to freshen up; I'll be back in a minute."

"Sure, Max, no problem."

He arose from his chair, placed his briefcase on the chair next to where he had been sitting, folded his jacket, placed it on top, and left Mr. Heart's office. He walked into the Men's Room and headed straight to stall number three, two stalls away from Josh, with stall number two still occupied by Irv.

As soon as Bartowski walked out, Hannah, who was keeping an eye on Mr. Heart's office, picked up her phone and called Marv. He picked up the phone immediately.

"You're on."

"Got it."

Marv had been waiting at a wall phone next to the Men's Room one floor below to save time. Hannah had copied that number earlier. He ran up the stairs and took a deep breath to ensure he looked calm before entering the reception area. He was dressed in a suit and tie. He had to borrow one from his brother because a suit and tie on Marv was like a Big Bird costume on most people, a very rare sight. He strode confidently to the receptionist's desk and announced himself.

The receptionist looked up from what she was doing.

"Charles Perkins to see Mr. Heart."

"Is he expecting you?"

"Just tell him it's Charlie Perkins; I was in the neighborhood, so I thought I'd stop by just a minute to say hello."

That was done because the receptionist did not have him on Mr. Heart's schedule.

She glanced at him while buzzing Mr. Heart's intercom.

"Mr. Heart, I have a Charlie Perkins who was in the neighborhood and wanted to say hello."

"Sure, I'm always happy to see Charlie; you can send him back."

"Of course, Mr. Heart… Mr. Perkins, his office is just down the hall on the right,"

"Thank you, Miss…?"

"My name is Evelyn."

"Thank you, Evelyn," said Marv, ever the charmer.

Josh was choking under the smell and sweating under the wig. If Irv didn't get out soon, the plan was dead. He had spotted Bartowski walk in through a small crack in his stall door. He was now the occupant of the stall on the other side of Carter.

At least he didn't head straight for the mirror and a quick splash of water on his face, thought Josh. *Here we are. In stall number three, the guy I've been waiting for that I have to keep in this Men's Room for as long as possible. In stall number two, Irv Carter who needs to exit the premises forthwith. And in stall number one, there's me, slowly losing consciousness and sweating up a storm.*

Suddenly, there was a flush.

As soon as Marv passed Hannah's office, she grabbed the large pile of paperwork she had assembled that suddenly needed copying and headed for the high-speed copier in the main office area. All she had to do was keep the copier available for when Jonah arrived to copy the contents of Bartowski's briefcase. Unfortunately, it was precisely where Jim, Simeon Tyler's assistant, stood with his own pile of papers he was busily feeding into the machine.

Marv knocked on Mr. Heart's door and walked in. As soon as he closed the door behind him, he carefully removed the jacket from the briefcase, placed it on the desk precisely as it was folded, and started working on the locks. Mr. Heart just stood and watched nervously, trying not to interrupt him.

"Hey Jim, could you do me a favor?" said Hannah. "I've got this large report I've got to get copied for Mr. Heart; he needs it for an important meeting tonight. Would you mind letting me get ahead of you? It won't take long."

Jim was well known as one of the most annoying people in the office. Everything was a federal case to him, so the answer she got didn't surprise her.

"Well, we've all got important things to do, Hannah; I guess you're just going to have to wait your turn."

Hannah glared at him. She didn't want to cause a scene, but if she could squeeze the little head that sat atop his oversized body as hard as she could, it would be her pleasure at that point. Hannah just stood there and looked at the clock on the wall. If she didn't get to the copier in time, she would not be able to step aside and allow Jonah, who was nervously waiting for the signal, to come to Mr. Heart's office, grab the paperwork, and head to the copier and start to copy Bartowski's reports as soon as he got to the machine. Hannah couldn't wait any longer and left the copy area, heading straight to Mr. Heart's office, and slipped in. She would have no choice but to go to Plan B.

"How's it going?" said Hannah.

"I've got one lock open and one more to go."

"Mr. Heart," said Hannah. "We have a problem."

❧

To Josh's great relief, the first out of the three-stall race was Irv, whom Josh spotted from his stall. He headed to the sink and was washing up when Bartowski flushed and exited.

Irv was drying his hands when he turned back and noticed Bartowski.

"Hey Max, nice to see you."

"Same here, Irv; how's the wife and kids?"

"Oh, the usual Max. I take it you're here for your Wednesday visit."

"Yep, the usual grind."

"Send my best to the Misses," said Irv as he exited the Men's Room.

This is it, thought Josh. *All that practice in front of the mirror comes down to this.*

Ping… the second lock popped open. Marv carefully emptied the briefcase and handed the contents to Mr. Heart. Without another word, he left the office and walked down the hallway. As he passed by the receptionist, he couldn't help but exercise his charm.

"Pleased to meet you, Evelyn."

"My pleasure, Mr. … Perkins, was it?"

"Charlie works fine."

"Charlie, it is; you have a nice day."

"And you do the same," said Marv as he stepped into the elevator in his snappy suit and tie.

Jonah saw Marv pass his office. He must have opened the briefcase, but Hannah hadn't called him to go to Mr. Heart's office yet.

Is there something wrong?

❧

"OK, I guess there's no other way to get this done," said Mr. Heart, who took the paperwork and walked out of his office, heading to the copier as Hannah returned to her office.

❧

Bartowski was admiring himself in the mirror as Josh nervously exited the stall and made his way to the sink next to him. His shirt was untucked on one side, and he looked and smelled like an office was the last place where he belonged. He was coughing, rocking back and forth, and making the biggest racket he could.

Bartowski looked to his right. The man next to him smelled like a cesspool.

"Hey Mister… can you help me… I don't feel so well."

Before Bartowski could respond, Josh lifted the arm with the clear tube hidden in his sleeve, held it against the side of his face next to his mouth, and turned toward Bartowski.

"I think I'm gonna be sick."

"Noooo!" yelled Bartowski, as he realized what was about to happen… but it was too late.

Josh pressed down as hard as he could on the rubber bladder attached to his stomach, and out of his outstretched hand, which was next to his mouth, gushed a geyser of sour milk, pulverized cat food, crackers, oatmeal, apple sauce, vegetable soup, mashed baby carrots, peas, and yogurt. Bartowski was covered from head to toe.

"Hey… what the hell is wrong with you?"

Bartowski started cursing like a drunken sailor.

"Eh… sorry sir… I guess I had too much to drink last night."

Bartowski had no time to deal with the guy next to him. He could not leave the Men's Room looking and smelling like he did. He started frantically dousing himself with water and paid little mind to Josh, who had moved to the other end of the room and was furiously working to remove the bladder, tubing, and disguise. The last thing he needed was for someone to walk into the Men's Room right then. He placed it all in a garbage bag he had folded in his pocket, which he stuffed into the trash can and walked out of the Men's Room. Bartowski was so busy cursing and washing that he had not noticed Josh's exit.

Josh was in panic mode as he moved like a cat down the hallway heading for his department while trying to keep his head down, hoping he looked clean enough to get by until he could get back to the small bathroom in the accounting office where he would finish cleaning up.

"Jim, I'm going to need this copier immediately; I have some important papers that need to be copied right now. Why don't you come back in twenty minutes and finish your project?"

Jim was startled to see it was Mr. Heart.

"Of course, Mr. Heart; it's all yours."

"Thank you, Jim."

Mr. Heart began to feed the high-speed copier quickly as Josh passed him by.

Meanwhile, in the Men's Room, Bartowski was practically taking a bath in the sink and continuing to curse like a sailor.

"That sonofabitch; if I catch up to him...."

&

Hannah called Jonah and filled him in on what was going on. Josh passed their offices on his way back to the accounting department and gave them the thumbs up. It was a race between Mr. Heart and Bartowski to see how it would all end. Mr. Heart completed making the copies, headed back to his office as quickly as possible, and closed the door.

He placed the originals back into the briefcase precisely as they were, locked the combination locks by spinning the dials, and placed the coat on top just as Bartowski had left it. He put the paperwork in his office safe and sat behind the desk, waiting for Bartowski's return.

About twenty minutes later, Bartowski burst into his office. He smelled like the homeless men Mr. Heart had often passed on the street. He looked utterly disheveled.

"Max, are you okay?"

"No, Franklin, some crazy maniac..."

He looked at Mr. Heart and decided to avoid the humiliation of a companywide investigation.

"Eh... never mind... there was some sort of plumbing accident in the lavatory... I... I... gotta go."

He quickly grabbed his coat and put it on in Mr. Heart's office, buttoning it to the top, and left without another word.

Mr. Heart could barely keep himself from bursting out laughing.

As Bartowski passed Hannah and Jonah's office, they

could see the bewildered look on his face and how quickly he made it down the hall and out the door.

They all breathed a sigh of relief. Part one was successfully completed; the meeting at Jonah's house that night would be fun, but their job was not complete without part two.

What did the Motley Crew have in mind for part two?

18

WHEN THE DAY was over, and everyone had left, Jonah knocked on Mr. Heart's office door.

"Quite a day today," said Mr. Heart. "The look on Bartowski's face as he scurried out of here was priceless."

"Yes, it was, Mr. Heart, and I appreciate your getting involved."

"Noah Tyler and Smokey would be very proud of what you did today, Jonah; I only hope it was worth it, and we put these people away where they belong."

"So do I, Mr. Heart."

Mr. Heart opened his safe and handed the papers to Jonah.

"What do you plan on doing with this?"

"The first thing I will do before I leave the office tonight is make a second copy. I will then hand one copy to Fred Watkins, who, having worked for the government in the past as a forensic accountant, will spend some time dissecting every line for proof of where the funds for financing this act of treason are coming from. Eventually, after part two of our plan is hopefully completed, all the evidence will go to the FBI, where they have many more tools than we have, to get to the bottom of this."

"I hope you are successful, Jonah."

"I will make some copies and head downstairs to where Watkins is hiding to hand him a set. My copy will be left in the safe deposit box at my bank in the morning. Tonight, we are all meeting again at my place to assess where we're at and begin planning part two of the operation."

"Good luck, Jonah."

"Thank you, Mr. Heart."

After making the copies, Jonah left the office and headed to the kosher deli, where Watkins insisted on meeting him; he was waiting in front. They stepped inside, and Jonah slipped the paperwork into Watkins's backpack.

"Aren't you going to stay for a bite?" said Watkins.

"Wish I could, but I've got to shop for another round of food tonight. Were you expecting to eat here and then again at my place?"

Watkins gave Jonah a sheepish grin. Jonah remembered what Josh had told him about Watkins's appetite and what he had already witnessed on his own. Jonah looked at the man behind the counter.

"Pastrami on rye with fries to go for my friend here."

Watkins couldn't resist.

"Can you add some kishke with gravy?"

"You heard the man," said Jonah.

He could see the smile on Fred's face.

Jonah paid the man behind the counter.

"Thanks, Jonah."

"Take the food home, Fred, and put the papers in a safe place. Make sure you don't get any gravy on it."

They shared a quick smile.

"I'll see you later, Fred."

Without another word, Jonah left the store. He headed to the supermarket for another load of dogs, wings, beer, and… Oreos.

The same kid was working the checkout line as the last few times. He was all smiles this time.

"Hey man, how's it goin'? I guess your nephews are over again."

At first, Jonah did not remember the excuse he gave the guy the last time for why he kept buying the same junk food. He clearly remembered Jonah's tip and was trying to make conversation. Jonah lowered his voice and leaned over to him.

"Listen, I'm in a big rush, you know, with the nephews being over again."

"Sure man, I get it; lemee get you outta here asap."

He quickly rushed Jonah through as others looked on curiously. When he checked Jonah out, he whispered to him.

"Hey man, anything for the college fund?"

Jonah remembered the five-dollar tip he gave him last time and reached into his pocket. All he could fish out was a ten-dollar bill. He was about to check his pocket for something smaller when the kid grabbed the bill.

"That'll do."

Jonah was about to protest when he noticed all the eyes looking at him. Suddenly, a few of them started clapping their hands as more and more joined in.

"That's very generous of you," said the old-timer next on line. I would do the same, but I'm on a fixed income."

The kid came around the counter and gave Jonah a big bear hug.

"Thanks, man; you are one special dude."

Jonah felt embarrassed.

"Eh… sure, kid, don't spend it all at once."

"You take care of those nephews of yours," he yelled after Jonah as he got out of there as fast as he could.

"Yeah, I'll do that," Jonah murmured to himself.

I'm either a very generous guy or one big shmuck.

Ryan grabbed a cab and took it across the border to New Jersey. He checked into a small motel near the George Washington Bridge, paid cash at the desk, and headed up to his new home for what he planned on being only one night; he had to keep moving. He had visited an ATM once the coast was clear and withdrew as much cash as possible. The man at the desk at the motel did not ask him any questions as he signed a fictitious name on the register. The best he could come up with was "Sam Smith." This was not an uncommon occurrence at the Galaxy Deluxe Motel. While hiding out, he hoped he would have a chance to do some thinking.

He had spotted a pay phone at the corner and decided to take a chance and use it to make an important call. It was his friend George, with whom he had attended the police academy. They became partners and walked the beat together while on the force. Although Ryan didn't make it as a cop and eventually left to pursue the opportunity at Tyler Technologies, George did.

"George, it's me, Ryan."

"Ryan, how've you been, buddy? I haven't heard from you in a while?"

"Yeah, well, it's been a little hectic."

"What do you mean?"

"I'll explain later. George, I need a big favor."

There was some quiet on the line. George was familiar with the lifestyle Ryan lived.

After a few beats, George asked.

"What kind of favor? Are you in trouble, Ryan?"

"Nothing serious, George. Can you run some plates for me?"

"Ryan, you know I can get into big trouble running plates outside an investigation?"

"Yeah, I know, George, but I'm all jammed up and have no one else to ask."

"I thought you said it was nothing serious?"

"It's not, George; can you help me... please... for old times' sake?"

George was quiet for another few seconds.

"Gimmee the numbers."

"Thanks, George, I owe you one."

"Right; I'll add it to your tab."

Ryan repeated the plate numbers he memorized off Angelo's limo and the car the two misfits drove that snatched him off the streets and had just chased him through midtown.

"Got it," said George. "Hold on a second."

After a five-minute wait, George was back on the line.

"OK, take this down."

George gave Ryan the information he was looking for.

"Thanks, George, you're a lifesaver."

"Where have I heard that before?" said an irritated George.

"I owe you one, George; I really do."

"Ryan, I don't know what kind of mess you're in, but do me a favor and lose my number."

"George, I really mean it; I owe you-"

George had hung up before Ryan could finish his sentence.

I can't blame the guy, thought Ryan. *I've been nothing but a pain to him and everyone else. I can't blame anyone for how they feel about me; I deserve it.*

Jonah was sick of all the dogs, wings, and beer he had purchased in the last few weeks. The mere smell of them made his stomach turn. But there was a different smell when he approached the door this time. He gave Hannah his key so she could hang out in his apartment while he was shopping. When he opened the door, he was startled to find everyone crowded around the stove. He could hear Hannah's voice above everyone else's.

"Now, the oil has to get really hot before you slowly place the Oreos in the pot. The secret is to take them out after they look plump and place them in the oven for another two minutes to get them crispy."

Jonah looked startled.

"And what have we got here?" he said.

"I'm just showing the guys how to make the world's favorite delicacy," said Hannah.

Fred wandered over to Jonah munching on an Oreo.

"She's a keeper."

"Yeah, thanks, Fred."

"And that kishke today… to die for!"

"Great to hear, Fred."

As the guys helped themselves to the Oreos, Hannah walked over to Jonah.

"You know, these guys aren't half bad."

"I knew you'd come around."

"They kind of grow on you, don't they?"

"Like mold on a piece of stale bread."

"I'm starting to see why you like them so much; these guys will do anything for you, and I'm sure you would do anything for them. I think that's great, Jonah. Loyalty like that is hard to find these days."

Jonah was taken aback by what Hannah said.

Maybe she's finally coming around.

"Thanks, Hannah; that means a lot."

They smiled at each other as if they had reached a new plateau in their relationship.

They both joined the party as it continued in the other room. Everyone laughed as Josh regaled them with the story of what happened in the Men's Room to Bartkowski, and he didn't leave out a single detail.

"You should have seen it!" said Josh. "It was like an explosion in a gut factory."

Everyone was doubled over in laughter.

"And the smell…"

"I would have paid to see it," said Pete.

"I think Mr. Heart took special delight in watching him quickly run out of his office."

As everyone was laughing, all Jonah could do was watch Hannah as she laughed along. She was so beautiful when she smiled. At some point, Hannah noticed; she looked over at Jonah and melted his heart with the warmest smile. She walked over to him as everyone was busy listening to Josh tell every angle of the story.

"You did good, partner," she said to Jonah.

"We couldn't have done it without you."

"What will you do for an encore?"

"I'll think of something."

Jonah gave her one last smile and yelled out to the group.

"Alright, everybody, it was a great opening act, but if we don't finish part two, that's all it will be. Fred, have you had a chance to look at the reports in Bartowski's briefcase yet?"

Fred quickly tossed a wing he was holding onto a plate and stepped in front of it. He made fast work of swallowing what he had in his mouth and swiftly wiped the barbecue sauce off his face.

"Well, being that I am, as they say, temporarily financially embarrassed, I had a few hours to spend with them," said Fred.

"So, what have you come up with so far?" asked Jonah.

"What we are looking for out of Bartowski's briefcase is some kind of lead to determine who is financing the operation to ship the illegal weapons and explosives to the Soviets."

"Yes, we know that, Fred," said Pete, who was starting to look annoyed. "So, what have you found so far?"

"Like I said," said Fred, looking sharply at Pete.

"I have been looking for those unexplained revenue items we talked about earlier; money that they are getting in that has nothing to do with their regular sources of income."

"Right, Fred; we already know that. Have you found anything yet?" said Pete.

Fred gave Pete another sharp look. He was trying to make a big production out of his presentation, and Pete was killing his mojo.

He ignored Pete and continued.

"Actually, I *have* found a company named AP Industrials. Heavy deposits are going into their books as regular income. Still, I can't match them up with anything Tyler Tech produces. And I don't remember ever hearing that company's name in all my years at Tyler Tech."

"Me neither," said Josh. "How heavy are the deposits, Fred?"

"We're talking tens of thousands of dollars every month."

That got everybody's attention.

"That's a lot of money, Fred," said Josh. "We need to somehow connect that company with what the Tylers are doing overseas."

"Well, I'm on it," said Fred.

Meanwhile," said Jonah, looking at the guys from the Motley Crew, "what have you guys come up with for part two of our plan to prove that the cargo the Tyler partners are shipping to Ukraine is being diverted in Turkey to our enemies?"

"Well, as luck would have it," said Mack, "we *have* come up with a little plan."

"We're all ears," said Jonah.

"OK," said Mack, "here goes."

"Hannah, you told us that the night you were hiding in the Ladies' Room, you heard Irv tell Simeon that he only gave lists of shipments to Ryan, but nothing with details that would be incriminating, so when Jonah and Ryan switched briefcases that time a few weeks back, Irv wasn't nervous that crucial information would fall into the wrong hands; like where the shipments were really headed for after being removed in Izmir, or anything else that would reveal the plot."

"That's true," said Hannah. "I remember him saying that the real dirt was on floppies that he kept in his own briefcase, which never left his sight."

Mack continued.

"So, what we have to do is another switcheroo."

"Another what?" said Josh.

"We need to get Irv's briefcase from him, get past the locks, and copy all the information about their previous illegal shipments and the upcoming ones off those floppies, and voila!"

"Voila?" said Josh.

"Voila, as in, *there it is… there you are!*"

"I'm familiar with the word. How do you propose to get this done? Will we ask Irv if we can borrow his briefcase for about a half hour while we copy all his files and send him off to jail?"

"Not the plan we have in mind, but a good try," said Mack with a hint of sarcasm.

"OK, Mack," said Josh. "Let's hear it."

"Alright, guys, in preparing for this plan, we asked you about any regular habits or routines Irv has, and you told us that he has a standing lunch at the Bristol Bar and Grill uptown every Thursday afternoon at one o'clock. And we know that wherever he goes, so goes the briefcase."

"True," said Josh, in an inquisitive tone.

He was beginning to feel uncomfortable about being the resident skeptic, and Mack was starting to look annoyed.

"OK, so next Thursday, Jonah, you will give me your identical company-issued briefcase, the same as the one you and Ryan and everyone else at Tyler Tech use. And while Irv stands outside waiting for his limo driver, we do the switcheroo."

"I'm going to need a few more details here," said Jonah.

"Uh… me too," said Josh.

"If you insist."

"I do," said both Jonah and Josh at the same time.

Mack glanced at the two of them and continued.

"We create a little diversion in front of the building to distract Irv while we switch your briefcase for his, Jonah. Then we copy the files, give him back the briefcase, and… voila."

"OK, enough with the voila," said Jonah, looking nervous.

Josh was glad Jonah had taken over the skeptic role.

"What if he doesn't put his briefcase down while he waits for the car?"

"Got that covered too; leave it to us."

"OK, assuming that part goes well, and that's a large assumption, we're going to first need to get past the locks on the case. Marv, you said that would only take you a few minutes, given how long it took you to get into Bartowski's similar style case," said Jonah.

"Right."

Jonah couldn't help but be impressed with Marv's confidence.

Mack continued.

"You will then copy the floppies, which you say will probably take about another twenty minutes or so, based on the number of floppies Ryan had in his briefcase, and then do another switch of briefcases. How is that going to take place?"

"A great question," said Mack.

"I tend to ask those."

"You, my friend, are referring to switcheroo part two."

"Switcheroo part two?" asked Jonah, looking even more nervous.

Mack continued.

"So, Marv copies all the information we need from Irv's floppies as he heads uptown to the Bristol, and then we return the briefcase."

"Return the briefcase?"

"Well, you don't want him to keep *your* briefcase, do you?"

Everyone in the room looked at Mack.

"Yes, anyway, we do a second switch to return the briefcases to their rightful owners."

"And how is that accomplished?" said Jonah.

"We did a little snooping last Thursday. He takes his coat and briefcase and checks them in at the coatroom before being escorted to his table. So, all we need to do is switch the briefcases again… and-"

"If you use the word voila again, I'm going to chase you with a bat," said Jonah.

"OK, there are many moving parts to this plan, and a lot can go wrong," said Mack.

"You are all going to be involved in one way or another, and it will take some choreography on everyone's part, just like in plan number one. We have decided who will do what, so the crew and I will work with you individually for a few nights. Then we will do a dry run right here next Wednesday night."

"I suppose you'll be expecting the same menu?" said Jonah.

Fred's eyes lit up.

"Great!"

The guys in the Crew spent a little more time reviewing the individual details for each player, gave them some homework, and then called it a night. As they were about to leave, Jonah approached Hannah.

"Can I walk you home?"

"That sounds like a plan."

Jonah held the door open for Hannah, and they left together. When they got outside, it was noticeably chilly, and Hannah was underdressed for the walk. Jonah took his jacket off and threw it over Hannah's shoulder. They both couldn't stop smiling as they went down the block.

"I kind of miss this," said Hannah.

"Me too."

"And they say chivalry is dead."

"What do *they* know?"

As they made their way through the streets, they both realized how comfortable they had become with each other.

"Ya know," said Hannah, "a girl can get used to this."

"So can a guy."

Ryan picked up the pay phone again and dialed Mr. Heart's number. He knew Mr. Heart wouldn't recognize the number, but he knew he was out there, so he prayed he would pick it up. His prayers were answered.

"Mr. Heart, it's Ryan," said the determined voice on the other end of the line.

"Ryan, I've been worried sick about you; where are you?"

"In a place they won't find me."

"Can I help you somehow?"

"The only way to help me now is to save this company and put some bad people out of business for good."

Ryan could hear the determination in his own voice, and he knew Mr. Heart would notice it too; this was a different Ryan.

"OK, Ryan, what do you need me to do?"

"Do you have a pen and paper?"

"Yes."

"Write this down and give it to the people who need it."

Ryan then told Mr. Heart what he needed to tell him as Mr. Heart copied it all down.

"Where did you get this from?" asked Mr. Heart.

"That will have to stay a secret; this information cannot

fall into the wrong hands. If something happens to me, you will be the only one who will have it."

"Understood, Ryan. Is there anything else-"

Ryan had already hung up. He was relieved he could pass the information to Mr. Heart, someone he knew he could trust. But he could not take the chance of being on any phone longer than he had to. He was exhausted from running and hiding; it was time to get a few hours of needed rest before moving to another place at the crack of dawn. He set the alarm on his watch for 5:00 AM. As his head hit the pillow, there was a knock on the door… and he knew it was over.

They had found him.

19

OVER THE NEXT few days, the guys from the Crew met with everyone individually to go over their part in the highly choreographed plan. Everyone had to know what to do and when to do it. This would be a joint effort between the guys in the Crew and everyone else. Their final run-through would take place the next night. All their efforts to this point would lead to nowhere unless they could complete part two of their plan.

Jonah sat at his desk. He had a view of Irv pacing around his office, and he knew that Ryan's absence was of great concern to him. Knowing of Ryan's earlier visit to Mr. Heart and what he had told him about the mess he was in, he could only imagine his predicament. It seemed to him that both sides were hunting Ryan, Irv, and whoever was behind all the illegal shipments. The thought of Ryan trying to bug Irv's office unsuccessfully and being called on by Irv really unnerved Jonah. As much as he wasn't Ryan's biggest fan, he was starting to feel sorry for him.

He must feel like a hunted animal.

Just then, Mr. Heart called Jonah on his intercom.

"Jonah, please come in here."

Jonah walked into Mr. Heart's office. Mr. Heart sat him down, closed the door, and told him about the phone call from Ryan. He handed him the information Ryan had related to him from the payphone.

"I think you could use this," said Mr. Heart.

Jonah looked down at the sheet of paper. A small smile began to form at the edge of his lip.

"I sure can."

Jonah looked at Mr. Heart; there was something he felt he had to say.

"Mr. Heart, you must be wondering about the rest of our plan."

"I know you are trying to protect me should things fall apart, Jonah, and I appreciate that. You're trying to give me plausible deniability."

As always, Mr. Heart is spot on, thought Jonah.

"Yes, sir."

"I appreciate that, Jonah, but I can handle myself."

"Someone needs to be able to run this company should things fall apart," said Jonah.

"You're trying to protect me because you think I've gone through enough with what happened to Smokey."

"Something like that, Mr. Heart; please accept my decision."

"But what if something goes wrong, Ryan? You need someone to warn you if something doesn't look right on this end; I'd feel a whole lot better if that was me."

"I'll tell you what, Mr. Heart. If things hit the crapper,

call this number. The guy on the other end will know what to do. We'll call it crapper insurance."

Jonah scribbled a number on a scrap of paper he fished out of his pocket and handed it to Mr. Heart.

"Good luck, son."

"Jonah did a double take when he heard those words."

"Thank you, sir."

He quickly left Mr. Heart's office, called Fred Watkins from his office phone, and asked him to meet him at the Kosher Deli for lunch. That got Watkin's attention.

"I've got something for you to see," said Jonah.

"I'll be there," said Fred.

Fred was waiting in front when Jonah got to the deli; they quickly took a table in the back and ordered some sandwiches. Fred no longer needed help with the menu; he had mastered the art of ordering kosher deli and was proud of it. As soon as they were served, Jonah took out the information he had been passed on by Mr. Heart and gave it to Fred.

Fred read the information and looked at Jonah.

"Where did you get this?"

"It's a long story, Fred; I'll fill you in later."

Fred was so excited by what Jonah had handed him that he almost didn't touch his sandwich.

Ryan had definitely come through, thought Jonah.

"Waiter," yelled Fred.

The waiter immediately came over.

"I'll take the rest of this to go."

I sure got his attention, thought Jonah.

"And if you don't mind, can you pack some extra gravy for that kishke?"

The waiter and Jonah looked at Fred's plate; his kishke was already smothered in gravy.

"I got work to do," said Fred, who took off as soon as he received his order.

⁂

Jonah headed to the supermarket that evening to pick up more snacks for the Wednesday night run-through. As he approached the checkout counter at the supermarket, he spotted the same college kid again. This time, he was determined not to be taken. He dropped the hot dogs, wings, and beer on the counter and tried not to make eye contact. The cashier noticed him right away.

"Hey dude, looks like the nephews are back in town."

"Looks like," said Jonah, determined not to look in his direction.

The kid had his eyes trained on Jonah.

Jonah stared at his sneakers.

"Can you hurry it up, please? I'm really late."

The guy hadn't listened to a word Jonah said.

"Hey dude, you were so nice to me the last time you were here, man; I really appreciate it."

Jonah made sure not to make eye contact.

"That's fine."

Others on the line, including some familiar faces, began to look up as the kid raised his voice so others could hear. Pretty soon, they all began to look up. There was no way to avoid it; it was like driving past a traffic accident. The kid looked at the man behind Jonah on line. He was a Vietnam

War vet proudly wearing his POW cap and his tattooed bulging biceps were displayed proudly.

Not falling for it this time… no way, muttered Jonah to himself.

"Do you know what this fine gentleman did the last time he was in here?" the kid announced to everyone within listening distance.

Nope,… not going for it this time. Once a shmuck is once too many.

The kid pointed to Jonah as his voice got louder.

"This man, right here."

He pointed to Jonah for all to see.

"This man, this American hero, took out his wallet and planted a tensky right here in this palm to help me with my future education. Is this man a hero or what?"

The customers behind him on line began to cheer.

"Hey, that's very kind of you, mister." Jonah looked down and saw a little boy around ten years old holding his grandpa's hand. He was the POW.

"An American hero, I tell you.…"

Jonah began to murmur to himself. *Cut it out… cut it out… cut it out!*

"Did you really do that, sir?" asked the elderly woman standing behind Jonah, now starting to sweat visibly.

"Well… I…"

"He sure did, ma'am, as sure as I am standing here today," interrupted the cashier.

"A true American hero."

He spelled it out for everyone to hear.

"H.E.R.O… HEEERO!"

More and more shoppers were cheering and whistling. Jonah just wanted to get out of there. He reached for his wallet to pay.

"And now he is reaching into his wallet again to help a young man working ten hours a day to make ends meet and pay for a decent education."

His voice began to crack; Jonah couldn't tell if it was real or not. He kept murmuring to himself.

Don't let him do this.

Don't be a shmuck.

Don't be a shmuck.

Don't be a shmuck!

"Look at him, ladies and gentlemen, what pure generosity; I think I'm gonna cry."

His voice broke with emotion as the entire store was cheering now.

As Jonah opened his wallet to pay, the kid's big grimy hand reached in and pulled out another ten-dollar bill as Jonah desperately tried to grab it out of his hands.

"No… no… no…."

The kid waived the ten-dollar bill as real or fake tears flowed from his eyes.

"Hey!"

It was too late. Jonah could not be heard above the cheers and whistles.

"Hee…ro, hee…ro… hee…ro!" everybody was chanting aloud.

Jonah had steam coming out of his ears.

Shmuck, shmuck… big stupid shmuck!

He grabbed his bag and waived back to the adoring crowd

serenading him with whistles and cheers as he walked out the door. As he looked back, his eyes met the cashier's eyes. The kid was grinning from ear to ear. Jonah still couldn't figure out if he was for real. But one thing he did know. He would no longer be shopping at this supermarket; he would have to find a place a little further from home. This one was too expensive.

An hour later, the apartment was beginning to fill up. This would be the final run-through before part two of their plan, which would take place tomorrow. The gang was all back. Jonah marveled at how much junk food they could all consume. Hannah was eating a bag of chips while everyone else ate the same exact food as the previous night as if they had never eaten it before.

"No fried Oreos?" asked Jonah.

"Do you think I want to burn a hole through my stomach? Who eats this stuff every night?"

Jonah looked at Hannah and smiled.

"OK, everybody, let's all pipe down," said Jonah. "Tomorrow is the big day; all our work until now will be a waste if we can't execute part two of the plan and give the FBI enough info to move on these people before they figure out where it came from. Pete, why don't you start us off."

Pete put down his food.

"OK, guys, we've worked with each of you separately on the plan that will allow us to get the information we need out of Irv Carter's briefcase. If you follow it to the letter, with some help from the three of us, you can expect to see these fine folks carted off to prison real soon."

For the next hour and a half, the three guys from the Crew ran through the scenario with all the players. If they noticed a mistake, they ran through it again. By the night's end, they were confident they could execute the plan.

"OK, everybody," said Jonah. "Go home and get some rest; this all goes down starting lunchtime tomorrow."

They all filed out of the apartment. To Jonah's astonishment, there was a mountain of chicken bones left over; everything edible had been consumed.

"How are you feeling?" said Hannah to Jonah; they were the only two remaining.

"Like the day I first saw you on the other end of the room at that singles mixer; lots of nerves mixed with a helping of confidence."

Hannah smiled.

"Why so confident? You know things can go wrong; there are many moving parts."

"That's true, but I've been thinking of Smokey a lot lately. I think he'll keep a good eye out for us."

"You never cease to amaze me, Jonah Mark."

"It's a gift; what can I say?"

Jonah faked some swagger, but Hannah knew how nervous he was.

"I better go," said Hannah. "I promised my mom that piece of salmon I put in your fridge."

Jonah walked Hannah downstairs, and they waited for her cab together.

"See you tomorrow," said Jonah as Hannah climbed into the cab.

"Count on it," said Hannah as the cab drove off.

Jonah watched the cab wind its way up the block until it was out of view.

I think I may just marry that girl!

❧

Jonah tossed and turned all night; it was impossible to sleep. There was so much on his mind. The plan the Crew guys had come up with was brilliant but daring. If it worked, the bad guys would be looking at lengthy prison sentences, and he and the others would never be suspected. If something went wrong… he didn't even want to think about it.

Nothing can go wrong; it's as simple as that. This needs to work for the sake of all of us, including Smokey, who can no longer speak for himself.

❧

Everyone was in the office bright and early the following day. The guys from the crew were getting ready and would be in position when it was time to execute the plan. Jonah, Josh, and Hannah were all nervously sitting at their desks and looking at their clocks.

At 11:55 AM, Jonah and Hannah saw Irv walking down the hallway briefcase in hand. Hannah quickly called Josh, while Jonah called Pete.

"It's a go," they each said and hung up.

They all headed to the vestibule, joining the other employees heading out to lunch. Irv was busy reading his newspaper when the first elevator arrived. Hannah took the same elevator as Irv and struck up a conversation with a coworker to keep Irv from starting one with her. Irv just stared at his newspaper, not bothering to look up.

As soon as the elevator door closed behind them on the tenth floor, Josh and Jonah discreetly headed for the stairwell and ran down the ten flights of stairs. They knew they would have a head start, as the lunchtime elevator would stop on practically every floor to pick up additional workers heading down to lunch. As soon as they got downstairs, they peeked into the main lobby to ensure the coast was clear. They spotted Pete and knew the other Crew guys were nearby and at their positions.

The elevator ping could be heard as it arrived in the main lobby, and its doors opened. Irv folded up his newspaper and headed outside to look for his driver. Hannah headed straight down the block to where Josh was waiting with a cab ready to go. They hopped into the cab and headed uptown to the Bristol while reviewing their carefully choreographed plan for Irv's arrival.

The street was teeming with people. Jonah stood off to the side with his briefcase slung over his shoulder, making sure not to face Irv as he exited the building. Marv was waiting at his position a few feet away from Jonah. Irv, briefcase in hand, saw his car pull up and the driver hopping out to open the back door for him. He started heading toward the car….

"Excuse me, sir."

Irv was startled by the mention of his name. He looked up to see a beautiful blond woman dressed to the nines in a fancy dress and trendy sunglasses that had pulled up next to him, seemingly out of nowhere.

"I hate to trouble you; you seem like a very busy man."

Irv was pleasantly intrigued and signaled his driver to wait as he stepped back toward the building.

"No trouble at all, sweetheart." Irv managed his most dashing smile.

"How can I help you?"

As Irv addressed the young lady, Jonah had positioned himself behind him, leaning against the wall and hiding behind a newspaper. He placed his briefcase on the ground between himself and Irv, whose eyes and attention were elsewhere, and slowly moved it into position with his right foot.

Come on, Irv, thought Jonah to himself, just *place your briefcase on the ground, and this will be over in no time.*

"Well, it's a little embarrassing."

"What is, sweetheart?"

The young lady looked shy yet sophisticated and spoke in a southern drawl. Her looks and demeanor intoxicated Irv as he was with every pretty woman. Pete had practiced every word and movement with his girlfriend Jill for the last three nights until she had it down perfectly. A tear began to make its way down her face, courtesy of a small amount of peppermint oil applied beneath her eye to create a watering effect, an actor's trick used to create fake tears that Pete had used before.

"I'm… sorry, would you happen to have a tissue? This is so embarrassing."

And then it happened, just as expected. Irv placed his briefcase on the ground as he searched his pocket for a tissue to help the distressed young lady. As soon as his case hit the ground, Jonah slid it away with his foot and slid his own briefcase in its place. Irv didn't notice a thing.

"Here you are, young lady." Irv handed her a clean tissue from a packet he had in his pocket.

By the time he handed her the tissue, Jonah had passed the case off to Pete, who took it and ran down the block to a nearby coffee shop where Marv was waiting in front. The owner was a good friend of his brother Mike. He agreed to look the other way for a small fee arranged in advance. At the same time, Marv used the back of the store to pick the locks on the briefcase and then used his computer to copy the disks onto a fresh set of floppies he had with him in his pocket.

Marv nodded to the owner as he walked into the store and headed to a door next to the men's room marked "Employees Only." He immediately began working on the briefcase locks. The case posed no challenge to an experienced lock picker like himself, and he was able to pop the locks quickly. The disks were in the same compartment under the snap where Jonah found Ryan's disks.

Pete waited nervously outside as Marv pecked away at the keyboard, copying Irv's disks as quickly as possible. As soon as he was done, the plan was to get the briefcase to Jonah, who would grab a cab and head to the Bristol and execute the plan to switch back the two briefcases before Irv would notice anything was awry. Jonah stood hidden behind Irv, listening in case of any hiccups.

"I'm from Alabama, and this is my first time in New York City. I was supposed to meet my brother, Max, he's from around here, in front of the public library. He said if I look out the taxi window, I will see two big lions right out front. He would be waiting in front of the one on the right. But, for some reason, the taxi driver dropped me off here. I don't know where I am or what to do; it's all so upsetting."

Jill's job was to keep Irv engaged for as long as possible, to delay him before he took his car across town to the Bristol, so the guys had enough time for Marv to get into the briefcase and copy the disks. But, as Jonah listened on, he heard the plan they had so carefully put together go completely off the rails.

"There, there, young lady; there is nothing to cry about. As a matter of fact, I have a great idea. I will skip my lunch and take you personally to the library; it's only a few blocks away. My driver will have us there in no time."

No, no, no, thought Jonah, *don't get into that car!*

Jonah thought to himself, *I should have figured Irv wouldn't let a beautiful young woman slip out of his hands so easily.*

He saw the expression on Jill's face; it was a look of confusion, desperation, and fear. It was not in the script Pete had practiced with her. She knew that Josh and Hannah were already on their way to the Bristol to carry out the rest of the plan once the guys were done with Irv's briefcase and passed it back to Jonah, who would then quickly head uptown with it. All she had to do was delay Irv as much as possible to give Jonah a head start to the Bristol. Instead, she was out of her league with Irv, a lecherous guy about to take her in the opposite direction to the New York Public Library. Who knew what he had in mind once he had her alone? As to the library, the lions would be there, but not her fictional brother Max. Even worse, he was now carrying Jonah's briefcase.

Jonah saw Jill desperately try to get out of Irv's clutches

as smoothly as possible, but she obviously didn't know what she was dealing with; he was like a dog on a bone.

"Please, you have been so kind already; I wouldn't want you to miss your lunch. Just point me in the right direction. If it's just a few blocks away, I am sure I'll find it."

"Nonsense, I have a driver who will get us there in no time."

Irv waved to his driver, who pulled the car up in front of him. To Jonah's horror, the driver leaped out and opened the back door before she could say anything.

Don't get in Jill, don't get in Jill, don't... get... in... Jill... damn it!

"After you," Jonah heard Irv say as they disappeared into the car's back seat. Jonah watched them head off in the opposite direction toward the New York Public Library with *his* briefcase. Jill looked back through the window with a desperate look, but she was no match for Irv.

As soon as the car had left, Pete came running up to Jonah with the case.

"All done!"

"I'd say," said Jonah.

He quickly told Pete what had just transpired; Pete did not look happy.

"What do we do now?" asked Jonah.

"Stay here for a second."

He ran back to the coffee shop and caught Marv as he was leaving.

"We have a problem."

Pete told Marv to grab Mack, head to the library steps, and sit there like they were enjoying their lunch break. Irv would not recognize them, and they could keep an eye on things up close.

"On it," said Marv.

Pete ran back to Jonah, who was frantic.

"What do we do now?" asked Jonah.

"We head to the library while I figure this out."

Jonah suddenly thought of something.

"Hold it! I've got to do something first; grab a cab; I'll be right there," said Jonah.

"You've gotta do what?"

Before Pete could respond, Jonah ran back into the building.

Pete ran to the phone at the corner and looked up the Bristol on the Manhattan phone book chained to the shelf beneath the phone. He looked up the number for the Bristol and dialed it. The receptionist answered on the first ring. Pete could hear the busy lunchtime crowd in the background.

"Bristol, how can I help you?"

"Hi, I'm looking for a young couple seated in the reception area; I will be late and wanted to-"

"Hold one moment, please."

"Maam, I jus-"

It was too late; Pete was suddenly listening to music on hold as Jonah pulled beside him. Pete quickly explained what he was doing and told Jonah to hail a cab meanwhile to save time. The woman finally came back on the line.

"Bristol, how can I help you?"

There was so much noise in the background that he could hardly hear her.

"Yes, I just called, and you put me on hold... I am looking-"

"Hold one moment, please."

He was listening to music on hold again. An electronic voice came on the line.

"Please deposit another ten cents for five more minutes."

Pete quickly searched his pocket and found a dime, which he dutifully deposited into the coin slot. He waited another minute before the woman came back on the line.

"Bristol, how can I help you?"

"Maam, you put me on hold twice. I need to speak to someone who is waiting in reception... now!"

"There's no need to be rude, sir; we are swamped here at this hour."

It was time for some charm from Pete.

"Listen, you sound like a very nice lady, and I can imagine you must be busy at this time of day, but this is an emergency; please don't hand up; I only have one more dime."

There was a quiet pause.

"Who are you looking for, sir."

"A young man and woman are probably sitting in the reception area; they will answer to the names Josh or Hannah. Can you please ask one of them to pick up the courtesy phone?"

"Hold one moment, please."

There was another minute of music on hold before Josh came on.

"Hello?"

"Josh, it's Pete."

"Pete, why are you calling me?"

"No time to explain… I-"

"Please deposit another ten cents."

Pete cursed under his breath as he went fishing through his pocket for his last dime, which he quickly deposited.

"Pete, what the hell is going on?"

"I need you both to grab a cab and head back downtown to the New York Public Library."

"The library? Pete, what are you talking about? We are supposed to…."

Pete was exhausted and was through explaining things.

"No questions; wait for us at the phone booth on the corner near the lion on the right side."

"The lion on the right side; what the hell are you talking about?"

"I said no questions!"

Pete had already hung up and ran over to Jonah, who had just hailed a cab.

He yelled at the cabbie.

"The library; if you do it really fast, I'll double the tip."

That's all he had to hear.

"You got it, bud."

They both entered the cab, which took off with a loud screech before Jonah could close the door. They both fell against the seats as the cabbie took off.

"What was that?" asked Jonah.

"I told Josh and Hannah to meet us. And why did you run into the building?"

"Crapper insurance."

"What insurance?"

"Pete, let's just concentrate on surviving this day. When I write a book about all of this in the unlikely event we survive this mess, you'll find it in one of the chapters."

Pete shot Jonah a sideways glance, but there was no time to talk. The cabbie was doing his best impersonation of a driver at the Indie 500… during lunch hour in New York City. They were each gripping their seats and saying their prayers.

✧

Mr. Heart's office phone buzzed; it was the receptionist.

"Mr. Heart, I have Paul Deluca on the phone for you."

It was Marco.

"Put it through, Evelyn."

Mr. Heart quickly closed his door and hustled back to his desk to pick up the phone.

"Marco, what's up?"

The voice on the other end spoke nervously and quickly.

"Mr. Heart, I just overheard a phone conversation between Carlos and Angelo. He told Angelo about your assistant Jonah Mark hanging out outside the partner's office and trying to listen in on their conversation when they were meeting. He also told him about discovering that Jonah hid in the office one night while they were having a late-night partners meeting and about catching him listening in from the empty office next door when he met with Carlos and me."

Mr. Heart was astounded by what he had heard about Jonah and remembered what he had told him about his background—the spy stuff.

"I could hear the boss yelling on the other end of the line. Trust me when I tell you, he is as paranoid as it gets."

"What did you hear him say, Marco?"

"It was pretty loud, Mr. Heart, so I know I got it right."

"What was it?"

"He said he was gonna find out exactly what that little Jew bastard knows, and then when he was done with him, he'd dispose of him like the others."

Mr. Heart felt the hairs on the back of his neck rise as Marco continued.

What others is he talking about?

"Then I heard him yell through the phone at whoever was with him: *you just get him to me; I don't care if you have to drag him through the streets; no damned kid is gonna mess this up for me; you got that? I want that kid dead, as in floating in the East River… understood? You get him over to me as fast as you can, and no mistakes. He can stick his crooked nose elsewhere!*"

Mr. Heart felt a shudder go through his body. Angelo was a ruthless killer who would take a life if someone looked the wrong way at him.

"And one more thing," said Marco.

"What's that?"

"They killed Ryan."

Mr. Heart gave out an audible gasp.

"Are you sure, Marco?"

"I heard Carlos talking about it on the phone. They tracked him down in some motel in New Jersey."

"OK, Marco, thanks for the info. I'll get back to you soon; give me the number you are calling from, and stay by the phone."

Marco gave him the information, and Mr. Heart hung up the phone; his hands shook. The news took the wind out of him, but there was no time to dwell on it. He quickly grabbed the piece of paper with the phone number Jonah had scribbled down for him, his crapper insurance. Jonah was in clear danger, and there was no way he would let anything happen to him, Hannah, or the others. Mr. Heart dialed the number.

"Hank speaking," said the voice on the other end of the line.

Mr. Heart was startled to hear the voice of Hank, the building security guard, on the other end of the line answering from his phone station in the lobby.

"Hank, is that you? This is Franklin Heart?"

"The one and only. Mr. Heart, how're you doin' today, sir? Do you need a car? I can have one for you in five minutes."

"Hank, this is very important. Did a young man from my office give you a message for me?"

"Oh, yes, sir, that nice young man Jonah did; I almost forgot. I wrote it down. Lemee see here."

Mr. Heart could hear Hank rustling through some papers. He was doing a silent prayer that Hank didn't throw the message away.

"Oh, here it is. It says: *We went to the library*. That's mighty nice of you giving library time to your employees, Mr. Heart. I sure wish the management of this building could do that for us. You know, my sister used to read a lot of books-"

Mr. Heart cut him off.

"The library? Why would he… never mind; Frank, did he say which library?"

"No, sir; I would have remembered that. But he did say something about the right lion. I'm not sure what he meant by that, but he was so rushed I didn't get a chance to ask him."

There was only one major library in the area, with two lions in front of it.

"Thank you, Hank."

"My pleasure, Mr. Heart… as I was sayin', my sister-"

He had hung up before Hank could say anything further. He quickly dialed Marco back; he answered on the first ring. Mr. Heart told him where Jonah was and that he better grab some guys and head over to the New York Public Library before Carlos and his men got to them first.

"On my way," said Marco.

"Marco."

"Yes, Mr. Heart."

"These guys are killers. I won't… I can't… lose any more."

"I understand, Mr. Heart."

They spotted Irv's car a block ahead. Jonah was amazed at what a New York Cabbie could do with a cash incentive; it felt like they had just been on a roller coaster ride. He was glad he skipped lunch, or they may have been looking at it in front of them.

"Pull over right here," said Pete.

They were two blocks from the library. They would walk the rest of the way to the phone booth at the corner, where Pete told Josh and Hannah to meet them and wait for their cab.

"Thanks a lot, bud; you did a great job."

"Yeah, well, let's see the tip, and I'll be the judge."

Pete started counting out some cash from his pocket as Jonah watched. He suddenly stopped and looked up at Jonah.

"You wanna get involved in this?"

"Oh, sorry!"

Jonah quickly started fishing through his wallet; he felt embarrassed that Pete was paying for what was Jonah's problem.

"My brains were elsewhere, Pete; you shouldn't be paying for any of this."

The cabbie looked back at them.

"The clock is ticking, gentlemen."

They both dumped a wad of cash in the man's lap. The cabbie counted the money, and a smile returned to his face.

"You fellas are men of your word; how about a return trip?"

"I've got a better idea," said Pete.

"What's that?"

"No driving involved. I'll…."

He looked at Jonah.

"He'll give you two hundred dollars for whatever we need from you for the next hour; interested?"

"I'm all yours fellas."

Jonah looked sharply at Pete; he wasn't so excited.

"OK, I want you to find a spot as close to the library as possible and sit tight; I'll get back to you."

"You know, there isn't much in the way of parking spaces on Fifth Avenue this time of day."

"Double park; tell any cop that stops you that you're waiting on a fare, do a waltz; I don't care. Improvise; he'll pay for any ticket you get."

Jonah looked over at Pete, who looked back at him.

"Hey, it's your rodeo!"

Jonah had no comeback.

"Sounds like a plan," said the cabbie; "I'm all yours."

"What's your name?" asked Pete.

"Fred."

"OK, Fred; keep your eyes open."

Pete and Jonah both left the cab. They watched the cabbie slowly pull away and look for a spot.

Pete told Jonah to scribble down the ID number of the cab since every New York City cab was yellow, and the last thing they wanted to do was lose him in a yellow cloud. They headed to the phone booth and waited for Josh and Jonah to appear.

OK, let's keep an eye on Irv's car and see where he goes," said Pete. "And let's try not to lose sight of our cab."

They started scanning the area around them but didn't notice anything unusual about the blue Honda parked between two cars a half block away. They spotted Jill and Irv leaving the car and heading toward the big lion on the right side of the long flight of stairs heading to the library entrance.

"What do we do now?" asked Jonah.

"We wait."

"For what?"

"For Jill's next move. We know she doesn't have a brother coming, and she's probably panic-stricken from being trapped with Irv; we'll have to play this one by ear. I'm guessing she will probably try to lose him as quickly as possible.

"How's she going to do that?"

"Knowing Jill, she'll probably say she needs to use the Ladies' Room in the library."

"How do you know that?"

"Because that's what she does to shake off a bad date, and this is one bad date!"

"Are you serious?"

"That's what she told me she used to do before she met me."

Suddenly, they noticed Jill heading up the stairs to the library while Irv stood there looking at his watch.

"What a creep!"

"You got that right," said Jonah.

"Do you notice something?" said Pete.

"What?"

"He doesn't have his briefcase."

"Son of a gun; you're right."

"He doesn't have to carry it with him because it's his car."

Just then, a cab pulled up and deposited Josh and Hannah, who both ran to the phone booth.

"OK, guys, what's going on?" said Josh.

Jonah filled them in on why they were suddenly at a phone booth in front of the library instead of at the Bristol executing their well-practiced plan. Josh and Hannah looked stunned, but there was no time for questions.

"We don't have much time," added Jonah. "Jill is probably hiding out in the Ladies' Room, and who knows what Irv might do next; we need to act fast," said Jonah.

"Thank you," said Pete, looking annoyed. "That's *my girl-friend* up there."

"Point taken," said Jonah, feeling a little embarrassed.

"We don't have time for anything elaborate," said Pete, "so we're going to go with something simple. We have no idea if we are being watched, so stay focused."

After dropping off his two passengers, Irv's driver parked his car across the street from the library; it was a black Chevy Tahoe with darkened windows, so someone would have to get close enough to the car to see the briefcase and would probably have to sneak in to make the switch. Pete then went over the plan he had just put together. They all listened carefully.

"Does everyone understand exactly what to do?"

Jonah, Josh, and Hannah answered yes; it was time to do a revised version of switcheroo number two.

"The cabbie is on the next block in front of the diner," said Pete.

Josh headed down the block to the cab, careful to stay out of Irv's line of sight, although his eyes were trained on the library. He filled Fred in on what they wanted him to do. He was out of his cab and on his way.

Hannah crossed the street and discreetly walked toward Irv's car.

⚘

"Hey Buddy," said Fred to Irv's driver, Mike. He was startled by the cabbie who had snuck up to his driver's side window, the side that could not be seen from the library. You scratched my cab."

344

"What are you talking about?"

"You sideswiped my cab back there when you pulled onto the block."

"I did no such thing!"

"You did no-such-thing? Who are you, Shakespeare?"

"I beg your pardon!"

"You beg my pardon; what the hell is that, more Shakespeare? Who's going to pay for my cab?"

"You are clearly mistaken, sir; I did no such thing!"

"Again, with the no-such-thing, I'll tell you what. How about you get your skinny little… derriere out of that monstrously oversized hunk of metal you're drivin' and follow me to my cab that's now up the block to survey the damage."

"As I said, I will do no such thing!"

"Or, you might opt for choice number two."

"What's that?"

"A nice New York-style knuckle sandwich on that pretty little mug of yours right there, and then we do the survey. Your choice, Buddy."

Before Mike could say anything further, Fred opened the door and invited Mike out of the car with a wave of his hand.

"This way, monsieur. Did I pronounce that right?"

Mike stepped out and was about to lock the door when Fred said:

"Let's go, buddy, no more wasting time. Us cabbies get paid by the minute."

The two of them headed up the block. Hannah had been standing under the awning of a store watching it all. As soon as they were far enough away, Hannah snuck up to the car door and opened it.

She immediately spotted the briefcase sitting on the seat on the back passenger side, the side that could be seen from the library if Irv looked across the street. She had been hiding her face behind a newspaper while waiting for Fred to do his thing.

Hannah quickly opened the driver-side back door, scooted across the seat, grabbed Jonah's briefcase, and placed Irv's briefcase in the same position. She then exited again on the driver's side.

Mike and Fred arrived at the cab. There was a ticket on the windshield for parking in a No Parking Zone, but Fred knew that was on Jonah's tab, so he wasn't concerned. He knew he had to move the cab ASAP before the cops called for a tow. He just had to lose Mike.

"OK, where is the damage, sir? This cab looks fine to me."

Fred had to think fast.

"Eh, what damage?"

"What damage? The damage you accused me of doing to your car."

"Not sure what you're talking about, mister. You must have me mixed up with some other guy."

"Some other guy? What other guy? You accused me of sideswiping your car."

Fred gave him a sheepish smile.

"Sorry, mister; gotta go."

"Gotta go; what the hell is wrong with you?"

Fred needed to come up with something.

"Eh, will there be anything else?"

"Anything else? Are you out of your… forget it."

Looking exasperated, Mike decided he was better off leaving this lunatic while he could and made his way back down the block.

Fred quickly got into his car and moved down the block to find another spot so he wouldn't be towed away.

Meanwhile, Hannah hailed a cab back to the office. She discreetly dropped Jonah's briefcase on his desk when she got upstairs.

❧

Being the only one Irv would not recognize, Pete crossed the street and headed down the block, scanning the street for Fred's cab, which he finally spotted double parked next to an unoccupied Lincoln Town Car.

"How'd it go?" asked Pete.

"Like a charm!"

He handed Fred the two hundred dollars he had taken from Jonah a few minutes earlier.

"Not so fast; there's the small matter of this forty-five-dollar ticket for parking in a No Standing Zone in Midtown."

Pete reached into his pocket and came up with the rest of the money.

Jonah better pay me back.

"Pleasure doing business with you," muttered Pete as he handed Fred the cash.

"Hey, the pleasure was all mine."

Fred drove off as Pete walked back down the block to Josh and Jonah.

"Job well done!" said Pete.

The guys high-fived each other, oblivious to the men watching them from the Honda across the street.

Pete looked up and saw Irv still standing by the lion.

"I can't believe he's still there."

"Believe it," said Jonah. "The guy's a pathetic loser, and I hope all of this work we've done will put him and the rest of them behind bars for a long time."

"Sounds like a plan," said Josh. "I just hope we have enough of the goods on them to put them away."

He also saw Mack sitting on the steps close enough to Irv to observe what was happening.

"Hang on, guys," said Pete.

He ran up the stairs to talk to Mack.

After a few minutes of conversation, he was back.

"OK, guys," said Pete; "it looks like Jill probably left the library through another exit; I'm going to try and track her down."

"Where's Marv?" said Josh.

"Double parked across the street in the grey Ford playing double park waltz with the traffic cops."

Jonah looked at Pete.

"Pete, I don't know how to thank you and the other guys for what you did."

"Me too," said Josh.

"I'll think of something, and by the way, Jonah, you owe me another forty-five dollars."

"What? Why?"

"Later," said Pete, as he started to walk away.

Jonah looked at Josh.

"It's just you and me again, buddy."

"Nothing ever changes. We should probably return to the office separately, just in case."

They both looked up at Irv, who was still standing there looking at his watch.

"What a loser!" said Jonah. "I'd love to confront that guy and give him a piece of my mind."

Josh quickly looked at Jonah. He had heard that tone from him before. It was Spy Novel Jonah talking.

"But of course, you *won't* do that, Jonah, because that's what they do in spy novels, not in real life where something like that would be frowned upon, not to mention getting a few people killed."

Jonah was feeling cocky; they had just pulled off two capers that some of his greatest spy novel heroes would be proud of.

"Relax; I'm just going to have some fun."

"Jonah… no!"

But it was too late; Jonah was already on his way up the stairs heading to the lion.

Josh took off down the block to catch Pete.

"Looking for something?" said a cocky Jonah to a startled Irv.

Irv spun around.

"What are *you* doing here, Jonah?"

"It's such a beautiful day; I thought I'd spend my lunch hour sitting on the library steps. The question is, what are *you* doing here?"

"None of your damned business," said Irv, who was irritated enough at that point waiting for Jill, who seemed to be taking a very long time in the Ladies' Room.

"Now, why don't you go eat your damned lunch elsewhere."

"Guarding the lion, are you?"

"What the hell is that supposed to mean?"

"Just asking."

Irv was in no mood to deal with Jonah; he was irritated enough with all the time he had just wasted and apparently being stood up.

"Listen, kid; I suggest you find an exit before I make life miserable for you and your girlfriend, Hannah."

The sound of Hannah's name coming out of Irv's mouth made him sick, but he was on a roll. Like a locomotive careening down the track, there was no stopping him.

"Hey," said a cocky Jonah, making a show of ignoring the last remark. "Guess what I just saw?"

"What?" said Irv, his curiosity piqued.

At this point, Josh had caught up with Pete, and Mack had approached them. They were in earshot, hiding a few feet below the lion.

"Are you hearing this?" said Mack.

"I'm gonna kill him," said Pete.

"Unless I get to him first," said Josh.

Irv's blood was boiling, but Jonah's locomotive only picked up speed.

"I saw this pretty young lady, maybe half your age, walking up these very steps with someone who looked just like you. And I thought to myself, that guy looks just like Mr. Carter from the office; I wonder if Mrs. Carter might be interested in hearing about how he spends his lunch hour."

"You miserable little…"

As Irv was about to lunge at Jonah, he suddenly stopped short as something behind Jonah caught his eye.

Jonah felt something hard and cold against his back.

"Don't turn around," said the voice behind him.

Jonah froze. The guy looked up at Irv.

"And you beat it."

Irv was panic-stricken. He didn't recognize the two guys but wasn't waiting for a second invitation; he high-tailed it out of there. Whether Jonah was being mugged or he owed these guys money was not his concern.

"OK, let's take a little trip down the steps. Any funny moves, and you'll be eatin' about five pounds of lead."

Jonah was speechless. A car pulled up to the curb. They tied his hands up behind him and dumped him into the back seat as the car screeched away into midtown traffic.

Jonah noticed the front passenger right away.

"It's you," said Jonah. "You're Carlos."

"Pleasure to make your acquaintance, kid, but this isn't a social call. You're a real smart ass; too bad where you're goin' your mouth won't help you."

Jonah was suddenly silent… and panicked.

Irv ran across the street and yelled at his driver, who was asleep at the wheel.

"Mike, take the long way back to the office; I just want to ensure no one is watching me."

"What about the young lady?"

"She'll find her way home."

"Yes, sir, Mr. Carter."

The three guys below the lion were startled by the sudden turn of events; they were franticly looking for Marv's double-parked car.

"There it is," yelled Mack.

"OK, Josh, I want you to call Mr. Heart from that phone booth at the corner and tell him everything that just happened and make it quick," said Pete.

A minute later, Josh gave a stunned Mr. Heart the details; there was no time to waste.

&

"…it looked like a blue Honda Accord, late model… please, Mr. Heart, hurry!"

After getting over the initial shock, Mr. Heart quickly called Marco on his car phone and related what happened.

"We saw it all from across the street, Mr. Heart, and we've got the car in our sights."

"Marco, please don't let anything happen to him; I couldn't live with myself if I lose Jonah too."

"I'll keep you informed," said Marco as he hung up the phone.

Mr. Heart was frantic. He had already lost his best friend in the world, Smokey, and was still digesting the news about Ryan. He opened the bottom drawer of his desk and pulled out some scotch. He wasn't much of a drinker but needed something to calm his nerves.

&

"OK, guys, we're looking for a late model Blue Honda," said Pete, as they were playing catch up through midtown traffic.

"Anything else of note?" asked Marv.

"Yeah, they've got Jonah in the back seat."

"Right!"

Pete took control of the situation.

"It's the usual heavy midtown traffic at this hour, and luckily, there's a lot of construction slowing things up even more, so they can't be that far ahead of us. Marv, start weaving through the lanes; we've gotta play some catch-up."

"On it," said Marv.

Pete hoped that Mr. Heart had alerted the feds and they were not the only ones on this chase.

⁂

Hannah sat in her office; something was not right. Jonah should have been back by now, and so should Josh. She decided she had no choice and knocked on Mr. Heart's door. One look at Mr. Heart drinking scotch confirmed her suspicions.

"Mr. Heart, I know something's wrong; where is Jonah?"

Mr. Heart did not try to hide it; he was as worried as she was.

"I'm sorry, Hannah, they've kidnapped Jonah."

"They did what?"

"Someone pulled a gun, and they threw him in the back of a car, and they're headed down Fifth Avenue."

"Oh no, this can't be happening; is anyone following them?"

"I heard from Josh about what happened and immediately informed some security people in the area; they are hot on their trail."

Mr. Heart's phone suddenly rang; he quickly picked it up. It was Marco from his car phone.

He put him on his speakerphone.

"Marco, what's going on? I have Jonah's girlfriend Hannah with me."

Hannah was startled to hear his name and surprised to hear Mr. Heart call her Jonah's girlfriend. But that was for a different time.

"We have the car in our sites," Mr. Heart. "It's a slow-speed chase; they are stuck in a mess of construction and traffic. We're about a block behind them."

"Please, Marco, don't let them out of your sight," Hannah yelled.

"Don't worry, Hannah; they won't get away. Listen, I need to keep this line open in case we need it."

"Keep us posted, Marco, please!"

"I will."

Mr. Heart hung up the phone.

Hannah was frozen in fear at the other side of Mr. Heart's desk. Tears started streaming down her face.

This can't be happening. I love Jonah; I always have, and I always will.

Mr. Heart handed her a handkerchief from his pocket. They were both too distraught to talk.

Jonah sat behind two large individuals who were not much for conversation. The nervous guy in the front passenger seat was Carlos, whom he had seen in the office a few times, meeting with the Tyler partners. He never noticed the tattoos that covered a good part of his neck, probably because they had been covered by his shirt collar when he was among the partners. The driver with the big cleaver hands and scar on his face he referred to as Frank in his conversations with him. They were frantically trying to make it through traffic but were going no faster than about fifteen miles an hour and stopping for traffic lights at each corner.

Although his hands were tied behind his back, Jonah had tried the doors earlier by discreetly leaning his back near each door and trying to work the locks; they must have fiddled with them, and the doors could not be opened from the inside.

I need to figure a way out of here while we're still in traffic. Once the roads clear up, they will take off, and I won't be able to do anything.

He started to think about all the spy books he read; maybe he could come up with an idea from one of them. He thought back to a spy handbook he once read when he was a kid that came free with a disguise kit he had bought with his allowance. He was so fascinated by it that he read the book over and over again. There was a chapter about what to do if you are ever held captive, including a checklist that he desperately tried to remember.

Let's see… Step One: Assess the situation.

Well, I'm stuck in the back of this car with no way to get out… no help there.

Step Two: Look around for any tools you can use to escape. Jonah looked around. There was nothing.

Step Three: Use the one thing they can't take away from

you… your head. I guess they must have meant what's in my head, maybe some mind games. I guess it's worth a try.

He took a deep breath and began.

"So, what's the deal, Carlos? How long have you been in bed with the Tylers?"

Carlos turned around and glared at Jonah. He looked sweaty and nervous, and his lisp was becoming more pronounced.

"Sssshhhhut up, kid!"

In for a dime, in for a dollar.

"You know, you're never going to get away with this; the feds are on to you."

"I said, ssssshhhhhut up!"

"What are you going to do, shoot me? If you were going to shoot me, you would have done it by now. I think Angelo has other ideas."

Carlos looked surprised when Jonah mentioned his name.

"Surprised, Carlos? Do you think I don't know about Angelo? You know what he does to guys like you if things don't go his way?"

"I'm warning you, kid… zzzzip it!"

This using your head thing is starting to show some dividends; at least I have their attention.

"We've been on to you the whole time. You know you're gonna fry for this, you and Frank, the Moron up there that's driving this piece of crap on wheels."

Frank heard the reference to his name and the adjective that came with it and squirmed in his seat but said nothing in return.

I need some more material here. Let's see….

"A Honda, are you kidding me? Is that all you're worth? That's what they gave you to pull off this caper? Where did you get it from, Rent-A-Wreck? I'm surprised Angelo didn't ask you to take a bus."

He heard Frank tell Carlos.

"If you don't shut that kid's mouth, I will."

Jonah heard him.

OK, now that I have his attention.

"Hey! Frank the Moron, where'd you get your license from a mail-order catalog? You're really breaking some speed records here. What are you doing, five… six miles an hour? My grandmother could probably beat you using her wheelchair."

Frank was starting to look agitated, and Jonah noticed.

"I'm tellin' you, Carlos, either you shut him up, or I put one right between his eyes."

That last line shook Jonah; he was sizing up the situation while hoping for one of them to lose it. He was walking a thin line, but he had no other choice. He decided to work on the driver a little more.

"Hey! Frank the Moron, it's hard to see past that big head of yours; you're blocking the view back here. It's like you've got a big melon sitting on top of your neck. And by the way, are you sure you know which foot is for the gas and which is for the brakes? Or do you need the other one for your mouth? Cause so far, from the cheap seats back here, it seems like you only know how to use the break. I'd be happy to give you a crash course; don't mind the pun."

Frank took a quick and menacing glance at Jonah.

"I'm warning you, kid, one more word…."

Jonah saw Frank gripping the wheel as hard as he could with his sweaty hands.

Jonah threw caution to the winds; it was his only chance, and time was running out.

"You know I once sat behind a guy with a fat head like yours at the movies. They had one of those really wide screens; I still couldn't see a thing. Ask me what happened at the end of Superman; I couldn't tell you."

There was steam coming out of Frank's ears. He was gripping the steering wheel while cursing under his breath.

Jonah waited for a green light, so the car was in motion.

"So ya know what I did?"

"I started kicking the back of his seat like this."

Jonah started kicking the back of Frank's seat with his legs as hard as he could.

"How about this one, melonhead; you… drive… like… my… little… sister."

Frank suddenly lost it; he yelled at the top of his lungs.

"That's it, kid… I warned you!"

Forgetting that the car was in motion, he lunged over the seat to try and grab Jonah by the neck. Meanwhile, the car was suddenly veering to the right.

"Ffffrank, what are you doin'?" yelled Carlos… "ttthe caaar!"

*This is my chance. The book was right, after all. I **can** use my head!*

Jonah waited until he had the perfect angle and slammed his head into Frank's nose as hard as possible. He could see Frank's glasses break off and his nose explode in blood.

Meanwhile, Carlos desperately tried to get his foot over to the driver's side to hit the brake somehow. In the commotion, he turned the steering wheel hard to the left and slammed into the car driving in the next lane. They could all hear the crash. Horns were now honking from all over.

Carlos was enraged. He took out his gun and waved it at Jonah.

"You missserable little-"

"Drop it!"

Someone yelled from outside the car as two people were pointing their guns directly at them. Both Carlos and Frank, who was wiping his bloody nose with his sleeve, looked stunned.

"Now, get out of the car slowly, both of you."

Carlos stepped out of the car first, startled to see who was holding the gun.

"Marco, what the hell?"

"Hey, Carlos; nice to see you again. Nice driving!"

"It was… Fffrank… nnnever mind."

Another car pulled up to the curb, and a stunned Carlos and Frank were handcuffed and placed in the back seat, and the car sped off.

"You must be Marco," said Jonah as he bent over to catch his breath.

"Yeah, I'm the guy that *supposedly* chased after you through the streets."

"Eh, sorry about that," said Jonah sheepishly. "How did you know where to find me?"

"Hank," they both said the name at the same time.

"Always carry crapper insurance," said Jonah.

Marco looked puzzled and was about to say something when Josh, Pete, Mack, and Marv came running up the sidewalk.

"Are you OK, buddy?" said Josh to Jonah.

"I'll live, but their car may need some work."

"How'd you get those guys to crash the car like that?" asked Josh.

"I used my head, Josh. I keep telling you to start reading some spy novels."

Jonah was suddenly feeling his oats. He had outwitted two dangerous guys that were probably taking him to be killed, and he was going to milk this for whatever he could.

"OK, guys. I think you both better get back to your office," said Marco. "I just got off the phone; Mr. Heart and Hannah are very worried about you. These guys will give you a lift."

The name Hannah got Jonah's attention.

A squad car pulled up.

"Thanks," said Jonah.

He gave Marco another look.

"For everything."

"Hey, kid, if you ever want a job in law enforcement, we may have something for you."

Jonah had been waiting all his life to hear those words.

"Are you serious?"

Marco looked at him with a smile.

"Nah!"

"You mind doing me a favor?" asked Jonah.

Marco knew what he wanted. He called over to Joe.

"Joe, let him use the car phone."

Jonah's eyes lit up.

"Be careful now; that's an expensive piece of equipment."

"You bet," said Jonah with a smile; he felt like Dick Tracy.

Jonah called Hannah at her desk; she had left Mr. Heart's office a few minutes earlier to get some quiet time. She answered on the first ring.

"Jonah, is that you?"

"In the flesh."

"Oh, thank goodness; I was worried sick about you. Are you alright?"

"Not a scratch on me, and I'm calling from a car phone!"

Suddenly, he felt a little uncomfortable as all eyes were on him. He lowered his voice and turned away.

"I'm heading back to the office, Hannah; I'll see you soon."

"I can't wait to see you, Jonah."

"Me too!"

As he hung up the phone, Jonah thought to himself. *She was really worried about me!*

Twenty minutes later, Jonah walked out of the tenth-floor elevator and headed straight to Hannah's office. He knocked on her door. Hannah practically knocked him over as she hugged him and cried on his shoulder.

"You're OK, Jonah; I was so worried about you. Let me look at you."

She stepped back and looked him up and down.

"Still in one piece," said Jonah. "And have I got a story to tell you!"

"Tonight, I'm making you the best dinner you ever had!" said Hannah.

"You mean french fries with melted cheese on top?"

"That's your favorite dinner? I figured hot dogs, wings, and beer."

"I don't want to see another wing as long as I live. And by the way, I will be doing my food shopping somewhere else from now on."

Hannah looked puzzled.

"How come?" said Hannah.

"I'll explain later. I better get over to Mr. Heart's office; I understand he's really freaked out."

"He is."

As he turned away, he heard Hannah say:

"It's so great to see you, sweetheart."

It stopped him cold.

Wow, she never called me that before!

He suddenly noticed dozens of eyes on him. He had no idea what his coworkers knew or didn't know, but he would play it cool, like just another day at the office.

"A piece of cake," he said as he headed to Mr. Heart's office. He thought he heard a smattering of applause but decided to keep walking.

Jonah knocked on Mr. Heart's door. He sprang out from behind his desk, and they both hugged. It was the type of hug Jonah used to get from his father, and it felt really good.

"Thank the Lord," said Mr. Heart. There were tears in his eyes, and Jonah suddenly felt emotional, too.

"Thanks for the idea of leaving the crapper insurance," said Jonah.

"I'm glad it worked," said Mr. Heart.

"Marco told me about what happened to Ryan; I can't believe it. Do you know anything more about it?"

"Not yet," said Mr. Heart. "But I'm sure we'll hear more soon."

They both looked up in time to see an irritated-looking Irv walk down the hallway and head straight to his office. Almost everyone could hear the slam of his office door.

"I suppose you know what that is all about," said Mr. Heart.

"Rough day at the library; I guess he couldn't find what he was looking for."

Mr. Heart gave him a puzzled look.

"If we all get out of this in one piece, there'll be stories to tell. I better get back to my office; there's still work to be done."

Jonah headed back to his desk. His briefcase was sitting where Hannah had left it. When the clock struck 5:00, Jonah left his office and took the elevator to the lobby. He headed to the corner of Fifth Avenue and Fifty-Seventh Street, where Fred Watkins was waiting in a cab on the corner. Fred rolled down the back window and accepted a paper bag filled with floppies and a summary file of information they had gathered so far. They didn't exchange a word. The window rolled up, and the cab headed to Brooklyn, where Fred would spend all night with the wealth of information he now possessed.

It was time to put these guys where they belonged.

20

FRED HAD BEEN up all night trying to connect the dots. He needed to figure out who AP Industrials was and why they made significant weekly deposits into the hidden Tyler accounts. He did some additional research and found that AP Industrials was a limousine company.

Why would a limousine company make regular large deposits into the Tyler accounts? thought Watkins.

He dug deeper and found the names of the principals of the company. There were about twenty names on the list. As he went through them, he found himself lingering on one name that caught his attention: Anthony Bernardi.

Where did I see that name before?

He started to go through the floppies Jonah had left him. And there it was, staring him in the face, the connection he was looking for. He grabbed his phone and called Jonah.

It was two in the morning, and Jonah was not very excited to be woken up at that hour, but if he was groggy when he answered the phone, the information Fred provided had him fully awake. There was no time to waste; he called

Mr. Heart at home. He would have never dreamed of doing it just a couple of weeks ago, but time was of the essence, and he needed his help ASAP.

❧

Mr. Heart got into the office early the following day. He had many friends and gained much respect in the Justice Department during his days at the pharmaceutical company. He would give them information from time to time on cases they were pursuing in getting black market drugs off the street. It was good for business on both ends. Mr. Heart waited until 9:00, picked up the phone, and called Assistant Attorney General Bob Strohman, a wet behind-the-ears staff attorney when he ran the pharmaceutical business years ago but had since moved up to a prestigious post in Washington DC. They often shared drinks when Strohman was in town.

"Franklin, to what do I owe the pleasure so early in the morning?" said Bob as he got on the line.

"Bob, any chance you can grab a plane and fly down to New York this afternoon?"

"You mean this afternoon as in *this* afternoon?"

There was no response from Mr. Heart.

"Sounds pretty serious; what's up, Franklin?"

"This one's too hot for the phone, Bob, but I think it will be worth your trip."

"Seriously?"

"Can you do Shaughnessy's at five?"

"You drive a hard bargain, Franklin, but for you, anything."

"See you then."

As Mr. Heart hung up the phone, there was a knock on his door; it was Jonah.

"Mr. Heart, do you have a minute?"

"Sure, Jonah, what's up?"

"I just wanted to ensure we were on the same page on what happens next."

"Well, I have contacted someone at the Justice Department I trust; we will meet this afternoon."

"That's great, Mr. Heart-"

As Jonah was about to finish his sentence, two men abruptly walked into Mr. Heart's office unannounced and flashed their New York City police detective shields. Evelyn, the receptionist, came running in, out of breath.

"I'm sorry, Mr. Heart, I couldn't stop them."

"That's fine, Evelyn."

Jonah had stood up and was about to leave the office when he heard one of the men address Mr. Heart. The man's question froze Jonah in place.

"Mr. Heart, do you know a man named Ryan Schapp?"

"Yes, I do; he works here."

"Well, I am sorry to inform you that he was found dead in a motel room in New Jersey last night."

Mr. Heart acted like he was shocked. Jonah was impressed by how Mr. Heart had handled the question, but the detectives… not so much.

"Were you close?"

"As I said, he was an employee here."

"Yes, *you did say that.*"

"How can I help you, gentlemen?" said Mr. Heart, ignoring the comment.

Jonah was surprised that he had not been asked to leave yet; it was almost as if the two men hadn't noticed him or didn't care.

"A note was found among Mr. Schapp's belongings; it was addressed to you."

One of the men handed Mr. Heart an envelope with his name on it.

"We've already read it; we thought you might be able to give us some insight. It seems to us he was more than *just another employee.*"

Mr. Heart took the handwritten note out of the envelope. Jonah was close enough to read it over his shoulder, and even though the note was private, curiosity got the better of him.

Dear Mr. Heart:

I wasn't sure who to send this note to, but you seemed like the most logical choice. If you are reading this, I am most likely no longer among the living. I assume the police probably found it among my possessions as I had left it, with the hope that if I were murdered, the police would discover it.

Mr. Heart, I am not proud of the life I have lived. It has been a life of poor choices and missed opportunities. It's too late to change any of that, so I hope the information I gave you a few days ago will allow you to get some bad people off the street and out of the Tyler company. Maybe my final act will do some good for a change.

I know my wife Sue deserved better. If I had the courage, I would have told her myself. Please tell her that I loved her and that I am so sorry for the miserable life I gave her. Tell her I hope she will find someone who will treat her with the dignity and respect she deserves. I left the number you can reach her at in the back of this note. It is the last favor I will ask of you.

Please do what you can to put these bad people away before they hurt anyone else.

Farewell,

Ryan

Mr. Heart couldn't help but wipe a tear from his eyes as he folded the note and placed it back in the envelope. Jonah was numb; he could not bring himself to say anything.

"*Just another employee, Mr. Heart?*"

Mr. Heart composed himself before answering.

"That's right."

The detectives weren't buying it, and Jonah realized how bad it sounded. But he knew Mr. Heart was not about to divulge anything about the case to anyone but his man at the Justice Department.

"Mind telling us what's going on here?"

Jonah could see Mr. Heart gathering himself. He always admired how he could take charge of a situation no matter how difficult.

"The Assistant Attorney General will be here in a few hours; I prefer to wait for him."

"You know, it doesn't work like that."

"I understand, gentlemen, but I am not prepared to talk

right now. So you can arrest me, I call my lawyer, and we do this dance downtown, at which point the feds will most likely take over this case anyway, or you allow me to have my meeting, and we see where things land."

The two cops looked at each other. They didn't have much to arrest him for at that point.

"I guess there's no harm in waiting a couple of hours," said one of them.

The other one shrugged his shoulder.

"Yeah, less paperwork, but we'll be back. Meanwhile, I think there's a young widow you probably need to call."

Mr. Heart nodded at them, but his thoughts were miles away.

"As I said, we'll be back."

As the two detectives saw themselves out, Jonah looked at Mr. Heart.

"I'm so sorry about how this worked out for Ryan; I guess he had a pretty rough life."

"Yes, he did, Jonah."

Mr. Heart seemed distracted.

"Jonah, will you excuse me?"

"Of course."

Jonah left Mr. Heart's office and quietly closed the door behind him. He knew the difficult task that lay in front of Mr. Heart. Calling a young widow to tell her such awful news would be tough, but Mr. Heart had been left with no choice.

Jonah walked into his office and sat at his desk. There were now two murders in this case. The thought of what Ryan must have gone through sent a chill up his spine. He couldn't wait for this all to be over. The longer it went, the more dangerous it became.

At 4:30, he saw Mr. Heart leave the office and guessed he was going to meet with the feds.

Bob Strohman was a middle-aged but well-preserved government employee with salt and pepper hair and a goatee that he was proud of. He had worked his way up the ranks in Washington DC and now sported the title of Assistant Attorney General. It was men like Franklin Heart to whom he owed his rapid rise to the top. The high-profile cases Mr. Heart had tipped him off on with information on black market drugs coming into the United States had given him a leg up in his career over others vying for the attention of his superiors. He was able to keep his eye on the top spot in the justice department someday because of men like him. He knew it would be worth the trip if Mr. Heart called him about something important that required him to grab a private government plane to meet him in New York on the same day.

He strode into Shaughnessy's at precisely five o'clock in his powder blue power suit. He headed straight to the table in the back, where he spotted Mr. Heart nursing a cocktail. He stood up, shook Strohman's hand, and waived over the waiter.

"He'll have a scotch on the rocks, and please get me another one of these."

"To what do I owe the pleasure, Franklin?"

"I was thinking, you don't get out enough, Bob."

They both laughed and made some small talk for a few minutes. Finally, Mr. Heart got to the point.

"Bob, I want to give you a complete file on a major case of corporate greed that involves our country's national security. The summary information you need to get started is contained in this file. I will send you the backup files by secure courier when you're ready. There are some bad actors involved here, Bob. They have murdered at least two people we know of and will stop at nothing to get at the people who have taken great risks to get this information to you. I want to ensure that the sources used to acquire this material are protected along with their families. These folks need to be taken off the streets quickly and permanently before more people are hurt."

"This sounds serious, Franklin."

Mr. Heart handed Strohman the file.

"I've got copies of all of this secured elsewhere. Bob, I need a heads up before you move on these people."

"Sure thing, Franklin; you have my word."

"It should make for some interesting reading on your way back to Washington."

Strohman placed the file in his attaché case.

"I wish we could spend more time together, Franklin, but I think this will keep my investigative team and me busy for a while."

"Always a pleasure, Bob, and thank you for coming on such short notice."

"The pleasure is always mine, Franklin."

The two men stood and shook hands. Mr. Heart watched

as Strohman walked out, attaché case in hand. He then called Jonah.

"The package has been delivered."

They each hung up the phone. The file Mr. Heart had just given the justice department and the following supporting files would contain all the evidence they had amassed over the last few months. Watkins had put together the summary file.

They included a sworn statement from Ryan Schapp that he had written on his legal pad before entering Mr. Heart's office to tell him he was being chased. He had it notarized and mailed it from the post office he spotted on his way to New Jersey. It was mailed to Mr. Heart and arrived the same morning the detectives visited him. As Ryan had requested, he was careful not to mention it to anyone. In it, he told his complete story, naming all the people involved in the plot. He also listed the license numbers of the two people who abducted him and the limo in which he met with Angelo Papatonis, along with the names the vehicles were registered under, which he stated came from an unnamed police source. He also related what took place in the limo with Angelo Papatonis, that he had taken credit for Smokey's murder, and how he was asked to spy on Irv Carter. The file also included a sworn witness statement from Hannah Weinberg, who overheard the entire plot in a conversation between Irv and Simeon Tyler the night she hid in the Ladies' Room. It was a damning indictment.

The evidence given to Strohman included a copy of the second set of books that could be found at Bartowski and Company, which showed regular large deposits from AP

Industrials, the same company the limo was registered under. It would come as no surprise that the owner of the limo, Angelo Papatonis, and the company name, AP Industrials, shared the same initials.

Late night over a hot pastrami sandwich, Fred Watkins had noticed Papatonis associate Anthony Bernardi's name on both the floppies and the list of limo company employees and made the connection.

The feds seized the motel cameras, which picked up the license plate of the car the two men who killed Ryan Schapp had sat in for over an hour before they entered right before he was killed. No doubt those license plate numbers would be familiar. The security cameras in Smokey's building were impounded, and the same two men who had visited Ryan at the hotel had been caught entering and leaving Smokey's building after the murder.

The evidence also included the list of dockworkers in Izmir, Turkey, whom the feds pressured the Turkish government to allow them to interview. The Turks did not look kindly on being the focus of an international incident to smuggle weapons and explosives to the Soviet Union. They ensured the dockworkers were happy to cooperate, further tying the Tylers to the plot.

Mr. Heart kept in close touch with Bob Strohman over the next few weeks as their task force painstakingly pursued their investigation. This was no small case, and the Attorney General was kept abreast of its progress. They would not move on anyone until they felt they had a strong enough case to keep all the culprits in prison until trial. However, they kept twenty-four-hour surveillance on Angelo Papatonis and the other principals to be indicted.

It was business as usual for Josh, Jonah, Hannah, and Mr. Heart at Tyler Technologies for the next few weeks. Everyone came and went to and from work as usual. There were no more clandestine meetings; they would all wait until the feds were ready. Jonah did his best to avoid Irv. Irv did his best to avoid Jonah, worried that he was crazy enough to call his wife and spill the beans on his clandestine lunch with a pretty young lady who was not his wife.

He had no idea what happened to Jonah when he was taken from in front of the library, but he was back in the office safe and sound, and Irv was not asking any questions. Given his apparent relationship with Angelo, Ryan's sudden absence was his only concern. He was doing his best to lay low.

Six weeks after Franklin Heart handed Bob Strohman the file, the feds had their indictments in hand and were ready to move. The call came to Mr. Heart at home just as he was retiring to bed one night. Everyone was to come to work, as usual, the following day and act as surprised as everyone else in the company. There would be extra surveillance outside their homes for an extended period until it was determined there were no loose ends left around should someone want to exact revenge if they caught on to whoever was involved in engineering their demise. Mr. Heart passed the message on to the others.

It was time for accountability for the Tylers, Irv Carter,

Max Bartowski, and the others. Justice would also come for the elusive Angelo Papatonis and his crew, whom the feds had their eyes on for quite some time on unrelated cases. It was time to send a message to those involved in the dangerous transfer of high technology to our enemies. It was time to restore the good name of Tyler Technologies as Noah Tyler had built it. Most of all, it was time for justice on behalf of Ryan Schapp and Smokey.

The hammer was about to come down.

21

AT TEN O'CLOCK the next morning, the three elevators on the tenth floor at Tyler Technologies pinged at almost the same moment as armed federal agents with jackets emblazoned with "FBI" across their backs stormed into the vestibule from the elevators and stairwell. The startled receptionist reached for her phone.

"Put the phone down, ma'am," said a burly bald-headed agent, "and kindly take a seat."

Joel, David, and Simeon Tyler were sitting in the conference room at a table with papers strewn across the desk, going over sales figures as armed agents stormed in and lifted each one of them off their seats. Before they could respond, they were each handcuffed behind their backs.

"What the hell is this?" yelled Joel Tyler.

"Gentlemen, you are all under arrest for conspiracy against the United States of America. The full list of charges will be read to you in the presence of your attorneys at the federal courthouse, should you desire counsel. Anything you say can and will be used against you in a court of law. You have the right to an attorney. If you cannot afford an attorney, one will be provided for you. Do you understand the rights as I have just read them to you?"

"I can afford a damned attorney. This is an outrage; we want our lawyers now!" demanded Simeon Tyler.

"You will give us their names and phone numbers, and we will see they meet you downtown, Mr. Tyler. Meanwhile, I suggest you remain silent."

Before they could say anything further, they were whisked into the arms of additional agents who had entered the corridor. At the same time, three agents burst into the office of Irv Carter just as he was preparing his morning coffee to go along with his prune danish minus one bite sitting on his desk. He was so startled by the sudden appearance of the armed officers that he spilled the coffee all over himself. Before he could say a word, he was removed from his seat and handcuffed behind his back.

I knew it was over once Ryan was missing, thought Irv. He decided that silence was the better part of valor and closed his lips tightly.

He was given the same charge and read the same instructions as the Tylers. He was then escorted down the hallway before an office full of startled workers. Mr. Heart, Jonah, Josh, and Hannah sat quietly in their offices, making sure not to make eye contact with any of the partners. A crew of agents then entered the offices and began seizing computers and files.

Max Bartowski was on the phone making an appointment with his massage therapist when three heavily armed agents entered his office.

"What the hell is this?" a startled Bartowski said while trying to catch some air as the scare knocked the wind out of him.

"Max Bartowski, you are under arrest for conspiracy against the United States of America. The full list of charges will be read to you in the presence of your attorney at the federal courthouse, should you desire counsel. Anything you say can and will be used against you in a court of law. You have the right to an attorney. If you cannot afford an attorney, one will be provided for you. Do you understand the rights I have just read to you?"

It began to dawn on Max what this was about. He decided to keep his mouth shut, too. He was cuffed and led out of his office in front of his employees. He decided that covering his face would be silly since they all knew who he was. He tried to force a smile, but that wasn't going over so well either. He noticed his personal secretary, Sheila, wiping her eyes with a tissue. Another group of feds then entered the office and began seizing his computers and files.

Vincent Papalone and Joseph Moretti, AKA Vinnie and Joe, the two goons Angelo used to carry out much of his dirty work, were each picked up at home and charged with the murders of Smokey and Ryan. They appeared to have been through similar routines like this before, but the word "murder" clearly got their attention.

❧

Angelo Papatonis, Tony Romano, and Carlos Martinez, who was out on bail on the charge of kidnapping Jonah, were hanging out at the downtown social club they frequented when a dozen armed FBI agents stormed inside. Most of the patrons dived under the tables, expecting gunfire to erupt.

"Calm down fellas," said Angelo, with a grin on his face; "these are friendly officers of the law just payin' us a visit."

"How can we be of help, gentlemen?"

Before they could say another word, the three men were physically removed from the table they were sitting at and handcuffed behind their backs.

"Hey, easy fellas, that's a five thousand dollar suit. What's the beef? Did we forget to pay for a parking ticket?"

"Angelo Papatonis, Tony Romano, and Carlos Martinez, you are all charged with conspiracy against the United States of America."

"Conspiracy? Are you kiddin' me, for what?" said Angelo.

"The full list of charges will be read to you when we get downtown. Meanwhile, anything you say can and will be used against you in a court of law. You have the right to an attorney. If you cannot afford an attorney, one will be provided for you. Do you understand the rights I have just read to you?"

"You guys are a piece of work. Georgie, get my lawyer on the phone and tell him to meet us downtown."

The three men were placed in a secure van outside, surrounded by police vehicles. A crowd had gathered and watched as they were each loaded inside. The sirens began to wail as the van started to move.

Justice had finally come to Angelo Papatonis.

22

IT WAS A sunny day in Washington, and a large press contingent was assembled in front of the Justice Department. The Attorney General was flanked by Assistant Attorney General Bob Strohman and other task force members working on the Tyler case ever since Bob Strohman had received the evidence from Franklin Heart. The Attorney General took the microphone.

"Ladies and gentlemen, we are here today to announce the results of an investigation into an incredible act of corporate and personal greed that involves issues of national security, fraud, deception, and murder."

He then detailed the case to the press and a national TV audience.

Watching it all from Jonah's mother's apartment were Jonah, Josh, Hannah, Mr. Heart, Fred Watkins, the three members of the Motley Crew, and Sue Schapp, whom Mr. Heart invited to join them in honor of her husband, without whom this celebration would not have been possible. Jonah had never told his mother about being kidnapped. It took her a few days to get over it when he finally told her.

There were plenty of hot dogs, wings, fried Oreos, and beer, along with some healthy food for the ladies and Mr. Heart, who was not a junk food kind of guy. Jonah ate a helping of his cheese fries. They toasted one another with champagne on a job well done.

When the proceedings were over on TV, Mr. Heart took the floor. He thanked everyone for all their sacrifice on behalf of the Tyler Company and the good name of Noah Tyler.

"I guess at this point, some of us are celebrating our unemployment," said Josh.

"Maybe we can start our own detective agency," said Fred, working through an overloaded plate of wings. The barbeque sauce around his lips was hard to miss.

They all looked at him, not knowing if he was serious.

"That's enough cloak and dagger for me," said Mr. Heart. "I've been thinking about retirement lately; maybe this is the right time."

Marv chimed in.

"I'd love to hear if anyone has any future plans?"

"Actually, I do," said Hannah.

"I'm going to spend the rest of my life with this guy," she said, looking at Jonah, standing beside her and grinning from ear to ear.

She waved her left hand, which sported a beautiful diamond ring. They all gasped as Jonah and Hannah were enveloped with hugs from everyone in the room.

"Everyone grab a glass of champagne; I'd like to make a toast," said Josh.

"To my best friend in the world and his beautiful fiancé; mazel tov!"

The night lasted another two hours. As they were all leaving and saying goodbye, Jonah walked over to Mr. Heart, who was putting on his coat.

"Mr. Heart," said Jonah, "do you mind if I ask you a question?"

"Sure."

"I have been thinking about this for so long."

"What's that Jonah?"

"On that day I came for my interview, was it that question I asked that got me the job?"

Mr. Heart looked at Jonah with a serious look that set Jonah back for an instant. Suddenly, a big smile appeared on Mr. Heart's face.

"Are you kidding me?"

Mr. Heart turned and walked out the door, leaving Jonah perplexed and everyone else laughing.

"And don't even try and use a line like that on me," said Hannah.

Josh grabbed Jonah and gave him a big hug.

"Hey buddy, I was just wondering."

"What's that?" said Jonah.

"Do you believe I possess the qualifications you are looking for to assume the position of being your best friend?"

Everyone had a big laugh except for Jonah, who was still trying to figure out Mr. Heart's answer.

EPILOGUE

THE TURKISH PRESIDENT spoke to his country 24 hours later and announced his shock that Turkish citizens could take part in such an egregious act against an ally. As their friends in Washington requested, they would cooperate fully in the investigation and extradite all involved in their crimes. The loss of a few dockworkers was a small price to pay to keep their honor. A news broadcast on the official Soviet news station that night read a quote from their President categorically denying any knowledge of the actions taken by these American mobsters.

All indicted received long sentences by the federal judge who showed no leniency for their crimes. They would all serve their sentences in a maximum-security prison. They would probably live out the rest of their lives behind bars. Tyler Technologies was closed by the feds, and their assets were sold, with some money earmarked to benefit the estates of Smokey and Ryan.

Jonah and Hannah were married three months later in a beautiful ceremony at the same temple in Brooklyn as David and Esther Weiss were married in 1949. It was what Hannah always wanted. Fred Watkins could be found sampling all the delicacies at the smorgasbord. At the same time, the Motley Crew guys sat together and shared stories about the old days with Jonah.

Josh Silberstein found a job in an accounting firm in Manhattan about four months later. Hannah and Jonah rented a small apartment in Brooklyn and eventually found employment in Midtown, working just three blocks away from each other. They would meet for lunch most days at their favorite kosher pizza shop.

A year and a half later, Hannah gave birth to a beautiful baby girl. They named her Esther, after Hannah's mother, who had passed on six months earlier. A few months later, they bought a small house in the Flatbush section of Brooklyn down the block from Mrs. Lichtenstein's old house; she had passed away many years earlier. Jonah would pass Mrs. Lichtenstein's house on his way home from the subway station and gaze at the front steps where he and Josh had spent so much time as kids. Josh now lived two blocks away from them and was a frequent guest for Sabbath meals.

Angelo Papatonis continued to proclaim his innocence until the day he was killed in prison by his bunkmate, who was annoyed that he kept his radio on too loud.

Once a year, on the anniversary of his death, a car would inch up to a small gravestone at Weeping Willow Cemetery in Hackensack, New Jersey. A stately man would step out of the car holding a bouquet of flowers and leave it at the headstone of Albert Bernstein.

On the stone, it read: "Albert (Smokey) Bernstein, Beloved Husband, Loving Father, and Loyal Friend."

"Rest in peace, my friend," Franklin Heart would say before stepping into his car and driving away.

AUTHORS NOTES

This is my first novel. It has been a bucket list item in my life that I was hoping to get to someday. I have always taught my kids to "leave footprints" to give people a reason to remember you after you've left this world. I can now cross this project off my list.

Although this book is not an autobiography by definition, it dovetails with an important period in my life. The main character is essentially me, with some bells and whistles added to keep things compelling. Jonah Mark was a young business student pursuing an MBA degree. He majored in accounting and worked in an accounting firm by day while pursuing his MBA at night. I graduated college in 1979, majored in accounting, and pursued my MBA at night. Like Jonah, I hated every minute spent in that accounting firm, and I realized on my first day on the job that visiting clients and going over their books was not for me.

After a few years, I found myself pounding the pavement, looking for a new job. In those days, practically no one owned a computer or a laptop. If you couldn't type, like yours truly, you had someone type up a resume for you on a typewriter. You then made yourself a hundred copies and either looked at the "Help Wanted" section in the newspaper and mailed out your resume in a freshly typed envelope to each company that you were interested in, in most cases never to see it again, or you visited an employment agency where hundreds of others sat in a large room waiting to speak to an employment counselor who would peruse your resume while looking you up and down to determine if you were a good fit for any of the jobs they had available. If you were a promising candidate, they would spin their Rolodex (look it up on Google) and set you up for an interview. More likely than not, they would keep your resume "on file" should something come up. That meant it was time to hit the next agency and repeat the process. I went through this degrading ritual for many weeks while walking the streets of Manhattan in my "interview suit."

I don't remember who, but someone recommended a small employment agency to me. So, I added it to my list and eventually found myself in an agency similar in size to Success Employment LLC., although I don't remember the name. The two women who ran the small office were very nice and certainly not as flamboyant as Millie Cohen and Sally Berkowitz. However, they did think I fit the description of the candidate a large family-owned swimsuit manufacturer based in Midtown Manhattan was looking for: someone young and energetic to assist the company controller, who was very detail-oriented and wanted things done exactly the way he wanted.

I did not know then that Mr. Heart (whose first name will remain anonymous and who has since passed on) would become one of the most influential people in my life. He taught me everything I know about acting professionally and taught me the self-confidence to take on many challenges in the future.

After a good spin of the Rolodex, an interview was set up with Mr. Heart. The magic sentence that the ladies in the book had taught Jonah would get him any job if he said it right was taught to me by someone at a previous employment agency during one of the interview practice sessions offered to potential candidates. It stuck with me for some reason. The interview with Mr. Heart was precisely the same as the one given to Jonah, although I didn't get a haircut or go through the other prep work the ladies in the book put Jonah through. I remember nervously launching "the question," and it went for me exactly as it went for Jonah. I got the job!

The dynamics of the company partners and Mr. Heart were similar to how they were portrayed in the book, although they did act professionally to each other. He told me in no uncertain terms on the first day that I worked for him and answered to him only. My office tour was the same as Jonah's. As a modern orthodox Jew, I wore my small knitted kipa around the office. There was a young and pretty religious girl that everyone in the office played cupid for, trying to fix her up with a nice Jewish boy. During my company tour, Mr. Heart knocked on her door, and the story of her being startled and knocking her papers to the floor was true, but unlike in the story, I had never met her before. She spotted my kipa as I entered with Mr. Heart, and I guess all that startled her. We actually dated for a while, although we never told anyone in the office. I would just smile when someone would offer the novel suggestion of dating the nice young Jewish girl in the small office down the hall. The inter-office mailbox (you might want to look that up on Google as well) was what we used to set up lunch and after-work dates.

The traffic manager at the company was indeed named Smokey. He was a really nice guy that I loved to spend time talking to whenever I got a chance. He always had great stories to tell. One day, Mr. Heart called me into his office; I had never seen him so upset. "They fired Smokey," he said. Smokey and Mr. Heart were very close, but there had been some budget cuts, and Smokey was let go. The good news is that he wasn't murdered, just fired, as most companies do it.

The sons of the company founder were not like the Tylers; they kept to themselves but honored their understanding with Mr. Heart that I was there to work for him, not them. The brother-in-law's office was directly across mine, and he could be heard yelling when things didn't go his way. But I found him to be nice, and we got along professionally.

The flashback to the pizza story was true, but it happened when I was much younger, maybe nine or ten years old. It was just me alone who found a quarter rather than a dollar, and I ordered a slice and a cup of Coke. That wasn't the actual amount they charged. The store owner was being nice to a little kid who found a quarter. But I remember how sitting at that counter, savoring my good fortune, made me feel like a million bucks.

The flashback to cheating on the history exam is also true, except that it did not happen in sixth grade; it happened during a high school geometry test. Those who recognize the story will know who it happened to. I won't spill the beans here.

A couple of other notes: Jonah and Josh are the names of two very likable young men who live in my community. They are the sons of some very good friends of ours. Gabe is the name of a dog that was very close to some other good friends. He was as loyal to them as Smokey's dog was to him until he passed on.

The license plate on Angelo Papatonis' car, 565-LOAN, may have been perfect for a loan shark like him, but it was also the phone number for a mortgage company I owned dating back to 1987. I used it for my own license plate as an effective marketing tool.

The reference to Bernie's Deli on Essex Street on the Lower East Side was my tribute to Bernstein's on Essex Street, which closed shortly before the timeline of this story. It was known as one of the most famous kosher delis in the history of New York kosher delis, where my wife and I spent much time devouring their incredible spare ribs and sino steak while we were going out.

I am the son of a Holocaust Survivor, just as my wife is the daughter of one. The chapter written about the Holocaust cannot do justice to the horrors they experienced. But it was my way of paying tribute to both of them and to all who suffered through that terrible period of Jewish history. I strongly believe in passing on this story to the next generation, and this was my way to do so. It is a story that must never be forgotten.

The story of Esther Mark going from knitting sweaters in a factory to opening a successful dress store is my mom's story. She taught me never to accept the status quo and to always reach for something better. She is responsible for my ambition and drive. You don't learn those things in textbooks.

I enjoyed this project, and although I can now check it off my bucket list, who knows, maybe I'll give it another shot one day… stay tuned.

ACKNOWLEDGEMENTS

Because this is my first book, I don't have a long list of professionals in the publishing industry that I can thank for their expertise except for one.

My editor, Nora Long Bellot, an industry veteran, worked with me throughout the four drafts of this book until it read like something I could be proud of. After reading my first draft, she took great care to keep my expectations low. As she wrote in her first editorial letter to me, "Make sure you're in the right frame of mind before taking a look at my letter; the standard advice is that if you're hungry, angry, lonely, or tired, HALT!" Talk about low expectations! Nora brought the best out of my writing by both being critical and inspiring. She noticed what can best be described as my quirky sense of humor in a few brief sentences in my first draft of what started as a serious thriller and encouraged me to tap into it. The result was a completely different book than what I originally wrote. I would also like to thank Cassie Gross, the only certified bookworm I ever met, who recommended Nora to me.

Speaking of that first draft, I'd like to thank the following friends for suffering through it and offering many helpful and encouraging suggestions. Chuck Weinstein, Elliott Friedman, Michael Paneth, and Ari Wein. Sorry to have put you guys through the pain of a new author's very first venture into the literary world. Thanks also to David Himber for his technical suggestions.

My family members have all experienced parts of this book in real life because, as expressed in my author's notes, this book is about me, or at least an alter ego. Although they never had it presented to them in book form, they have all experienced different parts of it in stories and anecdotes that I have shared with them through the years. I'd like to thank my daughters, Ariella and Lila, for their encouragement throughout this process.

Last but not least, the love of my life, Elane. No, that is not a typo; she actually spells it that way; don't get me started. Throughout the writing of this book, the line she kept repeating was "book tour." The idea that maybe some-day we would travel to exotic places to promote my book was enough to keep her happy. On a serious note, there is no one more giving, no one more encouraging, and no one more loving. I dedicate this book to her for being my lifelong partner, cheering section, consoler in chief, and best friend a guy can ever have. For all you do, sweetheart, this is for you.

Lester Bleich

Long Island, New York

A FINAL WORD…

As a new author, this has been a wonderful experience for me. The best part is knowing that people from all walks of life who don't know me, have taken the time to read the story I've created and the words I've written. It doesn't get much better than that.

If I can ask you one small favor, it would mean a lot if you would kindly take a few minutes and post a review on whatever platform you purchased this book. It would make my day.

And once again…thank you!

www.ingramcontent.com/pod-product-compliance
Lightning Source LLC
Chambersburg PA
CBHW062113290726
48975CB00001B/214